The Passion of Letty Fox

Also by Diana Saunders
TANA MAGUIRE

The Passion of Letty Fox

A NOVEL BY
DIANA SAUNDERS

DONALD I. FINE, INC. NEW YORK

Copyright © 1986 by Diana Saunders

All rights reserved, including the right of reproduction in whole or in part in any form. Published in the United States of America by Donald I. Fine, Inc. and in Canada by General Publishing Company Limited.

Library of Congress Catalogue Card Number: 86–81473

ISBN: 0–917657–74–8
Manufactured in the United States of America
10 9 8 7 6 5 4 3 2 1

This book is printed on acid free paper. The paper in this book meets the guidelines for permanence and durability of the Committee on Production Guidelines for Book Longevity of the Council on Library Resources.

BOOK One

CHAPTER *One*

*L*ETTY STOPPED fitting on her gloves long enough to watch the stranger as he climbed the hill toward her. She knew that word of the poster had traveled all around San Francisco, not to mention up and down the rugged California coast and probably as far away as the mining towns of Nevada. The parade of men streaming down from the hills to catch a look at the "portrait" of Letty posing as the Empress Eugenie had afforded her a certain cynical amusement, but for the most part she felt certain that Eugenie would have been as shocked by the poster as Letty herself still was. Knowing that she should feel flattered by the attention and, more importantly, by the business it brought to the theater where she performed, she still couldn't help wondering at times if it really was the right way to draw customers. Was the nudity *really* necessary? It seemed a cheap ploy; the theater troupe had received critical acclaim for their "high art," the upper-class audience never questioning their respectability.

Oh well. There was nothing she could do about the poster, so she turned her attention back to the man.

He was lean, well built, of no more than average height. But the face was arresting, faintly exotic, olive-skinned.

She tried to guess what his business was in San Francisco. Men who had failed in life usually wound up at the western edge of the continent, twenty years too late for the Gold Rush. Still, he didn't look like a man down to his last dollar. Maybe, she thought, he was an adventurer and gentleman, the sort of man she saw frequently in San Francisco these days, businessmen and newly rich miners.

Reaching the top of the hill, he passed beneath the long corrugated awning over the Chinese herbalist's shop and stopped. He looked around as if in search of someone or something.

"Six bits to a threepenny piece he's looking for my poster," she thought. And if that *was* the object of his search, would the painting be enough to entice him to buy a ticket for tonight's performance? She hoped so; there was something fascinating about him. He was handsome in an unconventional way: the lips were too full, the cheekbones too broad, yet the composite radiated a certain refinement.

Letty, standing on the opposite side of the street, was certain he hadn't noticed her, and she continued to watch as he crossed Dupont Street, the main thoroughfare of Chinatown. Letty wasn't the only woman to remark his passing; two of Madame Lu's girls, openly admiring, started to follow him in their noisy clogs. The sight of them made her uneasy; their brothel was less than a block from the resplendent Lyric Theater where Letty performed, and in her weaker moments she often felt that the semi-nudity Vincent insisted upon in certain scenes made her little better than the girls who now trailed after the stranger.

After passing a cherry-red Chinese pagoda whose sign proclaimed in English, "House of Thousand Flavor," he stopped in front of the entrance to the Lyric Theater, a huge new edifice whose twin turrets loomed over some of the noisier alleys of the city.

"I was right," Letty thought, though without any sense of genuine satisfaction. "He's hiked all the way through town to see that poster. I owe myself seventy-five cents."

He studied the impressive outer lobby of the building—the architecture marked the end of Chinatown proper and the beginning of Caucasian San Francisco—while ignoring the box office where Vincent Fairborne's wife Annabeth was on duty and oblivious to all but the more colorful passersby. The rich, the poverty-stricken and the endless degrees of people in between milled through the streets in a reasonably close harmony born of the Gold Rush. It was a feeling that although you may be down and out today, tomorrow you might strike it rich and become one of the lucky few to build the mansions high on the hills overlooking the harbor.

Now the stranger spotted the poster on the side of the building and stood off to study the headline: "Letty Fox, Queen of Impressionists." The wood-framed canvas that portrayed a voluptuous blonde clad only in a black Spanish lace shawl was twice life-size and as garish as the blue, red, black and flesh tones could make it. The loosely woven shawl revealed the subject's entire anatomy in a fleshy splendor that bore no resemblance to the delicate complexion and slender lines of the model. Unholy red nipples on great globular breasts peeked coyly through the black lace.

Letty had loathed it on first sight, the day Vincent and Annabeth first unrolled the canvas and held it up for her to admire. Even the muscular arms and legs were foreign to her anatomy. The eyes had been painted an unearthly blue, and Letty's small, proud chin exaggerated beyond recognition.

But, as Vincent had pointed out with his apologetic smile, "It will attract audiences."

And of course it had. In his quiet, persistent way Vincent always knew best. But admirers of the painting need not hope to win her respect.

Annabeth had finally noticed the man who stood studying the poster. Coughing a little with the exertion, she slipped off her stool and opened the door beside the booth. She was petite, with a fragility that was partially due to an chronic tubercular condition, arrested for now.

"Isn't it wonderful?" she called in a little-girl voice. "The picture of Miss Fox?"

Afraid that Annabeth might notice her and call her over as the subject of the poster, Letty backed away a few feet so she was not in her line of vision. It would be too embarrassing to be associated in this man's mind with that travesty of a portrait; Annabeth, in her curious innocence, never understood why Letty found the portrait so objectionable, especially since her husband had pronounced it satisfactory.

The man abruptly turned to Annabeth. "A wondrous picture, that. Tell me, is this creature human?"

"Oh yes, sir. Letty is almost as pretty as that picture. And she's very popular—and talented."

"I can imagine."

Letty flushed at the innuendo. Annabeth, however, took everything at face value.

"You ought to come and see her tonight, sir. She's absolutely thrilling. She plays queens and empresses and all sorts of famous people."

"Thanks just the same," the man said, shaking his head. Letty's unexpected disappointment quickly turned to curiosity as she watched him reach up with both hands and cover the portrait's face, all but the eyes. What on earth was he doing? He took his hands down and stood back, staring at the face, and said loudly, "Impossible. Good God, what an idea!"

Startled by the stranger's outburst, Annabeth jumped back, attempting to close the door.

"What the devil! I'm sorry, miss. Are you related in some way? If I've insulted—"

"She . . . she works for my husband."

Seeing how uncomfortable Annabeth was in the presence of the stranger, Letty decided she had better step in.

"He . . . you'd better talk to the gentleman," Annabeth said when she spotted Letty. Annabeth quietly moved back into the box office and shut the door.

The man scowled after her. "What am I, some sort of bogey? I merely remarked after this rather gaudy poster. Is she a relative of the woman? I apologized. But only a fool could admire that creature."

"I quite agree, sir," Letty said in a soft voice.

The man turned to face her. She was momentarily nonplussed by the piercing blue of his eyes, a startling contrast to his jet hair and dark skin. "Well, then, why did she take offense so?"

Annoyed that she had to explain Annabelle's actions—a woman whom everyone loved without question and treated with indulgence—to a stranger, Letty said curtly, "She is not well. And she's just recovering from a bout of consumption, following typhus last winter. She really isn't very strong."

"In that case, I do beg your pardon."

"You need not trouble. That was Mrs. Fairborne you frightened."

"I've no doubt you will make my apologies, Miss—?"

"Then you were not about to buy a ticket?"

"Good Lord, no! I didn't travel over those godforsaken plains and mountains to sit in flea-bitten discomfort, watching some third-rate baggage prance about in the nude."

Letty bristled—obviously he hadn't connected her with the poster—but chose to defend her country rather than herself to this foreigner.

"I can assure you, sir, we are not responsible for the fleas in San Francisco. And just what *did* prompt you to cross what you refer to as our godforsaken plains? Surely no one in San Francisco was foolish enough to invite you."

He agreed cheerfully. "Not in the least. It is entirely my fault that I didn't wait until the completion of your transcontinental railroad and make my arrival in some degree of comfort."

"You missed the joining of the tracks in the Utah Territory last year," she said, "though I daresay there are numerous places where the tracks or the railway cars are still unavailable. We're celebrating the first-year anniversary tomorrow."

"So I've heard. But if the date was May tenth, why aren't you celebrating today?"

"Because tomorrow is Saturday, of course."

This struck him as highly amusing. "There must be logic in that somewhere." Now he seemed to be appraising her. Letty knew she looked attractive in her walking-out dress of royal blue foulard. The fullness of the fabric was pulled back into a bustle that complemented her lithe figure. And she was glad she hadn't worn a dress with a bodice too low—it would only confirm that she could very well be the sort of woman the poster suggested. His eyes focused on her face for a long moment, making her self-conscious. Hoping to hide her nervousness, she said, "You are a stranger here, I presume?" She'd noted his accent, although she couldn't quite place it.

"I'm a foreigner everywhere. Max MacCroy. Born in County Sligo in the west of Ireland, though I've lived most of my life in France, where I work. Business brought me to Chicago . . . I failed to find what I was looking for, and a friend sent me to various towns in the West, pursuing this Letty Fox. It seems to have been a considerable waste of my time."

Surprised at his forthright manner of speaking about himself, she was about to blurt out, "What business have you with Letty Fox?" but thought better of it. Certainly she should find out more about this intriguing stranger before she revealed her identity. And he certainly wasn't the first man to seek her out.

"But this is hardly the district in which to find a young lady like yourself," he said. "I've been told that in Chinatown there's a crime every two minutes. Shouldn't you be a trifle more wary of these denizens?"

"Oh, but I am one of these denizens." With this remark Letty finally succeeded in shaking his brusque self-assurance. He frowned, looked her over again carefully in the bright sunlight. The wind whipped around her feathered bonnet and trim figure, but it wasn't the wind that made her cheeks redden as she guessed what he was thinking.

"No," she said. "I am an actress."

"An actress?"

Letty's face was burning. She remembered that every prostitute in the city's bordellos called herself an actress.

"*Yes.* An actress. I act. On stage. On *this* stage."

He opened his mouth to speak, seemed to think better of it, then took a step backward. He glanced at the poster, frowning, then studied Letty intently.

"You'll not be telling me—"

"No—I leave that for you to judge. What was it you called Letty Fox? A creature? Second-rate baggage?"

"Third-rate," he said. His mouth remained somber, but she could clearly read the amusement in his eyes.

"Are you really the Empress of Emotions?" he asked, quoting from the poster.

"By all means," she said, looking away as he finished reading it aloud:

> Presented by Vincent Fairborne
> THE CELEBRATED LETTY FOX
> Queen of Impressionists
> Empress of Emotions
> See her as she becomes the great women of the world: the revered Queen Victoria; the Roman Messalina, wickedest woman in the world; the tragic Empress Carlotta of Mexico; and the beautiful Eugenie de Montijo, empress of the French Performing with the distinguished star of Broadway and London, Vincent Fairborne.

"Impressive," he said. Letty couldn't tell if he was mocking her again. "Are you a good actress?"

"Tolerable."

"Only tolerable? I mean, when you transform yourself before our very eyes into Queen Victoria and—" he looked up at the poster "—the beautiful French empress, are you convincing?"

"Superbly," she said, "as an impressionist. There *is* a difference between an impression and an entire character."

"So I would imagine. However, I confess you don't particularly resemble any of those women. It may be your own blond hair. That and the fact that you are far more beautiful than most of the women you portray."

"And am I to assume you are acquainted with them all?"

"I've met all but Messalina," he said matter-of-factly.

Given the woman's reputation, his comment made her laugh. It was clear now why he wasn't going to bother to see her performance. Why should he?

Letty was anxious to be on her way; she saw little point in wasting any more time with him in spite of his interesting manner. She waved to

Annabeth in the box office, wished Max MacCroy a good day and left. Sensing his gaze on the sway of her bustle as she walked away, she was secretly pleased. By the time she crossed the street she felt she could risk a look backward without embarrassment. When she turned she was surprised to see him at the box office, pushing some coins through the window. Annabeth must have told him that gold and silver were much preferred over the new paper money, which most San Franciscans were reluctant to accept. So, she thought, he had decided to take a chance on the flea-bitten theater after all. Perhaps their paths would cross again, although she wasn't entirely sure she wanted them to. And what *had* he meant when he said he had come west in search of Letty Fox? Just another arrogant man, she decided, and with that continued on her way.

CHAPTER *Two*

*L*ETTY HURRIED toward distant Montgomery Street to meet Vincent Fairborne. A connection had informed him that a refugee Mexican hidalgo was willing to sell jewelry belonging to the widowed Empress Carlotta.

Letty was little concerned about the politics surrounding the jewelry Vincent hoped to buy, although she had developed a certain empathy for the imperial women she portrayed. This was especially so in the case of Princess Charlotte, who had by virtue of her marriage found herself a principal character in a politically motivated tragedy played out in Mexico, far from her native Belgium. Persuaded by Austrian and French imperials, the princess and her husband, an Austrian archduke, had accepted what proved to be nonexistent thrones as emperor and empress of Mexico. When the luckless archduke was executed by the victorious Republican army under their president Benito Juarez, the Empress Carlotta found it too much to bear. Rumor had it that she had gone mad.

Letty had thought the role of the Empress Carlotta a natural one for an actress, and since the execution had taken place only three years earlier, in 1867, it was still the topic of conversation in some quarters of San Francisco. Letty marveled at the international flavor her much-loved city possessed—the variety of life that teemed in the port—and reveled in the fact that today she, Letty Fox, illegitimate child, would be examining the jewels once worn by an actual princess.

She hurried past men setting up a hastily constructed grandstand and street decorations of red, white and blue crepe paper for the citywide celebration the next day. She knew that Vincent had already secured choice places for his company to view the parade and festivities, and the thought of being with him—even though they wouldn't be alone—pleased her even more.

Annabeth loved flags, banners and parades, and Letty knew it would be a special day for her. There were few things left that Annabeth could enjoy, and Letty took pleasure in the simple things that could add to her comfort. As much as Letty loved Vincent, she felt a deep affection and loyalty toward Annabeth, who had welcomed, encouraged and befriended her since the night Vincent had brought the fourteen-year-old Letty, hysterical and crying, home to their hotel in Virginia City. As Letty's talent developed and she came to be the starring attraction of Vincent's troupe, Annabeth was only pleased—in fact, she seemed clearly relieved to be in the background, assuming small parts in the sketches. But Letty knew that even if she wanted it otherwise, Vincent would never divorce his wife. By the time she was twenty-three she had accepted the fact that her love for Vincent would have to remain a deep longing and an unfulfilled dream.

Dreams were nothing new to Letty—dreams had rescued her from the sordid surroundings of her childhood. The product of a passionate affair between a young French seamstress and a Bonapartist student, Letty had been raised by her mother after her father was killed in the Paris uprisings of 1848. Sylvie Benoit took pains to see that her daughter, as she grew older, understood that her father had intended to marry her mother, and that Letty's illegitimacy was due to political circumstance alone. Nevertheless Letty, even at that young age, saw through the excuses. Furthermore, Sylvie had never been sure that the name her lover used was indeed his own.

Word of the California gold discoveries had been an answer to Sylvie's prayers. But in 1850 the dreadful voyage around Cape Horn in steerage used up all the money the young woman had been able to save from the sale of her lover's watch and fob, her father's Napoleonic medals and her actress mother's costumes. Sylvie quickly found upon her arrival in America that there was only one way to feed and house her child and herself: she married a friendly, grinning miner named Leonard Fox, who was willing to adopt Sylvie's exceptionally pretty three-year-old daughter.

The next five years passed in relative peace, but disaster struck again when Letty was eight. Her mother died during a typhoid epidemic that swept the new diggings at Virginia City, Nevada, and Letty found herself suddenly exposed to a lifestyle totally foreign to her upbringing. The prostitutes in the red-light district near the Fox cabin made it all too clear that Fox had given up mining to take up a more lucrative business, and Letty began to fear that at some point she, too, would be initiated into this life. She never knew when Leonard Fox would decide it was time for Letty to earn her keep. Her fear proved well founded—at the age of eleven she was dragged from her cot by her drunken stepfather and forced to parade in front of two miners in the kitchen. The rest of the scene was a blur: the lifting of her nightdress, the comments, the touch of their calloused hands. Ironically, it was her stepfather's greed that prevented her sale—Fox capriciously decided that Letty would be worth more when she filled out, and sent her to bed. The following night saw the first of her many attempts to run away.

Salvation came with the arrival of a tall, slender, graceful man—surely, the fourteen-year-old Letty thought, a gentleman—whose sun-burnished hair made him look like a saint in armor. And so her terror ended the night she was purchased by Vincent Fairborne. He had saved her, taken her to his wife Annabeth, made her part of their family; and Letty would never forget this, despite the different kind of love that gradually developed between her and Vincent as she blossomed into a young woman.

Vincent had asked nothing of her except respect and a willingness to learn. Vincent, who had come from a wealthy family in Virginia, trained her to act like a lady, to read, to study the world around her, and—most importantly, as far as Letty was concerned—taught her French. For Letty, learning Sylvie's native tongue was an irrevocable connection to her mother. But Vincent gave her more than a new life, he gave her the ability to dream something she would one day realize, though she had no idea how. Although her ancestors were forever lost to her, she was determined to return to France alone as a way of vindicating herself and her mother's painful exile from the land of her birth. Letty's plan for her return remained unformed until one night when Annabeth, early in her illness, asked that Letty replace her onstage. Even though the role was severely cut to make it easier for Letty, she knew immediately that acting was her future and that she would fulfill her vow to her mother by using her talent on stage.

When the War Between the States broke out, Vincent was forced to leave the company, which foundered without him. It was with a good deal of love and relief that Annabeth and Letty welcomed him back to restore his troupe to its former glory. He spent his early days home recuperating from a thigh wound received just before his capture in Chancellorsville. In exchange for his freedom he had been forced to take an oath never to reassume his old Confederate loyalties, but he managed to salve his conscience by giving much of the company's profits to southern sympathizers.

Once the company moved to San Francisco, Vincent used Letty's beauty and natural acting talents to the fullest. Her first attempts at impersonating well-known political ladies of the day proved popular, although the early audiences of rough miners and unsophisticated townspeople wanted something more. With that, Letty Fox the Impressionist was born. Before long it also became clear that the less the impressionist wore, the greater the box-office receipts. Since American political figures might protest too loudly, Vincent began turning out scripts about historical European ladies unlikely to be any the wiser for it.

A hundred of San Francisco's Gold Rush nobs might come to see a realistic portrait of the dazzling Empress Eugenie of France or the tragic Empress Carlotta of Mexico. But five hundred elegant San Franciscans lined up at night before the new Lyric Theater to see "The Theater at Its Best," as one San Francisco paper called it—and in particular to see Letty's body draped seductively in silk gauze as she played out high-born tragedy in faraway settings.

Letty's relations with the men who admired her meant nothing. Her most intense feelings—devotion and gratitude—were reserved for Vincent Fairborne. Occasionally in the past two years, driven by their needs and an attraction between them that Vincent as much as Letty tried to hide, they made love. Contrary to the beliefs of all who saw Letty onstage, Vincent had been her first and only lover. She told herself that these rare encounters were all she needed in her life, but that was a lie, and she knew it.

Remembering her debt to Annabeth, she tried to content herself with frequent public meetings, always for a legitimate reason, during which she and Vincent fell into the role of student and master. Letty understood that at no time should Annabeth ever guess that her beloved husband had made love to his star.

Then too, the bonds between Letty and her teacher were less sexual than mental and, in a sense, religious. She adored him. How could she ever forget that Vincent Fairborne had changed her life, persuaded her to educate herself with books and newspapers and careful observation, supported her and taught her how to perform, giving her the secrets of winning audiences?

Dreading her appearance in partial undress before the public, Letty reminded herself at the beginning of every half-nude scene: *I mustn't complain. I owe everything to Vincent. My life began when he bought me. I am doing this for him.* But the shame remained.

It was a bittersweet life, incomplete in some ways, but what life was perfect? And wasn't this one worlds better than the drudgery in the Virginia City miner's cabin Letty had known before?

On this bright, windy morning Letty arrived at the address she had been given by Annabeth and wondered if Annabeth might not have copied it down wrong. A solid brick business building three stories high occupied the corner that had been sketched for her on the back of a piece of Vincent's creamy white stationery. She studied the directory in the open foyer of the building, but the chalked names on the hanging board were those of local attorneys, a dentist and a shipping company for deepwater trade with the Hawaiian kingdom.

She went back out on the busy street, perplexed. A moment later she ducked back onto the sidewalk to avoid a crowded horsecar and suddenly caught sight of the narrow frame house that stood behind the business buildings of Montgomery Street. The house, like most San Francisco private residences, was built above a deep basement and what appeared to be an endless flight of stairs. It bore the same address as the business building and undoubtedly shared an owner in common.

As she started up the stairs, she heard booted steps behind her and looked back. A small, dark, ferretlike man in a sailor's short coat and a French matelot cap with a red pompom was behind her on the stairs. He looked up, met her eyes and behaved in a very odd fashion—he backed down two steps to the sidewalk, then hustled around the corner and out of sight.

Letty shrugged and knocked on the door. The house was dilapidated, the warped wood peeling and splitting and the uncurtained front window next to the porch badly cracked. Someone in the parlor crossed the dark room to the hall and the door slowly opened. She had begun to wonder if Max MacCroy was right when he warned her that these districts, perfectly safe for businessmen, were no place for an unescorted woman. But that was before she made out Vincent Fairborne's shadowed figure in the doorway. He stepped into the sunlight on the porch and greeted her, taking her gloved hand in his.

"Good. You are here in time. We must act fast. Apparently there are others after the jewelry."

"And not for sentimental reasons, I imagine."

"Obviously." He took her arm and walked her into the gloom of the house.

She had hoped he would take a minute to squeeze her hand or even to brush her forehead with his lips, any token of affection for her to treasure tonight in the cool dark of her bed. Such attentions were warm if inadequate substitutes for the sexual offers she refused daily from admiring males. Besides, it was not Vincent's modest sexual powers that she adored.

Today Vincent was preoccupied with the idea of the Fairborne Company's owning a necklace and tiara formerly worn by the Empress Carlotta of Mexico. She could understand that. It was Vincent, teacher and rescuer, who wanted it for his company.

The house smelled of boiled cabbage and potatoes; there had been a time when Letty Fox craved even the smell of such mundane food, but today the pungent odor dispelled any romantic notions about Vincent and imperial jewels.

"What a firetrap!" she murmured, thinking of the half dozen calamitous fires that had nearly destroyed the city during the twenty-one booming years since 1849.

"We needn't stay here long."

"Can you possibly afford the price he's sure to want for the jewels?"

Vincent squeezed her fingers, then let go of her hand. "I can if we all tighten our belts a trifle, my dear. It will mean a cut in profits for a few months, and of course it eats up the money I had reserved for refurbishing the scenery. But it will be worth it in publicity alone."

The profits made on the show were his in any case, but Letty was flattered by his reference to "our" belts, as if she were a part owner. Her small salary would be cut, but that was to be expected. And after all, she would be wearing the jewels onstage.

How dark the hall was! And the walls did not look clean. Here and there the blue striped wallpaper had been torn away, and fingermarks were everywhere. Letty took care to lift her skirts. She knew that one of the attractions of the expensive and glamorous Letty Fox show was the beauty of her costumes.

In the back bedroom they found the present roomer, presumably the possessor of the imperial necklace, a young man whose slender body was coiled on the cot like a serpent, whose black hair was unevenly cut. A complexion pale as milky china was offset by curious, slanting golden eyes. He got up from the bed, uncoiling himself, and greeted them with a graceful wave of the hand.

"Señor, señora . . . you honor this house."

Vincent regarded him with disdain, a manner reserved for the occasional juvenile he hired. Younger men were instinctively perceived as a threat in Vincent's profession. "I am told that you have in your possession some property formerly owned by the Princess Charlotte of Belgium," Vincent said. "Lately known as the Empress Carlotta of Mexico."

"How formal we are, señor!" the young man teased, somewhat to Letty's surprise. For some reason he seemed to find Vincent amusing. Not knowing that Vincent Fairborne was an actor, he probably found Vincent's style a trifle grandiloquent in a back bedroom like this one.

"Do you have the jewels, young man?"

"But of course, señor. And you may address me as the Con . . . the Conde Paolo Servandoni."

The title was Spanish but the name was Italian. Curious.

Letty watched the young man's graceful hands as he talked. Apparently the Conde Servandoni was an aristocrat. Letty guessed that he had been in the service of the Empress Carlotta and had remained in Mexico when she returned to Europe to get help for her husband. The imperial jewels fell into his hands and he was running away from the government of Mexican President Juarez—small wonder that he remained here in hiding. Undoubtedly he would take the money from the jewel sale and return to Europe by the first available ship.

"May we see the jewels, Your Excellency?" Letty asked, trying to hurry the matter through. She did not like this place, and for some reason she felt uncomfortable around the count. His golden eyes watched her with a kind of malicious amusement.

"But of course, señora." The count reached under the thin, lumpy mattress of the bed and withdrew a goatskin bag with drawstrings pulled tight. He shifted the bag from hand to hand as if weighing it, very obviously aware of Vincent's eyes following his every movement.

"Let me see them."

Letty was startled by Vincent's harsh tone. She hadn't realized how very much he wanted the empress's jewels. She did realize how important it was for him to achieve a financial success that would last, something he could bank and build upon. She knew he placed small amounts in the hands of San Francisco stockbrokers and checked with them regularly.

The count tossed the bag again—then, without warning, tossed it at Vincent. It hit the back of his hand and fell to the carpet with a thud. Vincent's handsome mouth tightened in anger, but he voiced no objection. He stooped, picked up the bag and emptied the contents over his fingers.

Letty could make out the web of many gems in graduated sizes, ending in what appeared to be a tear drop that looked as if it would nestle perfectly in the hollow of her throat. Impressive, and easy to wear without self-consciousness. She had been afraid the necklace would be too ostentatious for their purposes, a king's—or in this case an emperor's —ransom that had failed in its object.

Vincent was less impressed. "Let me see it in the light."

With the necklace looped through his fingers he walked to the window and held the jewels up in the shaft of sunlight. Every stone glittered. He wriggled his fingers, sending prisms of light arcing across the room. Letty had been warned not to show enthusiasm, but she couldn't help murmuring.

"Lovely!"

The count grinned. "Ah, but when you see the tiara! The necklace was originally part of a parure. I have the earrings and the tiara. For a price. There are other bidders, señor."

"Others? Who?" When the count did not answer Vincent dismissed his remark. "A bluff."

He glanced at Letty. "I can imagine you in these." He lowered his voice but there was no doubt the young count heard him. "And a new poster—you will be wearing the diamonds."

"A new poster? That I approve of."

"Dear child, do you think I've liked those foul beasts staring at you like that?"

She was quick with her denial, not wanting to hurt his feelings. "No, no. But something a little more . . . dignified, don't you think?"

He sighed, held the stones up to her bosom and studied them. "I wish you were right. Unhappily, you don't know the world as I do. Besides, no one really sees you as I do, in spite of that poster."

"No one ever will see me as you do, ever. Only you."

"*Diamonds usually produce that effect upon a female.*"

The remark was dry, cool, expressionless. Worst of all, it came from neither the count nor Vincent. Vincent turned abruptly toward the doorway across the room. He caught his breath and muttered something just as Letty recognized the man in the doorway.

Max MacCroy.

He leaned on one elbow against the door frame, grinning maliciously. He would be certain to think the worst of her now. No question but that in his eyes, the horrid poster was accurate.

Vincent raised his hand proudly. Beyond the area of light from the window, MacCroy stood in a shadowed portion of the room and Vincent scowled, trying to get a good look at him.

"Who are you—aside from an interfering busybody? Our conversation with this gentleman is private."

"Not private enough, I'm afraid. My dear fellow, I am a prospective buyer."

MacCroy's voice had an inflection that instantly aroused Vincent's antagonism—a vaguely British tone of mocking superiority.

"I was told I would be the only bidder this afternoon unless I failed to come up with the price. I don't propose to ask by what underhanded means you found out about this little matter."

"Just as well. I don't propose to tell you. I say, Miss Fox, that necklace was obviously made for you. What a pity!"

Before she could reply, Vincent turned to her.

"Has this fellow been formally introduced to you?"

"Formally?" She considered. "No. I can honestly say we have not been formally introduced."

Vincent turned back to MacCroy. "Then may I suggest, sir, that in San Francisco, unless you know a lady, do not address her by name."

MacCroy, as if determined to make things worse, protested with innocent bewilderment. "But I do know Miss Fox, sir. I might say there is nothing about her I do not know."

Letty blushed; she wanted to slap him but instead said quickly, "He must have seen the poster."

Vincent rushed on, obviously more interested in the subject at hand. "The Conde Servandoni has my offer. It is entirely in his hands. I was given reason to believe my offer would be accepted."

The count meanwhile had retreated into the shadow of the wall. Letty thought this odd. Was he afraid of the newcomer? Had MacCroy lied to her? Was he in the employ of the Mexican Juaristas? The young Conde would be in considerable danger for stealing confiscated government property.

"The Conde Servandoni," the Irishman repeated and moved further into the room.

No question about it: the young aristocrat did not want to be recognized. "*Si, señor,*" he began in a voice that sounded quite unlike the teasing tones he had formerly used. "I was told to keep them for myself. Anyone rather than the Juaristas, he said. He ... he wanted me to have them."

"I can imagine," MacCroy said. "By *him* I suppose you mean the late

Emperor Maximilian. And you've spent all this time nursing the little treasure."

Vincent and Letty exchanged a puzzled look, both of them bewildered by the radical change in the young count since MacCroy's arrival. Letty supposed their own chance of buying the jewels had vanished. She only hoped this mad Irishman wasn't violent.

But to her surprise and relief MacCroy laughed and proceeded to dig from his pocket an impressive roll of greenbacks.

"My dear conde, I offer cash. And no questions—"

Vincent interrupted, "I assure you, my check is fully as negotiable as this fellow's paper." Vincent played nervously with the necklace in his hands.

The count responded in a gruff tone, "I prefer to deal in cash."

"Ten thousand in cash," MacCroy put in. "And you are safe to return . . . home."

"Home? You swear?" The conde's voice rose almost an octave. Vincent and Letty were stunned.

I should have guessed, Letty thought. *All that grace and seductiveness. The conde is a contessa. When the sly creature looked at me in that impudent, knowing way, it was not, as I thought, with some lascivious idea, but something quite different, a woman challenging a rival.*

Vincent was indignant that he, an actor, had been duped, not to mention upset at the probability that he would lose the jewels.

"Can you afford to match his offer?" Letty dared to ask.

It was a humiliating question. Vincent answered with a shake of the head.

The Contessa Servandoni darted quick slanting looks from Vincent to Letty, but it was clear that she was aware of MacCroy behind her.

"You cannot raise Señor MacCroy's offer?"

"Mine is a legitimate offer," Vincent said stiffly. "I can pay you five thousand here and obtain five more—" He broke off at her expression.

The pretty contessa in her slim black trousers and white shirt made a disdainful movement.

"One must live, señor, and I am very expensive."

MacCroy said, "My ten thousand cash won't get you far, Pauline. Tell the nice gentleman and the beautiful lady that you really must get back to Rome."

"Paris!" the contessa burst out in sharp contradiction. "You and the empress cannot keep me away from my beloved Louis Napoleon."

"Try me," MacCroy promised grimly.

She boasted, "My Louis. He wants me. He will welcome me back in spite of your jealous empress, Max." The young woman's lip curled in contempt. "She gave him a son and then became too cold to share her husband's bed, as if one little prince imperial were enough. So he finds comfort where he can. Even emperors need warmth and love."

"I hope you don't expect to give him another heir to the throne, Pauline. Your bloodlines aren't quite pure enough."

"Do not be coarse, Max."

Letty wondered at the relationship between these two. She had heard the gossip about the Emperor Napoleon the Third and his notorious womanizing, and this feline creature was apparently one of his mistresses. Who could tell what she was to Max MacCroy. The golden-eyed Contessa Servandoni had seemed quite frightened of MacCroy; yet, now it appeared that their real relationship involved their mutual positions in imperial Paris. Had the contessa been afraid that MacCroy brought word from the emperor forbidding her return? Although it was obvious from the conversation that the real agent of the contessa's banishment was the empress.

Max continued, "The empress still has influence over His Majesty, and their son is heir to the throne. You cannot compete there. I doubt that you will be welcomed at the Tuileries Palace, my dear. You will have to entertain His Majesty elsewhere."

She grinned mischievously. "His Majesty has promised me a lovely flat within sight of the Tuileries. And I know the landlord."

"I don't doubt it."

It was astonishing to Letty how Europeans could discuss the most intimate details of their rulers' lives within earshot of strangers. Did everyone in France talk so freely about the imperial family?

But Letty was thrilled by this talk of her native land and its rulers. How proud her mother would have been to know that Letty was in the company of a man and woman who actually *knew* the emperor and empress of the French.

"We find ourselves in high company," she murmured to Vincent.

Vincent nodded, impressed in spite of himself, and his manner thawed perceptibly. As for Letty, her curiosity about the Irishman arose from her own interest in France. And, she had portrayed both empresses, Carlotta and Eugenie, so often that she felt she had a personal understanding of them surpassing all the others who saw them only as players in the contemporary political arena.

Even Vincent failed to understand that when she put on the paint, powder and black kohl, the elaborate costumes and jewels, she *became* these rulers, who were women first, empresses second.

"Well," MacCroy said, "what do you say, Pauline? I mean to have those jewels. I think you realize that."

Something menacing lurked beneath these words, and Letty congratulated herself on having labeled MacCroy so accurately the first time she met him. He *was* dangerous.

Wanting the truth, Letty suggested coldly, "As long as we are not to have the jewels, sir, perhaps you will tell us what you intend to do with them."

"I've no objection." MacCroy strode across the floor toward them while tossing the roll of bills into the contessa's lap. "I have imperial orders to return the jewels to their rightful owner, the Empress Carlotta."

"But I thought Carlotta had gone mad," Vincent interjected, then realizing how crude this sounded, apologized. "I beg your pardon. I realize it isn't generally discussed."

MacCroy corrected him indifferently. "On the contrary, it is on everyone's lips. However, the Empress Eugenie expressly commanded that the property be delivered to Carlotta, from whom it was taken. The entire parure was a gift from her late husband and the widow will treasure it, whatever her condition."

"Eugenie. Bah! That one," the contessa burst out. "She persuaded poor Carlotta to take an imaginary crown in Mexico and then abandoned her, all so the Mexicans would be forced to pay a few uncollected debts to France. The debts were never paid, in any case, and now she thinks to win forgiveness from Carlotta by returning her jewels."

"Enough," MacCroy snapped, but Letty noticed that he did not contradict the contessa, who went on.

"I shall return to France, you know. The emperor has given me permission. But I need the money for clothes and a few oddments."

"Is that why you entered Mexico in this disguise and wheedled those jewels from some hapless Mexican guard?"

"Please, Max." She smiled. "The *wife* of a hapless guard. A hidalga. She thought me very handsome. And it was only after I took the jewels that I asked Louis Napoleon if he was lonely for me. I have his letter. Very discreet, but it promises me a flat near the Tuileries and assures me of his continued regard."

MacCroy repeated flatly, "Regard. A pretty way of—" He broke off. "Ten thousand in cash. I assure you, the emperor will approve. He knows that Eugenie means to return them to Carlotta."

"In that case . . ."

Vincent, ever the playwright, nudged Letty and whispered, "I'll write a new scene to include talk of this link between the two empresses." Turning back to MacCroy, he said in a conciliatory tone, "I had hoped to have Miss Fox wear the stones when she portrayed the unfortunate Carlotta. But I do acknowledge the higher claims of the French empress."

"Good of you, my dear fellow."

Letty could read the sarcasm in that gracious remark.

"A great pity," Vincent sighed. He held the necklace up against Letty's throat and the contessa playfully threw him the tiara she had held out. It was a modest semicirclet of matched diamonds and pearls. Vincent pushed back Letty's bonnet and set the royal semicircle in her thick hair that, catching the sunlight, appeared almost auburn. The jewels sparkled among the brushed strands.

Letty felt a surge of regal splendor and looked directly at MacCroy. He stood spellbound, one hand frozen in the position where he had raised it to take possession of the jewels. He caught his breath.

Savoring the moment, Letty assumed the French accent she used as the Empress Eugenie.

"We receive you with pleasure, Monsieur MacCroy. You have carried out your commission with alacrity." Then she added, very American, very western, "Even though it did cost me ten thousand Yankee dollars . . . or should I mention such a crass detail?"

To Letty's surprise MacCroy frowned at the sudden change; the mood was broken. He recovered himself and held out his hand for the jewels.

Vincent removed the tiara and placed it, with the necklace, in MacCroy's outstretched hand.

"So!" The contessa's voice interrupted them sharply. "Everyone is happy but me. Me you have cheated. There are a hundred dollars missing here, Max."

MacCroy was cynical. "Up to your old tricks, Pauline? Fairborne, reach there between her breasts. You will find a hundred dollar note."

With a voluptuous smile the contessa challenged, "You do not dare!"

Vincent stiffened in disgust. "Really, sir!"

While Letty watched wide-eyed, MacCroy leaned over, put his hand down the front of her pleated Spanish shirt and, accompanied by the contessa's shriek, pulled out a crumpled hundred dollar bill.

"Now how did that come to be there?" the contessa asked in great astonishment.

Letty wanted to laugh at the bemusement in Vincent's face. But she herself wasn't the least surprised at the Irishman. It was all of a piece with his looks and previous conduct.

Of one thing she was sure. She had succeeded in interesting him in her acting ability. He would find out very soon that there was more to Letty Fox than an outsized and vulgar poster.

CHAPTER *Three*

*V*INCENT WAS surprisingly cheerful about the whole affair as they were leaving the house. He found a horse and buggy for hire on busy Montgomery Street, and they got in, giving orders for the theater a block above Chinatown's Dupont Street. Letty was impressed as always by the sophistication and affluence of this new financial district, reflected in both the buildings and especially the men (there were few women) striding past the buggy with not a glance at anyone else as they discussed stocks, bonds, the newest strike in the Nevada mines and the latest investments in the hills of San Francisco. Ten years ago that land had gone begging; now it was worth a hundred times its original price during the gold strikes.

Letty would have preferred to walk back to the theater—it had seemed the ideal opportunity to discuss with Vincent some of her feelings about her performances. It might be time to modify the Letty Fox impressions, if not the content of the playlets themselves. Bring them nearer the historic truth. Less blatant sex. More honest acting.

But if she and Vincent were seen alone, gossip was bound to spring up. She knew he feared gossip for several reasons. Having once supposed it was entirely out of regard for Annabeth's feelings, she knew better these days. Vincent Fairborne was a proud man, and he preferred to keep his affairs to himself.

The Fairbornes had been among the first settlers of the Middle Plantation along the Virginia Peninsula, a background which haunted Vincent. With the estate long since gone—gambled away by his high-living ancestors—Vincent had realized early that his real inheritance was a profile to make females swoon and a theatrical manner. The stage was his haven.

Letty respected the fact that Vincent took himself and his tiny company so very seriously. She was well aware that the stagehands and extras he hired in the towns they passed through found him pompous and frequently imitated him behind his back; she resented them even while sometimes secretly sharing their amusement. They had no idea how he had struggled.

Having arrived at the theater, Vincent dismissed the horsecab, carefully counting out the silver and copper coins for the driver, adding five cents as a tip. Letty heard one of the new stagehands call to him—at this hour of the afternoon it was sure to be trouble.

"Can't get the red curtains goin' by tonight, boss. Lemme use the old blue one fer tonight."

Vincent groaned. "Much good that will do. The entire Carlotta scene requires the crimson backdrop."

"I dunno," the burly young workman said. "Get it all shipshape tomorrow in time for the breakup of all the parades and such. Mighty big shindig goin' on tomorrow. T'aint ever'day we celebrate hooking up with back East by the steamcars. No sirree bob. I was drunk for a week last May when it come to happen." He shuffled toward the stage door.

"You may be right, Ted, but do what you can," Vincent called after him.

They found Annabeth asleep in the box office, her head on her arms. She looked so very young and fragile for her thirty-five years, partially because of her precarious health, but mostly as a result of her uncommon innocence, a simplicity that was reflected in her guileless eyes, in her plaited hair gleaming in a brown knot at her nape.

Letty was interrupted in her reverie by the lascivious chuckles of three men whose eyes were glued to the gaudy poster at the theater front. She was sickened; she turned her head and caught Vincent watching her expression. He put a protective arm out as she moved toward him.

Letty sighed. "It's shameful. Will I ever get away from the damned thing?"

"Someday," Vincent promised, "you will be world famous for your skill in pantomime and impression. You will see. The audiences will love you in London and New York as they do here. I haven't been wrong about your career yet, have I, dear child?"

"Never." But was this love? Three yokels drooling over that infernal poster?

Vincent was placating. "Being with you always makes me feel ambitious for the company. I have so many new ideas, for you, for all of us —I might even start you on Shakespeare's comedies. We could work up something humorous with only a little sex to entice them. I'll lend you my annotated copy of the Bard."

"Annotated? Wonderful." Whatever that meant. It didn't matter. Her teacher needed her. His desire for her company, his words—they were like sunlight in her shadowed world.

Suddenly Vincent seemed to straighten, become more authoritative, Annabeth's husband. He knocked on the box-office door. "Wake up, sleepyhead."

Annabeth raised her head with a nervous start and scrambled off the stool. She opened the door and stood there, rubbing the sleep from her eyes.

"Oh, you are back already. You look so nice in blue, Letty. I hope you got the necklace for the show. Was that blue too? I didn't mean to go to sleep, but it's so boring now. I sold a passel of tickets earlier." As Vincent kissed her gently on her broad forehead, she confided, "Two of the gentlemen didn't act very sober. But," she added in triumph, "they paid in gold. They were down from the Virginia City mines. I gave them silver change."

"That's my girl," Vincent said, putting an arm around her as they walked back into the box office, where he examined the proceeds for the day.

Letty saw the way Annabeth lovingly pushed a lock of sandy gold hair out of his eye. Not wanting to see any more, she went around the corner of the building to a street door of the Lyric House hotel.

The Fairborne Company had taken rooms in the newly remodeled Lyric House for their San Francisco engagement. Originally a two-story false-front wooden structure frequented by newly rich miners down from the gold country, the hotel was now an impressive four stories, its roof almost the height of the theater's twin towers. The recent discovery of the great Nevada silver lode had created a demand for luxury, and the splendid new brick structure advertised itself as "Fit for a king."

Vincent had justified the inordinate expense with the rationale that since the members of the Fairborne Company were on their way to the top—New York, Chicago—they must get used to living at the top. Letty and Vincent found themselves perfectly at home in the luxurious surroundings, and Annabeth enjoyed them for her husband's sake, worried as she was about their finances.

Unfortunately their feelings weren't shared by the rest of the troupe. Calla Skutnik, the only other woman in the company, and various handymen complained that they couldn't be themselves in these hallowed halls. They couldn't spit, except in the polished brass cuspidors, and they couldn't wear muddy boots in the lobby. And God forbid they raise their voices to cuss.

The dark, cavernous lobby was swathed in fabric: drapes perenially closed against the vagrant sunlight, emerald green velvet upholstering every piece of furniture in the room. Even the marble table was cloaked by a gold-tasseled table runner.

Letty padded across the carpeting to the staircase, bestowing her best stage smile on the little desk clerk and the portly couple waiting to register. She heard the whispers as she started up the staircase and wondered if they were discussing her. She hurried on. She swung around the newel post and stepped onto the cheaper carpeting of the third floor —the luxuriant green pile was confined to the first two. Here, the hall furniture—ladderback chairs, narrow credenza, and innumerable potted palms—was less elegant, the rooms lower priced. Vincent regarded this as shameful and persisted in remarking, "I'm damned if the Fairborne Company is going to remain third-floor tenants. It's going to be second floor for us one day soon."

But the expensive stage sets and carefully chosen costumes, the theater rental and salaries for twelve people, ate up most of the profits. All the troupe knew that the Fairborne Company would never make a big profit unless they went East, where the very fact of their being from the "wild" West would be enough to insure a huge volume of business.

Vincent's feelings notwithstanding, Letty considered her own third-floor room far more comfortable than any she had known on their tours before they reached San Francisco.

Despite the new grandeur of the hotel, the door to her room was opened by the usual skeleton key. Knowing that almost any key in the city would open the lock, and passionate as she was for privacy, Letty had taken all her savings at the end of her first year as company star and bought a clothespress with a secure lock and key. Although smaller than many, this oaken cupboard—as the others called it—was an encumbrance every time the Players moved on. All the same, it was home to her little personal treasures, the most fashionable of her dresses, and most important, every note, every gift ever given her by Vincent Fairborne.

Letty opened the door of her room and stopped in her tracks. The cupboard door was ajar, the afternoon sunlight slanting obliquely off the front. Two hours earlier she had closed and securely locked it, a routine from which she never faltered.

Alarmed and indignant, she examined the steel lock, which appeared untouched, and looked inside, breathless with anxiety. What would she do if her clothes had been stolen or ruined by vandals?

She ran her hands over the gowns, mantles and coats hanging on one side of the clothespress. None seemed to be missing, and they were just as she had left them. Her high-heeled shoes were all in their drawer below. Turning her attention to the several side drawers, she found the usual jumble of stockings topped by her one pair of patterned silks, which were still neatly wrapped in tissue.

No trinkets or jewelry appeared to be missing. Her most valuable pieces, a cameo framed in a thin web of gold and a topaz ring, were nestled in wads of cotton. She could not have borne losing them: the topaz was a gift from Vincent, celebrating the first time they made love, and the cameo was the only possession of her mother's that hadn't been pawned or sold outright.

She pulled open the next drawer. Behind an accumulation of souvenirs, playbills, reviews and fan letters were the notes to her from Vincent, all carefully "lost" among words from strangers.

In memory of those happy moments. They had spent three hours reading Dickens together, Vincent coaching her in her pronunciation of the various dialects.

I never knew what true beauty was until that hour today . . . Written after they had made love. Oh, how she craved his warmth and protection.

Adorable and adored. This had followed her first-night success as Messalina.

How I love your adoring eyes! If only things were otherwise. . . .

Nothing missing, so far as she could tell.

She mused for a moment, staring intently at the pile, and realized with a start that the last letters were on top; Letty had always kept the latest notes and fan letters on the bottom.

She took a step back from the cupboard, looking thoughtfully at the gowns. . . . As she thought back she realized that the last time she had put away the black-and-gold taffeta with the frilly bustle, she had placed it carefully against the wall of the cabinet. Now it was crushed between a dotted muslin and a furred mantle.

And yet nothing was missing.

Annabeth?

Panic coursed through her. Not Annabeth; please, God, not Annabeth. She could be so dreadfully hurt. But she had seen Annabeth in the theater box office only minutes ago, and she had been as friendly as always.

Not Annabeth, then. Besides, it was too professional a job, this neat opening of the door with a key. Nor were any of the notes missing. Letty counted them again; she knew by heart every line her beloved had ever written to her. Nothing missing.

What on earth was the vandal looking for? It was most unlikely that any of their Chinatown neighbors would commit such an outrage. They were coming to accept the Fairborne group as one of their own, in a manner of speaking. From the first, Vincent had paid his way, putting up money for neighborhood causes and otherwise making himself welcome, at least financially. He had even been nominated (or so he was led to believe) a member of the tong that currently ruled the area.

Ironically, Letty had observed that Vincent considered himself superior to the Asiatics. When she told Vincent of the break-in, he was liable, in his quiet, dignified way, to accuse first the Chinese and then the management, which could be disastrous.

Who could have done this? It was obviously not the work of a madman or someone who hated her; her property hadn't been attacked. Someone was curious and had rifled her belongings. It amounted to that.

Letty went to find Annabeth and Vincent and was disappointed at the cavalier way they treated the whole affair. When they found that no harm had been done to her clothing, nothing missing, no slashing or vandalism, the Fairbornes minimized the incident, Annabeth saying, "You've just forgotten how you put things, honey. That's all. You were in a hurry, you were excited about the jewels, and just threw things in. That's all, isn't it, Vincent?"

"I shouldn't think it matters too much," Vincent agreed. "So long as nothing was taken." He squeezed Letty's hand reassuringly. "You are joining us for dinner, aren't you?" But Letty couldn't pass it off so lightly; the memory remained, nagging her just as she thought she'd forgotten it.

Letty seldom ate much before a performance, but the prospect of lively conversation took her mind off the familiar stage fright that still, after all this time, engulfed her the instant before her first entrance. She changed to a lilac silk gown, whose bodice would be easy to remove for her first stage appearance. Her bonnet was not flattering, but it fitted very carefully over the dull brown wig that had already been carefully arranged for her first sketch.

When they met, Annabeth, as usual, giggled at the sight of her in the costume. They walked down the street with Calla Skutnik and Vincent, who, despite his claim that it was embarrassing to be seen in public with three women, seemed to thrive on the admiration of the passersby for carrying off this very feat. Because Annabeth tired easily, they walked slowly, chatting and joking the whole way to the restaurant. Annabeth delighted in calling everyone's attention to Letty's wig—"How funny you look, Letty! It changes you."

"It is *supposed* to change her, my dear," Vincent said. "Queen Victoria does not look in the least like the Empress Eugenie. Remember how we studied sketches of the two women that were made on their visits between London and Paris? Very different. And the wig helps this transformation."

"But it makes her look so ugly, and she's not, actually."

Everyone laughed, and Calla said in her gutteral voice, "That's no lie, girl. But it ain't acting when you keep lookin' like yourself."

Letty always felt awkward when her looks became the topic of conversation, but she was rescued by Calla, who wanted to know what happened about the jewels Letty was supposed to wear as the Empress Carlotta.

While Vincent herded his little group into a curtained-off booth in their favorite Chinese restaurant, he explained that the jewels had gone back to their original owner.

"I thought it appropriate," he added. "The poor woman has suffered enough."

"And he saw a lady dressed like a man," Annabeth put in. "I said he should have her in the show. Oh, and a man from the French emperor, he took the jewels. He really knows the Emperor What's-His-Name."

Letty said, "Napoleon the Third. Louis Napoleon."

"He was awfully rude, my Vincent says."

The wardrobe woman hooted. "Whyn't you argue him out of it? Your money's as good as his."

"Because," Letty explained, "the man was very tough. I think he's a secret imperial agent of some kind."

"Horrid!" Annabeth huddled against her husband. "These foreigners are dangerous."

"But interesting." Letty didn't know exactly why she made that comment; it was bound to irritate Vincent. "He knows all the crowned heads and he is likely to be critical of our show tonight."

Vincent stared thoughtfully at the green privacy curtain separating them from the other diners. Letty wondered what had intrigued him so about the idea of a critical audience, unless he thought Max MacCroy might be the harbinger of the imperial-class patron he hoped to win over. The women all looked at him expectantly.

He murmured, still deep in thought, "If he could spread the word about you—us, that is—we might even be invited to a command performance for Louis Napoleon and Eugenie."

"Wow!" Calla said. "That'd be somethin' to think on. Me in Paris, France."

Restraining her excitement at the thought of her birthplace, Letty asked, "What makes you think he will approve of our sketches? Eugenie sounds pretty calculating, the way you characterized her. And as I play her," she added quite honestly.

Annabeth insisted, "Vincent wrote her beautifully. Nobody could take offense at the truth."

Calla snorted, and Letty said, "Especially the truth."

She was remembering the Irishman's cynical manner and felt sure he could be trouble. Still, for reasons she could never have put a name to, she was anxious that he see how good she could be at her best, that he know that she was not the trollop he saw on the poster.

Without question, MacCroy had reacted when Vincent placed the tiara on her head in the room on Montgomery Street. But whether he approved or disapproved of her "imperial look" had been difficult to ascertain.

"How do you know the emperor's man is coming to the theater tonight?" Vincent asked suddenly.

"Because Annabeth sold him a ticket."

"I did?" Annabeth said, knitting her brow.

Letty reminded her, "The man who frightened you when you came out to talk to him."

"Oh ... him! The one with the scary blue eyes? They saw right through me. I didn't like him at first. But later when he bought the ticket and I had to tell him we liked silver, not paper money, he was real nice. He smiled at me."

"Well, well, well." Vincent kissed his wife's hand and gave Letty a puzzled look. She gazed back at him innocently and went on drinking the China tea that always soothed her before a performance.

The four returned to the theater by the alley entrance. This was directly opposite an obscure brothel door by which some of Madame Lu's more illustrious Nob Hill patrons came and went at odd hours. Nob Hill was beginning to attract a few of the men who had made their poke speculating, not on mines, but upon the future of the transcontinental railroad. It seemed pretty far away from the business and pleasures of Portsmouth Square, but that lively area was rapidly becoming passé.

The minute Letty stepped into the narrow passage backstage she began to stiffen with nervousness. She savored the strange backstage smells—the stale powder, the company costumes with their hint of perfume and sweat, the musty wood and canvas flats that made a palace out of a barn. All the same, the atmosphere made her legs feel prickly, the way they felt when she stood on a high ledge looking down. That terrible urge to jump into the valley below that some people experienced when standing on a cliff must be like her desire to plunge into her life onstage in front of all those elegant San Francisco swells and a few genuine theater-lovers.

She shared a dressing room with Annabeth and Calla. Annabeth played silent bit parts, and Calla was at once wardrobe mistress, dresser and small-parts actress. Neither of these women was nervous in the least but then neither was ambitious.

Tonight would be special. Letty did not need Vincent to tell her he was delighted that the company might impress the emperor's friend.

"And then," Annabeth had said, "we can all go over the ocean on a ship. That's like a ferryboat, only bigger."

Calla guffawed. "And a deal rougher, when it comes to that. You ever been seasick? . . . Hold still, Letty. You gotta hold your breath or you ain't gonna get these lacings tight enough."

"I was crazy to ever think I could shrink into a tiny creature like that —I'm a head taller than Victoria, for one thing." But she wore the small waist-cincher deliberately because it was the only opaque garment she could wear beneath the robes, and its presence next to her skin made her less naked. In spite of her flesh-colored tights she felt naked and from the audience reaction they shared her feeling.

"You get a tinier waistline," Calla said, "you gonna have nothin' to hold your bosom and butt together. And it's your bosom and butt gets them crowds in," Calla said as she pulled tight the strings of the busk around Letty's waist. Letty groaned. She walked up and down. But she was now little Queen Victoria. She slowed to a glide, pressing her ribs and taking long, gasping breaths.

"All right. Now the nightgown. Then the robe."

The filmy robes went on over her head and fell into place. They had been made up in what the seamstresses called silk gauze, an intriguing material for the purposes of the Letty Fox show.

Always superstitious, Letty called out, "Luck?" and bent her little finger, holding it out to the women. Annabeth hooked Letty's finger with her own. They turned to Calla Skutnik, whose stout finger repeated the gesture. Both women said brightly, "Good luck!" and Letty moved out into the passage with head raised and back regally straight. The gas globes around the stage and dimly lighting the wings provided an eerie effect that gave Letty chills. In a moment she would become Queen Victoria.

Calla Skutnik passed her, bundled in a long flannel nightgown and robes, her abundant gray hair piled into a ruffled nightcap. She played Victoria's mother, the duchess of Kent, a somewhat comic figure in the script. Annabeth scooted along in a maid's costume whose flowing black skirts made her look as if she were without feet.

The pianist, a local lady of uncertain years but enthusiastic touch, broke into a series of what she called "English country airs." The music managed to eclipse partially the drone of the audience—the talking, jokes and shouts of recognition of the predominantly male audience in the orchestra nearest the stage; nonetheless, Letty could still hear the buzz of ordinary conversation under the music.

Damn them! It always threw her off.

The music faded away and Annabeth came gliding onto the set, accompanied by a pleasant ripple of laughter. She gathered up scattered clothing and tidied the boudoir—the kitchen chairs, heavily gilded table and the much prized chaise lounge, its rich once-pink plush cushions now faded to a dull cream color.

Upstage left, six wooden steps climbed into the wings where Letty waited. One of the stage hands, a friendly, decent fellow with huge hands that minded their own business, stood by to lift Letty up to the top of the steps.

Meanwhile Calla entered the scene from stage level with a militant stride that clearly showed her authority and provoked a smattering of applause from her own small coterie of admirers—folks who enjoyed her ample curves and homey appearance. A couple of boos for the villainess could be heard from the balcony.

The sketch revealed a bossy mother who ordered every phase of her daughter's life. As a slightly absurd Teutonic character, Calla got some laughs for her grammatical mistakes, but her manner showed that once her daughter became queen—which was expected momentarily—it was mama who would rule the roost.

Just as those males who had come solely for sexual titillation began to grow restless, Letty Fox was lifted to the top of the steps. She drew a long breath and started down the steps onto the stage, all browbeaten innocence in her nightgown and robe. Thunderous applause met her appearance.

Letty walked downstage, talking to her mother, answering softly. The audience's murmur became interspersed with whistles. She walked directly in front of two oil lamps placed at the upstage walls, where, to some, the lighting suggested nudity beneath the translucent gown and robe. When she had first played this scene she was careful to walk with great precision, trying to reveal nothing of her body but the outlines. Since then she had realized that this prudery succeeded only in tantalizing the audiences; she now walked straight ahead, taking her normal steps, pretending she was actually the young Victoria.

As she moved forward, all the time exchanging short dutiful replies to her mother's tirade, it was impossible for her to distinguish individual faces beyond the dim gaslights. She was vaguely aware that the theater was about three-quarters filled. Not too bad. She wondered in passing if the Irishman was out there in the sea of faces.

Her fear and trembling had vanished the second she stepped out before the audience. She knew she controlled them, no matter what she thought of them. Pausing very close to the front row of repeat patrons, she felt their eyes boring through her gown, through the filmy robe. Two miners near the aisle were craning forward, practically falling out of their seats in their effort to see the *real* Letty. She slid back a step, reminding herself that she was close enough to be in danger if one of them reached for her in his drunken excitement.

Before things could get out of hand, Calla spoke the cue that brought Vincent onstage, as an emissary from the dying King William the Fourth. While Calla puffed up like a pouter pigeon and announced all the changes she would make in the palace when she was running things, Letty moved slowly away from the footlights and toward the backdrop. Waiting until the buzz and whistles faded after this movement, she spoke the line that closed the sketch—her first command as Queen of England —and sent her mother back to her own country. This historic inaccuracy satisfied the crowd, especially as Calla shrieked and fainted. The curtains were quickly drawn.

Laughter, followed by applause; the crowd was pleased.

The second sketch was brief. Catherine the Great, empress of Russia, signed numerous love notes promising her favors to various lovers and then walked off with the lackey who carried all these messages of eternal love. This time a good deal depended on her movements in picking up the amatory epistles that kept falling off her desk. Each time she bent over, the men seated in the front rows were graced with a whopping eyeful of her cleavage.

The last time she stooped over in this provocative routine, Letty found herself only inches from Max MacCroy's face. His eyes bore into hers, unnerving her, making her feel that her body was aflame. Those disturbing eyes followed every line of her body as she rose slowly, trying to recover herself.

CHAPTER *Four*

S*HE TRIED* not to look his way again; for once in her life she was glad of the whistles from her admirers in the audience, anything to take her mind off the Irishman.

She went through the motions of the scene. As soon as the curtains closed, she rushed to the dressing room with her arms folded over her bosom. Her reaction to MacCroy's presence took her completely by surprise.

He was in the theater. He had seen the sketches. This man who consorted freely with emperors and kings had every reason to think the poster revealed the true Letty Fox. Letty wanted so desperately for him to see that there was more to her than the vulgar behavior he had just witnessed.

It wasn't as if she liked him personally. He affected her in a disconcerting, even shocking way. She told herself he was like those few dirty fellows in the audience. Yet it seemed vitally important that he should respect her and know she was not what she might appear to be.

She had to concentrate. She could still hear the whistles and applause for Catherine the Great. But it didn't take her mind off the Irishman.

The Empress Carlotta was the subject of her next sketch. Because of the recent tragedy in Mexico, Vincent had agreed that it should be played comparatively straight, a rapid few minutes during which Carlotta's maid was substituted for the empress on a tryst with an adoring footman. Carlotta's only physical revelations were the two dainty limbs she showed while lending her shoes and stockings to the maid. This got the usual vociferous response, but Letty was trembling so much from nerves that she could hardly get the stockings off.

She had resolved not to look down again at the Irishman during the performance. In her efforts to avoid him, however, she was astonished to find another somewhat familiar face watching her from the audience, this time in one of the boxes elevated above both sides of the orchestra. Like the rest of the big, domed theater interior with its cluster of bright gaslights overhead, the boxes and railings were richly covered with crimson plush.

Letty usually anticipated eagerly the poignant farewell between Carlotta and Maximilian that followed the lighthearted maid-and-footman scene. Tonight other concerns made her forget Vincent's tender, protective embrace, his lips closing gently over hers. She whispered to him, "Look at the box. That woman today."

Vincent's blue-gray eyes wandered to the box while he continued declaiming his eternal love for her. What he saw was impressive. The Contessa Servandoni was stunning in black brocade with dazzling rubies at ears and throat. In fact, her throat was as bare as Letty's during her Catherine sketch, and a good half of her breasts could be seen.

But the woman was not completely foolish. Beside her sat a huge grizzled man with a face to match his size. Something about his ill-fitting evening clothes, and the way he stuck one thick finger into his collar every few minutes to loosen it suggested to Letty a type often seen here, a miner who had struck it rick and wasn't used to his rich man's uniform.

A movement near the footlights caught her eye. A grinning young man climbed over the back of what had been MacCroy's seat—now vacant—and slid into his place. All her fears had been justified.

She went up on her lines for the first time in more than two years, and Vincent was forced to cover for her with a quick, affectionate line that should have been hers. She recovered for the tragic finale, his departure and her "Farewell, my love," cried in heartbreaking crescendo after his tall, distinguished figure.

Letty rushed into the dressing room after the curtain-close to change into her most elaborate costume, that of Eugenie, empress of France. An exquisite ballgown skirted with thirty yards of gauze and tulle was festooned with tiny blue flocked flowers. The dress was difficult to clean, and since it was worn six times a week might not be said to be pristine, but those near her, whether onstage or in the first rows, were seduced by the tantalizing whiff of her most expensive perfume. The neckline and full corseting accentuated every voluptuous curve that was fully explored during this sketch by the roving hands of "Emperor Louis Napoleon."

Common gossip had it that the emperor had been forced to marry Eugenie because he couldn't get the fair Spanish countess to bed by any other means. Letty was at her best in this teasing, charming flirtation, in her skill at evading the imperial hands. It was not Vincent's favorite role: he abhorred the crude groping, considering it beneath the dignity of a gentleman, not to mention a monarch. But he knew what brought money into the Fairborne bank account, and he depended on this scene to help fill the coffers.

Though her jewels were paste, Letty's resemblance in her red-gold wig to the real empress had been frequently remarked, and she felt confident in the role, playing it with a hint of the proud Spanish grandee close to the teasing surface.

During an idle moment while the emperor received a jeweled necklace from his aide to use as a bribe for his fair prey, Letty allowed her attention to wander to the box seat where the Contessa Servandoni was enthroned. Her burly escort had moved away from her side and sat glowering at a newcomer—none other than Max MacCroy, who, leaning over the back of the contessa's chair, was engaged in conversation with her. The contessa had turned her back on the stage in order to accommodate him.

It was doubtful if she had seen Letty at all in her Empress Eugenie role. MacCroy, on the contrary, though deeply engrossed in the contessa, glanced often at Letty on the stage. In some ways she was relieved—at least he hadn't been disgusted enough to walk out on her.

With some difficulty, Letty turned her attention back to Eugenie and finished the sketch. By the time the curtains opened on the Messalina sketch, the favorite of many of Letty's admirers, both the contessa and MacCroy were gone, along with the contessa's burly guard. It was clear that despite the Irishman's obvious interest in Letty his real object had been to win over the contessa. Letty did not doubt his reason—she was a beauty.

She was relieved, however, that he would not see Messalina, though disappointed that he had not been more impressed by her ability to play the lady, as demonstrated by her Carlotta and Eugenie.

Vincent had chosen to write about Messalina, young wife of the aging Claudius, because the story contained both sexual and comic elements: Messalina's seduction of one of her husband's loyal slaves and her ensuing marriage to him in a mock ceremony. This conjugal debacle was accompanied by the pianist with the chorus of "Beautiful Dreamer," a recent hit back East that was making its way across the country in the track of the Transcontinental Railroad.

The sketch ended—and with it the show—with the shadowy figure of a headsman wielding a sword behind a scrim. The lighting brought the shadowy figure into relief only a minute or two before the final curtain.

Even as Messalina and her lover lay on a couch in the throes of lovemaking, the audience saw the executioner behind them and knew what end would befall the lovers. It brought the house down.

After the final curtain call, Vincent expressed his disappointment about MacCroy. "Evidently the Frenchman wasn't too impressed by the show," he muttered. "I wonder what we might have done to please the fellow. It would have been a triumph. You never know what it might lead to, in our profession."

Letty dismissed the idea brusquely. "Forget him. He came west to buy those jewels. That's all."

"I expect so. Do you suppose the contessa and that fellow are—"

"Lovers? What else?"

She marveled that a man who could write so explicitly about sex became such a prude in conversation. Was he as sexually restrained with Annabeth?

He shrugged at her comment. Then he shook her fingers playfully. "You were splendid tonight, Letty, as always. I was extremely proud of you. You have such great potential." He saw Annabeth. "Well, my sweet, how did it go? My little girl looks tired."

"Oh, not at all," Annabeth objected. "I loved it. You were thrilling —both of you." She clapped her hands. "Darling, you looked so handsome out there, I just wanted to . . . well . . . hug you."

"Then hug away, my pet." He kept his hold on Letty's hand but raised both arms high, leaving plenty of room around the waist of his Roman tunic for Annabeth to hug him with her cheek pressed hard against his shoulder. Over her head he looked at Letty.

For one timeless moment his eyes told Letty he loved her, an unmistakable look that asked for understanding. Guiltily, she freed her fingers from his and turned away.

She thought about it later, alone, when she went into her room again shortly after midnight and saw the cold starlight outside her window, the chilly white coverlet on her bed and the fashionable striped wallpaper that enclosed her on all sides.

She reminded herself impatiently that she was the luckiest woman in the world. If Vincent Fairborne hadn't gone into the Dry Run Saloon in Virginia City almost ten years ago to fetch one of his actresses, he would never have heard Letty's desperate pleas to her stepfather. Leonard Fox needed money. His good looks had rapidly gone to seed, and of late he had developed a wheedling voice that grew more irritable when he was opposed.

He had been opposed that frigid night by his stepdaughter, who refused to go to bed with a fifty-year-old miner who had just struck it rich. And Vincent Fairborne, golden knight, had heard and pitied, and eventually topped the miner's offer by one hundred dollars in gold. It was an enormous sum to Letty and, as it turned out, to Vincent Fairborne himself.

He could have seen very little that was prepossessing about the leggy, shivering adolescent girl. His treatment of her afterward demonstrated that he had no sexual interest in the gawky child; yet he had paid three hundred dollars. They walked down Virginia City's "C" Street to a hotel, where Annabeth and Calla Skutnik put Letty into a cot in the parlor of the Fairborne suite; she awoke the next day to find herself adopted by the company. Letty eagerly earned her keep, washing, ironing, running errands. But most of all she enjoyed sitting at Vincent's feet, learning more about the world than her mother had been able to teach her. She knew a little mathematics and much about her native France, but it was Vincent's reading of great classic and melodramatic roles that she enjoyed the most, and she soon committed the female roles to memory so she could give the appropriate responses to his readings.

He was as patient with her as he was with his wife, and if his manner became pedantic now and then, it seemed understandable. He was a teacher, and the teacher was always correct.

Whenever she found his manner cool, too authoritative or opinionated, she remembered that hideous night when Vincent had bargained for her virtue.

She never saw Leonard Fox again. He died two years after she left, in a mine cave-in at Gold Hill, Nevada. Letty did not weep for him. Rather, she was relieved.

Letty crossed the room in the darkness and fumbled for a match to light the oil lamp on the table near the bed. The flickering light through the frosted glass chimney had little effect on her spirits. Despite the chill of the San Francisco spring, she took off her coat and walked over to the window.

Pushing the shade aside, Letty looked out at the same view that had depressed her a minute before. Somewhere among the canyons nestled in the black hills Max MacCroy and the contessa were probably making love. Letty could imagine how violent and persistent the man would be. Nothing gentle or tender about that fellow.

She hugged her shoulders against the chill, thinking cynically that the one thing MacCroy would probably *not* do was ever let a female shiver with the cold . . . unintentionally.

Her thoughts drifted to Annabeth and Vincent in the two-room suite at the front of the building. What were they doing now? Talking companionably about the performance or about the midnight supper the company had gone to at an Italian restaurant below Portsmouth Square? Most of them, including Letty, had drunk a little too much red wine, and after the first comforting glow it left her depressed, as usual. The Fairbornes were wise; neither had drunk more than a glass of the strong, homemade wine.

Perhaps they were making love. She wondered, picturing it mentally, and felt gooseflesh prickle her upper arms.

"What a shame I have such selective tastes," Letty thought wryly. Probably half of tonight's audience would like to be sharing her bed at this very moment. She decided to take a hot tub and scent it with some of the perfume Vincent had given her for Christmas.

The third-floor bathroom was at the end of the hall, but at this late hour she could be sure of taking her bath without disturbance.

With a smear of face cream she removed the heavy stage paint that remained in spite of her efforts to scrub it off before they all went to supper. She wrapped herself in a heavy brown flannel robe that would have disgraced the empresses she portrayed and headed toward the clean, large bathroom with its clawfooted porcelain tub and "some of the finest indoor plumbing west of Denver."

She reached for the ornate brass doorknob, only to have the door swing open in her face as a man stepped out, towel circling his hips, satin robe thrown over one shoulder, Roman sandals on his feet. Nothing else. Letty was aware only of the expanse of his shoulder muscles and the clean lines of his neck and chest before she recovered enough from her shock to look into MacCroy's amused blue eyes.

Letty managed to sound more calm than she felt. "Are you everywhere, Mr. MacCroy? I seem to find you underfoot all over San Francisco."

"Not at all, Miss Fox. I am currently lodging at this palatial establishment."

"Why pick the Lyric House? It seems to me there are a good many other hotels dying to take you in."

"Let's say I was hoping to see more of you." He rubbed his tousled black hair with the robe, adding, "Not that it seems likely after your performance tonight."

She was mortified, but refused to let him see that his remark had struck home.

"Well, I am certainly seeing more of *you* than I intend to see in future."

"I wouldn't be too sure about that." He stepped aside, but did not leave her space to open the door wider. "You disappoint me, Miss Fox. I would have thought you believed in the equality of men and women. I have seen you, and now you see me." For a moment she wondered if he would drop the towel from around his hips. He put one arm and then the other into the sleeves of the expensive lounging robe before he swung the towel away. He grinned maliciously as she stared at him.

"Keep faith, Messalina. Maybe you will see more next time." As he turned his head, his face brushed her long, tumbled hair.

She tried to thrust past him but he was unyielding as steel. She felt the flesh of his chest, still damp from the bath. Suddenly he stepped aside. She bolted into the big, white bathroom and locked the door. In the dark she fumbled to turn the gas up from its faint blue glimmer.

She listened with her ear against the door and heard his footsteps retreating down the hall. Her heartbeat slowed to normal. She could take her bath without wondering if he was going to break in, but she wouldn't put it beyond him.

The water was heated by gas in an extremely modern way, probably because the hotel's lodgers were often star performers in the theater next door. They needed to wash off the makeup that stained the bodies of dancers who preferred paint to tights.

Reluctantly Letty shed the warmth of her bathrobe and, shivering a little, turned on the hot water tap.

To her disgust, little more than a dribble emerged from the faucet. The Irishman had used all the hot water, damn him!

She couldn't wait here all night for more water to heat. After all her exertions during the performance, her exhausted body ached for some of that warmth, but it was too late now.

She rewrapped the bathrobe tightly around her body, stepped into her slippers and unbolted the door. She hurried to her room down the dimly lighted hall. As she was closing her door she heard the betraying creak of another door along the hall. She hoped Mr. MacCroy had been disappointed. He probably thought she would come out of the bathroom like Messalina, this time without the protection of tights.

She realized that he was here on her account but something told her there was more to it than a desire to get her into bed. The city was full of women for that purpose, starting with the Contessa Servandoni. He had certainly been fawning over her in the theater tonight.

"What does he want with me . . . really?"

She had already gotten into bed when she heard the noise coming from the next room.

Whistling. At this hour.

Who the devil was in that room? It had been occupied until two days ago by a merchant from Hangchow and had been vacant since. Now, a whistler at one in the morning.

The tune . . . what was it? It sounded so familiar.

"Beautiful Dreamer."

In her opinion one whistler sounded very like another, and thanks to the Messalina sketch anyone connected with the Lyric Theatre was familiar with the song. There was no particular reason why she should be convinced that the whistler was Max MacCroy, but she knew it was.

A sudden thought made her sit up.

"He must have seen me as Messalina. He didn't leave the theater early after all."

She didn't know whether to be flattered or humiliated. No wonder he had talked to her in that insulting fashion outside the bathroom.

He had said he came west from Chicago because of something someone told him about her. A long way in order to whistle "Beautiful Dreamer" outside her door at one in the morning.

The fact that MacCroy had traveled that distance intrigued her. But the man was a mystery, and she wanted no part of any more mysteries. She stared at the clothespress and wondered.

CHAPTER *Five*

*C*HURCH BELLS, Chinese firecrackers, barking dogs, wind chimes, shouts and clanging fire bells . . . It was the first-year celebration of the joining of the Central Pacific and Union Pacific railroads. A great salute at dawn set off the San Francisco celebration on this May day in 1870.

Within a couple of hours the whole city had gone wild. Fighting the racket with pillows over her head had proved useless, so Letty Fox got up, washed with cold water and violet soap (a present from an admirer) and dressed for the parade she would watch later from the grandstands with the Fairborne Company.

Remembering the midnight whistler, Letty deliberately slammed the door as she went out, hoping he would think of her as he awoke. She usually ate her weekday breakfast at a little French café up the street, affording her the opportunity to practice that beloved language. The glamorous dining room of the Lyric House was reserved strictly for weekend repasts.

Letty hesitated in surprise at the door of the cafe—Vincent Fairborne was seated at the counter, attacking a plateful of the café's famous thin flapjacks. No Gold Town flannel cakes here, for which Letty was profoundly grateful.

Upon seeing her, Vincent's somber expression brightened.

"Couldn't sleep? I can't blame you. What a racket outside! It gave Annabeth a headache that brought on one of her spring coughs. Poor thing—she'll be devastated if she misses the parade."

"But she musn't." Letty perched herself on the stool beside him. "She's talked of nothing but the parade all week. Why not bring Annabeth some of Mathieu's good French cocoa? And some spice buns."

"Excellent." He smiled fondly at her. "You are so very good to Annabeth." His hand closed over hers on the bar. "If you hadn't nursed her through that typhus last winter in Oregon, she'd never have survived.

That was a close call, and no one knows it better than I. She still has that wretched cough."

"It's easy to be good to Annabeth," Letty said, knowing her feelings were genuine. "She has a rare simplicity."

Annabeth had to be aware that Letty was in love with her husband, but she never tried to place obstacles in the way of their meetings or time together. Annabeth even accepted their stage love scenes, with Letty only half-dressed.

"Without guile," Vincent said softly. "It was that naiveté that first drew me to her. I've told you how we met, haven't I? I had just come north to New York from Virginia, you know, in the hope of forming a company . . . a very serious, classical troupe."

"I remember . . ." She hesitated, then blurted out, "It seems such a pity you weren't able to have children. The miscarriages and all."

Vincent regarded the plate of food before him, then pushed it aside. "Two miscarriages. She just isn't strong enough. God knows, I dream of sons and daughters of my own. It's one of the reasons I married her. She seemed a perfect mother. But—" he touched her fingers again "—that's got nothing to do with today. This is a celebration. One year of the transcontinental trains. They've done wonders for San Francisco."

Behind him, two admiring schoolgirls in uniform pinafores and coiled braids over their ears giggled as Vincent turned. He heard the stifled sound and asked graciously, "Are you young ladies going to the parade?"

The girls could hardly answer, they were so enthralled with this handsome stranger. Vincent's attention to his admirers always pleased Letty, even when she found herself jealous of the time they took—time that he might have spent with her. She could never understand Annabeth's total lack of possessiveness.

A shadow crossed the window; a passerby had stopped and was peering in, his hands cupped around his eyes. Letty choked over her hot black coffee. Max MacCroy was staring in at her. No mistaking that. Vincent, meanwhile, had gotten up to autograph the girls' schoolbooks, so Letty was the only person in MacCroy's direct line of vision. But her first annoyed reaction was surmounted by a sudden impulse to confound him and possibly arouse Vincent's jealousy. She crooked her forefinger and beckoned him to join her.

The Irishman gave Letty a mock salute and strolled into the little café, passing between Vincent and Letty in order to take Vincent's empty stool. Vincent swung back from his admirers.

"I believe that is my seat," he said, frigidly polite.

"Certainly, sir." MacCroy slipped off the stool and immediately straddled the one on Letty's other side.

"Is there anything safe to eat in this place?"

Letty laughed. Something tough and daring inside her found his brash nerve appealing.

"Everything. Ask Mathieu."

He frowned, looking at her through narrowed eyes.

"You pronounced that very well. Do you speak French, by any chance?"

"Not by chance, no. I was born in France."

MacCroy's eyes widened; he seemed pleased out of all proportion to her simple statement.

"Ah! Excellent."

Vincent leaned around her to address MacCroy. "So we meet again," he said curtly. "Just what *is* your interest in the Fairborne Company, Mr. MacCroy?"

Max struck his forehead dramatically. "Good Lord! I believe I have forgotten to relay a message to you, Fairborne. Your wife seems to be looking for you down on Dupont Street."

Vincent raised his head, looking reflectively out the café window to the street.

Letty was disturbed; Annabeth had a history of unexpected wanderings. On one occasion she had gotten hopelessly lost, and they didn't find her until she was halfway down a hilly slope with a view of Fort Mason and the Presidio. They found her crouching in the grass, picking little yellow poppies. She had jumped up guiltily when Vincent ran toward her, Letty, Calla and two policemen in his wake. Annabeth simply explained that she was hungry for peaceful hillsides.

Vincent got up at once, his face momentarily cross. But his usual concern took over, just as her own impatience with the situation evaporated: Annabeth's innocent peccadillos were little enough to put up with when compared to the moody temperaments of some others in the company. "Including myself," Letty thought. She started to follow Vincent, but MacCroy took her wrist in a steely grasp.

Furiously jerking her arm, she said, "Let me go."

Vincent stopped her, saying to her in a whisper, "See what he wants. I don't like the fellow, but if there is a chance of a good engagement for the company, we can't afford to antagonize him."

"I wouldn't trust him two feet away."

"Don't worry, my dear. I assure you, I am his equal."

She devoutly hoped he was right. As Vincent reached the door, he turned and said, "I'm sure Annabeth hasn't gone far. They say the crowds are beginning to mob Stockton and Montgomery streets. She can't get through either street. And I saw them gathering at Jackson." He took his watch out and glanced at it. "I'd better hurry. We have to get to our places in the stands. We will meet you in front of the theater in half an hour. That sound right?"

"Fine. Hurry, now." She encouraged him, even nudged him onward because she was jealous and knew it. There wasn't a soul in the world, male or female, relative or otherwise, who cared that much for her. She thought about walking out of this place and back to her room, but pride stopped her.

Pride and the pleasant knowledge that at least someone wanted her! She went back to the bar and sat down beside MacCroy. Her coffee was cold but Mathieu refilled it with a decoction of repeatedly boiled coffee beans. She saw MacCroy eyeing it with interest.

"French?"

"So I'm told. Only Mathieu makes it strong enough."

He looked from her to the lean youth who was pouring the black liquid. "Don't tell me this child is the celebrated Mathieu."

"None other." She introduced them and discovered she had opened the way to some busy chatter in French. She tried to translate mentally. It wasn't as easy as she had hoped—occasionally she missed entire sentences. In the middle of this exchange Max MacCroy turned to Letty.

"Are you following this?"

"Yes. I know Mathieu's entire history, his birth in Lyons, his training in Paris, his arrival in the hold of a French bark that anchored in San Francisco after a merry trip around old Cape Horn."

"Excellent. Do you think you could attempt to speak French with just a smidgeon of a Spanish accent?"

She opened her mouth in surprise and almost forgot to close it.

"Me? Speak French with a—I've spent my whole life trying to speak French with a French accent."

He laughed. That broad, olive-skinned face of his softened a little. She caught herself staring at his mouth . . . sensuous and perhaps cruel, that was obvious. What would those lips feel like, crushed hard upon . . . She closed her eyes, smiled in what she hoped was lighthearted indifference.

"I trust you are going to tell me now why you would want anyone to speak French with a Spanish accent."

He was still studying her. "Your trust is misplaced."

While she fumed over that, he reached to touch her face. Startled, she waited an instant too long before she tried to draw back. He ran his blunt fingers over her profile from her forehead down to her chin. She licked her dry lips. His fingers hesitated, then they traced her mouth; she almost betrayed her feelings by a pleasurable shiver. She tried to regain command of the situation by a careless challenge, realizing paradoxically that she could hardly regain what she hadn't possessed in the first place.

"Are you quite satisfied? You don't have the look of a sculptor."

"Nor am I. Are you contracted to Fairborne?"

Surely this was the prelude to a legitimate offer. He was interested in her theatrical ability, not in mere sexual dalliance. Her dignified manner offstage must have wiped away the creature he saw onstage. His question gave her a chance to answer with the same dignity.

"I am committed by honor."

The pomposity brought a smile from him, which faded as he looked at her curiously. "That means you are not under contract."

"I am committed to Vincent's company. He's done a great deal for me." She tried to stare him down.

"That note of hauteur and the flashing eyes—really remarkable."

"Not at all. It is called sincerity."

"Of course. But you can adopt it at will?"

"If you mean, am I a good actress, the answer is yes."

He pinched her chin between his thumb and forefinger, dropped his hand and said, "I am looking for an impersonator. Not an actress. I don't want anyone who adds her own little touches to the portrait. You are not creative. You are imitative. That is in your favor, for my purposes."

"Your purposes. And I suppose I have nothing to say about it?"

His mouth was pursed in thought. He avoided her question at first, then shrugged too casually.

"I am thinking about employing you."

Simple as that. "You said yesterday that you had come west from—I think it was Chicago—to look me over. That seems a very long way just to see whether I would fit into your play or company, whatever it is. Actresses with my talents are certainly come by between Chicago and San Francisco."

"Not even between Paris and San Francisco."

It sounded like an overwhelming compliment. She started to thank him but broke off the words, reading cynicism in his expression.

"You aren't really complimenting me at all, are you?"

He shook his head. "No. But I did hear about you. A newly rich miner in a Chicago restaurant. He had a portrait of you about four feet long. He set it across the table from him and drank a champagne toast to it. Said he'd paid a thousand dollars for it and, as he put it, 'It's worth every goddamn penny of it.' I quote exactly."

"How sweet of him!"

"He was drunk."

She wanted to be angry with him but instead burst into laughter. "You came all the way out here just on the strength of that portrait. And then you saw that horrible poster at the theater."

"Well, not entirely. I was on the trail of the empress's jewels. I'd gotten word that my old friend the contessa smuggled them out of Mexico. And there was talk of killers on her trail." He looked into his coffee, poured in the hot milk Mathieu had set beside it and drank it rapidly. "Not that I blame them," he added.

She pushed back her own coffee cup. "At least you haven't failed in both missions. The poor empress will be glad to get her jewelry."

His gaze was probing. "I hope I haven't failed in either mission."

Here was her exit cue. She swung her skirts to one side and got off the stool. She was pleasantly aware that MacCroy had noticed her ankles with a gleam of interest.

"Going so soon?"

"I must. Vincent has reserved places for us in the stands over on Jackson Street."

"The same Mr. Fairborne who just hurried out after his wife?"

"The same." She looked back at him. "How did you know Annabeth was his wife?"

"The program last night."

So simple, after all. For a moment she had thought she caught him in a lie. There was nothing about him she understood, and the fact that he was such a mysterious figure in her life reminded her of another puzzle. Perhaps it was connected with him, too. She asked abruptly, "Why did you search my room? What were you looking for?"

He set his coffee cup down slowly. His voice had lost the teasing quality of moments before and reverted to a flat, expressionless tone. She thought of it as the voice of a man who had severed all warmth and humanity from his soul. It suited her first impression of him . . . a criminal, or a policeman.

"Someone searched your hotel room? When did it happen? Was anything missing?"

"While I was out yesterday. Nothing is missing, so far as I know. Was it you?"

He hesitated, then shook his head. "Not I." But she noted that her question troubled him. He added, "I hope you have a better lock now."

"Why trouble? He didn't break any locks. His key seems to work on anything." Her sarcasm wasn't lost on him.

Letty didn't wait to hear whatever he had to say to that. She walked out of the little café, aware of the sway of her gown and dust ruffle as she moved. He had upset her by his doubtless well-rehearsed tricks and she wanted to return the compliment. As she went gracefully down the street in the bright salt-tinged air, she wondered what MacCroy's invitation amounted to.

Not quite an acting role. He had made that much clear. More of an impersonation. She had heard about shows in Paris. All those nude women impersonating Greek statues or some other disgusting spectacle. But if so, why was he shocked when he saw the garish poster of her?

At the street corner she looked back toward Mathieu's café and saw that the Irishman had already left and was hailing a horse and cab halfway up Sacramento Street. He seemed to be in a great hurry.

By the time she reached the theater everyone was waiting for her. Vincent was in foul humor. "Thank God, Letty! I was about to go up and rescue you from that boor. What did the fellow have to say? Is he looking for a company of players?"

Annabeth, looking charming in a sunbonnet, was clutching Vincent's arm and beaming. Letty was suddenly angered.

"I thought Annabeth was wandering around Chinatown, lost."

Vincent waved aside this trifle. "Nothing of the sort. I found her waiting here with Calla, feeling better, and bound and determined to see the parade. I daresay that fellow MacCroy wanted merely to get rid of me. What did he want with you?"

He took her arm rather more forcefully than was his habit and looked into her eyes. "What did he do? Did he behave in any way disrespectfully?"

Deeply aware of her physical proximity to Vincent, she drew back, hoping Annabeth would not notice anything proprietary about his action. Nevertheless, Letty was delighted with Vincent's jealousy.

"He wasn't clear about the company," she said with strict attention to accuracy. Vincent let the matter drop.

The group, accompanied by a burly stagehand, Al Degnan, walked over to the grandstands on Jackson Street. They found themselves forcing their way through the crowds who had arrived first and who resented these moneyed newcomers.

Al Degnan proved a formidable guardian, muscling a path to their places on the flimsy wooden stands facing Stockton Street. Vincent thrust out a stiff arm and imperiously commanded his way through the unruly groups scrambling for seats on the planks.

Letty had never seen so many American flags, not even on the Fourth of July. Not only were most of the crowd waving flags, but flags and pennants decorated every building along the route. Each buggy in the parade carried a prominent San Franciscan. Since the celebrating had begun at midnight, most of these civic leaders looked a bit unsteady at the reins, to the immense glee of the bystanders who yelled out raucous encouragement from the sidelines.

Their self-aggrandizement was punctuated by the more interesting sight of horse-drawn floats carrying Chinese Central Pacific Railroad workers and Irish trackwalkers from the Union Pacific who were bowing to each other with crossed pickaxes. Floats with regal ladies bearing lilies represented the effete East, while the West was represented by gorgeous girls from the Barbary Coast, flipping their cancan skirts at the watchers.

A cannon from the Presidio rumbled along on a caisson, followed by marching units of the Union Army proudly flaunting the five-year-old victory.

Grizzled veterans of the Mexican War and the War of 1812, looking oddly noble in their old-fashioned, ill-fitting uniforms, rode in an open carriage. Then came more buggies and more pretty girls.

Letty was enjoying herself, but her thoughts kept wandering to that curious meeting with Max MacCroy. It seemed clear that he had gone to some effort to seek her out. He had even lied to Vincent, neatly getting rid of him. Yet so far as Letty could tell, the man was still uncertain about whether he was going to make her an offer at all.

Letty felt that she was being considered for the role and she resented it, although overriding this was her desire to see her mother's country, to arrive in triumph, whatever the price. She also realized she could not take such a job unless, of course, the entire company was invited.

Almost two hours had gone by and the parade showed every sign of rolling on and on. Annabeth began to complain that her headache had returned.

"I think I'd like to go home and lie down for a little while, darling. I'll come back later."

Vincent sighed. He got up, put his arm around Annabeth and prepared to lead her out to the end of the rickety stands. Letty said quickly, "I'll go with you," but Annabeth demurred.

"No, please. Letty, you and the others stay and tell me what happened. I'll be back in a little while. I heard that the best horses will be coming later. Oh, Vincent, I hate to miss them!"

"Yes, yes, darling. But you've been exerting yourself too much. I told you that only yesterday."

As they made their way down the stands Annabeth looked over her shoulder and called back, "I'll send him back, word of honor."

Letty watched them climb down, with Vincent lifting his wife the last four feet to the street. At that moment she envied Annabeth more than anyone in the world.

The parade had stopped between sections and Calla shifted her position next to Al Degnan. Her movement caused the board seat to creak ominously. She leaned over Al to complain.

"I'm sure goin' to starve right down to the bare bone 'fore this damn show is over."

"Be patriotic, hon," Al advised her. "There's folks here been looking at you. They're sayin' they seen you on the stage."

While these two discussed food versus public relations, Letty sat picking at the drawstrings of her handbag and wondered how she could get out of the stands gracefully.

Her departure was halted by the sight of Vincent Fairborne returning to the stands. He saw her and waved. While she settled down again, the band that had stopped just beyond Jackson Street began to tune up. Someone blew a whistle, cutting the air with the noise, and the parade marched on.

Letty watched Vincent on his way to the stands. He looked splendid striding along, gilded by the sun. Just at that moment she spied Max MacCroy sauntering along in the opposite direction, headed slowly up the street in front of the stands. He had no difficulty himself in getting through that crowd; he projected an authority—she had felt it herself—that commanded respect if not understanding.

He and Vincent met head-on; Vincent nodded coolly. MacCroy

saluted in response and continued on a few steps before stopping and watching Vincent climb up into the stands to sit beside Letty and Calla Skutnik. MacCroy caught Letty's eye and his unexpected grin was contagious. She smiled, only to have her sight of the Irishman blocked by Vincent as he moved in front of Letty and took his place between her and Calla. By the time he settled down, MacCroy had moved on.

The whistles blown by the parade directors and by the bands themselves were having their predictable effect on the nerves of the already skittish horses drawing caissons and buggies. Mounts reared and wheeled, and there were bets passed in the stands about the first mount likely to throw his rider.

After the next break in the parade half an hour later, several horses and buggies were caught between streets as the marchers started up. Buggies pulled up against the sidelines to await the conclusion of the parade, and arguments broke out between buggy owners and the crowd whose view they obstructed. Letty watched the conflict with mounting interest and some concern.

Suddenly the air was split by the din of several piercing whistles blown simultaneously by the division directors. Letty put her palms over her ears. Swearing and screaming erupted from the crowd.

Along the Stockton Street line of march a team of horses panicked and pulled forward, dragging a cart behind them. At the cross-street they ploughed into two buggies, overturning them on the crowd, and in the pandemonium that followed the outer planks of the grandstand broke away with a shriek of tearing wood.

Letty felt herself slipping and cried out. The plank under her feet disappeared. She groped in the air for support and was seized around the wrists by Vincent's straining arms.

Others had been trapped in a similar way. Panic and screaming surrounded them. When Vincent finally lifted Letty back onto a steady, reinforced plank that had been the seat of the row beneath them, she was able to look around in a daze. Then, after taking a few short breaths, she focused on one sight.

At the far end of the stands, on the wooden steps, Annabeth Fairborne, apparently on her way back to join her husband, had been caught in the collapse at the end of the stands. As they watched, she sagged into the arms of her rescuer, Max MacCroy.

CHAPTER *Six*

*L*IMPING PAINFULLY with what felt like a wrenched ankle, Letty followed Vincent as he made his way across the unbroken stands.

Annabeth had come to and looked pale and shaken. She stretched out both arms to Vincent, saying, "This man s-saved me. He p-pulled me away when the buggy turned over . . . oh, darling, I was so s-scared."

MacCroy deposited her into Vincent's arms in a flurry of petticoats, dismissing her husband's thanks with brusque indifference.

"It was all the little lady's doing. She leaped back just in time." He turned abruptly to Letty. "Are you all right? No broken bones?" He seemed tense, very much concerned.

Letty thought his sudden attention rude but flattering; she craved a little sympathy on her own behalf. At the same time the Irishman's manner seemed almost businesslike, as if a valuable stock might have taken a plunge in the market. Curious and a bit unnerving. She had no desire to be someone's commodity.

"I am perfectly well, thank you. Mr. Fairborne saved me from falling about ten feet."

"Our hero," MacCroy muttered. He took her arm and piloted her away from the pushing, shoving crowd. But meanwhile, concerned about the safety of the rest of the company, Letty kept stopping to crane her head and look for them.

MacCroy read her mind. "They're just fine. They seem to have performed a heroic rescue like your friend, the noble Fairborne."

"Good for Al. You mean he saved Calla?"

"No. The other way around. The redoubtable Miss Skutnik kept the headsman from going over."

She laughed. "I'm not surprised. Calla is capable of anything."

They started up the street. In spite of herself, Letty winced with every step. He paused at once, almost overly concerned.

"Your ankle? How bad?"

"Just painful. It happened when the plank first gave way. Don't fuss."

"Hold your foot up. Here."

To her astonishment he held his joined hands out for her foot, as if she would even consider exhibiting a bare ankle in public.

"Don't be silly. It's less than a block to my room."

"I don't want you walking on it until it's bound. You could dislocate several bones that way."

"*You* don't want me—what have you to say about my bones?"

She found his smile inscrutable. "Because I expect to own them very soon."

"Own! You couldn't be more—"

"Forgive me. A poor choice of words. I meant to say I hope to take your bones on lease, as it were."

He was just too absurd to bother being irate with. "Well then, I will protect them for your sake. Lend me your shoulder."

"This is a waste of time. Now, be quiet. No screams, for God's sake!" Allowing Letty no time to protest, he slipped one arm under her hips and the other around her shoulders and picked her up with remarkable ease.

"Don't struggle. You'll simply make yourself heavier."

No one had ever accused her of being heavy in her life and she was so deeply offended she said nothing until he crossed the street, just missing being hit by a team of horses drawing a fire engine. At the street doors of Lyric House, she said, "You may trust me to protect my ankle from here on. Unless, of course, you wish to carry me up two flights of stairs."

He grinned. "If I must, I must."

The toes of her shoes struck the polished wooden bannister several times on the way up the stairs, and he made no effort to keep her skirts from dragging along the stair carpeting. Reaching her door he ordered, "Give me your key."

She fumbled in her handbag, which was crushed against his chest, and unearthed her key, managing to slip it into his hand. He unlocked the door.

He dropped her on her bed with all the gentleness he'd have afforded a bale of hay and began to look around the austere, sparsely decorated room. She sat up while his back was turned and gingerly probed her ankle. Despite the pain and swelling, nothing seemed to be broken.

MacCroy returned to her bedside. "Remove the stocking. This needs cold water." Old Dr. Hinkle, at his sober best, could not have been more authoritative.

"Turn your back."

This time he actually chuckled, but obeyed; in any case he seemed safe enough. While he turned and examined the lock of the clothespress, she unpinned her stocking, slipped it down over her leg and dropped it on the bed.

"Very well. I am ready."

He rattled the steel lock. "Is this the best lock you could find?" He shook it again. "Was there anything important locked up?"

She hesitated. "Only a few old . . . love letters."

"Could they be used against you in some way? Blackmail?"

She laughed shortly. "No. I'm sure no one cares."

"I wouldn't say that." He came over to the bed. "How is it that this room isn't swarming with men who care? A woman like you."

"Don't be insulting."

He surprised her again by the quiet, matter-of-fact way he said, "I'm sorry. I certainly didn't mean to be." His hard fingers moved over her ankle in a practiced way. "Hurt?"

She groaned at the pressure of his fingers and said sourly, "No. It feels divine."

He slapped her knee. "Don't worry. It will be as beautiful as ever in a few days."

She threw her skirts over her leg. "I hope no one was badly hurt."

He went to the window, raised it and looked out.

"Fire wagons still coming. The people in the two buggies are the biggest problem, I imagine. A couple of horses trampled them."

"Horrible. Vincent had no way of knowing his wife was out there. He thought she was lying down. He is always dreadfully concerned about her."

"I can imagine."

"It's true."

"I'll get cold cloths." He started across the room.

She called after him, "I don't want you to have the wrong opinion about him. No man was ever—"

In the doorway he snapped, "I know of nothing more boring than a figure of nobility. And I have known plenty."

He slammed the door behind him.

Letty stared after him, wondering if what she had really heard was a certain jealousy. On the other hand, his antagonism might have something to do with his plans—whatever those were—for Letty Fox, Impressionist.

A series of light knocks on the door surprised her; it wasn't like MacCroy to be so polite. Perhaps this was his way of apologizing.

"Don't be silly. Come in."

Vincent Fairborne came in so quickly he didn't even close the door behind him. He strode to the bed, his eyes speaking volumes, his usual discretion abandoned. He took one of her hands and, bending over her, kissed her warmly on the lips. Her eyes shone.

"My darling, do you think I didn't care? I've been frantic about you. Tell me the truth. Were you hurt at all?"

She raised her skirt a few inches, exposing her bare leg and ankle.

"This is terrible. You *were* hurt."

"Not really. You mustn't worry." But she loved this display of concern. He patted her leg.

"I'm more glad than ever that I canceled tonight's performance. My lovely star deserves a rest."

She knew how much the profits from the show meant to him and was greatly touched by this sacrifice. Nevertheless the least she could do was protest to show him she understood what this would cost him.

"But you mustn't, my—" She broke off. She had always been afraid she would call him *darling* in public. "You mustn't do too much sacrificing or we will lose our audience. I can manage very well."

"Impossible, darling. I won't have you risking your health. I will always feel I did that with Annabeth. It isn't going to happen again. Not to anyone I love."

He caressed her leg just above the swelling until he reached the knee. His gentle, remote features looked deeply moved.

"How beautiful you are! If there is anything you need, just rap on the wall."

"That one?" Mischievously she pointed to the wall of Max MacCroy's room.

"No, darling. Don't be perverse. That room has been empty for a week."

"It isn't empty now."

He leaned over again to kiss her. "The wall of our parlor. I'll leave you, but as I said, if I can be of help in any way . . ." He straightened up to leave and found Max MacCroy standing a few feet behind him with a folded towel in his hands.

Vincent would not usually allow himself the indulgence of bad manners, but he demanded now, "What the devil do you mean, sneaking into rooms where you aren't wanted? Do you spend your life eavesdropping?"

"Run along and attend your wife where you belong, Mr. Fairborne, since you can do nothing useful here." He nudged Vincent aside, and went to the bed while Vincent watched in shock and disbelief.

"That's the girl. Hold your leg out. This may sting. I managed to get some ice from a fishmonger—it's wrapped in the towel. No, no! Get your skirts up. You want all that pretty lace water-soaked?"

"Now, see here."

"It's all right, Vincent. Mr. MacCroy is used to treating ladies with sprains. I suspect he used to be a physician, of sorts. Isn't that so, Mr. MacCroy?"

"I would never willingly contradict a lady. Hold still."

He was certainly not romantic. At least not when compared with Vincent Fairborne; but if she wanted to provoke Vincent's jealousy it seemed the aggressive and insolent MacCroy would do very well. She carefully obeyed him, raising endless ruffles to her knee while he applied the icy wet pad to the swelling.

Vincent came over, jerked her skirts down. "Kindly behave. You aren't exhibiting yourself on the stage now."

It was the first time he had ever said such a thing and it cut her to the quick. Even MacCroy's insolent mask seemed to slip a little, and she saw the muscles of his jaws tighten. She took a deep breath and said in her most theatrical voice, "Nor are you, sir. Would you mind closing the door? From the hall."

Vincent, who had appeared momentarily paralyzed after his outburst, took his cue and stalked out, slamming the door.

Letty lowered her skirts.

"I do believe that in the last six months I've never heard so much slamming of doors."

MacCroy laughed. He raised his head, staring at her face. "You are exactly what I have been searching for. That look. That voice. That manner. Everything. I really must have you, Letty Fox."

CHAPTER *Seven*

*H*OWEVER BRASH Max's statement, Letty was undeniably flattered. Assuming a coquettish air, she said, "But what if I do not wish you or anyone else to have me, Mr. MacCroy? Did you allow for that?"

He waved away her dismissal. "My dear girl, don't be tiresome. I'm not talking about physical possession." He took the sodden towel off her ankle and refolded it, his fingers grazing her flesh. Her resultant shiver was not entirely from pain, but Max apologized briskly as he replaced the towel.

"Sorry. The swelling will go down shortly."

"Good heavens! I can certainly stand a little pain. What kind of women have you been dealing with?"

She had managed to intrigue him. He looked into her eyes again. "None like you. Except one."

Letty demanded tartly, "A mistress of yours?"

His smile looked grim, and his answer, when it came, shook her. "I had in mind the empress of France."

So it was her resemblance to the Empress Eugenie that attracted him. Curious. Something about his answer made her suspect his interest in the empress was greater than that of the usual transplanted citizen toward his ruler.

"Then that is why you came across the country to see Letty Fox. Not me at all, but Letty Fox as the Empress Eugenie."

"Precisely."

"You need not be precise about it. It is positively insulting."

"Rubbish. I must find a female who closely resembles the empress. Some months ago I spoke with His Imperial Majesty about the possibility of an impersonator for the empress. It might prove useful in many ways. To relieve the boredom of social appearances. And to confuse a few of the empress's enemies."

She laughed, beginning to understand his disgust at their initial meeting.

"And then you came upon that poster and saw a garish creature not in the least like Her Majesty." She finished shaking her skirts down over her ankle. "Poor man. What a disappointment I must have been to you!"

"On the contrary. Time has shown me you are perfectly suited. Now if I can only teach you to speak fluent French with a slight Spanish accent, the matter is all settled."

He took far too much for granted.

"Spare yourself the trouble, Mr. MacCroy. I wonder why you thought I would be party to such a harebrained scheme."

"The pay is good, for one thing. For another, you will wear elaborate costumes and mingle in the highest society. Not at close range, of course. Even I couldn't bring that off. But the world will appear at a respectful distance around you and beneath you. You have the chance to play the greatest role of your life."

"And naturally I will accompany you halfway around the world to do this." She had heard a good many schemes either to pry her away from the Fairborne Company or to get her into bed, but she had to give MacCroy first place for originality. No one had ever approached her with a more fantastic proposition.

"The long trip home would give me the chance to drill you in your role. However, I haven't the time to spend, so the voyage will have to be made as swiftly as possible."

"*You* haven't the time to spend."

"That's what I said."

He seemed oblivious to her sarcasm. He got up to leave, took her hand and thanked her for what he called her cooperation. For just a few seconds Letty was fearful that she was passing up her only chance to return to France in triumph.

While MacCroy took her hand in farewell, she said firmly, "I consider myself contracted to the Fairborne Company, Mr. MacCroy. Where Mr. Fairborne goes, I go."

He nodded, grinned as if she had agreed to his little scheme, and was about to leave when he stopped at the clothespress and rattled the lock.

"Have you any idea who might have prowled through your things here? Or why?"

"Not in the least." No one seemed to take the invasion of her room seriously except Max MacCroy. She respected him for that. "Everyone tells me I imagined the whole thing."

He said, "I doubt it. Could it be anyone in the building? Another tenant? That desk clerk looks like a genial cutthroat."

She didn't think so. "It isn't like him. This was a furtive business. Someone sneaking around. Nothing was taken."

"And you haven't noticed anything else unusual in the last few days? Anyone watching you, seeming to follow you, for instance?"

She thought back, then smiled.

"Your friend, the Contessa Servandoni, has some sneaky friends."

That startled him. "How do you mean?"

She described the odd, ferret-faced little man who had been following her into the roominghouse the previous day. To her surprise MacCroy took the incident seriously.

"Ferret-faced. Yes. Very likely." A singularly unpleasant smile crossed his face. "I have led him a merry chase, but I scarcely expected to meet him in your bedroom. . . . Narrow eyes? Dark complexion?"

"More olive—like yours. And he looked back at me before he ran around the corner toward the Montgomery block. I didn't see him when we left."

"I knew he hadn't been on my trail the last few days."

This sounded like international intrigue of a sort that had never before come into Letty Fox's life. The scent of danger was provocative.

"Do you think the man was from the Juarez government in Mexico?"

He rubbed the lock with an absent gesture.

"No. It is very likely a Corsican spy named Rissoli. He has been following me. I intended for him to think my chief business in San Francisco was with the contessa—to retrieve the Carlotta jewels. I wanted him to report that to Prince Plonplon. But there must be nothing to do with you."

She laughed. *"Plonplon?* You *are* joking."

"It is a nickname for the emperor's cousin, Prince Napoleon. It seems that every second descendant of Napoleon Bonaparte has been named Napoleon. At any rate, he's determined to see the empress deposed. Preferably divorced, but certainly disgraced. It seems he'd like to see his sister, Princess Matilde, marry the emperor."

"Good heavens! What intrigue!"

"The emperor thinks so. Despite his dalliances with the contessa and a few hundred others, he is very fond of Eugenie, and the last thing on his mind these days is another marriage, least of all to his cousin Matilde."

"Well, then, why does this Plonplon even try?"

"It's in the blood, I suppose. And furthermore, some of Plonplon's very unpleasant friends suspect I am up to something that will ruin their schemes against Eugenie."

"Are you?" She had portrayed the Empress Eugenie long enough to be quite sympathetic to her.

He said blandly, "It is my *job* to protect her. I am the prefect of her private police, those charged with her protection. To this end, the emperor and I have been devising a little plan to confuse Plonplon and his plotters."

It was almost as if Letty herself were in danger; she was indignant. "I hope Her Majesty is safe while you are so far away."

"Spending the summer between Deauville and St. Cloud. Plonplon and his friends are not invited. But when she returns to the Tuileries it will be impossible to keep a Bonaparte prince out of the palace."

Letty couldn't imagine how she herself fitted into this sinister web. Unless . . .

"Do you intend to use me as a target in place of the empress?"

Her bluntness caught him unawares. He hesitated, then answered, "I might have, once. No longer. I see you rather as a complication, a diversion to confuse these idiots in their efforts to humiliate Eugenie. It is complicated. I will explain it to you at another time."

"You mean I would be humiliated instead of Her Majesty."

"No, damn it! You would make it impossible for them to move. They would never know—" He broke off, said abruptly, "You would be well paid, at least double your present salary. I would be with you at all times. Your shield. You would appear in Paris as a great lady, the lady you should be."

"Unless I were shot by this Plonplon's friends." She was fascinated by the scheme despite the probable danger to herself. Everything worth having cost something. She would be in service to her country. And it was the answer to all her dreams of vindicating her mother.

But leave the company? How could she tear Vincent from her heart, desert him, take away the star of his company? Or was the last merely conceit?

MacCroy's angry reactions continued to surprise her. "If you imagine I want to risk your life, you are as mad as Plonplon!" He recovered and said quietly, "Let me tell you what you may expect. During the great Paris Exposition three years ago in sixty-seven we found a female in Strasbourg who from a distance resembled the empress. Plonplon's agents broke into the woman's sleeping quarters, smuggling in papers that implicated the Empress Eugenie in treason—these papers thanked her for providing military information to the Spanish queen. We were able to prove the whole thing was a plot because at the time the real empress was across the country in Deauville."

"What happened to this look-alike Strasbourg woman?"

"She married a Rhinelander and left for Coblenz."

"Then the prince would not kill an impersonator."

"Certainly not."

But what about agents who might not be so fussy? Since she couldn't accept his proposition, Letty didn't bother to argue with his conclusions.

On a sudden impulse he said, "I've stayed too long in your intoxicating company. I have a few preparations to make for my friend Rissoli, if I can find him. I hope to speak to you and your noble mentor tonight. Meanwhile, if you see Ferret Face, don't antagonize him."

"Tell him not to antagonize me, if you please."

"Don't joke. I am serious. He is simply spying at the moment. But he may be dangerous if pushed to the wall. If you think you see him, leave a message under my door. A folded blank page will do. I'll contact you."

Then he was gone and she was sorry. She had found his visit stimulating in many ways and toward the end of his visit he had talked to her as if he actually cared what happened to her. She was exhilarated.

In accordance with the Irishman's plan to settle the matter soon, the following day he tracked down the Fairborne Company, but it was not quite the businesslike scene Letty envisioned.

The day was brisk and sunny, the wind scudding clouds through a piercing blue sky across the Golden Gate.

"I think I'd like a dress the color of this sky, with little white dots and a frill and a bustle."

Over Annabeth's head, Calla and Letty nodded to each other in a conspiratorial way—Annabeth's birthday was coming. The three women were riding in a hired buggy, while the two men sat on the box. Vincent handled the reins of the patient old horse and Al Degnan sat very still, nursing his back muscles, which had been wrenched during the parade disaster.

The Sunday traffic to Meiggs Wharf was at its height, and it was afternoon when they reached the long wharf with its swimming facilities, restaurants and the celebrated, if dusty, Cobweb Palace. In spite of the delicious chowders at the Palace, the ladies refused to enter the wooden hut; they contented themselves with an outdoor table and benches where they could enjoy the generous shells full of Dapper David's crab chowder.

Then Annabeth objected to sitting with her back to the Golden Gate; she exchanged seats with Calla, and now was facing Vincent and Letty.

"I want you to help me count the masts and spars and things on those schooners and barks. But with all the noise, it's hard to talk to you."

More shifting put Vincent beside her again, frowning with impatience. Moving slowly enough to conquer the painful throb of her twisted ankle, Letty would have welcomed her proximity to Vincent except that she caught the quick exchange of looks between Calla and Al Degnan. She shifted her position on the bench to put some distance between herself and Vincent, only to have him draw her in closer, saying, "Room for all of us. You'll fall off the bench if you aren't careful."

Her body stiffened, and when Vincent began to point out to his wife a particularly interesting four-master that was schooner-rigged, she took the opportunity to move again.

While Letty ate, she studied the noisy Sunday scene around them. She was intrigued by Max MacCroy's offer, the possibilities it seemed to hold. What could it possibly involve? Surely there were other women who resembled the empress. Why herself?

And furthermore, if MacCroy had tried to employ these other imperial copies, as he must have, why had they refused? And the Irishman did say the ridiculously nicknamed Plonplon's spies might be dangerous.

But the rewards—Paris, respectability, a name.

Her back to the Golden Gate, Letty stared out over the panorama of the San Francisco hills, bare in late spring, adorned by the scattered houses of the cliff-dwellers who desired the fabulous views. Between the hills, a beehive of shacks, solid stone office buildings, and everywhere, brick structures or earthquake-resistant wooden houses, cheek by jowl on incredibly narrow lots. The city had more than its share of church spires, comforting to Letty, though her childhood had weaned her away from that particular comfort.

She suddenly froze, spoon raised to her lips, and blinked, unable to believe what she saw across the pier. Squeezing his way through the hungry crowd that waited before the Cobweb Palace for seats to be vacated was the ferret-faced little Rissoli.

Although he hadn't seen her yet, she felt she was very possibly the object of his search. At the moment he was looking the wrong way, but she knew it was only a matter of seconds before he would turn in her direction and see her.

Instinctively she moved back into the shadow of the café roof with Vincent Fairborne's broad shoulders covering her side, vaguely ashamed of this cowardice.

Rissoli's glittering eyes wandered over to Vincent's party, and Letty was sure she saw his flash of recognition. Pride came to her rescue: she sat up and by an extreme effort managed to stare back at him without any sign of recognition. She began to talk, waving her hands and punctuating every few words with a laugh.

The rest of the party joined in what sounded to her like an absurd conversation but was apparently reasonable to them. Her own mind was far from this trivia, and her casual glance encompassed the area around the ferret-faced man.

Rissoli edged around to the outskirts of the crowd and, while a half dozen hungry patrons were ushered into the Cobweb Palace for a belated lunch, he slipped behind the old buildings. Letty stood suddenly; everyone at the table stared in surprise. A twinge of pain reminded her of her twisted ankle and she grabbed at that excuse.

"Sorry. I have a cramp in my foot. I want to walk it off. Go on eating, please."

"Want any company?" Calla asked, while Vincent got up to help her.

She waved them down again. "No. I feel like being alone. I just want to exercise my foot a bit."

Vincent objected. "You're liable to hurt it."

But Annabeth put a hand on his arm and said, "She knows what's best for her. Let her be."

Calla and Vincent reluctantly sat back down, Vincent watching as Letty limped away.

She pretended to test her ankle, but all her attention was focused on the scene, the bright parasols of the females in their Sunday best, usually black alpaca, and the men with their stiff white collars and confident swagger. Children were everywhere and, like the men, on their best behavior until they could break away and enjoy themselves.

Rissoli had scrambled down to the wharf, where several schooners and a ferryboat were tied up. Letty followed and almost missed seeing him climb the gangplank of a schooner named *Periere*. Foreign and probably French. MacCroy must be right—the fellow was an agent. She heard Vincent calling her name and turned back; there was nothing she could do alone, anyway.

Vincent met her at the corner of Meiggs Wharf. He looked concerned and started to put his arm around her, saying, "Letty, your ankle looks fine. Tell me what's wrong. What made you run away like that?"

After a satisfied instant she slipped out of his arm. "I'm fine. I just thought I saw the man who broke into my room."

"Oh, that. . . . But wait a minute. How could you possibly recognize someone you didn't even see?"

"Vincent, I have my reasons. I think it was that dark little man with the furtive eyes who was watching us a few minutes ago."

"What do you mean?"

"He—" She thought rapidly. "Mr. MacCroy says his room was also searched, and he described the man he suspected."

Vincent's clasp around her waist tightened. "Are you in danger in some way? Letty, if only I could take care of you, be with you more . . . but Annabeth—well, you see how she's been today. Up and down constantly, nervous as a cat. I don't dare leave her alone."

"I know. Here we are. They can see us."

"I think we had better go to the police. I don't like MacCroy's knowing all our affairs. He's much too interested in you."

She shook her head. "Never mind him. As for the police, I haven't enough proof." She began to favor her twisted ankle as they came into view of Annabeth and the others.

As they were leaving the pier less than a half hour later, they ran into MacCroy. He made a pretense of an accidental meeting, but Letty was sure he had tracked them by questioning some of the backstage crew. Vincent looked at him sourly.

MacCroy was charming, kissing each lady's hand, remarking that the coincidence of their meeting had worked out admirably, as he wanted to talk to Vincent about a matter of business.

Though the amenities took less than a minute, Letty couldn't wait for him to finish.

"Mr. MacCroy, I think I saw the man who went through my room the other day. He boarded a French ship here in the harbor. I haven't seen him pass this way since. He must still be aboard."

MacCroy reacted with that wary alertness she had noted in him before. But Vincent was furious. While she was directing MacCroy, Vincent demanded, "Why didn't you tell me? Where is he, damn it! You don't have to get your help from strangers."

"Don't swear at her, honey," Annabeth cut in, "it isn't nice."

Flustered, Letty started along the wharf with MacCroy, pointing to the battered old French schooner just as the ferry, on its return trip, entered its slip.

"Logical," MacCroy said. "He probably makes the French ship his home while he is watching me. And you too, I gather. Incidentally, if you must look so beautiful, I would appreciate it if it were not in public."

"I make my living in public."

He chuckled in spite of his tension. "I meant something else. Your resemblance . . . nothing. Don't come any farther. It may not be safe."

Vincent, following close behind them, interrupted loudly. "What do you mean, safe? Is Miss Fox in some kind of danger? Letty, leave this to that fellow and me. You run back to the others." He gave her a little shove, which she resented, even though she knew he behaved like this through concern for her.

But he hadn't reckoned on MacCroy.

"Fairborne," he said, putting out an arm to stop him, "I'd appreciate your taking Miss Fox out of this. It is strictly a French affair and it may also be a police matter. If you would just take care of the ladies and excuse me . . ."

Vincent frowned but tried to maneuver her back toward the wharf. She went reluctantly, looking behind her. MacCroy had already disappeared into the waist of the ship. Vincent was noticeably perturbed.

"What the devil is going on that I don't know about? Is he a detective of some kind?"

"I've no idea. But the man I saw sneak toward that ship has been following us all over town."

They both heard a crack that sounded like a loud slap, followed by others. Vincent turned sharply. "Those are pistol shots." Others on the wharf paused, looked back, but no one moved. "Your friend is liable to get his head blown off. The fool needs help." He went off on a run toward the gangplank of the French ship.

Another crack, closer and louder, made Letty jump.

As the crowd poured off the docked ferryboat, the wind swept in from the bay and across her face, so sharp and salty it stung her face. She raised a hand to her neck and then, almost absently, looked at her fingers. They were red.

CHAPTER *Eight*

*L*ETTY SWUNG around, gimlet-eyed, furious, looking for the person who had thrown the stone that cut her. The children pouring off the ferry didn't seem likely. In knitted caps and stockings, they were warmly bundled against the wind and hurrying along to reach Meiggs Wharf. Nobody was interested in her.

A chilling, if absurd, thought occurred to her. Had she been hit by Rissoli?

She couldn't possibly spot him now in the Sunday crowds, but if he had moved from the *Periere* to the ferryboat crowd while MacCroy was boarding the schooner, he might be anywhere on the waterfront. Letty found herself squeezed in among the giggling, chattering tourists, and after much too long a time she made her way back to Annabeth and the others. She found the two women puzzling over what was happening.

"Vincent said to wait," Annabeth was insisting, "not to move. I think we should listen to him."

Calla was less confident. "I don't trust that Irishman, or Frenchie, or whatever he is. There's something mighty funny about them foreigners. Letty! What the hell happened to you? You been in a fight?"

"I don't quite know." Letty looked at the handkerchief she had been holding to her neck. No more than a scratch, it had already stopped bleeding, but the whole affair was much too coincidental.

Al Degnan flexed his biceps. "Reckon I better go and get the boss out of trouble. These heroes ain't always able to handle things alone." He started toward the distant *Periere* but hadn't gotten far when he was caught in the crosscurrent of passengers heading for the Sausalito ferry. At the same time Letty saw both MacCroy and Vincent making their way through the crowd.

Letty hurried toward them. Vincent look disheveled but grimly satisfied. However, it was Max MacCroy she went to first, who frowned at the sight of her and caught her shoulders. He was staring at her hand.

"Is that blood on your fingers? How did that happen?"

"Something grazed my neck. Probably some boy throwing stones. Did you find Rissoli?"

He pointed to Vincent, who gave her a gallant stage bow and said, "I caught him only a minute ago, on the deck. With a pistol in his hand. He tried to shoot me—or maybe MacCroy here. I knocked him down. The San Francisco police have him now."

"Your employer saved my life, in a manner of speaking," MacCroy put in. He was still studying her face. His intense interest made her nervous. He politely dismissed Vincent with "Your wife is waving to you."

"Yes . . . in a minute." He lingered to ask, "Letty, are you sure you are all right?"

"Perfectly."

Off to Annabeth, always first, she thought. But he had touched her throat anxiously before he left.

"We'd better get some salve on that," MacCroy suggested.

When Vincent was beyond hearing she asked, "Was he Rissoli? Is he really in the hands of the police?"

"Yes on both counts. He was on the dock a few minutes ago. It may have been he who shot at you. Come along."

"If he did, and I was that close, he's a mighty poor shot. But then you mentioned dirks and daggers."

He disagreed. "If I read him rightly, his object would be to alter your appearance, not to kill you."

The very idea filled Letty with revulsion. That someone might want to kill her for devious international reasons was one thing—dangerous, but glamorous and exciting. To "alter her appearance" and scar her for life was quite another matter.

He took her back to the Fairborne group, adding wryly, "I must admit your dashing hero came flying to the rescue at exactly the instant I had persuaded the little ferret that I am as venal as he is. I was about to bribe the truth out of him. No matter. I'll have him another way. If the police do their part."

In spite of her fear, she laughed. "Vincent was reacting as one of his characters. Before the impressionist show became a success he played classic heroes. Shakespeare."

"I can imagine. Now, about the scratch on your pretty neck."

She bristled. "Are you interested in my welfare or in the welfare of my body?"

She caught him unawares. His hand fell away from her throat. "I beg your pardon. To be frank, a little of both."

Before she could say anything more, they reached Vincent Fairborne, who was hamming up his heroic deed for the little group gathered around him, showing how Rissoli was forced to give over the pistol. "Damned heavy for such a small affair."

"Like on the stage," Al said. "You grabbin' the gun and all." He pinched MacCroy's sleeve. "You been hanging around the company a lot, mister. You fixing to hire us Fairbornes for them Frenchies to see?"

Letty watched Vincent's reaction, the carefully controlled excitement, though he affected a tolerant amusement. She knew his hunger for recognition and sensed that MacCroy would not feed into it. It didn't seem fair, after all the good Vincent had done for so many . . . Annabeth . . . herself . . . even Calla Skutnik owed him her present position in life.

MacCroy surprised Letty by his affirmative answer to Al's question. "I do have something to tell you. However, I have been invited—shall we say?—to visit the local bastille for an hour or so. The police want to know the background of this Rissoli. Fairborne, I would like to discuss a business proposition with you this evening."

Letty flinched at what she suspected would be complete misunderstanding on Vincent's part. Letty knew it was not the Fairborne Company MacCroy wanted. He wanted the company's star.

"Certainly," Vincent answered. "Any time before six. Or after eleven. We usually have a midnight supper."

MacCroy didn't like this and Letty wondered why.

"Then you are going to perform tonight? I would think after the injuries at the parade yesterday, you wouldn't take the chance of further damage onstage. Isn't there a pretty high set of property steps for Miss Fox?"

"What do you think, Letty?" Vincent asked.

Letty was indifferent. She felt strangely removed, as though they were discussing a character she played, not herself.

"I've walked all over the wharves here. I think I can manage the scenes."

"Good." Vincent was obviously interested in one particular member of the audience. "MacCroy, may we count on you to see the entire performance tonight?"

MacCroy looked so long at Letty, she blushed.

"Would you like me to attend?"

She glanced at Vincent. His tawny eyebrows raised. She caught the merest suggestion of a nod.

She said, "Certainly, Mr. MacCroy. We always welcome another patron."

It was arranged then, and the group wandered back to the stables at the foot of Russian Hill where the horse and buggy were brought out. Just as Letty was about to get in with the other women, MacCroy drew her back, out of earshot.

"Look here," Letty said to MacCroy, "you aren't being very polite. What on earth do you want?"

"Give me your promise."

From anyone else these words might have been the prelude to something romantic, but coming from Max MacCroy . . . "What is it?"

"Promise to change your appearance for the Eugenie sketch. Wear your hair up, perhaps. Your makeup darker. Use a black wig."

"Why, for heaven's sake? Everyone knows she is auburn-haired. With a touch of gold, Vincent says."

"At this point your resemblance to the empress could give away our plans."

"Ours?"

"The emperor and I are the only ones who know. I cabled him in code this morning, according to our agreement. The contessa may be suspicious—she was close to the emperor before the empress made difficulties."

"Oh." It seemed cowardly to accept this advice, but it was sensible. She knew Vincent would disapprove; he had gone to great lengths to insure the accuracy of her makeup and costumes, and the empress was famous for her golden auburn hair. No matter.

She offered MacCroy a gloved hand. He took it, holding it in his while he stood there. He looked as if he wanted to say something, but he let go with a pat on her knuckles with his left hand. She supposed this a token of friendship.

Vincent, who had been standing off to the side, looked distinctly uncomfortable with their handholding. She smiled mischievously at MacCroy for Vincent's benefit and had the added satisfaction of seeing that she had flustered the coldblooded Max MacCroy as well. She picked up the ruffled train of her skirt and with a smart turn walked back to the buggy, well aware that both men were watching her.

Several times that evening, during the hiatus before curtain call, Vincent asked seemingly casual questions about her conversation with Mac-Croy. She was evasive, somewhat annoyed by the thought that both men wanted to use her for essentially selfish motives.

The little pianist played the first notes of the theme for the Victoria sketch. Taking this cue, Vincent hurried to the downstage wings to prompt Annabeth's entrance.

Letty pulled herself together and whispered, "All right, Asa. Get me up."

She felt her body in its shimmering gown lifted swiftly, easily, to the top of the entrance steps. She stood there collecting her thoughts, ready for her cue, but a feathery touch on her ankle made her look down into the semidarkness. Asa, a useful and loyal property man, had never attempted anything so forward.

But it was not Asa who had lifted her up here, and it certainly wasn't Asa's fingers that traced the curve of her bared ankle now. Max Mac-Croy gazed sweetly at Letty and grinned.

"You!" she whispered. "Don't. I'll go up on my lines."

He bent his head and before she could shrink away, placed his warm lips on her anklebone. She lingered, then stifled a sudden, ghastly desire to laugh, which would surely be heard onstage. Letty was so rattled she started down the steps and into the scene before her cue.

Calla Skutnik, as the duchess of Kent, missed a line but rumbled onward with such malevolent enthusiasm no one except the other players noticed it; in fact, the timing of the entire scene was off but the audience didn't seem to notice. The laughs, the shouts for more and the applause for Letty's seminudity came on schedule. When she made her exit, however, Vincent was waiting in the wings.

"What the devil happened, darling?"

She looked around nervously, knowing Vincent would never forgive himself if Annabeth heard these endearments.

"Nothing. I was thrown off-stride, that's all."

"But tonight we must be at our best. You do understand why."

"No. Why?" She said it flatly, without expression.

"You must realize MacCroy is wandering around, watching the show. If we fail tonight, we lose all chance of an imperial performance. That could mean everything to the company. Can you imagine, darling? My own Letty Fox, performing before the Emperor Louis Napoleon and the Empress Eugenie."

"Vincent, you may as well know, he isn't . . ." She couldn't continue

—this was no time to hurt him with the truth. He had several more sketches to play tonight.

He hugged her affectionately. "Later, darling. Run now. You've got that heavy Catherine costume to get into."

She raced for the stale-smelling little dressing room and hurried into the busk, bodice and heavy panniered skirts of Catherine the Great, relieved that Vincent had cut her off. While waiting for her cue she saw neither Vincent nor Max—it was just as well. She wanted nothing more to disturb her performance.

It was not until her appearance as the Empress Eugenie that she saw Max again. Normally she covered her own pale gold hair with a heavy auburn wig that gathered on the nape of her neck and below her ears in the style of the beautiful, fashion-conscious Eugenie.

Tonight she wore Carlotta's black wig piled high toward the crown of her head, and different makeup, much darker, the same paint she had used last year playing the Queen of Sheba.

She couldn't have less resembled the empress of France.

MacCroy waylaid her in the wings and nodded, pleased with what he saw. He rearranged the hair on top of her head so that the soft oval of the imperial face now looked slightly angular. Then, in what was becoming a habit, he slapped her hand lightly and made a gesture waving her onto the stage. Letty made her entrance and confronted a stupified Vincent in the Emperor Louis Napoleon's uniform, mustache and goatee.

He cried, *"Mon Dieu!"* fortunately remembering his role, if not his lines. Hearing the hum of the audience, many of whom were used to quite a different-looking Eugenie, he improvised, "Are you so anxious to avoid my attentions that you disguise yourself, Mademoiselle de Montijo?"

"I wanted to see if Your Majesty would still love me as a raven-haired Spaniard," she said with a flirtatious air.

After the totally ad-libbed beginning, she recovered her poise and worked into her well-rehearsed lines. The performance resumed its normal shape, but Letty, not wanting to make further explanations, took care to avoid Vincent between scenes. Luckily, he accepted her piquant change of costume as a whim.

Despite the success of that night's show—the audience that filled the old theater applauded thunderously—Letty grew more and more anxious about the expected meeting with Max MacCroy. She knew she would not betray Vincent by accepting MacCroy's offer, but she also knew how severe Vincent's disappointment would be that the offer was not for the whole company.

He was so sure they would be invited to France; it was better even than his dream of taking the company to Chicago and New York. No one deserved success more.

By the time the troupe had answered the last enthusiastic curtain call, everyone was keyed up, nervous, hopeful. Everyone except Letty. While the women were dressing for midnight supper Calla voiced her anticipation.

"One of these days we could all be so rich we'd be eating fancy every night. What say, Letty? You know that feller better than we do. What's chances?"

"Who knows what he wants? He seems like a very unreliable person to me."

"I like him," Annabeth said, and they stared at her. "Well, I do," she insisted. "He's been awfully nice to me. When I was in the wings tonight he said such a funny thing. He said it was a good thing I wasn't in Paris because Prince Plonplon or someone would eat me up. What do you think that meant?"

"It meant that the prince and others have good taste," Letty said. The remark made her wonder. Did Max intend to invite the whole Fairborne Company to entertain in Paris? She hoped so. It would make all the difference, and what a wonderful triumph for the company!

They all met MacCroy in the foyer of the theater. He had hired two horsecabs and insisted that the midnight supper be his treat.

"I owe it to Fairborne here for saving my life," he explained, and when Vincent passed off the Rissoli conflict as "really nothing" Max assured him that "I consider saving my life to be of the utmost importance to me."

Everyone laughed. When the company divided themselves up between the two buggies, however, Vincent dropped his beaver hat at the last minute and stepped back into the street to pick it up and dust it off. Then, in what appeared to be a mistake, he stepped into the cab to join Al Degnan and Letty, leaving one seat free in Annabeth's and Calla's carriage. After about two seconds MacCroy took the vacant place, and Letty heard him beginning a lighthearted flirtation with the ladies.

The driver of Letty's cab, bundled against the heavy white fog, gave the signal to his powerful black draft-horse and discussed with himself the pros and cons of shrimp scampi at the Family Albergo Inn. Vincent quietly took Letty's hand and raised it to his lips. Nervous at the possibility of Al's seeing this, Letty felt uncomfortable despite the thrill of Vincent's touch. MacCroy's kiss to her ankle a few hours earlier had aroused her senses, and she longed to share Vincent's bed tonight, though she knew there was little chance of that. But the sexual hunger held her.

Could this desire be what MacCroy felt for her? Indications were there —his interest in her did not seem solely for theatrical or political purposes. His concern about her looks troubled her, but this might be due to the nature of his business proposition. Those sensuous lips touching her ankle had not had business in mind.

No matter. Vincent, her mentor and protector, was beside her and there was no questioning his motives. He loved her, but his great compassion and loyalty would not permit him to give wholly of himself to anyone but the gentle wife who needed him. She wished it were otherwise, but her admiration for his character was all the greater. She stroked his hand surreptitiously with her fingers, and he looked at her.

Even in the dark of the buggy she could not mistake the love in his eyes.

They pulled up in front of an old frame house, the only one for what seemed miles among the dunes, facing the great gray Pacific. This long, narrow house with its bay windows upstairs and down was full of happy memories of many other visits for the company. Vincent leaped out and turned to lift Letty down. He set her on her feet, but his hands lingered around her waist for a long moment. The magic was shattered by a raspy "ahem" coming from the shadowy overhand of the porch.

Embarrassed, Letty broke away from Vincent and started to the house. Without seeing who watched them from the porch, Letty sensed it to be Max. Why he would spy on them and act so contemptuously she didn't know.

As she had guessed, Max MacCroy was waiting on the porch, smoking a cigarette like some elegant European aristocrat. He was all politeness.

"I told the ladies you would be here before dawn. They wondered, but I had faith."

She brushed past him, not bothering to reply. He must know perfectly well that she and Vincent had not lingered on the road out to Ocean Beach. They could hardly make love—or whatever he suspected—in the presence of Al Degnan. At this instant Al and Vincent came up the steps and greeted Max casually.

She wasn't exactly sure why she resented him so.

She slammed both the screen door and the glass-front door as she went in. Annabeth and Calla were standing with their backs to the crackling fire in what used to be the front room. It was now a family-style dining room with two long tables covered by red cloths and any number of chairs, none of which looked comfortable. Portraits of olive-skinned Latin women adorned the walls, all of them plump, all of them barebreasted.

Although Letty had been here before, she had never given much thought to these nudes; she knew that the newly rich miners down from the Comstock liked to spend their precious silver on such acquisitions. But tonight, the presence of Max MacCroy and his glances from the paintings to Letty made her feel acutely self-conscious, mindful of her own "portrait" adorning the theater.

They all took seats, and Letty found herself between Al Degnan and Max MacCroy, across the table from the other ladies. Vincent took his usual place at the head of the table. Watching him surreptitiously, Letty thought he looked nervous, though hardly for the same reason she was. He ate very little, passing around platters of bread and antipasto, of pasta and mushroom sauce. They washed this down with a strong local wine, fermented in the owner's own cellar if the smell issuing from the basement was any indication. Vincent kept pouring and sipping the sour red wine but ate little.

Letty's feelings were divided. The greatest professional thrill of her life would be an appearance in Paris as the Empress Eugenie, even if there was danger attached to it. Every time she had put on Eugenie's makeup and garments she had wondered what it would be like to *be* this woman. How would she feel? Would her reactions be different? And best of all, she would be treated with respect by those indifferent strangers who turned their gaze aside when the desperate Sylvie, with a three-year-old child in tow, fled the cold city. . . .

But she could not desert the company. Or Vincent.

Al finally pushed his chair back from the table, patted his substantial paunch, and remarked, "That was a supper."

Annabeth contentedly rearranged slices of a fresh apple on her plate before dipping each in a cut-glass dish of sugar and cinnamon and eating them one by one. Calla gulped down a fourth waterglass of wine, eyeing MacCroy furtively over the rim of her glass.

MacCroy said, "Now to business."

Someone dropped a spoon. It clattered in the silent room.

MacCroy leaned forward, folding both arms on the table and looked at each of them.

"As you may have guessed, I am in the market—so to speak—for a female with certain qualities."

Letty heard a sigh, more an exhalation of breath. Probably Vincent, realizing his dreams were about to be crushed. Her heart went out to him; how could she have been selfish enough to give any thought at all to leaving his company?

MacCroy went on, "Since this female is your leading moneymaker, I would appreciate your telling me in monetary terms what her loss would mean to your company and how much it would cost you to train another. I propose to recompense you amply."

Vincent was staring at a stain on the tablecloth as he said, "What you propose is a little like buying and selling human flesh. The Yankees were very severe with us recently on that point."

"Don't exaggerate," MacCroy said.

Vincent flushed. "I have always felt that Miss Fox would go far in the theater. You are referring to Miss Fox, I presume." He gazed along the table until he found Letty's eyes. His smile seemed wistful, but she felt her heart bursting with pride at his magnaminity, for he added, "Letty Fox is perfectly free to leave the company at any time. But as for me, I do not sell human beings."

No one else said anything, but all heads turned to Letty.

Others might call his reaction pompous, but Letty wanted Vincent to know she understood his generosity.

"How do you feel, Miss Fox?" MacCroy asked.

Letty smiled. "Everything good in my life comes from the Fairborne Company," she said with disdain. "Why on earth would I want to go clear over to France without them? No, thank you."

Max MacCroy did not seem too upset. He settled back, his arms still folded, and waited.

CHAPTER *Nine*

"THANK YOU, my dear," Vincent said, breaking the awkward silence. "But I'm sure you realize this is too big a decision to make on the spur of the moment."

Letty snapped, "My conversations with Mr. MacCroy have given me ample time to think about possibilities. I'm sure Mr. MacCroy understands how we all feel." She turned to him, adding, "We are a company, sir."

"And where you go, the company goes," MacCroy said, still without any sign of strong feeling.

"Precisely. Except for Mr. Fairborne, we are all equals in the company. Where one goes, we all go. Or none of us go. In this case—" she flashed a dazzling smile upon MacCroy "—we are like the characters in a novel by your French friend, Alexandre Dumas. 'All for one, and one for all.' "

Then MacCroy shattered the solemnity by chuckling. He unlocked his arms and casually examined his blunt, strong fingers.

"In that case—and with due thanks to Monsieur Dumas—I have a friend in Chicago who is on the lookout for new entertainment troupes. Chicago is quite the metropolis these days. You could pocket ten times what you are making here, and with a long-term contract, to boot. O'Halloran may be just the man to oblige me if I recommend you. I myself will stand as guarantor of your project . . . without Miss Fox, of course."

"I am acquainted with the reputation of this O'Halloran," Vincent said. "I have tried to meet him any number of times. Why should he oblige you, a foreigner?"

MacCroy refused to take umbrage at this. "I approached him a few weeks ago because he's an old friend. An acquaintance of his in a restaurant showed us the portrait of a woman with the type of appearance I've been searching for. O'Halloran's friend had seen Miss Fox with your company, and it was he who sent me west. That and another matter that has been settled."

"Then why would this O'Halloran take the company without Miss Fox?"

"Because I asked him to." The Irishman added, "Miss Fox would find herself in the highest company in France. Princes, nobles, ladies-in-waiting to the empress. Later, the empress herself."

Vincent bristled. "No! Letty goes with us. I don't abandon my people to fate."

"Miss Fox, as I said, will have free access to the Tuileries. I would hardly call that abandoning her to her fate."

Calla, Annabeth and Al sat in stunned silence while Vincent struggled with the decision. He was obviously in great conflict.

"Surely you have noted that the main attraction of the Fairborne Company is Letty Fox."

"I'm sure Chicago and a large purse can provide you with an adequate substitute."

"Substitute!" Vincent scoffed. He clenched and unclenched his hands. "Impossible. How do we know what will happen to Miss Fox?"

Letty knew deep down that the only noble thing to do would be to make it easier for Vincent to accept the offer. She knew there was no future in their relationship. And if she left the company, she would be fulfilling all her dreams of a return to France.

But to leave the only man she had ever loved?

She began to sketch trails on the tablecloth with her spoon. For the benefit of the others she asked, "Mr. MacCroy, just what would my tasks be if I went into service with Her Imperial Majesty? What exactly does this position entail?"

He was looking at her with an intensity she found unnerving.

"You are wanted as a lady of certain position, a lady with entrée to the imperial court. When your acting talents are needed, you will be informed. I can't tell you at the moment precisely what your duties will be, but they *do not* involve selling your body, naked or otherwise, for oafs to gawk at."

Everyone gasped. Vincent was ashen. Letty wondered if he had ever thought of himself in that light. He protested in a voice that shook slightly.

"I assure you, we regard Miss Fox's work as a form of art."

"And what I offer is a form of art, before an audience that will see her only in carriages or in an opera box, elegantly—and, may I say, fully clothed."

They finally began to understand that Letty's resemblance to the

French empress was the crux of the offer. This painted a much more acceptable picture since it seemed that MacCroy was not trying to buy their leading lady for sexual purposes.

Calla spoke with a relief that amused Letty.

"Then it'd be all right. Not . . . well . . . you know."

"What would be all right?" Vincent demanded. "To sell Letty? That's what it amounts to."

Annabeth tried to soothe everyone. "I'm sure she didn't mean that, honey. But if Letty can be a great lady and ride around like an empress, we must let her. Besides, you always said you would just die to play Chicago."

"I said nothing of the sort. I merely think we could do well there. But not at this price."

Letty watched his fingers closing nervously upon his palms, how unaware he was of this self-betrayal. She knew how very much he did want to better the lot of the company.

But it was also becoming apparent to her that since she could never have Vincent, it would be better to get away from the temptation, sever the ties. MacCroy's offer had been providential; the danger involved seemed unimportant.

Suddenly she heard her voice, falsely bright, animatedly cheerful. "No one seems to have consulted me. I'd love to go to France and meet the empress and ride around in carriages." She glanced at MacCroy. "Fully dressed."

Letty found the furore that followed, urging Vincent to say yes, an insult. Only Vincent reacted with a hurt, numb look that made her long to comfort him. Instead, she stressed the selfishness of her decision.

"That is, Mr. MacCroy, if I am suitably compensated."

No cynical smile this time. Perhaps he saw through her enthusiasm. He said quietly, "You may be sure of that."

She glanced at Vincent and watched him turn to the decanter and refill his wine glass. He stared morosely at the red liquid.

Al Degnan found his voice. "Looks like it's old Chi for us. What say, Vince? Plenty money there these days."

Annabeth added, "It would be awfully nice, honey. They say Chicago has a pretty lake and lovely stores and parks."

To everyone's surprise Vincent set his glass down, reached for Annabeth's hand and brought it to his lips. He became almost effusive. "If my dear wife wants Chicago, then Chicago it shall be. MacCroy, I'll discuss the terms with you tomorrow." He added on a note of deep bitterness, "I presume Miss Fox will be making her own arrangements with you."

MacCroy considered him thoughtfully. "You may well be right. Shall we celebrate? Do you suppose our innkeeper friend carries champagne?"

Eyes lighted. Vincent was a careful man with money and seldom threw it away on frivolities like champagne.

The proprietor appeared, agreed that he could produce a good French champagne and left the room with his stout, grinning little waiter. Mac-Croy remarked, "I only hope he hasn't been bottling the champagne in his cellar."

Everyone but Vincent laughed. Spirits rose even before the champagne appeared, and nobody said anything serious for the rest of what had proved to be a memorable midnight supper. The champagne bottles, which the proprietor said were the only ones in his cellar, proved adequate, and most of the company, including Letty, would not have known the difference, in any case.

It was not until the company arrived at their lodgings above the theater that Letty could find a moment to speak privately to MacCroy. She deliberately lingered, fussing with her key, until the others had closed their doors. Then she went down the hall to the Irishman's door and knocked.

He took his time answering. She had almost given up when he opened the door. His saturnine face gave her little encouragement, and she burst out nervously. "I just wanted to thank you, Mr. MacCroy. You can't imagine how happy you have made Vincent and . . ." She read something, some flicker of light in his hard blue eyes, and rushed on. ". . . Annabeth and all of them."

"Delighted. It is, of course, my mission in life to bring happiness to our hero and his little brood."

She bit her lip. "I only meant that we are so grateful to you. That's all."

"I supposed it was all." He said it so flatly she sensed his boredom or indifference or whatever, and she backed away, trying to bring a graceful end to this injudicious visit.

"Well then, goodnight, Mr. MacCroy."

She thought he was going to leave her without even a pleasant goodnight. Instead he astonished her by asking, "Have you considered the fact that your name and identity will follow you, perhaps even to France?"

She was confused. What was he trying to tell her? Didn't he want her, after all?

"I can change my name, but hardly my identity."

"You can if you are cloaked by a husband's identity."

"And if I don't wish to marry some oaf for his name? I should be giving up my identity and my body."

MacCroy persisted. His eyes were alight. Amused, no doubt.

"A marriage of convenience. It is common enough among the upper classes."

"Not in my neighborhood."

"Perhaps, as with warring nations, a treaty might be signed to assure that the husband will not violate the lady's bed." He added with a tigerish little grin, "And that she will not violate his bed. Naturally they do not commit any act that will reflect on the partner's honor."

She took a breath and spat out her opinion of his proposition.

"All this to cover the shame of remaining Letty Fox? I would rather remain shameless."

He seemed to find this quite amusing. "Ah, but you would be doing your husband a service as well. You must have the correct identity at the Tuileries. You can't very well appear as a single young female with no attachments. As for your husband, let us suppose he is in a profession famed for its ruthless character. A lovely, demure wife on his arm at public functions would soon act as an admirable cover for any of his more—shall we say—ruthless doings?"

"Horrible. Suppose he didn't really want me. I mean—as a wife."

"Suppose he did. In fact, I could almost give you my word."

"I could never marry a man I didn't love. Or who didn't love me."

"That could be rectified. It is even possible this elusive fellow loved you the moment he discovered you differed from your poster image."

"Highly unlikely."

He shrugged. "Even more unlikely things have been known to happen. I'll wager he could make you forget your noble hero if you gave him a chance."

"Very amusing."

All the same he still looked mighty pleased with himself when he closed the door.

Letty was confused; titillated by the entire conversation, her body betrayed her by its response to MacCroy. A dangerous situation.

There was a great deal of sense in his concern for her reputation, and in the case of most other women in a similar position, marriage had been the answer. But surely these women had not loved another man at the same time. Or had they? Could she marry a man whose attraction was purely physical, solely to protect herself?

She had her mother's example of what happened to an unprotected woman. Men like Leonard Fox waited in the wings. And marriage would offer a clean, unquestioned break with Vincent.

She swung around and started to her room, only to see Vincent standing near her doorway.

She wondered uneasily if the Irishman had caught a glimpse of him, which might explain MacCroy's cynical proposal. But when Vincent caressed her face gently and murmured in a heartbroken voice, "Why did you do it, my darling?" she could think of nothing but her love for him.

As they walked to her room, he drew her to him. She spoke the words he couldn't deny, "If we go on like this, where will it end? You love Annabeth—"

He hesitated, then said, "Not in the same way."

She ignored that. "I love her too. We must be honest. The only way out is for me to leave the company."

His grip tightened around her waist. "Don't!"

"You know it."

"I don't give a damn for the Chicago deal. I don't want it. Not at the price of losing you." He tried to kiss her. It hurt to turn away, to avoid his lips.

With a tremendous effort she reminded him, "It's impossible to go on like this. Suppose Annabeth found out."

Vincent, who never used violence, who was especially gentle to women, shook Letty now, and it shocked her.

"You want to go with MacCroy. That's the truth of it."

"I want to go, but not because of him. Just say it's to make up for things that happened to my mother."

He let her go and opened the door for her. She slipped inside, sweeping her skirt out of the doorway. The door closed behind Vincent and they were alone.

Before she could stop him he kissed her, his gentle lips lingering on hers as his hands carassed her cheeks. "My darling, don't leave me. I'll give up Chicago, or better yet, the Fairborne Company will get there without help."

He was only making it more painful. She struggled halfheartedly, wondering if she could bear to go on like this, with his touch, his kisses confined to dreams and promises and the occasional stolen moments.

She pleaded, "Please. I've got to leave you. I've got to regain my own self-respect."

"My sweet, someday, someday . . . God! I do love you so!" Perhaps it was the supper wine, or merely the warmth of their proximity, but his arms enclosed her and . . .

She felt the edge of the bed behind her and laughed when she lost her balance and fell backward onto the deep, welcoming mattress with Vincent's body above her.

He was not a man of great imagination, but since he was her first and only lover, the very touch of his flesh against hers satisfied her. When he took her body with his, for an eternal moment she became a part of him.

A lonely childhood in the grubby, greedy world of get-rich-quick miners had cut her off from any understanding of shared emotions. These brief sexual unions with Vincent Fairborne were the only times in her twenty-three years that she felt a part of another human being.

But Vincent's sexual appetite was soon satisfied. Minutes later, while Letty's flesh still quivered with anticipation he arose and began to adjust his clothing. She forced herself to look away. A fastidious man, he felt uncomfortable when she watched him dress after their lovemaking, even though his genitals were quite as perfect as the rest of his Adonislike features.

She wondered if he was equally modest with his wife.

Neatly dressed and looking very much his immaculate self, Vincent carefully covered her half-clothed body, saying, "Someday we will be together, darling."

"Whatever I do," she promised, "I'll always love you."

He looked back with a wistful smile and left to return to Annabeth. The room was now so silent that she heard the distant shouts of drunken sailors roaming along Dupont Street.

Dawn was breaking before she fell asleep. Sleepless, she thought of him lying with Annabeth in his arms, hers for the whole night. She pictured the joining of his body to Annabeth's, the way he must caress and stimulate and give her the satisfaction he was forced to withhold from Letty out of guilt.

If I were his wife, it would be different . . . There would be none of this furtiveness, none of this shameful haste.

Letty thought about Max MacCroy. She was not fooled by the Irishman's interest in her. He used his sexual allure for his own purposes, and at the moment they happened to include Letty. And his were far more selfish motives, far more reprehensible, than Vincent's honorable desire to remain faithful to his wife.

But her childhood dream—this flame burned more brightly than ever. It was so close.

The following day MacCroy remained out of her way until curtain time. It was just as well. How could she bring herself to agree to marry a man she didn't love, who might be totally alien to her nature and needs? He found her in the theater wings.

"Thought over my proposal yet? We could have a very successful relationship."

She was furious with herself for the excitement she felt at his words. He might not be a safe, trustworthy husband but she couldn't deny that living with him would be passionate, an adventure if nothing else. At least he would not have to keep her hidden from his wife. His ambition was to show her off, either as the empress or as his wife.

"Thought over what?" she asked to gain time.

"A marriage of convenience, to cover your position in France. You would remain as pure as you choose. And I would remain my—er—pristine self."

She laughed, and he continued. "Not that you will remain in that unhappy state very long. You will give me a dispensation fast enough."

"Such conceit."

"You will invite me for a number of reasons. And I—?"

"Well?" She pursued the joke.

"I may oblige you. If you insist."

"Don't wager on it," she said, still amused. Then she raised her voice for the property men. "Al! Harry! First curtain."

She heard Harry, one of the scene-shifters, lumber through the creaking passage, but he did not reach her quickly enough. She felt herself boosted up high to the steps for her first entrance and had to silently congratulate MacCroy for his dexterity.

No kiss on the ankle tonight, however.

She pulled herself together and waited for her entrance cue but couldn't resist looking back into the semidarkness where she expected to see Max MacCroy. He wasn't there. She heard her cue and moved down the steps onto the stage to the gratifying music of applause.

Inspired by the knowledge that they must be skilled enough to entertain the sophisticates of Chicago, the company proceeded through the sketches with more than usual dexterity. Only Letty Fox went through her roles without her usual enthusiasm. She wondered what life would be like in France without Vincent, and the obvious way out seemed more and more difficult.

Tonight, as the troupe sparkled onstage, she realized what it would mean to them if their one great chance were taken from them.

They had all so willingly accepted her rise to stardom, none resenting the way the Fairborne Company became known as "Letty Fox, Empress of Impressionists." She owed them all so much, and the Chicago offer was the first time she could repay them.

She tried to silence the inner conflict by concentrating on her roles, but she knew she was not at her best. By the time they reached the Eugenie sketch and nothing had happened, Letty lost her sense of foreboding. Fortunately, she remembered to mask her carefully imitative gestures and voice along with Eugenie's golden-auburn hair.

It was just at this time that Vincent, as the Emperor Louis Napoleon, began to appear absentminded. He dropped his line, took one from the Carlotta sequence and seemed unusually nervous. Every time Letty looked to him for a reply she caught him peering out over the footlights with a heavy frown. A few minutes later, in the middle of a dialogue, a scuffle began in the front rows of the theater. A woman screamed, and others in the audience began to shout. All action stopped onstage. And through the confusion of the two miners fighting in the pit came the crack of a gunshot.

His movements timed to the instant, Vincent pushed Letty to the floor and knelt between her and the audience.

He muttered, "MacCroy has the damned thing arranged. He warned me. Play dead."

She obeyed, but as she lay huddled on the stage, she raged. If this was indeed a Machiavellian attempt by MacCroy to destroy her identity, to silence the real Letty Fox, he was very much mistaken.

CHAPTER *Ten*

"*NEVER! NOT* in a million years." Letty heard herself, her voice shrill, hysterical, insistent, and in other circumstances would have been ashamed, but she was too angry to care.

She had just read her obituary in the San Francisco *Argonaut*. It was lavish and complimentary, praising her as an exquisite creature and "a credit to the wide-open freedom of San Francisco," a distinctly left-handed compliment. But she furiously resented the ghastly thing that had been done to her career and her life. MacCroy's machinations didn't surprise her; he was therefore not the real object of her scorn and indignation. The members of the company cooperating with him in this charade about shooting her accidentally during a fight in the theater were only human. They were thinking of money and travel and success. They owed her nothing. It wasn't they she scorned.

But Vincent Fairborne, who loved her, who had so often assured her that "If it weren't for Annabeth who needs me" he would marry her, had been party to this scheme against her, this charade that would destroy her identity. He was just like her stepfather and the men she had known on the Comstock . . . and MacCroy. When he talked of loving her, he meant something else entirely. He had used her.

"Can you honestly want Letty Fox to die and be reborn as some creation of MacCroy's? Why, in heaven's name? You, of all men."

"Because Letty Fox is in danger, my darling. MacCroy told us Rissoli may have a friend. Who knows?" Vincent repeated in a compassionate voice that had always convinced her before. "It is to protect you. And so much more."

"Not at all. It is to establish a new identity for me in France—so that no one can discover I was that awful actress, Letty Fox."

She crumpled the paper up, hurled it at the threadbare carpet and then tried to rise from her chair, but Vincent hovered over her with both hands on the arms of her chair, gently holding her prisoner.

"My darling, what you have performed is beautiful. It is art. The delicacy of your work—everything about it. I would never let you appear in anything obscene."

"Others call it disgusting," she insisted, remembering Max MacCroy.

He looked as if he had been slapped. His mouth worked painfully. "When MacCroy made that remark about the gawking at you, it hurt. How he could say it about your lovely performances, God only knows."

"I suppose MacCroy thinks he can buy us. He very nearly has."

He considered her sour comment and after a moment admitted with effort, "You will be paid enough, according to him, to keep you in the first rank of comfort and fashion for the rest of your life. I feel guilty at trying to hold you back from opportunity. But my darling, if you really want to go—" he added on a sudden hope, "it isn't too late for you to refuse. We can move on, somewhere beyond reach of these ruffians MacCroy has turned loose on us."

All I wanted before MacCroy came was to know you were near. A tiny room with you someday. Your love and care. Your company when I was lonely. Your voice to speak to me about the most humdrum, everyday things . . .

She loved Vincent for his willingness to put aside his dreams of Chicago. It made her more determined than ever to give him this opportunity for success.

Had MacCroy planned this from the beginning, making it impossible for Letty to remain in San Francisco where she was in danger? Maybe he had hired Rissoli as well. He had certainly arranged tonight's fight in the theater and the pistol shot. Worse, he had gotten Vincent to cooperate with him, on the spurious grounds that she was in danger.

She let Vincent kiss her without responding; she was too confused. Vincent got up and left the room.

MacCroy and Paris. She tried to think of it optimistically, to banish Vincent. MacCroy's physical attraction alone was not enough to sway her judgement, but if she added a triumphant return to Paris . . . ?

Most irksome to Letty was that while she sat here pondering her decision, the company—and perhaps MacCroy—were out under a cold blue sky on one of the endless hills of San Francisco, attending her funeral.

Timid upon their return, they tiptoed around her as though she were an invalid. Evidently Vincent had told the company that her decision to go to France was by no means certain; consequently they avoided speaking about the one thing that really obsessed them: would she or would she not agree to change all their lives? Letty was sickened.

Al Degnan and Calla Skutnik talked about everything under the sun except the matter at hand, describing how the police had hauled off the two miners last night. And how they had been released almost immediately, with no fanfare, after MacCroy had spoken to the police.

"It was so damned funny," Calla said, too loudly, "I mean, seein' all them men up there on the mountain around your coffin and things. Them long faces. It'd of done your heart good to see the tears them miners shed, all for you."

"Well, far as they're concerned," Al said, "you *are* dead. I mean, ain't likely any of them ever gets to see you again. You bein' a great lady 'way off in—" Calla nudged him. He stumbled. "That is—"

Letty's resentment was tempered by a strong urge to laugh at their efforts not to influence her. They were obviously afraid she would go back on her word to MacCroy and ruin their chances.

Maybe she could talk the Irishman out of the outrageous marriage scheme. She had almost settled in her mind that she would go along with the Paris political masquerade. The rest would be a natural result. Except for marriage to MacCroy.

Vincent and Annabeth came in, and Vincent, without preamble, said, "So far as any would-be spies are concerned, you were buried an hour ago. However, I don't think you have to worry about MacCroy's attentions if you insist on taking this French offer."

She raised her head sharply. "What on earth do you mean?"

"I have reason to believe, after seeing MacCroy and that woman at the funeral, that his affections are directed there. That pretty Contessa Servandoni, you remember."

She didn't know whether she believed that or not; yet she had assumed that the contessa would leave the country as soon as she got her ten thousand dollars. Her waiting for Max MacCroy certainly didn't fit Max's odd, romantic hints to Letty, or his recent proposal. Furthermore, how could MacCroy love a woman he knew to be the emperor's mistress? Or was his proposed marriage of convenience to Letty an attempt to cover an affair that was bound to anger the emperor?

It was difficult to know what to believe about Max and the contessa. Worst of all, her jealousy astonished her. A preposterous emotion, considering that she loved another man.

Letty tried to wheedle some further information from Annabeth—

famous for her frankness—to verify or give the lie to Vincent's suspicion. She chattered on about the funeral: "I could hardly keep a sober face, but don't you worry, Letty. Mr. MacCroy was there with a pretty lady and she kissed him in front of us. Most improper, but it *was* funny. Vincent kept his hand on my arm and he reminded me not to say a word. We are all packing, you know. Vincent says we'll lose money on the theater. Something about the lease. But that nice Mr. MacCroy will pay."

"Is he really nice to you?" Letty asked on a wistful note. Everyone was nice to Annabeth and no one ever expected anything of her in return except, perhaps, her smile.

Annabeth coughed while she thought about it. "Yes. He looks stern and cruel and sometimes his eyes scare me. But I think he'd make you a splendid husband, Letty, if it weren't for that contessa."

"Really, my darling," Vincent said, sighing. "Must you chatter so?"

"But it's quite true. He doesn't love that contessa, I'm sure. I think he would like to marry our Letty. He told me she would make a wonderful wife for a man worthy of her."

"Which certainly excludes MacCroy," Vincent said.

Annabeth hugged his arm. "I teased him a little, and Mr. MacCroy promised me something. He saw I was uneasy about a stranger like him wanting to escort our Letty to France. And he did promise me. He said, 'I swear to be as true to Miss Fox as your husband is to you.' Wasn't that dear? It does sound as if he might be courting Letty."

Letty and Vincent avoided each other's eyes. She wondered if Vincent knew how serious MacCroy was about this marriage of convenience. He had managed to weave his wiles around Annabeth and get her on his side. At all events, infidelity wasn't what she feared from MacCroy; what she feared was his sensual appetite, period. Her physical love had been reserved for one man, and unhappily, that man was Annabeth's husband.

At sunset Letty ventured out on the streets against MacCroy's strict instructions transmitted by Al Degnan. In fact, until Al said, "He absolutely forbids it!" she had no intention of going out.

While she wanted to flout MacCroy in any way possible, she was not foolish enough to appear in public as Letty Fox. She wore Annabeth's dull brown wig from the Victoria sketch and a plain alpaca dress. This was unruffled and without a bustle or even the passé crinolines and hoops. She threw an old knitted black shawl around her head and shoulders and walked down the street past the throngs of Orientals in their black pajamas, black skullcaps and queues.

Even though these local residents were well acquainted with her, they seldom spoke to her on the street, but she usually nodded and smiled when she recognized them. She had just turned the corner, walked under a corrugated tin awning and stopped to wonder at the strange, dried marine creatures displayed in the window of the herbalist's shop when she heard her name called.

"Miss Fox? Evidently resurrected from the dead."

She gave the slender youth a hard look. All in black and gold, with a flat-crowned black hat, the youth looked like the caballeros who had once owned this area. He looked familiar, yet strange. The golden eyes ... the Contessa Servandoni.

"Good heavens! I thought you would be halfway back to France with your ten thousand dollars."

"But you see, His Imperial Majesty trusts me. I doubt that he trusts his precious Eugenie as well. He sent me a cable." The contessa added with some pride, "Have you ever seen a cable? They are most impressive. He ordered me to offer his friend—Max, of course—any assistance in my power." Her businesslike manner changed; she became absurdly coquettish. "You may imagine with what pleasure I obey, Miss Fox."

"Miss Fox is dead. She was buried today. You might begin to help the emperor's friend by remembering that."

"I'll do much worse if you dare to marry Max, you silly little whore."

Letty brought her hand out of her shawl and slapped the woman as hard as she could. The contessa rocked on her neat, small boots. She looked around: the incurious Chinese went on their way. The contessa caught at Letty's wrist.

"Listen to me, you fool. If you marry him it will be playacting. Only that. I'll see to it. You cannot marry him."

"Suppose I choose to marry him. By him I presume you mean Mr. MacCroy?"

"I mean MacCroy, prefect of the empress's secret police. You will not marry Max. I forbid it!"

Letty could scarcely believe this nonsense. "What have *you* to say about it? I certainly will marry him if I choose."

"You dare not! You are too cowardly. You are afraid to marry Max. Not like me." She stared into Letty's face. "You, bah! In the end, you will do as I command you and refuse to marry him."

Letty laughed. She could never resist a dare, always fought back, always courted the forbidden. "I don't know what your grievances are, contessa, but if you hope to marry Max MacCroy, you will be disappointed. He is already betrothed to me."

Letty turned around and marched up the street, toward the Lyric House. Through the hum and buzz of the pedestrians, the sing-song of the local Chinese hurrying home to supper, she could hear the contessa calling after her with idiotic persistence. "You would not dare. You are too cowardly. No. You will refuse him. Because I order you."

The woman must be insane. Unless, of course, the contessa was acting, trying to goad her into the marriage as a favor to Max. A way to carry out the emperor's request to aid his emissary.

Letty had no chance to question the wisdom of her angry response to the contessa; just as she reached her room in the hotel, she saw Max MacCroy leaving his own room and starting for the stairs.

Too coincidental. A deliberate attempt to meet her just after her encounter with the contessa—it had to have been arranged. She felt flattered and amused.

He stopped, politely tipped his beaver hat to her and unfolded a newspaper that he had tucked under his arm.

"I'm afraid they've had to free Rissoli."

She panicked. "Why? How could they?"

"Someone paid his fine. They don't seem to believe I was in serious danger from the little rodent on the *Periere.*"

"Who paid the fine?"

He shrugged. "An interesting question, one I mean to pursue later. However, it does make the need for haste urgent."

Her departure and marriage to him was now imperative. She would need his close protection in France, and she did not want to turn back now. Not so close to the fulfillment of that childhood dream.

Letty raised her chin and said in the coolest tones she could muster, "It seems that I will have to go through that ridiculous pretend-marriage with you after all."

He didn't act very surprised. Why should he be? Nor was his voice the least bit excited as he said, "Before or after we leave for France?"

If he persisted in this indifference to her, perhaps she wouldn't have any trouble with him after all. But it *was* insulting.

"Not until we have left San Francisco. It might prove too much for even this wide-open city if a dead woman married an emissary of the emperor of France."

He laughed and put out a hand to her face. She jumped back instinctively, without quite knowing why. He stopped laughing abruptly and his voice assumed that now-familiar sardonic quality she dreaded.

"I feel you would look just a trifle more presentable if your wig weren't tilted over your left ear."

She stamped off to her room without another word. The man made her feel ridiculous.

CHAPTER *Eleven*

*L*ETTY FOX kept her head turned to the view out the window of the rocking, creaking stagecoach. After the monotony of the sagebrush desert, the wild terra-cotta beauty of the Mormon state was hypnotic and —thank heavens!—kept her from crying. This was their fifth day on the road and she felt as if the anguish at the parting should have abated days ago, especially as the short ride on the steam cars had been so very continental and elegant—and distracting.

But today's leg of the transcontinental crossing was, unfortunately, in the old-fashioned stagecoach—thanks to a herd of milk cows who had raised havoc on the newly laid tracks.

Beside her, Max MacCroy stretched his legs, boots pressed against the springs of the seat opposite, ankles crossed, reading a Salt Lake City newspaper. Across from Letty a somewhat avuncular old gentleman with sideburns leaned forward.

"Homesick, little lady?"

Embarrassed, Letty blinked, aware that the tears on her newly dyed dark lashes had betrayed her. Her laughing denial sounded theatrical even to herself.

"Heavens, no! It was just the sun on those red rocks."

He reached across, patted her gloved hands. "That's the brave girl. Nobody wants to see those pretty eyes filled with tears."

MacCroy sat up with a casual movement, dropping his feet to the floor. He said nothing, looking at neither Letty nor the old gentleman, but his subtle hint was understood and the gentleman backed up into his seat precipitously.

Letty smiled. In spite of her homesickness she was beginning to think she could do far worse than trust her life and career to Max MacCroy. Five nights of travel, five nights of sharing shabby frontier hotels and quaint, barnlike way stations hadn't changed his casual manner; he was rather like a brusque and indifferent brother. It was curious that she should now feel safer with him than with anyone else, certainly anyone she had encountered on the road.

She would never afterward remember quite when or where she and Max had been married. It was carefully planned to take place somewhere in the High Sierras at an hour when the patrons who might recognize Letty Fox were all snoring away in their cabins.

The setting was depressing enough, a bar called Youngblood, or some such name with *blood* in it. The minister, who claimed to be "of no denomination and all of them," recited the words and officialized their marriage with a wildly ornate certificate with pink ribbons, which he presented grandly to Letty. It was certainly not the way Letty had expected to be married.

Nor was her wedding night at all as she had romantically pictured it in her youth. Camped in an old mining town in western Nevada, appropriately named Petered Out, Letty went to bed in a tent with all her clothes on, while Max strolled to the adjoining saloon and spent his wedding night at the faro table. After two hours of tears for what she had left behind in San Francisco, Letty went to sleep. She awoke with a start to find Max standing over her bed.

"What do you want?"

"Just your signature, my dear wife. If you have forgotten our little contract, I haven't. It came back to me rather forcibly during the night."

He handed the two sheets to her. He had written them both and the paragraphs were identical. He had even struck out one word on the second sheet to match the first.

Letty began to read by the light streaming in the uncurtained room:

> I, the aforesaid Letice Jane Fox, do swear upon my honor never to intrude upon the privacy of my husband, Maximilian Liam MacCroy, in either the physical or mental state, until and unless I am given dispensation from this oath by the aforesaid husband.

She began to laugh so hard she couldn't hold the pen steady. "What is the penalty if one of us fails to keep this oath?"

"This requires consideration. What penalty do you propose? Be frank. Of course, the worst penalty—but even you would not stoop to that."

"What penalty?"

He turned away. She could not see his face, but she heard an echo of emotion in his voice.

"I shouldn't like this paper to be made public. It would sit very badly with those I am supposed to terrify. The shame of it! But I'm afraid a female wouldn't understand."

She knew he was making fun at her expense, but there might be a good deal in what he said. He again offered her the spattering pen and inkwell —the ink was already coagulating—and she signed.

Early in the evening of a bright, glorious June day Mr. and Mrs. Max MacCroy reached a way station somewhere in the Wyoming Territory, and it was here Letty discovered her husband had merely been saving his energies until she was unprepared, defenseless and vulnerable.

He ordered two rooms from a fat, pockmark innkeeper obviously more used to serving rum and whisky than waiting upon ladies of Madame MacCroy's unusual good looks. Letty, certain that there was still no danger of Max's creeping into her bed at night—not that there was much to be said for the bed, in any case—bounced on it, saying to Max who stood in the doorway between the two rooms, "Well, it's not the Lyric House, but it will do."

"Trade you."

She laughed but refused. "You say that with too much enthusiasm. I'll wager it's worse than mine."

"It is. Filled with corncobs, I suspect. But the food smells good. Some sort of stew. Dare we eat our supper down in the so-called dining room?"

She looked around at the drafty, austere room with its high ceiling and narrow leaded window.

"Let's be brave and chance it. No one has recognized me so far."

Actually, as she was well aware, they were lucky not to find themselves in a sod house. It wouldn't be her first experience of those dark, dank dwellings, but she couldn't imagine Max MacCroy at home in one. Certainly not after the elegance of the imperial courts at the Tuileries, St. Cloud and Compiègne.

He was pleased. "Good. Freshen yourself and let me know when you are ready. We have a great deal to do this evening."

"What do you mean?"

"I mean a few lessons in manners. You will be rehearsing during the rest of our journey. Manners, etiquette, everything you will need to adorn the imperial court with quiet elegance."

"I don't wish to adorn the court, quiet or otherwise."

"You will, though. Now, hurry."

"Yes, master." She curtsied deeply, her ruffled black skirts billowing out around her.

But she might have known he would have the last word.

"Amateur theatrics, I see. But don't concern yourself too much. Before we are through, you will do it properly."

Letty slammed the door in his face but not before she saw his grin. She knew she shouldn't let him incite her this way; the trouble was, he knew exactly how to do it.

Letty didn't dare change for supper or make herself more attractive in any way. It was vital that she not call attention to herself except as Mr. MacCroy's wife. Thus far, luckily, no one had proved more than casually interested.

But when she looked into the cracked and unsilvered little shaving mirror on the tabletop and smoothed her hair, she rolled her eyes in disgust: she had never allowed herself to look so plain. Until this journey east, her looks had been her only passport. And now, no lip rouge, no black kohl to give her eyes the exotic slant that critics often mentioned. Nothing remained but to pinch some color into her cheeks, which she did in spite of Max's instructions to make herself as plain as possible.

She ignored his knock on the connecting door and waited until he had knocked twice on the hall door. Then she swept regally out, waving a black lace fan. Max looked her over.

"You move too rapidly. You are not a barmaid hurrying to a customer but a lady of considerable grace and dignity. Again. And slowly."

Letty gave him a look of unadulterated disgust, went back into her room and came out in a leisurely glide, eyebrows raised and a look of disdain for the world.

"Good God, no! That look would get you guillotined in short order. You are dealing with a rough citizenry who have overturned three thrones and a republic in the last eighty years."

A chilling notion. MacCroy followed Letty to her room and pushed the door open, bowing deliberately like a badly trained lackey. Inspired by his amateurish pretense, she tried again, moving more slowly this time, bestowing upon her audience a gracious smile.

He gave her what she imagined was probably his supreme accolade. "It might have been worse."

"It is so false. I felt what a lie it was, even while I smiled."

"The lady you are imitating is not false. She has many things on her mind. Her days are extremely full, but she manages a smile, an acknowledgement for each of her guests—hundreds. She—"

"Oh, good God, a paragon!"

"Not a paragon at all," Max said, obviously annoyed. "Her curtsy is considered the most beautiful in the world. It requires a great deal of practice. Once more . . . I am the Emperor Louis Napoleon. You glide across the floor to greet me."

She shrugged and took a breath. Moving toward him, Letty stopped and swept a deep curtsy while retaining her gracious smile.

This time, say what he might, she was positive he had been pleased.

"Well, so much for that. I suppose you were born to it. Everything is so easy for people like you."

"More especially for aristocrats like you!"

"Naturally. All the urchins who lived in the coteens curtsied and bowed to the wreckers of the Coast."

Letty's eyes widened. "You knew men who deliberately wrecked ships? How did they do it?"

"Men *and* women. My dear child, I grew up among them. They merely shifted the lamps and other lights on the cliffs. It was blood money that sent me to school in Dublin."

"No!" She wondered if he himself was guilty of this monstrous crime; she wouldn't put it past him. "Didn't you realize how terrible it was? All those innocent victims!"

His thoughts seemed to be far away. "To a child without parents it was a way of life. My father drowned when his curragh was swamped in a storm off the coast. I don't remember my mother." He slapped the wall beside him, making her jump. "It was not until I came to Dublin that I knew a different life was possible. Later, I turned my face against my past, probably as violent a reversal as I could make. I grew into my present profession."

"And now you are a policeman."

"In a sense. Not in uniform. I am the perfect of the empress's police, though you might say my business is still furtive. In the beginning a friend in London paid me to rescue Louis Napoleon from Ham Fortress where the French king had imprisoned him."

"Then it isn't loyalty but money that motivates you?" She felt a curious twinge of regret.

"You may believe what you like. My motives are of no concern to anyone." His vehemence surprised her and she suspected, for this reason, that loyalty had replaced mercenary motives. She hoped so.

He sidestepped the subject. "Shall we practice descending the stairs without looking down?"

Maddening creature. She managed to descend the steep, twisting flight of stairs without looking down, until she reached the third step from the bottom; she caught her heel in the stair runner. Max's hand gripped her upper arm. She was not grateful for the support.

Just because she knew he didn't want her to do so, she continued to play the great lady after they entered what the innkeeper hopefully called his hotel dining room, a sizable lean-to grafted onto the main two-story building. Although it probably leaked unmercifully during the Wyoming winter, on this June evening it graced the room with slivers of blue sky just turning gold from the reflected sunset light.

Max followed her gaze and noted a phenomenon.

"I do believe the heavens have provided you with a halo, ma'am."

She would have dropped a mock curtsy in thanks, but he held her arms up so securely she'd have looked ridiculous in a curtsy that left her arm high in the air.

The dining room was already full—never had she seen so many cowhands in one place. At one table, roughly constructed of sawhorses and planks and covered by a stained tablecloth, three men wearing short, drab coats, probably cattle dealers, sat discussing beef prices. All three men eyed Letty with the same hard-faced speculation they probably used to bid on steers, but they did not stop talking. The range cowboys, eight at one table, seemed much freer, louder and drunker. Her entrance caused a general buzz among the men and some craning of necks.

When one friendly soul bellowed, "Hi there, honey!" he reminded Letty so much of her vociferous but admiring theater followers that she called back, "Hi yourself, handsome!"

Max's eyebrows raised but he looked amused and made no objection.

There was one other woman in the room, dining in a corner with a gentleman in a Prince Albert frock coat who sported a goatee obviously trained to resemble that of the French emperor. The woman was overdressed and the brassy hair under her coquettish, dated bonnet looked no more natural to Letty than her own dyed black hair.

"What on earth does a gentleman like that see in such a woman?" she whispered.

"That elegant gentleman is undoubtedly a gambler out to fleece the cowboys."

"He doesn't look like any gambler I ever saw in Virginia City or even San Francisco."

"From the East Coast, I would say. Possibly even England. Liverpool, perhaps."

Letty was not convinced, but an hour later when she and Max were walking out of the dining room she saw the frock-coated gentleman setting up a faro game at a table in the bar. Max MacCroy certainly knew the world.

The gentleman scrutinized her face as she passed on Max's arm, and for the first time since her anguished parting from Vincent in San Francisco she was afraid. Max wanted them to walk outside to view the breathtaking expanse of open range country after sunset, but she pulled at his sleeve.

"Let's go back. He's still watching. I think he knows me."

"I doubt it. However, if you would rather work—"

She hadn't said a word about work, but she preferred that to the flinty gaze of the gambler. It was at moments like this that she appreciated her husband's efforts to conceal her real identity.

They returned to her room, and she was about to say a firm goodnight when she found he had not been joking when he said "work."

"Come now," he taunted her. "Growing lazy just because you are playing empress?"

So it was back to bowing, proper use of a fan, an occasional—"not too often, mind"—flirtatious tilt of the head, and worst of all, the Castilian lisp. As a tribute to her mother Letty had spent most of her life trying to speak flawless conversational French, which she now had to adulterate with a Spanish accent. So far, so good. But in the middle of what she considered to be an excellent attempt, Max said suddenly, "You will continue to speak your conversational French as my wife, and when talking to English or American people you will speak almost flawless English with just a trace of a Spanish accent."

"When do I lisp?"

"Only when you are onstage, so to speak, as the empress. It is not a lisp, but merely the Spanish way of saying c's and z's in Castile. And for God's sake, don't mimic the empress if you are both together in public."

She hesitated. "Is it going to be dangerous after all?"

"I won't let you be a target. I've made up my mind to that."

"Thank you." She was demure. "You are *so* generous."

But he refused to joke about it. "Any time you play Eugenie, I intend to play your shield, so to speak."

"Gallant. I feel as safe as if I were in church."

"Safer, I hope. There have been times when I didn't even trust Notre Dame." He reached for her hand. "I'm not going to lose you. I will not!"

Then he grinned. "You've slacked off. Here we go again—no laziness now."

She was tired and worn when he finally gave up his coaching and started for his room with a somewhat preoccupied goodnight. When she did not answer he looked back from the doorway. She was surprised to glimpse sympathy in his face. He stopped, came back to her. "Are you crying?"

"Certainly not."

He raised her chin and examined her face, then said something so unexpected she blinked with the shock and pleasure of it.

"How lovely you are!"

Self-consciously, she moistened her lips and gave him a tremulous smile. "How surprising! You actually can be nice."

"I'm often nice, as you put it. I know you are homesick, and I'm sorry for that. But the hurt will go away. It takes time. And new scenes. You'll soon forget all about the old life. Has it been so very bad, traveling with me?"

"No. You've been splendid. Like a wonderful and generous brother."

"Good God! A brother."

He pinched her chin hard, turned away, and suddenly swung around again.

"A very loving brother."

Before she could jump out of his reach he cupped one hand around her neck and pulled her to him.

"We'll see about that."

Startled and a bit afraid, she sealed her lips stubbornly as his mouth closed on hers. She tried to kick out at him but became entangled in her skirts and thought her back would break as his sudden assault pushed her over the table behind her.

To keep from falling she reached around his body, clawing at the back of his coat. If he had been Vincent, he would have understood that this was merely a desperate attempt to keep from falling, but MacCroy was quite another man. He forced her lips apart with surprising ease and she felt the heat of his mouth cutting off her protests and her breath.

She had a burning sensation that left her body quivering with the hunger she had felt when left so unsatisfied by Vincent, a merely physical response that she resented, especially for this man, the wrong one. She had left Vincent only five days ago, had even today been crying over him. She would never forget Vincent's face during that last painful good-bye.

Yet she was capable of being aroused by a stranger. She hated herself for her betrayal and tried to draw her thighs away from the pressure of his groin.

He let her go, took a deep breath and then released her fingers, embarrassingly tightened on his shoulders.

"Brotherly?" he asked while she sucked a broken nail on her finger.

"We had an agreement. If you do that again, I'll march right back to —to the Fairborne Company."

He stared at her. There was nothing of the passionate romantic about his eyes now.

"You'll march back to your precious hero. Was that what you meant to say?"

"Certainly not. When I make a bargain I keep it, which is more than I can say for you."

He went out through the hall door, slamming it behind him.

It wasn't until later, when she figured out that jealousy had triggered his anger, that she was able to find some forgiveness for him.

To her intense irritation, they seemed to have bypassed Chicago. She had been thinking that she might cross paths with the Fairbornes when the company met with the all-powerful O'Halloran to plan their show in the great midwestern metropolis. In fact, after questioning a lady on the steam cars about the best way to get to their destination, New York, and learning that "Everyone these days goes by way of Chicago, dearie," Letty had assumed they would pass through.

But not Max MacCroy.

They arrived in New York and even here he found reason to hurry her directly to their ship. According to Max, New York was full of people who might question her masquerade as the black-haired Midwest beauty who had so unexpectedly become Madame Jane MacCroy.

"Ours was a whirlwind romance," he reminded her in his sardonic way.

She snorted.

As they were riding down Fifth Avenue in a hired buggy, he did oblige her with the news that the Fairborne troupe would appear at the Grand Union Theater in Chicago within the week, and with no less than the celebrated soubrette, Nell Talley. The article he showed her in the Chicago *Tribune* impressed her, but she couldn't help resenting the "celebrated soubrette."

"What does she do?"

"Removes her clothing. Artistically."

Not as well as I do, she thought, but at least Vincent and the others hadn't been deserted.

As the buggy passed along the wide boulevard, Max pointed out the elegant mansions with their cupolas, towers, and prisonlike gray-stone fronts, and mentioned the great families living there. She had heard of the Vanderbilts and Whitneys and so many others, but it still seemed incredible to her. They were all ugly buildings, overdecorated and not nearly as beautiful as those in San Francisco.

Max found this naive but he didn't seem to mind.

"It doesn't matter except that it will make it easier for you to embark now without regretting all those marvelous things you wanted to see in Chicago."

"This town doesn't even have a lake."

"It has an ocean and a few rivers."

"It isn't the same thing at all. Anyway, Chicago was different. The company would have been there."

"And would unintentionally have led any of our enemies directly to you."

"All the same, I wish I could have seen . . . them."

That silenced him for a few minutes, and she looked out once more at the great, gray mansions, the five- and six-story hotels, one of which had little moving rooms that went up and down from one floor to another in place of stairs.

"I do wish I could have ridden in an elevator," she sighed.

"If you want movement, you will get it soon enough aboard the *Nouvelle Heloise.* She is a sturdy ship, but I don't doubt that there will be rough weather. It can be mighty foggy, even in June."

This was depressing news, which she distracted herself from by studying the ladies promenading along the avenue. In the environs of the hotels and mansions the women were exceedingly well dressed—judging by the Fifth Avenue Hotel the bustle was certainly "in." She didn't see one crinoline in a block and a half. But the atmosphere changed as the two buggy horses trotted off to the left, turned a corner and made their way toward the East River docks.

Here she saw the other side of New York, the pushcarts, the aging tenements, the rabbis in heavy black beards and strange hats. And children everywhere, barefoot, running, playing, shouting, working. She saw some of the bitterness in those faces that she was sure had been in her own at that age.

A little further east and they came into sight of the river. Even in San Francisco Letty had never seen so many spars and empty masts as there were on the horizon today. Where had they come from; where were they all going?

She sat up straight, for the first time really feeling the magic of this journey. How exciting to be alive! It was wonderful to know she was going to meet an emperor and empress, to wear beautiful clothes. All she had to do in exchange was play the part of the empress. Everyone would bow and curtsy to her, and she would smile, nod, flirt a little. The exchange was in her favor.

"I can't wait," she cried to Max. "It's so exciting."

He touched a curl of her hair with one finger. She did not pull away; she wanted him to know she appreciated what he was doing for her.

"Stay excited," he said. She was surprised at the troubled depths in his voice as he added, "And keep enjoying it."

Why shouldn't she? What an odd, unpredictable man!

When they reached the noisy, crowded waterfront she was surprised to find herself actually walking under the long bowsprit of a sailing vessel, so close she felt that if she stood on her toes she could reach it.

"Is it ours?"

"This one is English. Ours is French." He stood behind her, shifting her slightly so she could get a better look at the big ship riding the river current in the morning sunlight.

"Just remember, Letty. By the time you set foot on those shores you will be Madame Jane MacCroy, my wife. At least in name. You will have learned your role so well, no one will be able to trip you up, even in the slightest detail. But there can be no more Letty Fox. In manner, speech or conduct. You understand, love?"

"Perfectly, monsieur. Is that our rowboat coming up to the wharf?"

"One of our boats, yes. By the way, Madame MacCroy, I assume you mean to keep to the terms of our contract."

"Absolutely." He had done everything in his power to keep her from seeing Vincent on their journey. The least she could do was remain faithful to Vincent.

He nodded. His cheek brushed her head. "Then you will surely not object if I take my pleasure where I can find it."

She was so taken aback she blurted, "What pleasure?"

She suspected he was playacting again—he was far too casual to be genuine.

"The usual pleasure. For example, one of the other passengers."

She stared at him, then followed his gaze to a woman in robin's-egg blue making her way saucily through a crowd of sailors. She was followed by several lackeys carrying trunks and smaller cases.

The Contessa Pauline Servandoni.

Was the woman here again at her imperial lover's order? Max's hints about the contessa had unfortunately succeeded in piquing her jealousy, and for a moment or two Letty lost some of her enthusiasm for this voyage. She could hardly wait to reach France where she would begin her new life and not be locked up on a rocking, leaking sailboat with these two.

But Letty's competitive spirit rose to the occasion . . . and the memory of Max's kisses.

As the contessa drifted toward the longboat rocking on the swells against the pilings, Letty raised her chin, answering the challenge she thought she saw in the contessa's golden eyes with her own silent oath.

You are not going to steal my husband. I'll learn to hold him in ways you've never dreamed of. She turned to Max with a smile full of promise, her lips moist.

He did not look very surprised. "Playing the coquette, Letty?"

The snub wasn't going to stop her. "Have you forgotten? You told me there must be no more Letty Fox. You see how obedient I am as Madame Max MacCroy?"

He laughed. "Obedient? You? Take care. You may find yourself outfoxed."

"And I suppose you think yourself the fox?"

"Like you, my love, I always accept a challenge."

He hustled her over to the edge of the wharf.

A ruddy, grinning sailor in a stocking cap looked up from the boat below, having just lifted down the contessa and her little maid who was bundled in her own stuff cloak and starting uneasily at the movements of the boat.

Max descended the ladder with admirable skill, his body holding Letty in place as she moved down gingerly rung by rung, seeing between the rungs of the ladder the foul debris of a big city washed into this sparkling green darkness under the wharf.

As they joined the contessa in the boat she said, "I saw one of Plonplon's cronies at the Fifth Avenue Hotel while I was here. General Hugo Darlincourt. I will confess to you, my friend, he paid for my dinner last night. But still I learned nothing from him, and need I say, he learned nothing from me." She glanced around her at the oblivious French sailor. "Not that I have any secrets to hide. Heavens! How disappointing if General Hugo should prove to be a false trail for me! I was so sure I could help you by my friendly approach."

Max was getting Letty seated on a hard, damp thwart beside the contessa in the stern of the boat. He said, "We avoided Chicago completely and came directly to the New York docks. Newlyweds, you know."

"No one should know better, my dear contessa," Letty said, smiling sweetly. "Since it was your persuasive manner that convinced me to say yes to this gentleman."

The contessa laughed and shrugged. "Max asked me. And I have orders from my beloved Louis Nap—well, I must be discreet. I am trying not to be ordered out of France again for my indiscretions."

"I am assured that Monsieur MacCroy will be—what did you call it, sweetheart?—my shield."

He raised his eyebrows at the endearment but agreed with some amusement. "Just so. By the way, you have not congratulated us on our wedding."

"Poor dear! My sympathies. Max is quite impossible, you know."

Letty played along. "Then you no longer are madly determined to marry him?"

The contessa's trill of laughter was surprisingly pleasant. "No. I fear I led you astray there."

"Not as far as you might imagine."

Both Max and the contessa stared at her, and Letty said serenely, "Shall we be on our way?"

CHAPTER *Twelve*

*L*ETTY HAD heard so much about seasickness in San Francisco, where even sailing out of the Golden Gate was hazardous to the stomach, that she could hardly believe she was enjoying her first night at sea. And, to her great satisfaction, both Pauline Servandoni and her maid had been had been confined to the contessa's cabin from the time the *Nouvelle Heloise,* with all sails set, passed through the narrows and headed for the open Atlantic.

It was long past midnight, but the moon was up and the stars had never seemed so bright. Letty felt the same excitement she had known when she celebrated her first Christmas in the Fairborne Company—a glorious evening of stringing popcorn and cranberries, exchanging precious little gifts, hugs and kisses . . . the warmth and companionship . . . and the final kiss from Vincent.

She blinked, held out her arms over the weatherbeaten wooden rail and heard Max's voice behind her.

"Embracing the moon? How poetic."

Feeling foolish, she dropped her arms.

"The air is so wonderful. That salty taste. Does the air normally smell like this?"

"Sometimes. Matter of fact, you can slice the air if we sail into fog."

He put his arm around her, and she realized that she had been a bit chilled. She welcomed his warmth, but it reminded her of his first concern. She asked, "How is the contessa?"

"How would I know? I do not linger in bedrooms or the cabins of seasick beauties. I'll stop by her cabin in an hour. She may be more receptive by then."

Receptive, indeed. He seemed to be getting a great deal of mileage from Letty's jealousy. Truth to tell, however, his affair with his own wife had scarcely begun. She would give a great deal to know just how much he cared about that.

A fleet little schooner bound for New York passed on the horizon, its triangular topsails edged with silver. For a moment Letty thought, "If I were on that ship, I'd be heading toward Vincent." Then she banished the idea. Someday she and Vincent might meet again, with all the sweet, comforting love they had once known. But not now, nor any time in the foreseeable future.

She looked into Max's face and gave him a beaming smile. "You can be awfully nice, monsieur my husband. Is it because you need me for some devious scheme, or by some odd chance do you love me?"

"My dear, I never do anything by chance." He traced her profile with his finger. "Your face might have been a work in silver by Cellini."

"Who?"

"Never mind. Your face is cold. Shall we go below?"

The wind had picked up. The sails billowed and she heard the creaking of the shifting yards. She gave the scene one last look, sniffed the air again and wrapped herself closer in the blue velvet shoulder cape with its luxurious sable collar—a wedding present from Max. An entire wardrobe was still waiting to be unpacked in her tiny cabin.

She did not fool herself, however, that this luxurious wardrobe was a present to Letty Fox. Rather, it was a present to the fictional character she would play in Paris. He insisted that very little effort need be made to fit this wardrobe to her lissome figure, as he put it, but she had no doubt she would be sewing and stitching and hemming in her cabin for most of the voyage.

Then, if she failed to convince anyone at court and in Paris, she would be packed off back to the United States, without the elegant wardrobe. And without this tentative, attractive husband as well?

She was thrown against Max as the ship suddenly heeled over in the trough of a wave. Max was right. Time to go below. The silver light had faded.

The companion ladder was steep and the ship listed as the narrows caught the Atlantic current, but with Max's help she made her way along the passage to her cabin. Max opened the door, looked in and whistled.

"Can you turn around in there? I ordered everything from a dress-maker friend of mine in Chicago, but I didn't ask her to turn you out onto the deck to sleep!"

She grinned. "I don't mind. It's the adventure of it, as I often tell myself when I feel inclined to throw it in your face." She suggested hopefully, "I don't imagine yours is bigger." No point in asking to trade, but still . . .

"You have the owner's cabin. Pauline and her maid have the captain's cabin. I share a coffin of a space with Pauline's dinner companion of last night, General Darlincourt. Call that a coincidence, if you will. His valet is stuffed in also."

"Do you think the general is on board to do some mischief?"

"I don't believe it's a coincidence. The general used to be for hire, and long ago he attached himself to Louis Napoleon. When he felt he wasn't properly rewarded—he wanted to be a marshal of France, if you please —he dropped away from the emperor's party. Lately, he seems to have joined forces with Prince Plonplon, and I guarantee he will certainly report that Pauline has been invited back to court. It will make Plonplon happy because, in a sense, it is a triumph over the empress."

She never could understand why Plonplon hated the Empress Eugenie, even though to Max it was so simple.

"Eugenie is conservative, Catholic and a strong influence on the emperor. Prince Plonplon is liberal because he chooses to be the exact opposite politically of his cousin the emperor. In my opinion, Plonplon is jealous of anyone's influence but his own."

His expression softened. The lightness and humor returned to his hard face. "I don't suppose you feel inclined to share that spacious bunk of yours."

"I couldn't. That would be violating your contract. You were very specific about that."

"But you signed as Letice Jane Fox. That was not your correct name when you signed. You were at that time Madame Maximilian MacCroy, or Letice Jane MacCroy, as you please."

Her eyes opened wide; she wanted to laugh. "You rogue! Is there no honesty in you?"

"I played strictly by the rules. I wrote the contract before our marriage. It was your responsibility to make any changes you chose. You chose not to. Can it be that you subconsciously preferred to abrogate our little contract?"

"Abrogate, indeed! I don't even know what it means. Go to your seasick siren. Besides, there isn't room in here for two."

"Let me show you how that might—"

"Get out!"

She saw the humorous but determined air about him and closed the door before she betrayed her own feelings by asking him to stay.

Afterward in her bunk, with the bedclothes piled around her against the cold that seeped through the wooden hull and under the door, she wondered what he was doing with the contessa in the captain's cabin. Did he make love like Vincent, or in some more exotic way? Probably he was aggressive and quickly satisfied. Hadn't Calla Skutnick said that all men were like that?

Trying to fall asleep, Letty found the ship rolling so much she could hardly keep from falling out of her bunk. The night with its frequent interruptions made her aware that it was not wise to scoff at the sufferings of others. During the early morning hours she was mercifully spared seasickness, but she nonetheless had moments of sheer terror as she rolled from side to side and up and down.

She had just finished dressing when a brisk knock on her door was followed by Max's voice.

"Bonjour, my love."

"Who is it?"

He pushed the door open.

"How many loves do you own to at this hour? I am instructed to ask if you wish Claud-Ange to bring a tray of breakfast, or will you dine with us peasants?"

"Don't be ridiculous. I shall certainly dine at the table. I'm very much afraid a tray would be useless in that bed."

"Rather like your husband, madame."

She snickered, ignored the arm he offered and started proudly down the passage with him in a sway of skirts and petticoats.

The elegance was short-lived. As they started in the direction of the crew's quarters in the fo'c'sle, the ship shuddered, caught in a crosscurrent. Letty pitched forward along the passage and tumbled against the galley door.

When Max pulled her to her feet he said, rather ungenerously, "You deserve it after refusing my arm."

But she was not the only one who hadn't gotten sea legs yet. A huge gentleman, made huger by dint of a velvet-striped travel cape, lurched out of Max's tiny cabin and jammed his elbow into a bulkhead. His cape flew out around him so far it almost enveloped the passage. Letty envisaged a gigantic bat hovering over them.

He picked himself up, dusted himself off and made a bow to Letty that was surprisingly graceful for so large a man.

"Max, you scoundrel! You did not tell me your bride was a beauty." He took up her fingers and touched them with his lips. "No. I was in error. A very queen of beauty. Venus herself."

The only Venuses Letty had ever seen were nude and she gave Max a sidewise look of alarm but he merely remarked, "Hugo has poetic leanings. My dear, it seems I must present General Hugo Darlincourt, since this ship is too small for us happily to ignore him. He is an old friend of the emperor and his cousin, Prince Napoleon. Their friendship dates back to His Majesty's London days."

"My dear boy, Plonplon makes enemies everywhere. It is an art with him. However, if I may flatter myself, I make friends everywhere. Indeed, the emperor himself would have been cut by all the really important members of London society but for me. That is, before he made himself an emperor, you understand."

"You haven't a modest bone in your body," Max said.

"Unkind. I am a very tolerable fellow, until you know me well."

Letty laughed, and the general released her fingers from his grip, which was surprisingly strong despite his fleshy appearance. He took a tiny, square monocle out of a slit pocket in his waistcoat and looked her over.

"Excellent, my boy. The little man will be overjoyed. I'm very much afraid his present bouquet is a trifle wilted now from so much sniffing."

She wondered if he meant what she thought, and for a horrified moment she suspected this might be her real task at court, to succeed the contessa as the emperor's mistress. She was relieved when Max snapped, "My wife is not part of his bouquet. Are you going to breakfast or do we spend the day prattling in the passage?"

Ignoring this ill-natured comment, the general addressed the lady present. "Forgive me, dear Madame Max. Let me show you the way. So." Before either she or Max could stop him, he had placed her hand on his arm and was escorting her into the cold, swaying little cabin that was the dining saloon.

Hazy morning sun streamed through the two cabin windows framed by very faded chintz curtains that had been tied back. Obviously some woman's touch long ago. The room was more cheerful than Letty's own stern cabin with its northerly light.

Captain Henri de Sens, a lean, aristocratic gentleman, was just leaving as they walked in. He seemed surprised, if not too pleased, to see them. Acknowledging in French his introduction to madame MacCroy, he nodded briefly to the men, saluted Letty and excused himself on the grounds that there were many tasks to be performed.

"Including, I regret to say, a ghost." All ears perked up. He explained with distate, "Undoubtedly a stowaway my superstitious sailors have taken for an apparition. They have not yet located him. He came aboard ship in New York by a method as yet unknown to us."

"Then how do you know he exists?" Max asked.

"He was seen sneaking about in the hold. He escaped, but unless he has gone over the side he is still somewhere about."

"I prefer to think of him as an apparition," the general said with enthusiasm. "Always wanted to meet one. But I'm afraid your crew has mistaken my valet for this ghost. I sent him to the hold to fetch up another change in my wardrobe. What with two beauties aboard, one must try to make a suitable appearance."

Captain de Sens said repressively, "My men should have been notified. In any case, the entire vessel must be combed to be quite certain there is no stowaway."

He bowed stiffly and left them. General Darlincourt could hardly contain his excitement. "I do believe the crew of the *Nouvelle Heloise* has provided me with a subject that will occupy me on this boring voyage. I would never have believed it possible. Damme! It almost makes up for the discomfort of that miserable, miniscule bunk."

"He talks of bunks while they had to string up a hammock for me," Max complained to Letty.

"I told you to let my valet Simkins take the hammock. You might have slept in the other bunk."

"I prefer to be near the door."

Letty had no idea whether Darlincourt understood that Max did not trust his two cabinmates, but she was sure of his meaning.

As for the general, he eyed them with interest. He was already halfway through the pewter plate of sweet honeycakes when he suggested casually, "Curious business, your marriage. One would think any red-blooded man like you, Max, might prefer a bunk with Madame to a hammock with Simkins and me."

"He snores," Letty explained. Max responded with an indignant stare, but clearly he appreciated her quick reply—even if it was disparaging.

The food in this small dining saloon was far better than its San Francisco reputation; General Darlincourt explained that since French ships carried only French crews, it was necessary to furnish better food than that doled out to the international British crews.

"No crimps and shanghaiing for these ships," the general boasted. "Better made, too. Much bigger deckhouses and cabins. That makes for safety."

"Bigger!" Letty choked on her light, beaten eggs.

Hours later when Max was showing Letty around the tight little ship they discussed their meeting with Darlincourt.

"Don't believe a word Hugo says about safety and size and the popularity of French ships," Max said. "It's the Gallic food."

"So I noticed." But she was distracted by the loping run of two crewmen who passed her and rattled down the companion ladder.

"Wait here. Near the man on watch. Don't go near the rail."

"Why not?"

Too late. He had gone after the sailors.

She suspected that they were chasing the stowaway. Why was Max so concerned, unless he thought there was personal danger involved? The officer on watch, a stocky Breton with a square, windburned face, squinted into the horizon as he paced the deck. He seemed to have no curiosity about the running sailors.

The youth at the wheel was not quite so disciplined. A stocking cap pulled over his wildly flying red hair gave him a jaunty look and this, combined with wide brown eyes, made him appear friendly. Considering his age, she was impressed by his handling of the wheel. He gave Letty a shy grin as his hands eased over the spokes with the vagrant running of the sea.

Following the height of the mast to the high royals snapping in the wind, Letty was awed by the size of the *Nouvelle Heloise,* but when she lowered her gaze to the horizon she saw how tiny the bark really was. The watery sunlight cut the distant view even more, making her uncomfortably aware that she was sailing into the unknown; that, in fact, the unknown was all about her and included her husband.

CHAPTER *Thirteen*

*L*ETTY GREW more and more anxious over Max's pursuit of the stowaway. Did he suspect the stowaway's identity? She was distracted from her thoughts by the sudden appearance of Pauline Servandoni's beautiful head above the companionway, and Letty staggered across the slanting deck to meet her.

"Contessa, have you heard anything about a stowaway?"

The contessa waved this aside. She was heavily bundled in furs but neither the blowing sables nor the aftermath of her seasickness had taken away an iota of her feline attraction. She began to rattle in French, " *Chérie,* forget these, what one calls stowaways. My maid Beata has seen an odd thing. That stout Hugo, sneaking about in passageways. Max suspects him of working against the empress. He is too friendly with Prince Plonplon. But the emperor also owes him favors from the past."

"I thought you shared Max's suspicion. Never mind. What of the stowaway?"

The contessa glanced over her shoulder and down to the deck below. "Very likely it is General Hugo's valet fetching up his clothing, or something of that nature."

"Is this Prince Napoleon—Plonplon—actually a *traitor* against the emperor?"

The contessa was impatient. "You are not listening, *chérie.* It is Eugenie that the Bonaparte family wishes to be rid of. In a perfectly respectable way. After all, Eugenie's son will be emperor one day. Such a charming little boy—Lou-Lou, they call him, for Eugene Louis. But the emperor's family believes Eugenie is pro-Spain. They also think she has too much political influence with the emperor."

"And has she?"

The contessa shrugged. "It is possible. But I have learned my lesson. If I wish to hold the affections of the emperor, I do not conspire against his wife. Not that I ever have. He is very loyal to her. He exiled me solely because Eugenie asked him to."

"Aren't you afraid to return?"

The contessa laughed, and then choked as the ship heeled over and then righted itself. When she could breathe once more she shook her head.

"No. That is the doing of your Max. He informed Eugene that it was I who had recovered the jewels she is returning to the poor Empress Carlotta. I am rewarded. I may return to Paris. I owe much to your Monsieur Max."

Letty wasn't at all sure the contessa herself could be trusted, any more than the fat general. Both had reason to root out the empress and her influence. "I can't quite picture General Hugo Darlincourt, with his weight, sneaking about anywhere. What does he do? How does he work for Prince Plonplon, if he does?"

"He profits by dealing in secrets. We are old acquaintances, and have been in the same profession at one time or another. This time I am definitely on my poor Louis Napoleon's side, and that means the side of Eugenie. But Hugo has his ways of adding to his income, and I have mine. We each recognize the danger in the other."

"You have not told me what you know about a stowaway, if there is one," Letty reminded her.

The contessa frowned. "This is not a city, only a small ship. How do you think a man could hide here and not be found? In a cabin, perhaps? But Max is fool enough to share the cabin of the stout one. Max may wake up with the throat cut. But we know the stowaway is not there with those three men. Where would he hide? Then there is my cabin, which my maid, that ugly Beata, shares. The stowaway cannot be there." She looked around and raised her voice. "Beata?"

The ship had begun to pitch and toss, forward and back, up and down. The contessa, holding a lace handkerchief to her mouth, begged, "Beata! I am sick."

But across the deck the luckless Beata leaned over the rail, groaning.

The contessa mumbled, *"Je m'excuse,"* and waved Letty away in a panic.

Letty asked, "Shall I bring you something for your stomach?"

"S'il vous plaît. In my cabin. A brandy decanter. Near the bunk. *Mon Dieu!"* She grasped the rail and bent her head over it.

Letty started across the deck. A man in a great hurry had suddenly run ahead of her. She assumed he was a crew member also in search of the stowaway. She found herself sliding down toward the companionway, then plodding up with enormous difficulty over the freshly holystoned deck. She reached the steps and managed the descent to the deck below, not without trouble.

The crewman ahead of her was out of sight. The passage was ill-lighted by the companionway and she had to feel her way to the door Max had pointed out as the contessa's port stern cabin. The ship heeled over to whatever Max had called the right side. Yes, the starboard, she reminded herself as she fell away from the contessa's door.

She climbed back to the door and threw it open. She looked around, finding the place in a worse state than her own. At least her cabin was lined with trunks or boxes. The contessa's gowns, cloaks and furbelows hung from every conceivable object. One of her very fashionable feathered hats sat precariously on top of an oil lamp, and the captain's precious books and ancient charts had been piled up haphazardly beneath the desk, obviously as a footstool for the contessa. The desk was littered with cosmetics and perfume-scented stationery.

The servant's bunk was a makeshift cot in a corner of the cabin now shrouded in gloom by the fog pressing at the large cabin window. A great bundle of what appeared to be bedclothes was crumpled up on the cot.

Letty found the brandy decanter and poured the golden liqueur into a pewter cup, wondering if she could get the cup up to the deck without spilling it.

Carefully balancing the cup, Letty was just about to turn toward the door when she became aware of a sound in the cabin, near the maid's cot, quite distinct from the creaking of timbers and the moan of the wind. Someone was moving behind her.

She glanced over her shoulder and stared into the muddy, narrow eyes of the grinning Rissoli.

He waved a long knife blade before her.

"Do not be surprised, madame. My ears are very sharp. Sharp as this blade. It will keep you from making fools of those who are your betters."

He had to be the crewman she saw hurrying down the ladder. Even in the foggy gloom that filled the cabin she was aware of the double blade, each edge honed to a razor sharpness.

She screamed with such ear-splitting force Rissoli took a quick swipe at her, catching her sleeve but missing the flesh. She could see his small, yellow teeth as his lips pulled back.

"No scream. Or I will have to kill you."

She knew perfectly well he would have to kill her. There was no way for him to escape from the ship in mid-Atlantic if she remained alive to point him out. Evidently he had been biding his time, waiting to scar or kill her before the *Heloise* dropped anchor at Le Havre.

Letty was shaking with terror, but instinct prevailed. She threw the cup of brandy in his face and screamed with all the theatrical force she could muster, while she pulled her jacket off and tried to protect her hands with the many folds of velvet and fur.

"Silence, damn you! Quiet. You want to die? Come close. Closer. Just . . . so."

He swung the knife like a scythe. She heard the tearing of material and kept screaming hoarsely while she darted this way and that to elude the deadly blade.

Encouraged by a near miss, he tried a wider arc, slicing through the folds of velvet and fur. She was breathless now, helpless against the double blade that was everywhere, dancing through the air.

Suddenly the door burst open and two men rushed into the cabin. Max MacCroy caught Rissoli in a choking grip, enclosing his neck in the angle of his elbow and wrist; the knife blade, now flashing vainly, was twisted out of Rissoli's fingers by the powerful hand of General Darlincourt.

"Take him," Max ordered. "I want to see to my wife."

The general took charge of the little man, who had been possessed by a fit of coughing and choking. It stopped just as abruptly: Rissoli slipped through Darlincourt's hands and crumpled in a dingy heap on the cabin deck.

Letty cried, "Oh, Max!" and threw her arms around him spontaneously.

He opened his arms to embrace her, remarking, "You were bound to appreciate my sterling qualities sooner or later. I must say, after one night of that hammock, I am glad it was sooner rather than later."

Darlincourt had gone down on one knee, with much creaking of joints, to examine Rissoli. A minute later he cleared his throat and said apologetically, "Max, your friend here seems to be dead. Don't know your own strength, old boy, and there's the truth of it."

Still with his wife in his arms, Max turned. "Damn it! I wanted him alive, to talk. Well, too late now. Better get the captain, Hugo. I don't want the maritime company accusing us of murdering some poor stowaway."

General Darlincourt paused in the passage to ask, "Could the contessa have known? This is her cabin."

Max looked at Letty who shook her head. "The contessa was seasick almost from the moment of sailing. She was most definitely sick when I left her on the deck."

"Benefit of the doubt?" the general suggested. "I've known Pauline for a long time. Not her sort of mischief, knife blades and such."

"But she did send me down to her cabin," Letty thought.

"Obviously this was the stowaway," Max said, "prowling around after hours. I imagine he planned to dispose of anyone who caught him stealing."

"What the devil could he have been looking for? And why try to kill your wife, Max?"

"He may have been the commonest of thieves. As for killing my wife, he knew she could identify him." As the general was heading away again, Max added, "I hope you won't be alarmed, Hugo, if I hint that the fellow just may have been after you. Are you carrying secrets?"

The general looked uneasily around the dark passage. "I've no secrets. Just a friendly voyager going to Paris for the food and those pretty females one sees at Vefour and the other restaurants." But he kept glancing over his shoulder until he had knocked and was admitted to the captain's makeshift cabin.

Letty recovered enough to laugh at Max's trick.

"You know perfectly well he was after me."

"Let Hugo worry a trifle. It will do him good. May even burn off some of that blubber he carries around. Besides, he might be Rissoli's employer. Certainly Pauline isn't guilty. She wouldn't jeopardize her position with the emperor."

She resented his quick defense of the woman and almost wished she hadn't brought up anything in the contessa's favor.

Captain de Sens appeared in the doorway of the contessa's cabin along with Darlincourt. He looked impassive as he studied the crumpled heap. "It would seem obvious that this is our ghost—our stowaway."

De Sens strolled around the cabin. Despite his effort to hide it, Letty was sure his aesthetic sensibilities had been shocked at the condition of his books and maps, the devastation of his quarters.

"How did the victim meet his end?" de Sens asked, turning Rissoli over with the toe of his boot.

"Excuse me," Letty said, "but I believe *I* was the victim. Madame Servandoni was seasick on deck, and I came to find brandy for her. I discovered this man and he tried to kill me. I screamed." She added, in a tone of accusation, "I thought perhaps you might have heard me screaming."

Captain de Sens made a rapid negative motion.

"I have only just returned from the forward hold."

"His neck seems to have been broken," Darlincourt observed with interest. "Max seized him and I got the fellow's knife away. Between us, we apparently lost him."

"Very well. I will have your stories taken down by my supercargo. The matter will have to be brought before the prefecture when we anchor." He glanced at Max. "Although I imagine you, Monsieur MacCroy, will take precedence—since you are a prefect of the imperial police."

It was clear to Letty that the captain, like most seamen, resented the higher judicial claims of landsmen. De Sens ordered the body removed, to be stored in a barrel of spirits for the rest of the voyage.

Letty whispered to Max, "It looks like he had no particular sympathy for Rissoli, either."

"He reserves his sympathy for the crew," Max replied. "Rissoli will be pickled in a barrel of their spirits."

She wanted to laugh at the grotesque joke, but forced herself to keep a sober mien.

"We had better notify the contessa," she suggested. "It might be interesting to watch her reaction when you tell her."

Letty was grateful for his arm around her as they left the cabin; in fact, she wondered if she could have walked at all without him. Her knees shook and a nerve in her right leg kept twitching wildly.

Out on deck the weather had rapidly worsened since Letty went below. The fog was everywhere—great, ghostly puffs along the deck, swallowing up both the wheelman and the contessa, who was leaning over the rail, resting disconsolately on her elbows. They all could hear the unfortunate maid Beata gulping and retching further along the deck.

Max said to Letty, "The contessa looks as though she were suffering the pangs of hell, and she's not the least bit curious. She hasn't looked back once."

Letty agreed. They made their way toward the contessa just as she straightened with an effort and headed for the waist of the ship. The rough seas made it difficult for Max and Letty to reach her. Letty found herself climbing what appeared to be mountains of deck space before she could call to the contessa.

"I'm afraid I dropped the brandy. . . . I found the stowaway in your cabin. He tried to kill me."

"Madre de Dios!" the contessa went off suddenly in her native Italian. "Tell me you are joking." The words barely out of her mouth, she was thrown against the rail by a sudden roll, and Max caught her.

Pauline was either completely surprised or an incredibly good actress, for she shook Max, crying, "You do not see the full horror. If I had gone to my cabin he might have killed *me!*"

Max glanced at Letty. She saw Max's grin but was not amused.

After they had taken the contessa to her cabin, the "death cabin," as she now called it, Max insisted that Letty would be unsafe in her own cabin without a man to protect her. When she scoffed at the idea, he came into the cabin with her, made a great pretense of looking into corners and then agreed.

"You seem to be safe."

"Not quite. You are still in my cabin."

"True." But the teasing manner did not match the hard look in his eyes. It excited her, even while she knew the danger of yielding to his sexual magnetism.

Letty realized that it was with this power that he hoped to make her forget the past, all Vincent and the company had done for her. The company had given her the family she had never known, and Vincent . . . Vincent had taught her what loving was.

From her experience as Vincent's mistress she had learned that true love demanded passivity on her part. Although this defied all her passionate instincts, anything else could only be classed as sexual gratification and had nothing to do with the adoration she felt for her knightly lover.

All this reasoning was necessary to assuage the guilt Letty felt at feeling this sexual stirring in the wake of such a horrifying experience.

Max's hands, those same capable, strong hands that excited her, had snapped a man's neck not an hour before. Whatever desires he aroused in her, she had seen him kill a man so easily. Yet he had done it to save her life. Surely that must be taken into account. Torn, she said, "Try your hammock again, Max. It won't seem so hard the second night."

He had his back to the door. There was humorous purpose in his attitude. "What if another Rissoli is hiding under that bunk? Or in this trunk?"

"Unlikely." But she gave the big trunk a suspicious glance.

He rubbed his shoulder. "Have you no compassion for my back?"

"It isn't your back that concerns me."

His laughter was startling. She wondered what the crew or their fellow passengers thought and waved him to be silent. He caught her hands and lightly imprisoned her against the bunk. A part of her wanted this—to be forced to submit to this rogue. Afterward she could tell herself she had been faithful in spirit to her true love.

Shocked by her own duplicity, she pleaded, "I can't. It wouldn't be fair."

"To whom, my love?"

"To you."

He was angry now. "Let me worry about that." Before she could make further protest, he kissed her. Nothing gentle or knightly about his rough mouth; nothing maidenly about the swiftness with which she found herself drained of resistance. Instead of fighting off this advance, she fell back onto the bunk, drawing him to her, locking her arms around his back. Her body reacted to his touch; his lips brushed her throat as he tore away the lace at the neckline of her gown.

Closing her eyes, she pretended she was in Vincent's bed, his wife. But she realized in Max MacCroy's arms that there had been something furtive about Vincent's lovemaking—his insistance on darkness while Letty disrobed, and the brevity of their union.

For all Max's force and insistence, he made no effort to hasten a climax. Her senses had never been aroused in this way before; his fingers expertly probed the deepest recesses of her body while his mouth provoked the wild, erotic excitement she had heretofore reserved for her most private fantasies.

She caressed his shoulders and neck, brought her hands around to his groin and felt the hardness that she had aroused in him. A tongue of fire seemed to play about her loins before he was ready to enter her body. She heard herself mutter hoarsely, as she would never have done to Vincent, "Now. Please—now."

"You love me. Say it!"

"I want you."

"Say it."

She repeated, "Darling, I want you, please."

He entered her body roughly, grinding and hard, an angry man. But she was ready for him; she had known it would be like this. She tried to enclose him within her, to make him a part of her, prolonging the climax. With the bursting of Max's power within her, she felt an ecstasy she had never known before.

She knew when it was over, as she sensed his glittering eyes watching her while she lay with her eyes closed, that she would want him again. And again.

BOOK Two

CHAPTER *One*

"**H**OW WRONG Vincent was!" Sitting forward, Letty looked out of the horse-cab window at the fantastic buildings in the French capital. "When I told him how mother loved Paris, he said I'd imagined it all."

Max had been watching her face with an intensity that at any other time would have unnerved her.

"I am happy to hear that this Achilles of yours has a heel somewhere."

She took his hand and squeezed it. During the many days and nights they had shared since that hour in her cabin, she had often wished that when he asked her if she loved him she could say yes. A lie would be easier for them both to live with.

She liked Max enormously, and their sex life was the greatest thing that had happened to her since her rescue from her stepfather so long ago. But Max was a policeman. Policemen had a way of recalling all the small remarks you didn't want them to remember.

She tried again. "I wish I could remember something. I was about three . . . all these wide avenues and the hotels . . . I don't know . . . Look! There, across from the huge building that's half-finished. That's a hotel. Why, it's bigger than the Fifth Avenue in New York and the Lick House in San Francisco!"

He smiled at her exuberance. "That half-built monstrosity is the new opera house. The building on this side is the Grand Hotel—they say it's the largest one in Europe. And you are certainly right. It is elegant. More elegant than my rooms, I'm afraid."

She looked at him, trying not to show her disappointment. "You should have seen where mother and I lived—at the top of an old, fallen-down building in the Temple district. We had to climb endless stairs . . . and so dark . . . I remember that very well. But when we got to our room we had a wonderful view. All the chimney pots and church spires and domes, and the sparrows on the roof next door . . . I wouldn't know how to act in a place like the Grand Hotel."

He shook her hand roughly. "Yes, you would. You've been acting correctly everywhere else. You are as good as they are. Never forget that. Wasn't a triumphant return to Paris one of your ambitions?"

"I know." She tried to laugh. "I must remember that, and that now I am the empress—at least once in a while."

"As good as the empress."

"Better."

"Absolutely." But she wasn't sure he agreed because he really thought so or if he was simply humoring her.

"When I said Vin—my friend had been wrong, I meant about Paris. He said it had narrow streets and medieval buildings and was terribly crowded."

"Your—friend wasn't far from the truth. You will still find his Paris in the Marais and on the Cité and the Left Bank. In fact, here to your right, along St. Honoré. This is the street the tumbrels took on their way to the guillotine. It looks very much the same today—minus the tumbrels. And the guillotine. We keep our guillotine a trifle more private nowadays, but it does exist."

She looked along the serpentine street, with its ancient cobblestones, its narrow houses huddled together, and shuddered.

"Don't tell me such things. I like your new Paris."

"Artistically it belongs to two men—the recent prefect of the city, Baron Haussmann, and, of course, the emperor. It is his child. When did Vincent visit Paris?"

"A few years after mother and I left. He came in steerage in the early fifties, when he was young."

"How young is he now?"

"He isn't young at all. He is very mature. Thirty-six. He'll be thirty-seven on July twentieth."

"While I, a truly mature man, was forty on my last birthday. Last January, in fact."

Did he care? Was he, perhaps sensitive about his age? At least she could let him know it didn't matter to her.

"I admire older men. I've had men fifty and sixty years old—perfect gentlemen—come to me in the theater and say the nicest things about my performances. Of course, at that age, you could hardly expect them to—well, you know."

He winced. "We oldsters do have our uses."

The late June day was sultry, the sun hidden behind a thick haze, and yet there were few light, summery dresses in sight. Nothing looked familiar. Thus far, Letty had found that the darkly clad, hurrying people on the streets seemed very like those in New York, perhaps not as richly dressed as those on Fifth Avenue but more impressive than the poorly dressed foreign-looking people she had seen on the way to the docks. In fact, at the time, Letty had been surprised by the number of Levantine and Mediterranean immigrants she saw when they left behind the moneyed section of New York.

In San Francisco, despite its heavily Italian population, the "exotics" had all been Chinese, with a light sprinkling of other Orientals. The Parisian street throngs were reminiscent of San Francisco's Market Street, except that they were more conservatively dressed. Letty even saw some women still in crinolines. She wondered if her elegant bustle gowns made her look overdressed.

The horse and cab jogged into the rue de Rivoli, which paralleled the Louvre and Tuileries palaces. Max pointed out that the latter, a great stone rectangle which housed the imperial family, closed the courtyard of the Louvre.

"There, between the Louvre and the Tuileries, was one of the worst slums in France. But we've done away with that."

"Where did the slum dwellers go? Does His Majesty care?"

He started to say something, stopped, and said, "He cares. Much good has been done. Believe me."

She looked skeptical and he changed the subject suddenly. "The emperor is in Paris. His flag is flying from the Tuileries. So I can report directly to him."

But Letty's attention had been caught by the marvelous arcades lining the near side of the street, all of which faced the imperial palaces across the avenue. Standing between the two, she felt overwhelmed by the splendor, and hoped she didn't seem too mercenary when she asked if she could go shopping.

"Look at those gloves. Like melting butter, so soft. And the bonnets. That pink one with the plume would look perfect on Annabeth. And how Calla would strut in the red one!"

"What? Nothing for the noble Vincent?"

She hesitated. "I thought maybe some gloves. For Al Degnan too." Her husband had given her so much, the splendid wardrobe, even a pearl necklace and earrings and a small diamond parure, that she felt guilty in talking business. But she went on. "When you give me my salary, I shan't trouble you about trifles. I know you have a great deal to do, now that you are home."

"And if I like to be troubled about trifles?"

He was teasing, but she felt the sincerity behind his banter. Now, however, his attention was directed to the forbidding gray edifice in front of them that was the imperial Tuileries. He would have to report to the emperor about Rissoli . . . and also, perhaps, about the American woman who had been brought here to impersonate the emperor's wife. Her hands felt damp inside her new kid gloves. Suppose the emperor disapproved of Max's choice! She must make the emperor like her.

For blocks on end, the roofs with their chimney pots rose evenly above the shops. What would it be like to stay in those hotels and privately owned salons as a foreign visitor? She reminded herself that her husband was not rich and that the closest she would probably get to this luxurious life was a brief outing in one of the celebrated parks of Paris while she pretended to be someone else. Still, she had already returned in triumph compared to the gray morning she and Sylvie had crept out.

Beyond the Tuileries Palace the rue de'Rivoli eventually opened out past long, formal gardens into an enormous square. Letty's dazzled eyes took in only bits and pieces, formal buildings on one side, the gray-green busy river on her left. But ahead, as the cab rattled around the square toward the great ornate bridge, she gasped at the sight of a wide carriageway in the distance rising to the biggest arch Letty could possibly imagine. She stuck her head out the cab window and stared.

"It's it. I've seen sketches. I know I'm being too enthusiastic, but the Arch of Triumph! I mean the Arc de Triomphe—you know."

"I know," he said and surprised her by kissing her cheek. "Be as enthusiastic as you like. I'll wager this is much more the real Letty Fox than that creature I saw displaying her body to the mob."

She appreciated the unexpected tenderness in Max but resented his occasional gibes at her past. She had tried to be genuinely creative when she played those women. The nudity had been an embarrassment, but she wasn't a bit ashamed of her acting performances.

"I assure you, I was very much myself in those days."

He said nothing to that. It annoyed her that he seemed to despise what she considered to be the real Letty Fox. Apparently all Max loved was the masquerade, the Letty pretending to be something she wasn't. All in all, the reality of her life in Paris might not be quite the glorious conquest she had dreamed of.

The cab crossed the Concorde bridge and weaved down along the Left Bank quais. Letty made it a point not to openly admire anything else, although this was difficult when she spied the mansard roofs, obviously created for artists' studios, and Romanesque palaces that seemed to be government buildings.

Max, after watching her a few minutes, began to look out his own window. After passing more stone bridges, Letty saw something in the distance that appeared to be the stone and grass prow of a ship. This must be the Ile de la Cité, the island in the Seine that was the site of the most beautiful edifice she had ever seen in a picture book.

"Notre Dame! There they are. The two towers." She didn't continue, embarrassed by her outburst.

He leaned out the window again, signaling the cab driver on his high perch. The horse pulled up obediently before an ancient three-story building that faced the quai; another half story nestled under a mansard roof. Letty found this grim, medieval exterior ominous. A minute later Max got out and turned to assist Letty to the pavement.

It was only then that she saw how Max's home was situated. Across the quai and beyond the Seine loomed the flying buttresses at the rear of Notre Dame cathedral. Letty stood almost opposite the Ile de la Cité where, according to Vincent, Paris had begun over two thousand years before. She clapped her hands in delight, then, recalling her sophisticated pose, turned to enter the old building.

"I do hope your room has a view of Notre Dame and the islands in the Seine," Letty said casually.

"My . . . uh . . . room overlooks this view. You see that top floor? No. Not the attic rooms."

She looked up, impressed by the grandeur of the floor-length windows framed by open shutters. Six windows. It must be a huge room. She began to feel better about her life in one room with Max.

While he paid the cabby, a petite, dark woman at Letty's elbow spoke to her. "Madame will point out her cases for immediate use?" Max turned back.

"Good. You remember. As I told you in my letter, Claudel," he said, unexpectedly jovial, "I have brought you home a new mistress. You must now check everything with Madame MacCroy."

But Letty, having no idea what she would be doing immediately, was forced to turn the matter over to Max. Max sent the cab on its way and checked over the bags, then surprised Letty by embracing a huge bear of a man, heavily bearded and wearing baggy breeches beneath a faded blue smock.

"This is Fedor," Max said. "He and Madame Genevieve Claudel run the household. Anything new during my absence, Claudel?" He added to Letty, "Nothing passes those dark eyes of hers."

The woman was over thirty, perhaps thirty-five, very good-looking in a small, trim way. Letty could sense the woman's pleasure at Max's return and wondered if she had ever been his mistress, but then caught herself. Was she going to feel suspicious of every female Max had dealings with? Ridiculous thought.

Madame Claudel indicated a crowd of violently gesticulating men standing around the abutments of a stone bridge to the Ile de la Cité a block away.

"As you see, monsieur. Small riots since the last elections. His Majesty talked so much about the new liberal empire, as the newspapers call it."

"It could scarcely be more liberal," he muttered. "What can they want? He has given the people more freedom than these damned republicans ever promised. I know the combined vote in last May's elections exceeded the vote for the empire, but it also involved considerable pressure from the radicals."

"Lucky for His Majesty," Fedor said as he lifted one of Letty's big trunks onto his shoulder. "Their Majesties took a drive last month, out through the Bois and back along the Champs-Élysées, and were cheered, such cheers as you would never believe. The citizens do not want the radicals and their revolutions."

Letty hadn't the least idea what they were talking about, and was surprised that her husband should be bandying political ideas with a foreign-born porter. Getting to know Max was a constant surprise—he was so multifaceted. She admired and respected him but was keenly aware that her part in his life was probably no more than political, despite those exciting nights. At least now she could remain true to Vincent in heart if not body. Max would be too busy to care.

Lifting the hem of her full black skirt, Madame Claudel started up the stairs. Halfway up she slowed her steps and warned Max, "The Bonaparte prince, the one they call Plonplon, he has been spreading stories that the empress should go."

"He is always spreading stories about Eugenie."

"But now he says she is a threat to His Majesty's liberal government. He says she is priest-ridden and wishes to destroy France."

Max snapped, "He would like nothing better than that Eugenie should go the route of Marie Antoinette. If he could bring her to the guillotine himself, I would not put it beyond him. Well, we have a few schemes to confuse Cousin Plonplon, my wife and I."

Letty wondered. It began to look as if Rissoli had been the least of her worries.

She felt the strain in the tendons of her legs long before they reached the top floor but was impelled to keep going by the sight, when she looked over her shoulder, of Fedor balancing the trunk and marching so easily behind her. Though the staircase wound upward toward what appeared to be eternity, it was reinforced and reasonably modern. She had expected seamed walls and an occasional flickering candle but found the stairs amply illuminated by gas jets in small, opalescent, lantern-shaped fixtures.

They passed other doors, one to each floor, heavy oaken panels that looked forbidding and very private. Max pointed them out.

"My tenants."

So he owned this building. It came as a pleasant surprise.

"On the street floor," he went on, "an ex-prefect of police, a friend of mine from the old days. We both worked to free His Majesty from the prison fortress at Ham."

Claudel said repressively, "The gentleman has sublet his rooms by request of the emperor. His Majesty said you would not object. Your original tenant is currently in Prussia on some business with Chancellor Bismarck."

"Harmless business, I hope," Max said. "The emperor doesn't trust that Prussian Bismarck, and I certainly don't."

"The emperor asked him to sublet his apartments—to a female, of course," Fedor said, his mustache quivering. "His Majesty came personally to inspect them. In disguise as a *flaneur,* a wealthy street idler—one of those fellows who sit all day at the sidewalk cafés gazing at the females passing by."

Max seemed to accept this as commonplace.

"Who is the female involved?"

Madame Claudel took out a card from her pocket. He read, laughed, and said, "Very like Louis Napoleon. I might have expected it. . . . But to move on. Here on the next floor, these are the apartments of the old marquise." He chuckled and Letty caught him exchanging a glance with Fedor. "Madame la Marquise has a taste for young males. She is in

London at present, satisfying that taste. Now, the top floor. Enter, madame."

By this time Letty realized her idea that she would be sharing an attic garret with a poverty-stricken prefect had been somewhat distorted.

Madame Claudel pushed the door open and stood aside, brushing her skirts out of Letty's way in a manner that suggested Letty's touch was to be avoided.

Letty forgot the gesture entirely as she stared at a long salon that occupied the entire front of what she called, in the American fashion, the third floor. The white plaster walls with their gilt-framed panels were elegant enough to belong to the emperor himself. The small gas jets, which Claudel proceeded to light, gave the room a fairytale luminescence, bright against the hazy, almost gloomy weather outside.

The furnishings, though, looked uncomfortable. The silk-padded gilt chairs and shining inlaid tables were the kind Letty had seen in museums with signs reading Do Not Touch.

The fireplace and mantel were whitewashed, setting off a gilt-framed portrait that hung above. It dominated the room. For an instant Letty caught her breath. Letty Fox looked down at her, her head tilted a little, her mouth serious and her eyes amused, a glorious crown of light auburn hair—yes, it was Letty Fox in a teasing scene from her Eugenie sketch. The gown was a white tulle crinoline that revealed flawless shoulders and bosom.

Madame Claudel made a small gesture toward the painting.

"Her Imperial Majesty."

Letty's smile remained firm upon her lips but the light in her eyes died. She was furious with herself for not having guessed the identity of the subject at once.

"Charming," she agreed somewhat inadequately. She became fascinated by the opposite side of the room. "And what a splendid view!"

Meanwhile, Max took the trunk from Fedor and disappeared along a white passage toward the back of the apartment. Fedor hurried down the stairs again. The view was all that Letty had hoped for, but unfortunately, Madame Claudel seemed to feel it her duty to remain as companion and instructor. She pointed out, beyond the river, the incredible number of domes, towers and, in the greater distance, open spaces, explaining, "They are parks and squares. His Majesty says they give the breathing space to Paris."

"Very nice." In spite of the magnificence around her and the view from

from this apartment, Letty felt lost. She had believed that something about the city of her birth would be familiar. She had forgotten that the "elegance" she wanted to offer to her mother's memory would be so foreign to herself and certainly to Sylvie.

Max called to her from another room. "Where do you want these gewgaws, love? And the ball gowns?"

Before she could start along the darkly elegant inner hall to the rest of the rooms, the outer door opened again. Fedor unloaded a box and two portmanteaux, and stood aside, bowing deeply to the man behind him.

Letty wondered if the emperor himself could have followed Fedor up the stairs, but this man was clean-shaven, square-faced, dark, and taller than the emperor was said to be. It was his curious, distorted resemblance to his uncle, the great Napoleon, that told Letty who he was, despite the severe, unadorned black frock-coat, buttoned up to his chin, and his scowl which totally lacked the much-vaunted charm of Napoleon the First.

So this was Prince Napoleon—the much discussed Plonplon.

Letty was far more intimidated by him than she would have been at meeting the emperor himself. She sank in a low curtsy, well aware of his penetrating gaze.

CHAPTER *Two*

*A*T FIRST she thought he wasn't going to offer her his hand. A bit shakily, she started to rise. But Plonplon's hand was there before her. If she kept rising in this humiliating position her lips would touch his fingertips. She raised her head, just avoiding his fingers by an inch or two.

"Your Highness. I have only just arrived in my husband's house, else I would be honored to receive Your Highness as my guest."

"I quite understand, Madame MacCroy. But this is not an official visit." His voice was harsh, his manner abrupt. "I come to see the—ah—lady Max chose to marry. My cousin the emperor has not yet seen you. That is evident."

"Evident, Your Highness?"

"—or you would not have been bedded so far from the Tuileries. You see, I know my cousin's appetites."

She flushed angrily, surprised at his flippancy. There seemed to be very little difference between crude San Francisco frontiersmen and crude French princes.

"Your Highness must be better acquainted with the Bonaparte appetites than I. As Madame MacCroy, I share only one bed, that of my husband."

They were both startled by an unexpected burst of laughter from the interior hall.

"Your Highness has the answer, I think."

Max stepped forward, putting an arm around Letty, drawing her to him. "My wife and I are on our honeymoon. I suggest you consult your agents as to the date of our marriage and my wife's background."

"Background? Agents?" the prince echoed.

Letty wondered if Max was trying to make Prince Plonplon betray the fact that Rissoli had been his spy.

"My wife's father—he is in cattle, you know—insisted that the ceremony take place at the ranch. Or do you call it a farm, my love? In a province called Wyoming."

"A territory, darling."

"Enormous wealth in Janie's family. You know how people eat beef, Your Highness."

Letty was thankful that Max had so carefully altered her appearance. Clearly the prince saw little in her that reminded him of the empress, although the fact that he came to examine her so soon was proof that Rissoli, and perhaps others, had notified him of the resemblance. She wondered if the prince always sent agents to spy on Max MacCroy's wanderings outside France.

"I am told by a loyal friend in the prefecture that either you or that fat rascal, General Darlincourt, murdered a man at sea. But no matter. Do you still have any of that brandy left, the year my uncle preferred?"

"By all means, Your Highness, and perhaps you will be so good as to give me your view of what has been happening in Paris during my absence."

"Nothing would give me more pleasure. First of importance, my poor cousin will end by bringing down the dynasty if he doesn't put aside that Spanish wife of his."

The prince strolled into the salon, making his way like an habitué to a sofa across the far end of the long room. Fedor, after a look at Madame Claudel, took His Highness's top hat, gloves and walking stick. Max went off to find His Highness's preferred brandy.

Letty had no idea of what to do next or even where Fedor and Max had put her luggage, although she was not precisely overjoyed when Claudel urged her in a low but officious voice, "If Madame will follow me, we may unpack and arrange your things."

"Thank you, but that won't be necessary. I'm used to unpacking for myself. Just tell me which is my bedchamber."

But Claudel was not so easily banished. "This way. Monsieur and Madame's chamber overlooks the inner courtyard where it is more quiet. The dining salon overlooks the courtyard and the easterly view as well."

They passed what appeared to be a comfortable study and library, then a small parlor. Letty did not see whatever lay behind the doors on the other side of the hall. It did not matter, she told herself. Her role was only temporary. All anyone wanted from her was a performance.

Even Vincent. She had been Vincent's important moneymaker. Was it this he had really valued in her?

What made that preposterous idea pop into her head? She felt desperately alone, an entire ocean and a continent away from her "family," those who, she thought, loved her. But in her present mood she questioned even that, the one truth she had clung to.

In the years since her mother's death she had sought only one thing, to belong. Surely, she had belonged in the Fairborne Company, but at this moment all that came to mind was how they had all urged her to leave them, to go far away, across half the world. They had been happy to trade her for a chance to appear in a Chicago theater. Maybe it was time to belong to something—or someone—else.

Her husband?

In spite of their conjugal raptures she knew with each further step onto French soil that she was merely an object he had purchased for his political purposes.

The bedchamber was lovely with its view of a chestnut tree, a pleasant, cobbled courtyard and attic windows across the court. The bed was big and comfortable, with a lofty mattress and four short, thick bedposts. The shaving stand and its wood-framed portable looking-glass were pushed into one corner to make room for a brass-fitted mahogany chest-on-chest, so tall it looked as if it could hold all the possessions of her lifetime, and a matching bureau with a mahogany-framed mirror that gave back her reflection from head to foot. An easychair covered in green silk damask and a small triangular table with a sewing basket sat beside the window. Max's instructions to Genevieve Claudel must have been thorough.

"How very thoughtful of my husband!"

Madame Claudel gave the arrangement a casual glance.

"Yes, madame. They were gifts from Her Imperial Majesty. Private gifts. That is to say, the table and chair. Monsieur MacCroy is exceedingly devoted to Her Majesty. He felt that your tastes might be similar."

After that piece of information, Letty ignored the carefully chosen place by the widow. Was it possible the empress had a private interest in Max? Perhaps there was a relationship between them. It didn't at all match the portrait of the cold, haughty Spaniard that gossip described. But it might be Eugenie's way of paying back her husband for his notorious liaisons.

But why should she care that Max and the empress of the French, as she called herself, were lovers? If they were . . .

But I am alone again.

She knew the absurdity of this thought. All around her was a splendid, rich life in her mother's Paris. She might ask for almost anything, except the one thing she had been searching for all her life.

Claudel asked, "Shall I hang the ballgowns, madame? There is a long closet across the hall. Monsieur MacCroy thought it might be suitable."

"Yes. Wherever seems appropriate." It was like discussing the costumes for her elaborate charades on stage; the wardrobe did not really belong to her. She removed her new hat with its tilted brim and green plume.

Claudel watched her, an apricot tulle-and-satin gown draped over her arm. "Monsieur MacCroy informed us that you would be choosing a maid shortly. French, of course."

"Of course." But Letty determined that second to thwart this woman, if only by hiring someone who was not French.

She was rummaging through her old carpetbag when her husband came in, passing the housekeeper in the hall. "Ah, Claudel. Good. I knew you would have my wife settled in no time."

"Is the prince gone?" Letty asked coldly.

Max looked over his shoulder. "Shhh, love. Voices carry." He took her by the wrist. "Come along. We must give His Highness a polite farewell."

She wrinkled her nose.

"Remember," he warned her in a low voice, "you are Janie MacCroy. We don't want him to see any more resemblance to the empress than necessary at this time. He will find out soon enough just how remarkable it is."

"Janie. Ugh!" She rolled her eyes, then abruptly simpered as she came into view of Plonplon, who stood in the salon easing on his gloves.

This time His Highness was somewhat better mannered. When she reached him, aware that he had watched her approach along the open hall and undoubtedly was studying her, he looked as malign as ever but extended a hand.

"I had not intended to stay so long, madame. I trust you will forgive me for having deprived you of your bridegroom. But business and politics—you understand."

She decided to be charming—perhaps this surly fellow could be broken down. He wouldn't be the first of his sort that she had subdued with sweet words. She curtsied and rose up under his eyes with the celebrated Letty Fox smile.

"Your Highness is too kind."

It may have been the first time anyone ever accused him of being too kind. He was caught unaware, blinked and very nearly returned her smile.

She waved Fedor aside and said, "Such long, tiresome stairs. Permit me to keep you company, Monsieur le Prince."

"That won't be necessary." He licked his red lips, added stiffly, "very kind, I am sure. Max, you have found an American with the charm of a Frenchwoman. My congratulations."

Behind the prince's broad back Max winked at Letty, and then, bowing respectfully, moved ahead of them while they descended to the street in regal fashion. In the passage leading to the courtyard His Highness stopped and squinted at a card stuck under the brass knocker of the ex-prefect's street-floor rooms. He remarked in his rasping voice, "I congratulate you again, Max. Your wife is more broadminded than mine. Or has that nauseous prefect sublet his apartments?"

Letty read the card over Max's shoulder.

"SERVANDONI, MADAME LA CONTESSA PAULINE"

This must have been information on the calling card the servants had conveyed to Max when they arrived at the house. Max hadn't seemed upset. But of course he could hardly countermand the emperor's own arrangements, even assuming he might want to.

"I believe the contessa has business in Paris," Max said.

"Not when the Spanish woman discovers she has returned. Eugenie has a Spaniard's jealousy."

Max remained undisturbed. "I think we can agree that the contessa will not be a guest at the Tuileries."

Prince Plonplon laughed shortly. "My cousin may find he is in more danger between these two women than he ever was thirty years ago in prison."

Max summoned the prince's horse and groom. Letty was surprised to see this man, nephew of the great Napoleon and cousin to the present emperor, calmly riding away on a respectable hack, with no one but his groom in attendance. She remarked on his apparently democratic principles but Max scoffed at them.

"The fellow would do anything if it made him more the opposite of his cousin, Louis Napoleon. The emperor is more clever, more indirect, and Plonplon despises that. Plonplon seems to have no executive abilities of his own, except to disagree."

"Why does he hate the empress so much?"

Max placed his arm around her waist and walked back into the entryway while Letty gave a regretful look at a little café sign swinging from an ancient building a few doors away.

"I'm afraid that began long ago in Spain. Our clumsy Plonplon made advances to Eugenie, so the story goes. Eugenie found him repulsive. Then she capped her first error by marrying his cousin and producing an heir to the throne. You see, Plonplon was quite sure he would reign one day."

Letty asked him if he thought the prince had ordered Rissoli to kill her, but Max shook his head.

"I've considered it. But Plonplon has never hired assassins, except of character. We have no proof Rissoli didn't plan this as a blackmail attempt. Then he could report to Plonplon and demand a reward for killing you, a woman who, by her resemblance to Eugenie, might cause Plonplon trouble. Plonplon cannot create his lies about both of you at once."

"What kind of evidence does he create, this Prince Plonplon?"

"Forged letters from His Holiness, hinting that the pope has been advising Her Majesty on political affairs. Secret cover letters in Spanish found in Eugenie's wardrobe. Supposedly from the Spanish queen. One of these charming little bits of forgery thanked Eugenie for the border fortification plans. Fortunately we caught the spy while he was placing them in one of Eugenie's Spanish lace fans."

"And I am to expect them in my fans?"

"If so, you will say at once that Her Majesty heard nothing about the matter—whatever it may be. That you yourself acted in order to trap our princely friend. Then, no matter what Plonplon may claim, it will be obvious that he has been trapped in something devious and evil. On his part."

"I only hope he doesn't get so angry with me that he really does send someone to kill me."

"Louis Napoleon insists it is not his way, sweetheart. He does have his honor to think of."

She laughed. "Honor among princes."

"Be that as it may. But if Rissoli had killed you, there are many in court who would suspect Plonplon of having hired him."

"Your friends are so charming."

As they passed the door of the ex-prefect's apartments Letty remarked, "Evidently your influence in Le Havre wasn't as great as you thought. The contessa was not held. She seems to have beaten us to Paris."

He shrugged. "There is only one man who could countermand my order. The emperor."

"Good Lord! It all sounds like a cheap triangle on the Lyric Theater stage."

"Not cheap," he grinned. "Pauline is an expensive mistress."

"Aren't you going to visit her immediately? She may be expecting you."

"On the contrary. If I know Louis Napoleon, he is probably there now. But he knows his duty. By the time I've been interrogated by a half dozen members of the chamber of deputies, and I myself have questioned a few palace functionaries, the emperor will be back at the Tuileries, ready for business."

They reached the rooms on the upper floor, and Max took her in his arms. "Now, my girl, I'm going to leave you. I have a great deal to report. Louis Napoleon must decide how much to tell the ministers and any members of the legislature he chooses. There is a real danger from the reds. The radicals. Even Plonplon has noticed them, and he is all for democracy in its noisiest forms. He says the public is terrified of the empire falling, and if it falls it may fall into the hands of radicals like those in ninety-three."

"Ninety-three?"

He ran his forefinger rapidly across his throat.

She was not enthusiastic about his leaving, even if it was to go and pay a call on a real live emperor. Letty wondered what would be proper to do about dinner, but she didn't want to mention it in the same breath with his talk about government ministers, the legislature and the possible fall of the greatest empire in Europe.

When he was ready to leave she walked with him to the door like a good bourgeois wife, and asked, "Will you tell the emperor about his cousin's visit?"

"Of course. And Plonplon knows I will tell him. This is how the prince reaches the emperor's ear without directly approaching him."

She laughed, kissed him good-bye and found Madame Claudel beside her when he had gone.

"Does Madame wish a dinner tray served?"

Eating alone wasn't at all what Letty had envisaged for her first night in fabulous Paris. So on the spur of the moment she said, "Never mind. I will eat at a restaurant on the quai."

Claudel almost gasped. "Not alone, madame."

"Certainly alone." She hadn't the slightest idea what other American women did in Paris, but she didn't care very much. She was going to do at least one of the things she had always wanted to do, sit in a café that was open to the world and watch the cream of Paris ride by in their fancy carriages behind magnificent matched bays, or stroll along, the men in high hats and gloves and swinging canes, the women glorious in fashionable French gowns.

Before she could lose her nerve, she scrambled into a fringed black moiré jacket that would subdue the effect of her emerald green watered-silk travel dress. A black hat with a wide, tilted brim and emerald feather that matched her costume completed her outfit.

She did not forget gloves. No mistakes—she was determined to play the lady. She owed Max that.

Claudel followed her halfway down the stairs, obviously hoping she would change her mind. Letty waved good-bye, promising, "I am perfectly all right. Don't concern yourself."

As she left, she overheard an unintelligible exchange in French between Claudel and Fedor.

Not that it mattered. If no one really wanted her for herself, she still had one great advantage: she could do anything she wanted. She owed no one her allegiance or explanations.

The late afternoon was still sultry and Paris looked like a painting seen through a bronze-tinted screen. Letty crossed the quai, walking amidst a throng she guessed were both Parisians and visitors. Dressed in dark colors, even on this summer day, the young women who were genuinely Parisian had a special look about them.

Their coiffures, under an assortment of hats and bonnets, looked stylish; the faces were supercilious, arrogant, superbly confident; and yet, as Letty knew, most of these young women were walking homeward to a single, stifling room with no water and no heat, carrying string bags full of vegetables, a little veal or fish, and loaves of bread, all for their husbands, children, parents and perhaps grandparents.

Letty crossed the nearest bridge, looking down at the water and barges both the same golden hue. Minutes later she passed the enormous basilica she recognized as Notre-Dame de Paris. But even this could not delay her. There was too much to see. She began to walk faster, making her way around wreckage and appalling destruction where whole slum areas had been razed and lay everywhere in great piles of debris.

Looking out from yet another bridge, Letty saw the sumptuous buildings that guarded the Right Bank. She hurried on. A café on the street, a café that welcomed her . . . where?

She approached the Right Bank, and decided to have tea in the fabulous Grand Hotel she had seen as she and Max rode through Paris.

Hurrying past the last colonnades of the Palace of the Louvre, Letty entered the wide, splendid avenue leading to the half-finished opera house and the Grand Hotel. She stopped for a moment to get her bearings. Simple enough—the huge bulk of the Louvre would be her landmark. After that, the two bridges, one onto the Ile de la Cité, and the other off to the Left Bank and Max's house.

Her way blocked by another pile of aged wood and stone on the sidewalk, she turned down a narrow, intriguing side street, and turned again at a right angle to get back to the avenue.

Suddenly the gaslights lining the streets began to glow. Pools of brightness punctuated areas that were darker than she had thought they would be. She counted three cafés in one block and all of them well patronized, mostly by men. Very much like San Francisco's Barbary Coast, though these patrons appeared to be better dressed and more languid.

It was time to turn back. She had a stitch in her side, and common sense told her this was no place for an unescorted woman. However, she was too tired to start the long walk back without at least a cup of tea, and a tiny white table was just being vacated by an old man with an imperial goatee and a young, overdressed woman. Near the street, the table was close enough that she wouldn't have to squeeze her way between all those crowded tables. Picking up her skirts, she hurriedly slid onto the wicker chair, feeling like a native.

Most of the tables were occupied by couples keeping up a running commentary on the passersby, but the man at the table next to hers was alone. Middle-aged and respectably dressed in black, he wore a wide-brimmed soft hat tilted to one side that left his eyes in shadow. In imitation of the emperor he wore a goatee and a graying mustache.

This was Paris and he seemed the embodiment of a French artist. It was so exciting. But when the waiter approached her brusquely, she became flustered and stumbled over the pronunciation of "tea." The waiter shook his head and said that this was not a tea salon.

"*Très bien,*" she managed more confidently than she felt and added in English, "Give me one of those." She pointed to the little cordial glasses of green liquid she saw on a nearby table.

The waiter raised his eyebrows but started away. To Letty's surprise the man sitting alone signaled the waiter, said something to him; the waiter looked back at her, grinning. Then he shrugged and went on. Tense and angry, Letty turned to the man.

"Did you say something about my drink?" She realized she had spoken in English and started to translate but he raised a hand to stop her.

"Please, I do not mean to interfere, but I didn't think you were aware that you ordered absinthe." His English was excellent, with just a hint of an accent, more German than French.

She knew all too well how deadly absinthe could be. Vincent claimed it rotted away the brain. She tried to recover her sophisticated pose but it was a bit late for that.

"I didn't know. I'm sorry. It was kind of you to notice." She remembered his remarks to the waiter. "What did you order for me?"

"A pleasant *vin blanc ordinaire*. A light wine. You are new to Paris?"

"I only arrived today with my husband, but he has gone off to report to the—to his superiors. Are you English? Or German?"

His smile was warm, almost seductive; it made her slightly uncomfortable.

"Neither English nor German, madame. Actually, I was born in Paris. But circumstances forced me to live abroad when I was young. You are not English, I think?"

"American." She said it proudly.

"The United States. I have a real fondness for your country. My uncle too, often—" He broke off as though he had said too much. "Ah, here is your wine. You must tell me if you approve my choice."

She sipped, enjoyed the dry, pleasing bouquet and said, "I approve. It is better than what we get at home. Not as strong."

The waiter had slipped a stained piece of paper onto a small saucer and stood expectantly while she examined it. She opened the drawstrings of her fringed handbag and drew out a silver dollar. She knew this was far too much, but no doubt they would rob her in the exchange.

The waiter took the heavy silver piece, tossed it contemptuously and returned it to her angrily.

"No foreign coins. Only French."

She was shocked and pointed out to him, "It's perfectly good. I know. We don't take paper money in San Francisco. But this is silver. You see?"

The stranger watched this scene with amusement. She sensed that his eyes, shaded by that hat brim, had not missed a single line of her face or nuance of her actions. An extraordinarily observant man. When she began to panic and the waiter grew nastier, the gentleman touched the waiter's sleeve, offered him a coin.

"Take this and leave the young lady."

The waiter looked at the coin, bit it, nodded and went away after giving the man a smirking grin. Letty understood that smirk very well.

"My husband would never approve of your paying for my drink. You must take this dollar. It's perfectly good."

"Certainly, madame. Who knows? The way the world is going, I may end my days in your lovely United States."

She tried to laugh but the encounter had left her nervous and frightened, and it was a long way home along the gaslit streets. She started to get up.

"I am late. Max—I mean, my husband—will be worried. We arrived only today."

He looked at her a long time, as if memorizing her features. "You have arrived only today? Would your name, by chance, be Letty?"

She was suddenly terrified. Could this nice, gentle boulevardier be a killer like Rissoli? How had he known her real name?

"Certainly not. My Christian name is Jane. Not that it is any concern of yours, monsieur."

He arose too, throwing several large silver five-franc pieces on his own small saucer. "I beg your pardon, madame. It is just that I believe I am acquainted with your husband, an Irishman. Monsieur MacCroy."

"How do you know my husband?"

"He is a close friend. I owe him a debt that nothing can repay. I may safely say it is due to Monsieur MacCroy and a few others—But if you are wise, madame, you will not trust me or any other stranger until you know us better."

He was being very kind. Sensible, too. When she started to walk toward the river, he called out, "No. To your right, now, and forward. You will cut off many blocks. Or better yet, let me call a *fiacre* and send you home." He added in a gently teasing way, "I would accompany you, but I am afraid you would suspect my motives."

It was true. On the other hand, she didn't see what harm it would do if she herself gave the cabman his orders. To her new friend she said, "My husband must repay you, monsieur. May I have your card?"

"Max and I are sure to meet soon. I will explain your problem. Ah! This fellow will do, I think."

While she was giving the grizzled cabman her address—"the third house beyond the square on the Left Bank opposite Notre Dame"—she saw the artist give the cabby a gold piece before he left her. It was embarrassing. She wished she could be sure he and Max would meet so that they wouldn't be beholden to a stranger.

Riding through the streets with their fairytale glow, hearing the clip-clop of the horse and creak of the wheels over pavement and cobblestones, Letty finally relaxed. These moments were almost perfectly romantic; they lacked only a partner. If she could share this ride and this memory with Vincent—or even Max—then it would be perfection.

The cab crossed another bridge at the Seine, splendid, uncluttered. "The Pont Neuf," the cabby announced loudly, proud of his Paris. With his whip he pointed out a curious series of buildings to her left. Their pepperpot towers told her he was correct when he said "the Concièrgerie." Even Letty knew this was the dreadful last stop before the guillotine during the Great Revolution. She looked away quickly, then back again, mesmerized.

As they approached the Left Bank the surroundings once again became familiar. Just as Letty's driver pulled up, another cab stopped, and a man stepped out to pay the cabby. Letty got down without help and walked toward Max's house, wondering if the visitor who had just arrived was heading for the MacCroy rooms.

Evidently not. He walked through the entry hall ahead of Letty, and by the time she reached the staircase he was being admitted to Pauline Servandoni's apartments. Just as he was about to enter, he raised his head, looked back at Letty and smiled.

It was the man—her Good Samaritan.

Of course. She had seen this man long before, or at any event, his portrait. The eyes, the goatee and mustache all had been depicted in San Francisco newspapers, his portrait printed in magazines, especially during the recent Austro-Prussian War where he had acted as mediator. And according to Max and Plonplon, the Emperor Louis Napoleon had a penchant for disguising himself and going about the city, enjoying the hospitality of the cafés.

She grinned and waved to him.

As she went up the stairs she felt exuberant. The emperor was under the same roof, probably about to spend a few hours with his mistress, the Contessa Servandoni.

Sylvie Benoit's daughter had actually met the Emperor Louis Napoleon.

CHAPTER *Three*

*L*ETTY WAITED impatiently, triumphantly, for Max to come home from his visit to the Tuileries. Claudel brought her a tray of dinner from the restaurant on the quai; it was much more practical for Letty to visit the restaurant, but she had caused so many hard feelings by her abrupt departure that she felt it best to stay put.

The meal itself was unlike anything she had ever tasted. That little restaurant Le Petit Prince, despite its modest facade—ancient casement windows and a tiny sign swinging over the door—had to be one of the best in Paris. When she said this to Claudel and Fedor while enjoying the boeuf bourguignon after a heavenly fresh fish grilled over coals, the woman looked superior and Fedor threw back his big head and laughed.

"No, no, madame. A most ordinary café. Not one of the great. No. It is a laugh, that."

Feeling foolish, she reminded herself not to praise anything French. She did not even hint her satisfaction with the simple beaujolais, or the champagne that accompanied the cherry tart.

Letty passed a pleasant evening, despite her loneliness and an awful feeling of foreignness. She sat by the front windows looking down at the endlessly fascinating river, which seemed to be busy at all hours of the day and night. At night an extraordinary number of tramps and derelicts bundled up and slept along the quai and under the bridges. She wondered if the kind, friendly emperor who liked to wander the city incognito was actually aware of all the poor of Paris.

Max returned late in the evening. Not knowing in what kind of mood he would be, Letty was nervous about broaching the subject of her acquaintance with Louis Napoleon. He wouldn't like the fact that she had gone out alone.

Letty played the dutiful wife. Claudel had rushed to remove his coat but Letty was there first.

Max kissed her and asked if she had enjoyed her evening.

She said hesitantly, "I enjoyed my walk . . . and that sidewalk café.

Terrasses, they call them. The gentleman was so kind, not like most French people I've seen."

He hadn't heard a word. His thoughts were elsewhere.

"Good, I knew Claudel would see to your wants. Tomorrow, if I can arrange it, I will present you to His Imperial Majesty. You may imagine how busy he is. He's spent the last few weeks working on the plans for the liberalization of the empire."

"Did you see him tonight?"

"No. But I talked with Emile Olivier, who represents the opposition —the moderates. He is the new prime minister. I had interviews with the court chamberlain and some of my men."

"I do believe that if I applied myself I could probably find His Majesty at this very minute," she boasted.

"Very likely." He took the coat from her and gave it and his hat to Claudel. "As if that weren't enough, Darlincourt is free to roam about wherever he takes the notion."

"Poor man. It isn't as if he had committed a crime. My bets are on your friend, the contessa. Are you sure you don't want to hear my theory about how to find the emperor?"

"No more theories, please. I'm damned hungry. I haven't eaten since the train. Fedor, how about another tray from The Little Prince?"

"I sent him for a tray a moment since, monsieur," Claudel said. Letty thought she sounded mighty pleased. Letty turned away but Max caught her.

"Not so fast, my love. You are about to earn your salary. For a very short time I want you to be seen from a distance as the empress. A kind of rehearsal. Matter of fact, we may need a rehearsal right here tonight."

"I thought the empress was at St. Cloud."

"Exactly. But, you will remember, it is our plan to confuse her enemies. Beginning with Prince Napoleon. Our Plonplon would lose some of his power to spread malicious gossip if he spread a story about her and then we proved the empress was elsewhere."

Letty was willing to begin—at least, she would feel more independent when she was doing what she had been brought to France to do. If her marriage had been contracted for reasons of love, companionship and children it might have been different.

"I'm ready. Where shall we rehearse?"

Fedor came in in triumph, bearing a covered tray and a bottle hanging from his neck by the strap of a string bag.

"Excellent," Max exclaimed, clapping his hands. "Give me time to eat this and I am at your service."

"Five minutes," she said playfully.

"Why not? Napoleon the First made love in five minutes. But he had empires to run." He sat down to eat.

"So have you."

"If you repeat that I'll deny it, my love."

From the joking way in which he used the endearment she knew it meant nothing. She must always remember that or she would let herself be hurt again. Falling in love with Vincent had caused her enough anguish.

As if he could read her mind, Max suddenly looked up from his ragout of mutton.

"By the way, Fedor . . ." He raised his voice. "Fedor! There are letters in the pocket of my coat. Get them for Madame."

"For me?" She was delighted. The only letters she ever got were from strange men, a few with not-so-delicate notions of what they'd like to do to her.

Fedor brought four letters over to her, three of which were in Vincent's handwriting. She was so glad to see that splendid hand, beautiful as an engraving, that she almost put the envelopes to her lips. But something made her look up from the letters, and she found Max staring at her. She had no idea what that direct, unblinking stare was about.

"Good news?" he asked as she shuffled the letters nervously.

"I suppose—I don't know. What shall we do? About the rehearsal, I mean? Would you like me to change?"

"Not necessarily." He cut and chewed another piece of mutton. "Tough old girl."

"What?"

"This old sheep. Aren't you going to read your letters?"

Letty broke the seals with affected indifference and took a quick look at them. "All about the Fairborne Company. And this one is from . . . somebody I never—" She turned it over. "Good heavens! It's Calla Skutnick. I didn't know she could write. Bless her! She says she is so popular she never would have believed it. She had three gentlemen quarreling over her at the stage door. She wishes . . ." She read more closely. "She wishes the climate agreed with Annabeth. Her cough is worse and Vincent wants to go west again, this time where it's dry, but

Annabeth refuses to leave Chicago. She is so proud of her husband's success."

"Like the success of Mademoiselle Skutnik." Max set his tray on the inlaid gaming table. "Does it say that three ladies quarrel over him at the stage door?"

"He was always popular," she reminded him stiffly.

"So I understand. I could never see it myself."

She wanted to smile but did not. She began to read the first of Vincent's letters. It was friendly, impersonal and might have been written to Calla Skutnik, or even to Max MacCroy. The second spoke of doubts about Annabeth's health.

> My poor girl has not been well. One cold after another in this climate that is intermittently too hot, then too windy, and finally too smoky from all the industrial activity. The company has been surprisingly popular, and the new actress does moderately well. Audiences call us the Gold Camp Players. Rather amusing for a man like myself, whose ancestors settled in Virginia in 1650, but at any event, they like us.
>
> I must go now—Annabeth is calling. I do not like her cough, nor am I impressed by the local doctors. Syrups and powders are not the answer.
>
> I must go.
>
> Good-bye, my darling.

My darling. It was the only personal remark in the letter.

She refolded the letter and put it in with the first. She would have read the third, but Max had set aside his dinner tray and was striding around the room impatiently, picking up objects and setting them down with noisy clicks and cracks of sound that made her jump.

Her thoughts still on the letters, Letty put on a false brightness.

"What shall we do? How can I rehearse?"

He motioned to Claudel, who nudged Fedor, and they left the apartment. Letty wondered if they slept together and if so, where. Probably in all those rooms under the mansard roof.

Max pulled out a chair with two substantial arms. Had it been on stage of the Lyric Theater, Vincent would have called it a throne. However, Max had different ideas.

"You are seated in an open carriage. People are cheering you."

"What if they aren't? I mean, suppose they shoot at me?"

"Your nearest footman will be on the watch. His body will stand between the assassins and the . . . target."

"Me." She added skeptically, "How do we know we can trust this footman?"

"Because I will be the footman."

She felt better. "Good. Then the bullet must go through you to get to me. That seems fair enough."

"I am touched by your solicitude. Very well . . . the slight smile. Not too broad. Gracious, I think."

She turned her head, smiling graciously but not too broadly, trying to imagine she was a proud Spaniard and the most celebrated female on a European throne.

"Softer. Eugenie can be democratic. In fact, you may like her very much. Many women do."

Jealousy prejudiced her; she disliked the empress already.

Max was reasonably satisfied. "Well done. And another matter. When you are presented to the emperor, you must try not to be intimidated. He is a kindly man. He lived many years in bourgeois surroundings before he won the French elections in 1850. He lived in the United States a short time, so he may want to question you about your country."

She was demure. Since Max had twice prevented her from telling him about her meeting with the emperor, some perverse humor made her say nothing about it now. "I'll try not to be frightened of him. Of course, he may overwhelm me with his regal bearing and all that." Max was being much too pompous about her intimidation by the imperial presence.

"Remember. I'll be there to present you, and if conversing with him should be a little too much, I'll take over the matter."

"You are so good to me. I'll count on you to protect me from him. They say he is irresistible to women."

He considered. "Louis Napoleon is popular with women, I'll admit. And God knows he adores them."

In fact, she thought with smug satisfaction, the emperor was exactly what he had appeared to be tonight at the sidewalk café.

When they went to bed Letty was in excellent spirits. She couldn't wait until Max presented her to the emperor with due formality and his usual arrogant confidence.

Max was still upset at not having talked with the emperor at the Tuileries and his mood didn't improve when, as she was undressing, the letters from Vincent fell out of her pocket. He picked them up for her, glanced at the superscription on each before returning them.

"Incredible that he has that much to say," he commented.

"He is writing mostly about Annabeth."

"Thoughtless of him, writing to you about his wife. It was my impression he was so popular with his ladies at the stage door that he wouldn't have time to write to one of his ex-actresses."

"Ex-star!"

"Well, Madame Star, we will need you to give your greatest performance tomorrow. So, by all means, sleep well tonight." His voice was so heavy with sarcasm that she felt hurt.

He slapped the letters into her hand and walked out of the bedroom.

She spent a long time combing and brushing her hair, hoping he would return to share her bed. Their hearts might be elsewhere, as she realized every time she thought of his devotion to the empress, or her own letters from Vincent, but they were marvelously compatible in bed.

Max did not return to the room. After a while she crawled between the cool sheets of the bed, a pleasant haven on a sultry night, and unfolded Vincent's third letter. It filled her with guilt:

> My darling,
> I wrote this salutation in spite of myself. My Annabeth is still unwell. I have called in new doctors, and they are horribly inept. Including one from New York. She needs certain foods, a great deal of milk to restore her dear color. We supply it. Very well. My poor girl almost drowns in it. But the coughing . . .
> And here I betray her by calling to you longingly, desperately, but, my darling, the memory of you is the only beauty left in my life.
> You sacrificed yourself for us. I realize that now. But if you find some small measure of happiness in your new role, I can console myself with that. I only ask that you think of your old mentor occasionally, and remember.
> We all love you, even though you are so far from us.

My poor Vincent, she thought, but her heart went out to Annabeth, her kindness, her generous nature and trusting affection. Letty prayed, "Don't let her die . . . Please protect her."

A troublesome thought came to the fore: was it possible that what she loved and missed and longed for was not so much Vincent as the "family," the Fairborne Company? And Annabeth was its heart.

She slept at last.

Letty's dreams, however were far from San Francisco and the Fairborne Company.

She dreamed that Louis Napoleon, in a sparkling robe of cloth-of-gold, stepped down from his lofty throne and bowed over her hand, saying, "I am a common fellow at heart, and my wife simply doesn't understand me. But you, my dear, are so different."

The next morning, Letty awoke excited by the prospect of going to the Tuileries, of meeting her acquaintance of the sidewalk café, and of confounding Max MacCroy, who never dreamed she had met him.

Having heard that His Majesty, like the first Napoleon, strongly supported French industry, she thought it would be a good political move to wear the deep rose walking dress that Max had said was made of Lyons silk.

When Max came in from heaven knew where, he was pleased with her choice and seemed to be in a good mood.

"Unfortunately only the servants in the palace will see it, because I want to sneak you inside. I have personally appointed the servants who will receive you."

"But when do I pretend to be the empress?"

He fingered the wide, square neckline of her gown. His touch sent delightful warmth through her body, reminding her of what she had missed last night.

"My love, you change in the palace. I don't want to present you for the first time as yourself. The emperor must see you first as a replica of his wife."

"For heaven's sake, why? I should think it would be better if he came to know me as I am."

"No!"

She was startled. "Why ever not? He might like me. In fact, I'll wager he does."

He laughed shortly. "I don't doubt it."

"Well, then."

"My dear innocent, if he sees you as Eugenie, he will be inhibited. You've heard it yourself, Louis Napoleon eats up pretty girls. There must be hundreds he has bedded. Sometimes once, sometimes, in the case of women like Pauline Servandoni, for years, off and on. Now, one other thing. You are not to be seen by anyone on the way to the Tuileries today. I've managed that, I hope."

The affair was growing less and less romantic.

"What am I to do, crawl through the sewers of Paris, like that poor man in the book?"

He lifted her chin with his forefinger. "You are too pretty to waste in the sewers, and for God's sake, don't mention books about men in sewers to the emperor. The author has written some very harsh things about our Louis Napoleon, from the safe haven of the Channel Islands. . . . Come now. Breakfast is here."

The morning seemed eternal. More rehearsals, and worse, another series of curtsies, over and over. It amused her to think that she had not curtsied even once to the emperor when they spoke together last evening.

Shortly after noon Max gave the cue to leave and Letty's nervousness rivaled any she had ever experienced before going on stage. After one last glance in the long mirror, she was satisfied that nothing more could be done.

"Just look out the windows occasionally," Max said to Claudel. "Nothing else will be necessary." Letty was puzzled by these instructions and by the fact that Claudel was carrying the green dress Letty had worn yesterday.

She waited until they were in the hall beyond Claudel's hearing before she asked about the dress.

"Quite simple," Max said. "The house may be watched. Claudel will simply pass by the windows, at various times glancing out. You may have noticed that she is no longer wearing her hair high and tightly braided, but more loosely around her cheeks, like yours. . . . Have I told you, Madame MacCroy, you are looking especially delectable today?"

It was not so much his flattery as the warmth and lightness in his voice that cheered her, despite her uneasiness about Claudel playing Letty, while Letty played empress—perhaps against assassins.

"Wouldn't it be simpler just to let me play myself and give Claudel the role of the empress?" She couldn't help the shrewish tone her voice carried. Letty intensely disliked the idea of her own identity being absorbed by someone else.

"Because, my love, in spite of Genevieve Claudel's efforts, there is only one Letty—pardon me—only one Jane MacCroy. Unlike Eugenie de Montijo, there are no imitations."

"Thank you. You did mean that as a compliment?"

He lowered his head. For an instant she thought he was about to kiss her, but they had reached the ground-floor entryway and Fedor called to them from the courtyard.

"Clear ahead, monsieur. This way, madame, if you please."

She began to panic. "Aren't you going with me, Max?"

"No. If any of Plonplon's men are watching the house, I want them to see me leave alone."

"Of course. I'm sorry. Will I see you at the palace?"

"I'll be there." He looked at her a long moment. "My good soldier."

She laughed and walked around the old fountain in the center of the small square while Fedor pointed out the beauties around them. The vine-covered walls and the splash of the fountain gave the place a cool, verdant feeling on this hot day. In the winter, she suspected, it would be damp and depressing.

"The flowers, they are of a great perfume." Fedor pointed to the tiny, sweet flowers among the vines. "Mimosa. Very popular in Spain. They make the empress sad for her old home in Madrid."

The empress. Always Eugenie.

Nevertheless, Letty had to admit that the scent of the tiny, pale gold flowers was delightful. She reached out, broke off a small branch and stuck it into the thick strands of hair that covered her ears, furthering the illusion of Eugenie de Montijo.

Before going on with Fedor, Letty looked up at the windows of Max's apartment and wondered for the first time if he had concocted this entire game of two Eugenies so that he might possess one for himself, since the real one so clearly belonged to someone else. "No wonder he enjoys making love to me. He must be pretending I'm his Eugenie! It needs only that I pretend he is Vincent, and we'll both live double lives."

"Hurry, madame," Fedor called. "It is safe now."

She went obediently but without enthusiasm. One end of the alley beyond was blocked with building materials—crumbled plaster and worm-eaten wood that smelled of age and many lifetimes. No windows looked down on the near end of the alley, and no one was in sight.

What a great bother about nothing!

But Fedor had his orders, and he obeyed them. Letty was led past a wrought-iron gate and through a small enclosed garden in very unkempt condition. Apparently the occupants of this particular house or series of lodgings threw their trash out the windows to land in this pretty cul-de-sac. It seemed a shame.

They emerged onto a busy street and Letty was hustled into a closed cab, which took off immediately with Letty alone in the cab. She caught sight of a wide square filled with young people, all of whom seemed to be waving flags or quarreling, against the backdrop of the massive Louvre across the river. Beyond the riverside arose the Tuileries.

Suddenly she thought of the polite and gentle emperor. How could Max have told her scandalous gossip about a man who had gone out of his way last night to see that Letty got safely home without being molested?

Whatever Max might tell her, it didn't alter her opinion of Louis Napoleon. The Contessa Servandoni was probably the one mistress that all rulers had—no more than what one expected of a king or an emperor.

Letty was hurried into the Palace of the Tuileries through a side door and was relieved to find Max, true to his promise, waiting for her in the obscure and ill-lighted passage, which looked as though even the palace servants avoided it.

"Heavens! I feel as if I were in a Lyric Theater melodrama," she whispered to Max.

"You are. Believe me."

Nevertheless, she felt considerably more assured when she locked her hand in the crook of Max's arm and heard his confident "You will do very well." But she had to smother a laugh when he continued, "You mustn't be frightened of His Majesty. He will understand your natural timidity at meeting him—he has the common touch. Remember, he is a Bonaparte, not a pompous Bourbon."

"I will try hard not to be terrified."

"That's my girl."

She seemed to hear Vincent speaking tenderly of his wife and the memory made her wince.

"I'm not *your* girl. I'm myself."

"On the contrary. You are not yourself. You are Eugenie." But he stared at her while he knocked twice and then twice more on a carved oaken door. The lackey who admitted them into a spacious salon wore the imperial livery embroidered with the gold B's symbolizing the Bonaparte family. While they waited, Max pursued a matter that puzzled him.

"What did I say to offend you a minute ago?"

She answered with a shrug. She was too busy speculating about the hard face and powerful, lean body of the lackey. She suspected he was one of Max's men. Had things gone so far that even some of the imperial servants must be policemen?

A gaunt, stern woman, dressed completely in black with a lace mantilla pinned to her graying hair, entered the room and greeted them. Her sibilant Castilian "s" gave her away as a fellow countrywoman of Eugenie's.

"Doña Catalina de Sanchez, my wife, Madame Jane MacCroy. I leave her in Your Ladyship's hands."

"Very good, monsieur." The woman gave him a stiff curtsy. It pleased Letty to note the respect Max commanded.

Doña Catalina led her across the long leaf-green salon. Golden B's were embroidered on drapes, table runners and the backs of some very uncomfortable-looking gilt chairs. Two long windows looked out on the wide, tree-lined expanse of the Tuileries Gardens toward the Place de la Concorde in the distance. But there was no tarrying here. Doña Catalina nudged her on through twin gilt-framed doors to a large dressing room.

A gown of white Lyons silk embroidered with Bonaparte green sprigs had been chosen for Letty to wear. The full overskirts were pulled to the back to reveal a green silk underskirt.

"For the rest, the undergarments, you may wear your own, madame."

It was exactly like her first day on the stage, Letty thought, as, with Doña Catalina's help, she exchanged her pink gown for Eugenie's summer carriage dress. Once again, she was on exhibition before a critical audience who might or might not approve. And there were so many instructions, she would never remember them all. A green bolero jacket was slipped over her shoulders and Letty thought she was ready.

"*Madre de Dios!*" Doña Catalina muttered, pushing her into a chair before the long pier glass. "You are only begun. Now comes the wig, of a golden auburn like Her Imperial Majesty. *Exactamente*. So."

Letty's hair, which had been dyed from blonde to black before she left San Francisco, was now swept up and pinned tightly against her scalp so that the light auburn Eugenie wig would fit. There was no doubt it made all the difference. A plump, pretty little girl, who also spoke French with a heavy Spanish accent, helped give the finishing touches, a hint of rouge and a pale color that played down the soft curve of Letty's mouth. A little plumed hat with a saucy brim was the final touch, lending just the right nuance of imperial arrogance to counter her flirtatious smile.

Letty arose and extended her hand with haughty condescension to the Spanish maid, who curtsied and burst into giggles. Letty strutted around, knowing she annoyed Doña Catalina, partly out of defiance, but also to get the feel of her costume.

She received imaginary guests as Eugenie de Montijo, empress of France, chattering away in Spanish-accented French.

"My dear Prince Napoleon, how sweet of you to wish me well when I know you hate me! . . . And if it isn't, of all people, my dear sister-monarch, Queen Victoria! . . . How dowdy you look, *chérie!* . . . I greet you, Chancellor Bismarck! . . . Welcome to the Tuileries . . ."

Doña Catalina was stiff-lipped but thorough. "Not, I think, the Prussians. Her Imperial Majesty does not trust them. And with good reason. It is said that the Prussians would like to put a German on the Spanish throne. This is not good for France."

"Stand aside, if you please. Make way for the empress of the French. I assure you, we Bonapartes are not afraid of mere Prussians."

She had certainly impressed them. The Spanish maid stared in her direction open-mouthed and sank down in a deep curtsy. Doña Catalina dropped a hand mirror that shattered as she too curtsied to the floor.

Behind Letty, in the doorway, a woman spoke. Her words were in flawless French with just a hint of a Spanish accent.

"Catalina, why is this woman dressed in that absurd jacket I particularly dislike?"

CHAPTER *Four*

*E*VERYTHING SEEMED quite mad. In the pier glass, she saw reflected the unmistakably regal and elegant Empress Eugenie. But this was her own reflection.

Across the room, flanked by two lackeys in the doorway who were dismissed at once, stood a slim beauty with red-gold hair crowned by a flat-topped, wide-brimmed Spanish hat, of the type often worn by Mexican caballeros. A black bolero jacket covered a white shirt, and her black skirt was short enough for boots to be seen. Her slender waist was accentuated by a wide red leather belt.

She was a magnificent sight and would have looked quite at home in an equestrian ring, but anyone seeing Maria Eugenia Ignacia Augustina, Countess de Montijo, Countess of Teba, at this moment might be pardoned for supposing that she was the actress and Letty Fox the empress.

Showing every drop of her ancestral blood, fiery Spanish and stubborn Scot, the empress walked across the floor and circled Letty, whose knees trembled as she started to curtsy.

"No. Stand. Let me look at you."

In spite of all her preconceptions Letty was awed by the splendor of the woman's bearing and the infinite self-confidence that spoke nothing of the days when the English queen called her "timid and shy." Letty was also well aware how far she herself was from truly playing the role.

She attempted an explanation.

"If . . . if Your Majesty will call in my husband, Monsieur MacCroy or His Imperial—"

Eugenie pointed her riding crop at Doña Catalina.

"Has my impersonator no training in court etiquette? Haven't you told her not to speak until she is spoken to?"

Doña Catalina, her lips pulled thin, crossed her hands against the passementerie beads at the waist of her black taffeta gown. Clearly she did not take lightly to being scolded.

"Majesty, I understand that the young person is trained only to appear at a distance."

The empress frowned. "His Majesty sketched the plan to me, and so long as the young woman is in no danger, I make no objections. But if there is a danger of assassins and the like, it becomes my affair. I am not lacking in courage, I think." She looked around as if daring anyone to deny her staunch heart.

She tapped Letty here and there with her riding crop, not hard, but as though testing ripe fruit. "She is twenty years too young. Anyone may see that. Plonplon is always the first to remind me that time is a woman's enemy. Heaven knows he never sees that brutal face of his when he looks into his own mirror."

Letty stifled a laugh and Eugenie looked at her. Her own eyes sparkled with sudden humor.

"Your first lesson, Madame Max. I may be insulted. My son, Eugene Louis, who is only fourteen, may be insulted. His Majesty as well—he may even join you in the joke. But no one laughs at Plonplon to his face. It is dangerous. He fancies he should have been in his cousin's shoes, and he never forgets. You are acquainted with my husband's cousin?" She remarked to Doña Catalina as she turned away, "I shudder when he hovers over my son."

Max had taught her how to *be* an empress, but he hadn't told her a word about getting along with an empress. None of the little nuances, the flirtations and the half-teasing manner would do here. She was forced to rely on nothing but her instinct. She had known many Mexican Californians and two qualities were common to all who had Spanish blood, their pride and their courage. She therefore doubted very much if the empress would like her to cringe and crawl.

Respect was the key word and perhaps a bit of humor. Eugenie had made her own feelings for her husband's cousin perfectly clear.

"Yes, ma'am," Letty said carefully. "His Imperial Highness came to visit my husband only minutes after we arrived in Paris. He was curious to see Monsieur MacCroy's wife, he said."

"And was he satisfied?" Her Majesty asked with some slight tension.

"Yes, ma'am. I was wearing a heavy travel gown and my hair—it is dyed black—was worn to cover my ears entirely." It was the nearest she could get in her suggestion that though she naturally looked like the empress, she had not done so yesterday.

Eugenie studied her. "Did he seem . . . drawn to you?"

"Perhaps. A little. I could not say, ma'am."

Eugenie nodded to Doña Catalina. "It would satisfy his arrogant streak. If not the original, then the copy. He has not forgotten the setdown I gave him so many years ago in Madrid . . . Take care, Madame Max, especially after he sees your resemblance to myself. He is not a man to trifle with."

"No, indeed, Your Majesty." *Even I know that.* She thought the empress's smile was a trifle grim.

Doña Catalina cleared her throat, drawing Eugenie's attention to her.

"Your Majesty, having someone in the enemy camp might be advantageous. If His Highness, the prince, developed a—an acquaintance with the wife of your loyal Monsieur MacCroy . . ."

Letty refrained from shivering, but only just.

Eugenie's answer was quick. "One does not ask acquaintances to serve one in such a fashion."

"Still—"

"Max's wife is a lady. Not a common prostitute. It would be different if she were from a different background."

Ah! Letty thought, half amused, half alarmed . . . if she only knew about Letty Fox!

Letty's tension was relieved by the sound of Max's voice in the big salon beyond the dressing room. "Good God! When? She wasn't expected until Friday."

This was followed by the lackey's much quieter assurance that Her Imperial Majesty had arrived incognito.

Letty eyed the empress furtively and saw Eugenie raise her head, look toward the open door, and close her lips, as if to force back a smile. Her eyebrows lifted in disapproval when Max came in.

Max bowed—respectfully, but not obsequiously as Letty had expected —and straightened, after touching the empress's fingers.

"We are not in a police prefecture, Monsieur Max. Kindly watch your language."

"Your Majesty took us all by surprise. Incidentally, may I have the honor of presenting my wife?"

"We have met. Let me know quite clearly what is her purpose in imitating me—to confuse Plonplon when he tries his tricks against me or to deflect attacks on me? If so, I will not permit it, as you well know."

Max glanced at Doña Catalina, who shrugged.

"No one could imitate Your Majesty. You are inimitable. However . . ."

"Come, come." Eugenie clapped her hands, the reverberation crackling through the room. "Reserve your flattery. There can be but two reasons. I hope you do not mean to use the one which would shame His Majesty and me. We do not use human beings as shields. As I hope we have proven on more than one occasion."

"Certainly not, Your Majesty. All I hope is to confuse various parties who have been spreading troublesome gossip and planting forged papers in Your Majesty's suite."

"Say Plonplon and be done." She looked doubtful while they all held their breath. She said at last, "I have your word that this child is not intended as a shield for my safety?"

"I would hope that I will always be Your Majesty's shield. I will certainly be a shield to my wife, whatever the political climate."

"We will not let this matter die. Your wife's safety is in your hands."

Letty said quietly, "I will be most happy to act in any capacity, ma'am."

Eugenie shrugged. "Since His Majesty is involved in all this chicanery, my opinion does not seem to matter. Though I am astonished at you, Max. It is not healthy to resemble heads that are highly placed. They make excellent targets."

"I hope to be a barrier between the assassin and the target."

Her bright blue eyes looked Letty over in what seemed a calculating way. When she spoke her tone, but not the words, was indifferent.

"We cannot afford to lose you, Monsieur Max. So I advise you to take care."

"It is a habit of mine, ma'am. . . . By your leave." He bowed and then offered a hand to Letty, who took it while she curtsied in a circle of skirts and frills.

The empress nodded. "Very well, run off and play your absurd games for Plonplon's benefit. Just one thing—"

"Ma'am?"

She ignored him, motioning to Doña Catalina who had knelt to pick up the shards of glass from the broken mirror.

"Catalina. Forget that. The bad luck will come. We can do nothing about it. See to it that this person"—she corrected herself—"Madame MacCroy does not wear that detestable jacket. I always looked hideous in it."

The mistress of robes signaled to the little Spanish maid and poured broken glass into her apron. Then she opened a tall armoire and took out a close-fitting jacket in white moire that, held up to the light, possessed a pale greenish hue. Max smiled at all this, and, upon being dismissed, started out with Letty.

The empress surprised them by calling out, "Madame Max, you pleased me with your proud boast about the Bonapartes and the Prussians." She added to Max, "She is of good breeding. Good family. Luckily for you, Monsieur Max."

In the big salon Letty took a long breath.

"I was never so scared. Good family! If only my mother could have heard her, how happy she would have been!"

"Come along. She will have to change from that ridiculous riding costume before she meets the emperor—so we may as well carry out our original plan. Can you face a second imperial presentation in one day?"

"I'll brace myself for the terrifying prospect."

He looked at her quizzically, as if he suspected sarcasm. The idea pleased her. She had certainly been uneasy during her unexpected interview with Eugenie, and she still wasn't sure just what the empress's relationship to Max was.

They descended a servants' staircase. A handsome, blond young man in livery passed them, carrying a tray with sweet biscuits and a curious bottle shaped like a Spanish peasant's leather wine flask.

"A fruity Spanish wine. Very sweet," Max explained. "For Eugenie. What did you think of her?"

"I'm not sure. She is everything you said, and more. And I was surprised to see that."

Max stopped in his tracks. "What the devil do you mean by that? Don't you trust my judgment? She's an extraordinary woman."

She said nothing. She didn't like his quick defense of Eugenie.

A short distance away, Letty caught sight of an enormous staircase with pillars and high light globe standards. It must be awe-inspiring at night by gaslight, she thought. Contrasts abounded in the Tuileries—the passage they walked through now still employed whale oil for lighting, and it filled the hall with an unpleasant odor. Letty hoped the smell wouldn't cling to the empress's lovely gown.

A gentleman with a chest full of medals passed them, bowing deeply from the waist. Throwing herself into her role, Letty nodded to the gentleman and gave him her practiced imperial smile.

"Well done," Max said. "I think Louis Napoleon will be surprised at your talent."

He signaled to a pair of elaborately uniformed Cent-Gards who had just come out of a room on the first floor. They both saluted Max, which made Letty proud of him.

"I wish you wore one of those glorious silvery helmets. The guards all look like statues of Greek gods."

"Not really my style. I'm useful, not ornamental."

She laughed. "Men like that are impressive to women. They add to the imperial flavor of the court."

"Perhaps so. I am more interested in the ability of agents and prefects. And of horsemen to stop street riots. We have had no revolutions since Louis Napoleon was voted complete power."

"You are hard."

"Life in the ruling business is hard. Since His Majesty liberalized the imperial government we have had every conceivable splinter party trying to take over the country. From Karl Marx's friends to those royalists who still think they can turn the calendar back to 1788."

All the same, Letty looked back at the handsome guards, with their glittering cuirasses and helmets, standing in the sunlight of two long windows.

Max stopped before a centuries-old door whose wooden surface appeared to be splintered in places. As if someone had sensed his approach, the door opened. A dark, chunky little man greeted Max in a familiar way.

"His Majesty is expecting you. This is the woman?"

Max said edgily, "This is Madame MacCroy. My wife."

"But of course. Madame." The emperor's secretary carefully closed the door behind him while he looked her over. Letty got the distinct feeling that he was analyzing her potential in quite another field. He made no attempt to disguise his leer. "Perfectly satisfactory, I would say, knowing his tastes." He stuck a thumb into Max's ribs. "Can't get his own wife into bed, so he does the next best thing. He takes the young copy."

The muscles in Max's face froze. He caught the man by the shoulders.

"Madame MacCroy's services are in public. Not in private. Pietro, you are detaining us, I think."

While Letty stared, Max whirled the little man around and moved him out of the way. Then he knocked twice and opened the inner door.

"Monsieur?"

"What, Max? Waiting for the formalities? It isn't like you."

Max ushered Letty into a book-lined study furnished with Moroccan leather and mementos of the First Empire. She recognized the black, metallic bust on the desk as the Little Corporal. A standard heavily embroidered with gold and trimmed with gold fringe hung behind the emperor's chair. Dingy and faded, the tarnished gold standard even had a hole in it. Why would anyone want to keep such a thing in view?

The emperor looked up from his chair and gave Max his hand. Over Max's bowed head he gazed at Letty. He looked drawn and tired. She wondered if he was suffering physical pain. There was a peculiar mesmeric quality about his gray eyes that she did not remember noticing before. She had expected the emperor to acknowledge their acquaintance, perhaps to make a little joke, and was prepared to remind Max that she had tried to tell him the truth and he had silenced her.

But those strange eyes, gray with flecks of green, appeared speculative, as if Louis Napoleon were considering his own reactions to her. He smiled at Letty, but said nothing until Max had introduced her.

"May I present my wife, Madame MacCroy, to Your Majesty?"

"Beauty is always a pleasure to behold, madame," the emperor said as he took Letty's fingers in his hand and brought them to his lips. His mustache tickled her and she wanted to laugh. She was enormously flattered. *How they would stare at me at the Bucket of Blood in Virginia City if they could see me now! The French emperor, the real emperor, not a stage actor, has just kissed my hand.*

For the first time Max seemed slightly nervous.

"What is Your Majesty's opinion of the resemblance? Is it strong enough? It fooled a servant a few minutes ago."

The emperor came around the long desk, which was crowded with souvenirs, and looked Letty over from head to foot. There was something sensual about his gaze, and yet, she did not feel offended. It was the look of a man who enjoyed collecting objects d'art, a man who loved and cherished his possessions.

He turned his attention reluctantly to Max. "Max, you have done well. An exquisite . . . resemblance."

"Thank you, Your Highness."

The emperor piled a sheaf of papers together on his desk, neatly tapping them together with his fingertips. He was still looking down at the papers, some of them scrawled over with corrections and notes, when he said, "The empress has arrived, looking like a circus equestrienne. She wants to visit our son at his school. I confess I am proud of Eugene Louis, but like all boys, he is embarrassed by formal visits in the presence of other youngsters his age. So the empress visits his school more or less incognito."

"Yes, monsieur. So I understand."

The emperor paused. Letty felt that he was waiting for some reaction from Max, who was deliberately being dense.

"Well, Max, I hope you will not permit the empress to ride out in this radical atmosphere without your sharp eyes and right arm as her shield."

Max looked at Letty. She smiled brightly and nodded, trying to let him know by her expression that she did not need him at all. Then too, it was almost insulting the way he acted as if she needed protection from his friend, the emperor.

Max's mouth set. "Then my wife will not be seen today in her—transformation?"

Louis Napoleon seemed surprised. "But yes, Max, while Her Majesty is traveling in disguise to see our boy, Lou-Lou." He chuckled. "It should throw our enemies off. And confound my cousin, the prince."

"Then have I your leave to retire, monsieur?"

"Certainly, my friend. Run along. And you might tell the empress I have decided to turn over to our boy's care the sword his great-uncle wore at Jena. Eugenie will like that. I sometimes think her reverence for the great emperor is as keen as my own."

"Yes, Your Majesty." Max glanced once more at Letty. He frowned slightly. She gave him what she hoped was a reassuring nod. He bowed and retired, leaving Letty and Louis Napoleon alone.

The emperor smiled at her. It was a singularly sweet smile, and she understood the attraction this man of very moderate looks held for females of all classes.

"I believe our Max is jealous. He suspects I am about to seduce his wife." Letty stiffened uneasily. Was this why he hadn't told Max of his earlier meeting with Letty? It was flattering but a little alarming.

He rang for his secretary, who popped in looking wise and rolling his bulbous eyes.

"Her Imperial Majesty will be riding in the Bois, Pietro. I am joining her. And Pietro—"

She realized that the emperor had lied to Max when he assured him she would not be playing the empress in public without Max. But the secretary was all ears.

"Yes, Majesty."

"You have just been honored by the presence of the empress. You understand?"

"Perfectly. Monsieur . . . madame." But he left no doubt to Letty of what *he* thought she was about with the emperor. He bowed and left the room.

The emperor assured her, "I have done all I can to preserve your reputation, Madame MacCroy. But I very much fear that with my secretaries it will be in vain. They prefer to think the worst." He added on a lightly wistful note, "Or the best, depending upon one's viewpoint." She laughed. "Ah, but you must not be amused by my little jokes. The empress never is, and you will give the show away."

He was so unpretentious she forgave his lie to Max and burst out ingenuously, "How kind you were to me last evening, sir—Your Majesty! I would never have gotten home without your help."

"Was he very cross with you?"

"He doesn't know."

For some reason he liked that. "Then it will be our secret. I thought perhaps it explained his jealousy a moment ago. At my age it is something of an achievement to arouse the jealousy of a vigorous fellow like Max MacCroy."

"Forgive me, but Your Majesty's gallantry to me last night makes me suspect you will always arouse jealousy in lesser men."

She was rather proud of that speech, but he reached out and shook her gloved hand with playful impatience.

"No, no. I like you better the way you were a moment since, all bubbling with young honesty. Just now you sounded like a courtier. Come. I will ring and have myself decked in my imperial plumes and we will ride together."

CHAPTER *Five*

THE OPEN carriage was flanked fore and aft by mounted horsemen; another cantered along beside them. He might so easily have been Max if only the emperor hadn't forced him to attend the empress.

But maybe it was just as well. Max had never been with her on the stage in her sketches, and today she felt that all these trappings were part of a new set for a new sketch in a much bigger, more elaborate theatre —the wooded paths of the Bois de Boulogne. She quieted her sudden stagefright by telling herself she was really just Letty Fox on the stage of the Lyric Theater, playing a character called the Empress Eugenie.

She heard them cheering for herself—no, for her character. She twirled her green-and-white silk parasol and flashed a tremulous smile at the crowds who gathered on the paths under the sunlit trees. The emperor either praised her or advised her on changes, exactly as Max would have done. Actually, he was nicer.

"You must not be frightened, my little friend. Your role requires great authority." Scarcely moving his lips, he murmured, "You are acquainted with the empress? She is afraid of almost nothing. Always bear that in mind." He pressed her hand in his fingers playfully and let it go before she could draw away. He looked so like a mischievous boy that she grinned back at him and idly pursued something he had said.

"Her Majesty is afraid of *almost* nothing. What is there that can frighten an empress?"

He pressed his fist into his side and winced. "Definitely not her health. No. Oddly enough, ever since the coronation she has been obsessed with the memory of Marie Antoinette. She seems to see a parallel. Sometimes, she tells me, she sees herself running in flight from the Tuileries, with mobs pursuing, crying 'To the guillotine!' The usual thing."

"How terrible!" The idea was enough to chill her impersonation.

"Yes. Because it is unjust. Eugenie has never been indifferent to the sufferings of others. From the day she turned over the wedding gift from the City of Paris to the city poor—an amount that did enormous good—she has always done much for the people. Every year she is generous. Not stupid or extravagant like the other one. But her air of confidence, that Spanish pride . . . people misunderstand it." He studied her, as if seeing another face, his wife's, behind Letty's carefully disguised facade.

She was moved. "I will remember, Your Maj—"

"Ah?"

Flustered, she corrected herself. "I will remember, because it makes me understand her better." She reminded him in a low voice, "As an actress I add details to the picture in my mind. She isn't quite the marble lady on the throne."

"Far from it. Wave. Just the last two joints of the fingers. Excellent . . . Good day . . . Good day . . ."

Though the crowds were kept from impinging on the road, Letty could hear the shouts of *"Vive l'Empereur!"* and less frequently, *"Vive l'Imperatrice!"*

The emperor nodded, acknowledging faces, distant shouted cries. To each he seemed to give something of himself, recognition, a special little smile, a name.

"I never realized how many things an emperor must learn to do. I'm surprised anyone ever wants to be one."

He smiled. "Try and convince my beloved cousin Plonplon of that."

The situation had grown more comfortable. Letty was finding conversation with the emperor much easier than she had expected, and she laughed now.

"I met His Highness on my arrival in Paris. He did not look like a happy man."

"Nor is he. But I'll wager your presence cheered him."

She shook her head. "Though I should not contradict royalty."

He was amused and started to take her hand but thought better of it. Several voices called, *"Vive l'Empereur!"* and he nodded and waved gently. On Letty's side of the carriage, the horseman rode ahead a few paces around an ancient landaulet that had broken down and been deserted.

"Death to the Spaniard!"

Letty knew she had paled with terror and that this was not the manner of spirit of Eugenie de Montijo. Sitting up perfectly straight, Letty made every effort to ignore that female voice.

A whirring sliced the air. Something crossed her vision, so close she felt a blow across her forehead and tried to cry out, but her vocal cords seemed paralyzed.

Everything stopped for an instant. Somebody screamed. Then people were running, and Letty heard hoofbeats madly beating over the paths in the Bois. She raised her white-gloved hand to her forehead. She was unhurt. Her flesh did not even sting. But for some reason she found herself crying at the indignity of the whole business.

"I've been shot," she whispered.

The horsemen were hovering around the coach; the emperor was dabbing at her cheek with his handkerchief—he was the only one who kept his head. He murmured as if to a child, "No, no, my poor little one. I heard them called 'love apples' in your country. It was a tomato fruit. But I am very much afraid the stains have ruined your gown." He looked over her head at the mounted escort.

"Who was it? Have you caught him?"

One of the horsemen leaned down. "A female, Your Majesty. Distraught over the loss of her lodgings—an attic room on the Cité. Those slums were all torn down and carted away. I believe the last have just gone."

Letty began to recover. She was ashamed of her reaction to the attack, but oddly enough she felt sympathy for her attacker. She had lived in many rooms in many a western slum and couldn't find it in her to blame the woman. There was such a crowd now that the attacker was hidden in a nest of helmets with great horsehair plumes. Chattering witnesses tried to give their version of the assault.

"Cover your face," the emperor whispered.

She didn't understand why until she realized her proximity to the crowd, some of whom would certainly recognize her as an imitation Eugenie. She covered one side of her face with outspread fingers. The emperor gave the signal and the procession started up again.

Trotting out from under the lacy greenery, the team moved around the enormous Arc de Tromphe and down the Champs-Élysées toward the distant Tuileries. At first sight of the Renaissance building, Letty felt a twinge of disappointment that her "reign" was so soon over. Aside from the terrifying fear that she had been shot, and the humiliation of the stained dress, she had never felt so much the star of a stage drama.

She sighed. Louis Napoleon studied her.

"You are relieved that your time with me is over, is that not so, madame?"

She was so surprised at his misreading of her mood that she burst out spontaneously, "Oh, no, monsieur. It's just the opposite. I was sad. It is all over."

He liked that and the unconscious flattery of it. He bowed over her hand, and again his mustache tickled her knuckles as he brought her fingers to his lips. She took this opportunity to ask him for clemency.

"Could Your Majesty be generous with that woman who threw the fruit? After all, she's lost the only hovel she had to live in. It must be so dreadful, all those people having their houses torn down!"

It occurred to her that this was not very diplomatic; since his administration and his prefect of the city were responsible for what tourists were beginning to call "the glorious New Paris."

The emperor did not take offense, however. Maybe he thought she was too stupid to count as a dangerous critic.

"My child, the rebuilding of Paris gave work to over a third of the city. The restoration of housing is an urgent need, but everything takes time . . . time." She suspected he was no longer thinking of her words but of some greater dream that encompassed the nation, a dream rapidly receding under the present discontent. The current anti-government wave had been spurred partly by the industrialization of Europe and partly by the Marxists and disgruntled Orléanists and Bourbons who dreamed of a prerevolutionary France.

Inequity was everywhere, but . . . She said aloud, "It's the same in San Francisco politics."

"In San Fran—? Doubtless, very similar." She didn't know if he had been taken aback by the comparison or amused, but he added, "I promise you, the woman will not be punished. In fact, we might use her as an example. Hundreds, even thousands, have been resettled since the building began. But here we are, madame. My wife has a notable grace in descending from a carriage. I know I may count upon your own charming movements."

This well-meant remark had a crushing effect upon her, but luckily, just as she was about to descend, she saw Max waiting to help her down.

She was about to cry, "Oh, thank God, Max!" But she stopped herself before finishing. He looked unusually stern, even angry and his manner toward the emperor was far more familiar than would be permitted in any relationship not based on many years of trust.

"It might have been a bullet, Your Majesty."

"Very true, Max. But it wasn't."

She nudged her husband. "Really, I'm fine. No harm done, except to this dress, and a stain on my bonnet."

The emperor placed his hand on her wrist. "Quite true, my dear. Max, do come along, old fellow. I want to discuss the fate of that wretched woman. We must be certain the unfortunate creature is not chastised for the business. The empress"—he indicated Letty—"has expressed a charitable interest in her."

"Indeed, monsieur." Max didn't seem to like this at all. But Letty knew that, in his profession, he had to be hard, a little ruthless. He walked behind them as they passed beyond what appeared to be hundreds of people on the street and in the courtyard, to the equally crowded but darker galleries of the old palace.

The emperor bowed, left her in Max's charge and said he was going off to change before meeting the trade delegations of the Hawaiian and Siamese kingdoms.

"Fortunately, the one group speaks English and the other French," he remarked. "For I speak neither Siamese nor Hawaiian."

Max, unusually quiet as he returned Letty to the empress's apartments on the first floor, said suddenly, in English, "What the devil did you say to Plonplon? He has persuaded his sister, Princess Matilde, to invite us to one of her soirées. Matilde and I haven't exchanged a polite word in ten years. She has a virulent hatred for the empress."

"What a coup," Letty said, "to be welcomed into the enemy camp! Does Plonplon's sister have a nickname too? I shouldn't like to make a mistake."

He laughed. "No nickname, but she came within inches of capping her title of princess with that of empress."

"What? Impossible." Letty had seen portraits of the Bonaparte princess, niece of the great Napoleon, and the stout, heavy-jawed woman would hardly attract Louis Napoleon.

"When they were younger she refused the emperor. They are first cousins, of course, but such a marriage would have cemented the Bonaparte dynasty. She never thought he'd go as far as he has. You know she and Plonplon regard Eugenie as an interloper. Watch when they are at a Tuileries ball or a court function—Matilde does her best to take center stage."

"Max, do you want to go to the princess's party?"

"Very much so. I'd like to win her confidence, find out if she is up to any tricks." He stopped suddenly, realizing what she was leading up to. "Now, see here. You were in enough danger today."

"A fruit thrown at me. A tomato."

"Next time, a bullet. A dagger. No, thank you. I hired you to confuse Plonplon and make nonsense out of his lies about the empress. Not to risk your life. Eugenie is furious."

Always Eugenie. "Eugenie ought to consider herself lucky."

"She thinks it makes her appear a coward."

"Well, let her think it. What an odd thing for an empress to worry about! Not where she would if her house were torn down. Not what she would eat if she had only three sous in her purse."

Max shrugged, not knowing how to respond to this, and left Letty in the changing room, where Doña Catalina and the maid awaited her.

"It is ruined, utterly," Doña Catalina grumbled. "The overskirt, the busk. Even the bonnet is stained. And Her Majesty wishes it had been she!"

"So angry, madame!" the maid confided in Letty's ear. "She says they will think Eugenie de Montijo cannot face a tomato."

Letty burst out laughing, interfering with Doña Catalina who was removing the offended parts of the empress's wardrobe. She pinched Letty to make her behave and Letty yelped just as the door opened from a small salon. Eugenie's reflection appeared in the mirror opposite Letty. She caught Letty's eye in the glass and laughed at Letty's indignant expression.

"Do not be shocked, Madame Max. Catalina behaves exactly the same way to me. I am one mass of bruises from all those pinches."

"Her Imperial Majesty is pleased to exaggerate," Doña Catalina muttered and showed the empress the stained garments.

Eugenie would not touch them, clearly revolted by the affront. "Humiliating. Better to be struck by a gun shot."

"Not to me, Your Majesty."

The empress recovered herself. "Certainly not. You should never have been the target." Eugenie was elegantly dressed in a white, summery dress whose bustled skirts stood out like the crinolines she had made famous. She looked down at the elaborate layers of tulle as if seeing that pristine whiteness spattered with rotting fruit. Or perhaps blood.

While the maid helped Letty back into her own gown and combed out her thick black hair when the wig was removed, Letty remembered the invitation to the Princess Matilde's house.

"Your Majesty mentioned Prince Napoleon today. You wondered

how anyone could know what he thinks and does these days. Well, his sister, the Princess Matilde, has invited my husband and me to her house. A soirée, she called it."

Eugenie was very interested in this information. "They will say nothing in front of Max, that is certain. But—if you are a good listener—" She hesitated. "I suspect Her Highness will attempt to quiz you about me."

"I hope Your Majesty knows I would say nothing that she could use against the imperial family. Naturally, my husband won't accept the invitation if you or His Majesty should object."

"On the contrary." The empress looked at Doña Catalina and a mischievous look came over her face.

"I'm afraid I don't understand Your Majesty."

The smile remained. The empress glided the length of the narrow room toward her. Watching her, Letty wondered if she could ever copy those movements precisely.

"Madame Max, I am anxious that you should understand." Without looking around, the empress said, "Catalina, go. And take the little poppet with you."

Doña Catalina curtsied deeply, her face showing resentment. She snapped her fingers and the jolly Spanish maid followed her out, not without some eager backward glances.

The empress then tapped Letty's arm.

"If you do accept Her Highness's invitation, I warn you, her tongue can be sharp as a viper's. But she will also try to gain your confidence, to learn any petty, unpleasant gossip about me."

"But ma'am, I don't know any unpleasant gossip about Your Majesty."

Eugenie's smile had an edge to it and her eyes sparkled with doubt. "Nicely spoken, my child. I ask only one thing of you. I wish to know what is said of me. Even what is asked *about* me. I'm afraid I often use my acquaintances in this fashion. But knowledge of the enemy is my only real weapon."

Letty sighed. "And I have been jealous of Your Majesty."

That startled the empress. "My jewels and this palace? They are trappings lent to me for the time my husband lives." She turned away from Letty with a shudder. "I sometimes dream that we are plunged into revolution and I am riding in the tumbril to that guillotine these French are so fond of."

"But Your Majesty—"

"With all my charities, it is never enough. Good works count for nothing." She set her teeth in a kind of angry desperation. "I will always be thought of as the Spaniard. Just as Marie Antoinette was always the Austrian."

"I wasn't jealous of the jewels and this palace, ma'am. But of something else."

Eugenie turned back to face her. "Of what, then? My son, of course."

"No. I was jealous because my husband admires you very much."

Eugenie's cheeks colored a bit. She was not displeased. She said after a short pause, "It is easy to admire an empress. But that is not at all the love of a man for a woman. You are young. You will learn. You may ring for Catalina now. And one more thing—"

"Yes, ma'am?"

"This will be our little secret."

Letty realized that she was trusted. Either that, or the empress was testing her.

"We will talk again," the empress said in dismissal.

Max was waiting for Letty in the salon. He bowed slightly to Eugenie, who stood in the doorway, took his wife's hand and hustled her out.

After the tiresome, intricate series of corridors, galleries and staircases Letty once again was seated in the closed carriage. Sighing for vanished glory, she looked out one last time and saw Louis Napoleon standing by a ground-floor window, not an area of the palace where one would expect to find the emperor. And better still, he actually waved to her. She thought for an instant that he might be saluting his old friend, Max. But no. He seemed to be looking directly at her.

She laughed and raised her own hand.

Max said, "Careful."

Feeling awkward, she lowered her hand, and not knowing what else to do with it, touched her lips with her gloved fingers. Too late, she realized the implication; she could have sworn the emperor smiled.

Max gave the briefest of replies all the way back across the river and through the narrow Latin Quarter. Letty felt like a child about to be chastised for a fancied wrong, and she resented it. After all, it was she who had been attacked today, she who had won the friendship of the emperor, and above all, she who had become a confidante of the empress.

Having arrived back at Max's house, they were passing through the ground-floor corridor just as the Contessa Servandoni came out dressed for the street.

The contessa snatched at Max's sleeve. "My friend, I warned you. General Hugo, that fat fool—I saw him with Plonplon an hour ago. Heads together, at a café in the Bois. The one beside the big cascade."

"Quite legal," Max was impatient.

"Max, the good general had high influence to free him from house arrest in Le Havre."

"And so did you. Even higher."

"You do not understand. I believe Rissoli was General Hugo's man."

"We'll talk about it later."

Letty started toward the stairs. Max did not stay to argue with the contessa but went after his wife, taking her arm; she drew it away pettishly. Letty had come down too rapidly from her high throne as consort of an emperor.

Before they reached the door of his apartment, he demanded, "What happened between you and Louis Napoleon?"

"Don't be ridiculous. Nothing. We were in a public vehicle, very much on display."

"I mean last night. At the café."

"What?"

"He told me."

Men simply could not keep secrets. She was annoyed, but it was too late to do anything about it now, and there was no mistaking Max's scowl. Good heavens! Was he jealous?

The absence of the servants was a relief; she didn't want them to hear her husband talking in this fashion. She twisted her arm out of his grasp and moved along the hall to the bedroom which they had not yet shared. She walked, as she thought, the way she always did, but somehow even that upset him. He came after her in two or three strides.

"And don't play the wanton with me. I didn't teach you that walk. I'm only your husband."

Maybe he was drunk. She had never seen him in a worse mood. She defended her walk, of all things, with indignation.

"It's never been criticized before, and I don't propose to change it now. Vincent taught me to—"

That was a mistake. He looked at the high ceiling.

"Vincent says. Vincent taught me. Are we never to be rid of the noble Vincent? I didn't hire Vincent. I hired Letty MacCroy."

She stopped in the middle of the bedroom, furiously angry but remembering that only an hour ago she had been empress of the French. She must keep her dignity.

"Thank you for reminding me, Monsieur MacCroy. I am never likely to forget that I was hired to play your wife."

He waved this away.

"You know I didn't mean that. We were talking about Louis Napoleon. I told you what he is with females."

"A perfect gentleman."

"And I am not, I suppose."

She had thrown aside her bonnet and was unhooking the tight basque of her silk dress. "I don't recall that we were discussing you."

This rubbed him on the raw. He reached for her, pulling her back against his body with such force she protested, "These manners may appeal to your other women, but they are too imperious for me, if you don't—"

She got no further. His lips were hot upon the back of her neck, beneath the soft pile of her hair.

"No!" She tried to break free, but she was caught in waters beyond her depth. She felt the dampness of his lips upon her throat and the muscles of his body pressing hard against hers; she remembered the delicious pleasures in the bunks of the *Nouvelle Heloise* and at the inns on the high road to Paris.

"No, I—"

But his mouth was firm on hers. He picked her up and dropped her onto the bed with no ceremony whatever—she might have been a bundle of old clothes. No time to straighten out the wrinkles in her gown—he was there at once, one knee pressing down all the skirts and ruffles, the other knee imprinting the coverlet beside her slender waist, imprisoning her.

CHAPTER Six

*M*AX HAD proved often enough that Letty was physically no match for him and he demonstrated it yet again, fastening her beneath him while she struggled. Struggled for her freedom to love Vincent, her freedom to be the emperor's friend and beyond suspicion. But the warm touch of his lips undermined her resistance. Her anger ebbed as she felt her skirts pulled away and her warm body exposed to his hands.

The only thing she was aware of was her passionate hunger to take him within her body, to feel all the wild, driving force in her vitals, to strain against him, fighting, loving . . .

All this she would teach to Vincent one day.

They took possession of each other, she and Vincent. *No.* She and Max —her husband. The fierce, wild force was briefly hers. Simultaneously they reached the climax of their ecstatic struggle.

Once more he whispered that strange, passionate plea, "Love me, sweet . . . love *me.* Not that damned ghost."

She reached for him, brought her hands up and delicately traced his features, trying to erase that somber, unhappy look from his face.

"Darling, you made me so happy. Aren't you happy?"

He shrugged. He turned his head slightly and touched her fingertips with his lips, but nothing changed; he still looked sad.

"What we have is almost love, isn't it?"

He stared at her without answering. Then he completed dressing, picked up his coat from the floor, slung it over his shoulder and walked out.

Why was I so tactless?

Letty did not know what to expect, either of him or her career, although she did feel that the more successful she became, the better Max liked it. At least, he worked hard to instill in her all the airs of an aristocrat. She knew he wanted her to impress Matilde and her cronies, who were said to be so disloyal to the empress. And Letty wanted to be able to return to the Tuileries and report their treacherous gossip to the Empress Eugenie.

Max was generous; he gave her what he called her allowance and what she called her salary for the first quarter. She immediately went shopping along the Rue de Rivoli with Fedor accompanying her on the carriage box, and, as usual, she appeared as the brunette self that had never seemed real to her.

But even with her dark hair she was stunning, and it was flattering to be stared at as a lady and not as Letty Fox, the half-nude star of the Lyric Theater. Thank heaven that ghastly business was ended!

She visited the milliner's shop and found that the cherry-red bonnet she had wanted for Calla Skutnik was gone, but the one she had picked out for Annabeth was still in the window. She bought the pink-plumed bonnet, marveling that for the first time in her life she could pay an enormous sum for a hat.

She owed Max MacCroy a great deal, only wishing he would stop behaving so oddly and begin to act as if he were enjoying her little triumph here in Paris. Because she knew it wouldn't last; someone would reveal her true identity. But until that happened, she went about the city, suitably chaperoned by Fedor, with the certainty that her mother had finally been avenged for the terrible way in which she had had to leave Paris. And it was heavenly.

The fear of discovery was always near the surface of her mind. One day, while she was in a narrow but shockingly expensive glove shop near the luxurious Hotel Meurice, a stout lady tapped her arm with the handle of her parasol.

"I know you, miss," she said in English, obviously a tourist.

Letty tried not to preen.

"Do you, ma'am?"

"Orville." The lady called her husband away from the pretty salesclerk. "Isn't she the spitting image of that one we saw last night? You know. At the Variètés. That Offenbach thing. She did the cancan."

It was bad enough to have seen the provocative—some said lewd—dance, and all Paris had, but to be accused of performing the cancan, with its baring of the dancer's buttocks, was a vile offense.

Letty was shocked, enraged. About to explode in a wild and indignant denial, she was held back by something, perhaps Max's training. Letty drew herself up to her full height and became the Empress Eugenie.

"Madame? I trust I have misunderstood you."

Orville nudged his wife. "Nothing like her. This lady's thinner and darker. She's got an air that—well, she sure ain't a cancan dancer."

The fat lady studied her from head to foot with a brazen stare while Letty, with great relish, laid down a handful of gold twenty-franc pieces.

"A dozen pairs of gloves, if you please. One wears out so many at court functions."

The gentleman understood this, whether the woman did or not. He tried again with his wife, *sotto voce*. "Come on, Effie."

It was not an easy victory but by the time the packets were laid in Letty's hands, Orville and his wife had exited into the crowded arcades of the Rue de Rivoli, Effie still insisting she had seen "that creature" before.

After that experience, Letty was more careful in her trips about the city. She had been anticipating an invitation back to the Tuileries for another performance as the Empress Eugenie, but according to the court calendar, Eugenie and the excited young prince imperial were in Corsica to celebrate the centennial of Napoleon Bonaparte's birth.

The empress, despite her present difficulties with the Bonaparte family, had been a passionate partisan of the late emperor, "The Great Napoleon."

Since Letty's acquaintance with Eugenie's husband, Louis Napoleon, she thought his almost equally popular nickname—Napoleon the Little —somewhat insulting. She thought that in both intention and act Louis Napoleon had done as much as his uncle had for France.

Letty expressed this sentiment to Max one day and was delighted to find that he agreed; she knew his peculiar prejudices. He could not serve those whom he felt to be politically wrong. She decided this was due to what she called his policeman's nature.

It continued to puzzle her that Max could be so jealous of her innocent relationship with this man he served so loyally. Perhaps he was jealous on Eugenie's behalf, not wanting her to be humiliated by gossip, groundless though it might be.

But shopping and sending presents overseas could not occupy all her time, and she was delighted when Max one night took her to the theater on the spur of the moment. In spite of the insult she had received from Effie, she soon shared the Parisians' love for the light, tuneful, danceable music of Jacques Offenbach and rode home humming while she displayed for her husband's delectation a neat ankle that she turned as if in dance.

Max seemed to come out of the gloomy, set anger that had absorbed him lately. He grinned at her display, reached down and gripped her ankle, holding it captive. "That last champagne cup must have done this."

"Oh, no! Am I drunk? I don't feel like it."

His hand traveled up to her knee. She slapped it, amused. His other hand slipped easily over the soft satin and rough tulle skirts to her waist, under the white-and-silver brocaded evening cloak.

"What a tiny waist!"

"Now you'll understand why corsets are so expensive."

He leaned over her body, pressing against her, close enough so that she felt his heartbeat. They kissed as the horse and buggy rattled over the cobblestones. Letty welcomed his passion; perhaps due to the champagne, she found herself able to return that passionate exploration without letting her thoughts go wistfully to her far-off hero. But a disquieting darkness nibbled around the brightest edges of the scene, and Letty thought, *It is like one of my stage scenes. Not real. My whole life here is a masquerade, with Vincent floating further and further out of my reach . . . I shouldn't be enjoying this performance so much . . .*

Ashamed of her excitement, she nonetheless couldn't reject it.

Fedor leaned back and interrupted them.

"Monsieur? Madame? You expect a summons from the palace?"

Max stirred, sighed and sat forward. "Fedor, if you haven't an earth-shaking excuse for this interruption, tomorrow you go to the Concièrgerie, if not the guillotine."

Fedor grinned. He pointed his coiled whip in the direction of the Tuileries gardens. At this hour they looked alive with gently waving trees and bushes. Long shadows crawled across the patterned brickwork of the walks, haunting the carefully fenced and locked park.

"One of His Majesty's coachmen has just signaled me. I think someone in that coach wishes us to stop."

A closed carriage and team pulled out of the Place de la Concorde to cut off the MacCroy horse and buggy. Letty pulled herself together and tried to look more like the respectable Madame Max MacCroy and less like the wanton Empress of Impressionists.

Max muttered, "Damn! At this hour." But he got down from the buggy and went to the closed carriage while, to Letty's surprise, Fedor and the coachman of the other carriage got into a heated argument about rights of way, thus presenting an excuse for the sudden confluence of two carriages in the middle of the street. Most curious of all, until Letty understood that they were playacting, the argument seemed to begin in the middle, as though by common consent. Max returned to the carriage two minutes later, still scowling.

"Politics. Murderous politics. If only Louis Napoleon weren't so enthralled with all this absurd Arabian Nights business! We might as easily have met at the Tuileries."

"Is it bad?"

"As bad as possible. Some months ago the Spanish threw out their queen for one reason or another. Now Bismarck and the Russians insist on putting up a German prince for the Spanish throne, and the Spanish government may accept. This would trap France between two German armies. Naturally, we can't permit that."

"But you aren't in the army. Your job is the protection of the empress."

He shrugged. "True. But Spain spells Eugenie. She has nothing to do with it, but that doesn't prevent lunatics and political opportunitists from using her as a scapegoat. There have been new threats. So I will have to accompany her to St. Cloud."

"Was that the emperor you were talking to?"

"God knows why he persists in these night meetings."

"He is off to a rendezvous with some lady, I expect." She said this dryly.

"Undoubtedly. And he shouldn't be. He isn't all that well. That kidney stone will kill him if he isn't careful, damn it!"

"Kidney stone, how awful!"

He looked at her sharply. "Only his physicians know about this. I learned of it during one of his attacks. Pauline doesn't know. Even the empress has no idea. For God's sake, don't mention it to anyone."

"Certainly not. You must think I am a leaky jug."

"A what?" He laughed. "Just forget I said anything, my beautiful leaky jug."

Letty hated to sound selfish when he was concerned with matters of far greater importance but she couldn't help asking in a small voice, "Does that mean you can't go with me to the Princess Matilde's soirée?"

"I'm afraid so." He slapped her hands playfully. "You wouldn't have a good time, anyway. They are all pretentious intellectuals. They pride themselves on insults and filth against the government. You wouldn't feel comfortable with them."

What made him think she had no intellect of her own?

"I really have matched wits before," Letty said. "With critics, for instance. And with men who wrote nasty things about me in the newspaper columns."

"It isn't the same thing at all, my love. You don't know the French wit. There is no one in the world who can be more cutting. Forget it. When the present crisis is over I'll take you to the Variètés again. Maybe next time we'll go to Maison Dorée or the Café Anglais. You'll like that. And you can appear in all your splendor."

He must think she was very naive. Going in all her splendor to a public restaurant was not the same thing as being invited to a private soirée by the niece of Napoleon Bonaparte. She pretended to consider his patronizing offer.

"I suppose I could wait. At least the emperor will be in Paris. He might need me to ride through the Bois with him."

"Are you so fond of being pelted with tomato fruit?" His mouth was set irritably.

He really wants to keep me locked up like Bluebeard's wife, she thought, and the idea brought her independent streak to the fore. She said, "Of course, I can't refuse if the empress asks me to visit Princess Matilde. And she has."

"I forbid it!"

She made no more protests; although she did not say it aloud, she knew that if the emperor needed her for an appearance, she would go. He had always behaved like a perfect gentleman with her and besides, it wasn't good politics to offend the greatest ruler in Europe.

Matters did not improve when they returned home and found a letter waiting from the Fairborne Company. It was signed by Vincent for the entire company and described the company's modest but heartening success, which no one could appreciate due to the rapid decline of Annabeth's health. A young actress from downstate Illinois, who had worked as a costume seamstress for the various Fairborne plays, was currently standing in for her.

"We are desperate about Annabeth," Vincent wrote.

> The progress of the wretched disease is alarming. Yes, the sanitorium doctors confirm the frightening truth. It is what they call galloping consumption. This despite the fact that she seems in excellent spirits. Her color is high. Surprisingly high. The dear child has never been more loving. But they have prepared us for the worst.

We haven't heard from you in weeks. Are you well? Have you played your role often? Are you a success?

Have you forgotten us? Annabeth sends you her love, in which we all join.

Vincent

Annabeth dying? It couldn't be true. Annabeth had been ill for years and always recovered. Letty refused to believe it. The idea preyed upon her conscience. She loved Annabeth, but she had betrayed her with Vincent, time after time.

Max asked too casually, "Does the noble Vincent express the proper affection at this distance?"

Still numbed by the news, she handed the letter to him. It was as if even more of her past was slipping away, leaving her bereft of one more friend. "Read it yourself. There is nothing secret about it. Vincent is above that sort of thing."

Her honesty was wasted, however. A fast reader, Max merely glanced over the letter. He handed it back, noted her eyes and dismissed the matter.

"Not much of a love letter. Even I could do better."

She folded the letter and put it away in her jewel case.

Two days later, amid much publicity and many crowds—which always troubled Max—the empress and the teenage prince imperial left for a brief vacation at their summer residence at St. Cloud. Boyishly proud of his accession to manhood, the slender prince was marching around in his new military uniform, as a genuine officer of France.

Ten years ago Letty had seen the results of the war fever in the United States and thus felt heartsick at the sight of a uniform on anyone so young; in this, she was supported by the boy's parents. Max said both Louis Napoleon and Eugenie were much opposed to the passionate opinion, both in the streets and in the chamber of deputies, that "sooner or later, we must show these Prussians they cannot rule the whole of Europe."

"Louis may talk and exhort and reason," Max said, "but if Europe wants war, nothing can stop the tide. My agents tell me Bismarck is determined to push us until we behave exactly as he wants us to behave."

"Can we—I mean, can the French—win?"

Max looked grim. "To judge by appearances, yes. We have the finest army in Europe. We proved that at Sebastopol and the Crimea in fifty-six."

"But this isn't fifty-six."

"And Louis is ill. That is the worst of it. Eugenie is beginning to ask questions. She must not know," he reminded Letty. "She has enough to concern her."

For a split second all Letty could think was "always Eugenie" but she caught herself, ashamed.

Max thought it wise that the empress would be out of Paris for a few days; it would allow time for talk of the emperor's ill health to die down. "The rumor that he is dying—which is wildly untrue at the moment—serves our friend Plonplon very well. He has begun to promote himself as regent to the young prince."

Intelligent as Max was about most things, Letty thought him naive about this. The departure of Eugenie in no way stopped the rumors.

She and Max said good-bye in the Cour du Carrousel, in front of the gray east face of the Tuileries. The area swarmed with the usual sightseers, tourists, loyal citizens, and new reinforcements of the imperial guard—and with Max's plainclothes agents. The knowledge of their presence was a bit unnerving.

Max gave Letty a long, affectionate hug and a good-bye kiss, but she was puzzled by the way he studied her face, as if he wanted to sketch it. Even more puzzling was that she felt the same way about him; it was amazing how central he had become to her life.

She kept waving until she saw him swing up into the empress's carriage to join the empress, her two ladies and the young prince imperial.

Fedor's big, bearish figure was close beside her as she left the courtyard. It seemed that he was becoming truly fond of her. He was beginning to like her for herself. As they walked out of the courtyard, the dear fellow brought her a small nosegay of violets to pin on her mantle.

"Parma violets," he said, smiling. "The flower of the Bonapartes, madame. It symbolizes, 'He will return in the spring.'"

"He?" she asked, wondering if this was some religious gesture.

"The Little Corporal. The return from Elba, you know."

"Oh. It was so sweet of you." She concealed her smile by burying her nose in the fragrant flowers. It had been a kind of religious gesture, after all, from a follower of the great emperor.

After Max's departure Letty spent her first night straightening house, rehanging her fine new wardrobe, and moving furniture around—to Genevieve Claudel's acute discomfort. Though the night was humid and warm, the bed felt cold and extraordinarily large.

The next day, armed with a basket, she walked up past endless churches and the gray medieval tenements of the Sorbonne and found several markets where she purchased fruits and vegetables that might be eaten raw. It was such a treat to be able to purchase tropical beauties like bananas, pineapples and pawpaws with their deep orange flesh. But later that afternoon, back at home, she began to feel deeply depressed. Not for the first time, she wished herself back with Annabeth and Vincent and the others, with Annabeth reasonably well, everything as it had once been.

Would she *ever* learn what it was like to be truly loved for herself? The closest she had ever come was her relationship to Vincent Fairborne and even there she had often wondered in her heart of hearts how much was love for her and how much was his pride in a half-educated little urchin whom he had rescued from defilement and molded into a popular actress.

Then, on her second night alone, came the summons to the Tuileries, at His Imperial Majesty's own command. Lest she be concerned about her—or his—reputation, she was assured in the note delivered to her by a lackey dressed in neat black, that His Majesty wished to discuss with her the beauties of her country, and perhaps learn something about America's innovative ideas. There would be a companionable group of ladies and gentlemen in the small party.

She most certainly would accept the royal invitation. At last, here was a man, and the greatest of all, who enjoyed her company as a conversationalist. So much for Max's impression that she would not be able to hold her own with French intellectuals!

CHAPTER *Seven*

*L*EAVING THE house for the evening was not as easy as she had imagined, unlike her years with the Fairborne Company when she might have been lectured and warned by Vincent but was certainly free to visit whomever she chose.

Not here, and not with Fedor on the watch.

"Madame, your pardon, but M'sieu Max, he would not permit."

"We are speaking of the Emperor Napoleon the Third."

"No, madame. I speak of Louis Napoleon Bonaparte. I have served this good man as long as I serve M'sieu Max, and he is to be much admired for his efforts to help all men. But all women?" He shook his head. "Different."

He kept repeating this. She could get nothing else out of him; so she decided to surrender—on the surface.

"Very well." She shrugged, looking disgruntled. "I will go to bed early and be bored to death."

"A pity, ma'am. One wonders why His Majesty chose to change his mind and send M'sieu Max after all. It was not at first intended."

She heaved a great sigh, bestowing on him a wistful smile when he and Claudel left for the evening.

"Think of me, Fedor, when you and Madame Claudel are out enjoying that famous nightlife of Paris."

Claudel's black eyes squinted at Letty, but Fedor chuckled good-naturedly at what he rightly took to be a joke.

When they were gone she changed carefully into a shimmering taffeta gown of that shade named magenta in honor of the emperor's late victory. She took care not to douse herself with the Eau de Fleur de Lys that Max had bought her last week. It seemed to her that when she and Max visited the theater or restaurants they were surrounded by people who preferred wearing perfume to bathing.

If it had been after dark she might have hesitated about her visit, not because she mistrusted the emperor, but because, if his other guests were not discreet, it would reflect badly on her reputation. However, the sun had barely gone down behind the distant trees of the Champs-Élysées, and the garden restaurants had not yet turned on their tiny lights that glowed like fireflies amid the trees. Even the Tuileries gardens were still touched with a burning vermilion glow when Letty reached the unobtrusive door on the side of the palace facing the Louvre and the Arc du Carrousel.

The closed carriage was far from the handsome barouche she would have preferred and it made her seem like an upper servant arriving for an interview. She began to wonder how she could gracefully turn back without offending the emperor.

The coachman was elderly, heavily mustached, and appeared to find her quite interesting; she hoped he was not an incurable gossip. Max would probably be furious to think she had gone against his firm instructions.

"Well, he may have married me, but he doesn't own me."

Once more she was hustled into the palace by the unobtrusive door probably used by servants. It was discomfiting tonight because it suggested something furtive and dishonorable. What if Max and Fedor had been right and Louis Napoleon's interest in her was less than honorable?

No matter. She couldn't very well turn back at this point. She would recoil from him indignantly at the first overture. If he tried force, she would threaten to scream. Surely he wouldn't want word of such a scene to reach Eugenie.

There were no proud masters of ceremonies with pristine gloves, no chamberlains to greet her. She was relieved to be met by a lady in the obscure gallery by which she entered, even though the lady's sophistication and blonde beauty seemed unlikely to commend her to the empress. The lady turned her over to an usher in livery who led Letty through a small anteroom that was airless and ovenlike, to an imperial study. This room was too big for a seduction. One hardly seduced a female under a gigantic map of the city marking the various districts that made Paris look like a series of wheels—the *arrondissements.*

This was not the same library where she had met the emperor the first time. The desk looked even longer. There were walls full of shiny wooden file cabinets, but everywhere were scattered papers, drawings, elaborate plans with hundreds of inked notations.

She was startled by a voice explaining the reason for this hopeless disarray.

"A war on filth and disease and overcrowded tenements, my dear Madame Max."

The emperor had been standing at the long windows that illuminated the far end of the salon. He signaled and a fat little man in livery too tight for him hastily closed the drapes in the already overheated room.

She swung around, open-mouthed, and curtsied low, noticing that his other guests, if any, were suspiciously missing. Louis Napoleon strode toward her over the carpet. He seemed to move with unnatural deliberation, and she remembered what Max had said about his kidney stone. How could she, or Max, or Fedor suspect this sick man of having sexual designs on her? It was clear that the emperor's overriding concern was the welfare of his subjects. It was said that he looked best on horseback, but from the lines of fatigue in his face and his measured steps, he was in no condition to ride horses.

His hand made a slight movement. Both the lady and the two men in livery vanished, leaving Letty alone with the emperor and suddenly terrified that she would forget the habits and customs appropriate to the situation.

"Sir," she began in a shaky voice, correcting herself in French, "that is to say, Your Imperial—"

He raised his hand. "Let us speak in English, my little friend. I was happy in England. Yes, and in the States as well. What a vast country!" He looked around and then ventured, after an awkward moment, "I did not quite tell you the truth, as you see, Madame Max. We are alone. But please regard me as a sincere friend, interested in your country's welfare and that of my own. Do you forgive my little subterfuge?"

Imagine an emperor asking her pardon! "Of course, sir. And I would love to discuss these things with Your Majesty."

He made an open-handed gesture. "Come. You must not stand. We are friends. You must tell me—has your country recovered from its tragic revolution?"

"Civil War." She corrected him without thinking. Vincent never referred to the War Between the States as the Civil War. Then she hesitated, not knowing where to sit. The emperor indicated a satin brocade sofa that was dwarfed by a world map hanging on the wall above. She moved toward the sofa with her hand on his arm; started to sit down, waited uncertainly, but caught his smile and collapsed onto the sofa in relief. He reached around beside the sofa to a silver tray with several cut-glass decanters and two delicate, extraordinarily long-stemmed glasses. He poured a green cordial for her and laughed.

"No. It is not absinthe. I hope the ladies who visit me do not have to go that far to prepare for an audience with their emperor."

Letty sipped the sweet, not unpleasant drink while he settled beside her with his back to the gilt arm of the sofa and one arm thrown over the sofa behind her.

"So that I may gain a better view of your lovely profile." He smiled. "Is it something in the air that gives young American ladies such innocent freedom?"

"My husband says I have a strong . . . left." Grinning with mischief, she held up her fist in its magenta glove. "Very strong—so Max says."

In mock terror he started back, then took her fist, closed his fingers around it, and brought it down to his upper thigh in friendly conquest.

"Very strong, except for the right man. And he so far away."

What should she do? Her fingers were uncomfortably close to his groin. She rattled on hurriedly. "Yes. And his wife is a friend of mine. A dear person. So all he can do is only write to me, little snippets of gossip. About the players, you know."

"The—ah—players. Yes." Clearly mystified, he tried to make sense of this. "Then I take it, this man you speak of so eloquently is not my friend Max."

She had said more than she intended to, but in any case he now knew the truth. "Max married me to get me over here respectably. He needed me in Her Majesty's service. He said you agreed."

"Quite true. I cabled my consent. I even asked a loyal friend to help him in his quest. The Contessa Servandoni. But you say this marriage is purely a formality. If you will forgive me, how can he resist you?"

She laughed. "That's the easiest part of it. He adores—" She caught her breath, and wondered if the color left her face. "—his work and all."

He squeezed her fingers sympathetically. "It sounds like dear old Max. There is no man more loyal to me. But I'm afraid it leaves him little time for other emotions." Letty's gaze became fixed by the gray-green depths of his eyes; she found herself behaving as if hypnotized.

Her lips trembled, but she managed to say in a hoarse, uncontrolled voice, "I'm quite h—happy with my h—husband. I mean—Max."

"I should be disappointed if you were not. He deserves all that is good. Tell me about this man you . . ." She felt him very close beside her. "He is your true love, as you might say? Does Max know about him?"

It took a minute for her to realize that pursuing this line of conversation could be dangerous. She tried to wriggle her fingers from his grasp and assume a naive, ingenuous look.

"My husband knows everything about me. He—he has a great affection for me."

"And not surprisingly."

The ensuing silence felt charged.

"America—that is to say, the United States, is a very interesting place, monsieur. Did you get a chance to go west?"

"No. I must always regret I missed that. Most especially as those great wilds produced so much grace and dignity."

He seemed simply overpowering, and worse, she found it hard to resist him. Something about his eyes, his sweet, gentle manner. She could not imagine herself letting him make love to her, but she had a panicky feeling that she might not be in a position to stop him. If his behavior weren't otherwise so gentle, she would swear that she was the helpless prey of a spider.

She forced herself to realize that it didn't matter if this man sitting next to her was the emperor; he was an elderly gentleman, named Louis Napoleon Bonaparte, who was sitting *too* close and breathing *too* hard.

In his curiously persuasive voice he continued, "Max must be blind not to see the loveliness in his own home. I myself would never be guilty of such callous indifference."

She sat forward and put down her glass. "But Your Majesty is fortunate. You have the most beautiful women in Europe in your bed—I mean, your house."

He sat back more comfortably, watching her movements, but with one hand idly over the back of the sofa.

"You do well to hesitate, my dear. My wife's unfortunate difficulties at the birth of the prince imperial have made it impossible for her to enjoy the conjugal relations that . . . But I need say no more. The empress is my staunch friend, my faithful companion, my wise adviser in so many ways. Above all, she is the mother of the prince imperial."

And Letty Fox was his diversion. One could scarcely blame him.

"You are much admired by the French community in San Francisco. They even have shops that are French. Not like the Paris stores, mind you, but they are very progressive."

His hand played with the chignon on the nape of her neck, below her bonnet.

"Have you seen our Bon Marché?" he said. "A magnificent creation. The first of its kind. We are very proud of it. If I were to give the word and send you with my chamberlain, I am certain you would be permitted to wander up that great staircase under the dazzling glass dome at an hour when the usual sightseers are gone."

She chattered rapidly, trying to keep in mind how Max would disapprove of this visit.

"I read somewhere that the great staircases of Bon Marché and the others are grander than the Tuileries."

"Not . . . quite. We must rectify your impression by inviting you to supper here at the Tuileries."

His other hand was around her upper arm and his face close to hers. Letty was terribly frightened. It was not the blind, defensive anger and fear she had known when she fought off Risolli. It was worse—fear that she would offend him *and* ruin Max in the bargain.

The hand that had held hers shifted her fingers to his groin, resting them on his swollen member. Paralyzed by fear and a curious, terrible lassitude, she wondered, "What if I yielded?" She shuddered . . . she could never do that. . . . But he was the emperor, could destroy Max if she refused him. But if she let him . . . besides the obvious shame . . . she could never face Max again.

He leaned a trifle nearer and kissed her, his lips touching the edge of her mouth. Had he kissed her hard and violently, as Max often did, she wouldn't have had time to notice any related sensations, but the emperor's kiss, doubtless through hundreds of similar seductions, was soft and, again, gentle. And before she could be stirred in an erotic way, she was stirred by his carefully waxed mustache and his neat goatee.

She burst into giggles.

He drew back, undoubtedly affronted. It was hard to know. Max had once said, "Louis Napoleon never looks where he strikes. You can't read his thoughts by his face." With much difficulty, she stifled her giggling.

"I'm very ticklish, sir. I hope I haven't offended you."

There was an awful stillness. The idea of looking him in the eyes terrified her, but she turned her head and was astonished by his faint, self-deprecating smile. He lifted her fingers away from his groin and shook her hand teasingly, almost as Max might have done. "Do not look so stricken, little one. I am not the English Bluebeard."

"English?"

"Henry the Eighth. I do not inspire such awe. Now, are we friends?"

She laughed and agreed.

"Is that the color our fashion patriots call magenta?" he asked.

"Yes, monsieur."

"May I take this as a compliment to the nation?"

She smiled her answer. He got up, reached for another decanter that held a ruby red liqueur.

"If you will forgive me, Madame Max, I will just refresh myself with a drop of something my self-esteem badly needs."

"You are awfully—" She searched for the word. "—nice. I was afraid you would be angry. To tell the truth, Your Majesty, I never really thought kings and queens were people one could talk to."

"Another compliment of rare distinction." He raised his glass, touched hers with it, and then drank. She repeated his motion, toasting him proudly, *"Vive l'Empereur!"*

"Thank you, my dear. That was spoken like a Frenchman. Or rather —as I wish a Frenchman might say it. And now, perhaps, we should see to your reputation. We mustn't have you gossiped about." He added, "Falsely, alas!" with a rueful look that made her smile.

He stood up to summon the lackey to show her out, and she rearranged her bonnet and mantle. But he did not get as far as the big desk before he stopped and doubled over with a groan. Grasping the edge of the desk, he tried to speak. His face was beaded with sweat.

Panicking, Letty tried to support him, but he waved her away. "Evans . . . friend. Dentist friend. He knows. Was to see him later. Discreet."

She had no idea of how to summon his servants or his court physician, so she ran out of the big salon, though the stifling little anteroom, and into the gallery beyond.

Two of the gorgeously uniformed Cent-Guards were on duty in a cross-gallery at the bottom of a magnificent flight of stairs.

"The emperor. Quick. He is ill. Hurry." As an afterthought she added, "I must find a dentist, a Dr. Evans. I have a message."

The two guards had already started off on a loping run, holding their swords at their hips, but one of them gestured toward a single door on the left of the gallery. She rushed to the door just as it opened and a dark, bearded man came out. They collided and she cried out in a burst of French, "I pray your pardon, monsieur. I must find Dr. Evans."

The bearded man caught her. "Slowly, madame, if you please. I am American. My French is not so rapid. But I am Thomas Evans."

"Thank God. I'm American too," she said in English. "His Majesty asked for you. This way. He is ill."

Letty tugged at his sleeve, and he hurried along behind her.

"We were just talking. That's all. And he bent over, and he was in such pain!"

"I know. That is why the empress delegated for him so many times this past year. Has anyone seen you?"

"Two guards. The ones with the plumes."

"There must be no gossip. The opposition would ruin him if they heard of this."

She pushed open the door of the anteroom. They could hear voices in the big salon—and thank God!—one of them was the emperor's, weak, but unmistakably his voice.

"Much better . . . Thank you, no. Better now. A pinch of dyspepsia. Madame MacCroy came with a message from her husband. The message about the—er—Corsican extremists was a shock."

Dr. Evans stopped before they entered the salon. "I had better see you out, madame. That is undoubtedly why he sent you to find me."

"But shouldn't I—"

"No. The less you are seen with His Majesty, the better. Come. Is there a carriage waiting?"

"I think so. Off the Place du Carrousel."

The dentist led her toward an anteroom door she hadn't noticed before. Feeling much like a criminal, she stepped out the door.

The old coachman looked back curiously as she climbed into the closed carriage. She took care to keep her face averted from any tourists and curiousity-seekers who might be strolling along the streets on this warm summer evening.

The quai was crowded with strollers when Letty arrived home, making it easy enough for her to slip into the courtyard passage and up the stairs unnoticed. This was a great relief; she didn't want Fedor or Madame Claudel adding their two bits to any gossip Max might hear.

It was, therefore, a considerable shock to find the door to the upper floor apartment blocked by a motionless figure standing with arms folded in a belligerent posture that allowed for no compromise.

"Good evening, Mrs. MacCroy. I hope I didn't startle you. I seem to have arrived inopportunely, as they say in the French farces."

She recovered with difficulty, determined not to let herself be humiliated by this man who came home from several days with the woman he idolized to play the indignant husband with her. Worse than indignant. Sarcastic.

"Don't be so cat-and-mousy. I'm tired and I've had a perfectly horrendous evening. Do move aside so I can go in."

"And go to bed with your long-lost husband? Won't that be a trifle crowded—you, your memories of the evening, and me?"

She moved toward the door. His arm was thrown across the door, casually resting against the opposite doorjamb. She snapped. "Don't be so vulgar. It looks to me as if we are going to spend the night out here in the passage."

He raised his arm and pushed the door open. She ducked under his arm and went in, taking off her mantle and bonnet and hurling them both onto an armchair. After an uncomfortable minute or two Max came in, closing the door behind him. She had expected a slam.

Max finally broke the silence. "I take it that you aren't going to tell me where you have been this evening."

"Of course I am. You might have asked; I would have told you at once." She thought he looked a trifle relieved. "I might have said I was touring the sights of the new Paris at twilight. It would be the most logical thing."

"Were you?"

"No. I was given an imperial invitation"—she saw that he was growing tense again—"to come and discuss the changes and advancements in America since the War Between the States."

"Did it occur to you that he might have asked me? I've been in the States any number of times since sixty-five."

"I consider an invitation from the emperor a command."

"Rubbish."

"Well, I don't know your stupid rules, your protocol, but I thought there was no harm in obeying an imperial command."

There was an odd look in his eyes and she couldn't trust his smile. "And was there?"

"Yes."

He opened his mouth abruptly and then closed it. He fingered the candlestick on the mantelpiece but kept watching her.

"He was feeling alone and deserted. And unwell, I think. He asked me about America, gave me a few silly compliments like old men always do."

"Old men? Yes. I suppose they do. And then?"

"He tried to—in fact, he kissed me."

He shifted the candlestick an inch to the left without looking at it. "Was it an enjoyable kiss?"

She shrugged. "I can't quite say. It really depends on the viewpoint. You see, I started laughing." She saw his eyes widen, and explained with sweet innocence, "You do see; it was his waxed mustache. I'm extremely ticklish."

He burst out laughing. The candlestick rolled over the mantelpiece and landed on the hearth, the candle broken in two. He paid no attention to it.

"I would dearly love to know what Louis did then. The beau of the boulevards, the master of the bedroom, gives a young woman a fit of the giggles."

"He was very nice about it. I told him so. We are friends now. He knows I'm not like your old contessa."

"Not *my* old contessa, thank God! I can't imagine what you talked about afterward."

"We didn't talk much. He was about to ring and have me taken home when he had an attack. He suffered terribly, poor man! The thing you told me about, I expect." She saw from his look of consternation that his focus had shifted, and felt piqued for a moment at how readily his concern for the emperor supplanted his concern for his wife, as preposterous as her annoyance was. But her basic affection for Max superseded her other feelings, and she picked up her discarded cloak and bonnet, which she didn't want Madame Claudel to find.

"He recovered, I trust."

"Certainly. I wouldn't have just left him to suffer, would I? A dentist, a friend of the emperor's, took me to the carriage secretly."

"A dentist. Yes. I know the man. An American. Edmonds . . . no, Evans. Medium tall. Heavy beard. Friendly manner, but no nonsense."

"That's the man."

"You did right, my love." He held out his two arms. "Come. Time for bed."

She felt her pulse throbbing in her throat.

"I know it wasn't long in hours, less than two days, but I discovered something. While you were away, it seemed a long time."

"For me, too. The empress is safe, so she sent me back—I wanted to get back to you as fast as I could."

They walked to the bedchamber together, his arm around her, holding her close. As they reached the door, he began to chuckle.

"What is it?"

"Tell me again what Louis said when you started giggling."

She laughed. "He said he wasn't Henry the Eighth and my head was safe on my shoulders, or something like that. So I said he was awfully nice."

"Nice! Good Lord! It's a wonder he didn't strangle you."

He was still chuckling as he helped her undress. "I hope you aren't going to tell me I'm nice."

"Certainly not in bed. And please don't try to be."

"You have my word on that."

Later on, as they rested quietly, Max remembered the news he had for her.

"The most elaborate ball of the year is to occur soon at the Tuileries."

She stiffened, fearing what was to come. "I know. You are invited and it is a great honor. To you. And you're going to be away all evening while I stay here locked up. I'd be better off back on the stage."

"If you prefer. However, Her Majesty did have a thought."

"Ha. I've no doubt." He pulled her head down, cushioning it on his shoulder.

"Of course, if you feel so strongly about Eugenie's company, we will have to refuse for you. That's all."

She tried to see his face in the bar of moonlight falling through partially closed portieres.

"We?"

"She has taken a fancy to you. God knows why. Says you are a very obliging young woman. She is going to have an invitation issued to you."

Because I am going to do her a favor at Princess Matilde's house. Still, it was pleasant to be in Eugenie's good graces.

"Go on."

"Why bother? If you feel so strongly against the whole affair."

She pounded his bare chest. "You dreadful beast! Why didn't you tell me straight off?"

"I had something else on my mind."

Her thoughts leaped to her mission for the empress. "It won't interfere with the evening affair given by the Princess Matilde, will it?"

"Why should it? We don't go to the Tuileries ball until July eighteenth."

"Then you will take me to the Bonaparte princess?"

"It seems inevitable."

Some time later he sighed. "I wish I hadn't told you tonight about the ball."

"Why, for heaven's sake?"

"Because you're not here. You're there."

"I was just wondering if they could possibly find out about me."

"They can try. They won't succeed." He grinned. "All our secrets are buried." He shook her playfully. "Still planning your wardrobe, or thinking of banquets? You're not keeping your mind on the work at hand."

"Not precisely *at hand,* darling."

This time she gave their lovemaking her all.

There was no doubt about it. Max might not be the man she adored, but she had more fun with him than with anyone ever, even Vincent.

CHAPTER *Eight*

*T*WO *MORNINGS* later, when Max brought up the mail, he was unexpectedly tense. Letty was puzzled until she saw the black border on one of the envelopes.

"I'm afraid your friend is gone." He handed the letter to her.

She stared at the envelope for a long time without opening it, realizing that with Annabeth dead, Vincent was free.

She became aware that Max was watching her, and blushed. But perhaps the idea had crossed his own mind.

Carefully opening the letter, she discovered, to her surprise, that it was written by Calla Skutnik.

> Letty, honey:
>
> I reckon you can see from this that Annabeth died. It was a week ago, come Sunday. We all took it right hard, she's such a dear little thing. "Galloping consumption," they call it. Her old tubercular problem.
>
> She passed away in Vincent's arms. He cried—reckon we all did. We said his little girl was now in heaven, but you know how them things are. It don't help none.
>
> He took her to New York for burying in her family's plot. He seemed so lost. I think he needs someone to comfort him.
>
> And that makes me open my big mouth, like Al says. We ~~aint~~ arent blind and we sure saw that you two was mighty close.
>
> Vincent asked O'Halloran for time off. He said if he was in New York he could take a boat to London and do poetry readings until fall, if O'Halloran could get him any bookings. But we think he's on his way to Paris. He knows you're playing a part, so to speak, and he won't betray you. But he sure as hell wants to see you. And Annabeth not cold in her grave. Just thought you ought to know.
>
> > Lots of love from us.
> > Yours sincerely,
> > Callantha R. Skutnik

Her voice choked, Letty said, half to herself, "I was gone when they all needed me most."

"Don't be silly. Truth is, they were a greedy pack, looking after their own interests."

"Not—all of them."

He turned away and began to riffle through his mail. "Are we to hear the virtues of the noble Vincent extolled once more?" He looked up, but not at her. "I have an appointment at the prefecture. But I warn you, you had better lay aside this business for the evening. If a message from Rissoli got through to them, Matilde and Plonplon may be exceedingly interested in any mention of the noble Vincent. From his name it is even possible they might make the short jump to Letty Fox. They play cat-and-mouse, that pair."

"I understand. I'll take care. Whatever you may think, it is Annabeth I was—"

But he was already out the door.

For a long time she stared at Calla's letter, remembering what Vincent and Annabeth had meant to her.

Her future was an uncharted sea. Max must have been as surprised as she by the success of their marriage of convenience.

At odd moments she even wondered if he had possibly married her out of love rather than expedience. But she had no real idea how deep his feelings ran for her. Her feelings for him had evolved to the point where now she could truthfully say that in many ways she loved Max.

Vincent was free now, and she knew Vincent loved her. And Calla had said he might be coming to claim her in Paris. Surely that was what it amounted to, that anxious trip across the ocean! To think that soon she might see him again, even briefly! Her knight in armor.

Freed by Annabeth's death, he had thought first of Letty. But could she ever be happy with him again, haunted as she was by the memory of Annabeth and all that Letty owed her?

The letter fluttered to the carpet. She stooped to pick it up and started to cry, not only for the lost Annabeth but for the lost Letty Fox. Life had been so simple for the Letty who had adored only one person, Vincent Fairborne.

Nothing was simple any more. Not even her love for Vincent.

The whole day was hers to think, to grieve, to wonder what Max's mood would be tonight. At the very least, her nervousness about the evening's soirée didn't surface until late in the afternoon. Not realizing that Max had returned, Letty overheard him discussing with Fedor the order for a new carriage. She walked out to the salon, wanting to tell them how she felt about the matter.

"You mustn't sell the old carriage. We're used to it. It's comfortable, and I don't like those landaus and barouches and all." She walked up to Max and kissed him lightly.

Fedor was triumphant. "You see, M'sieu Max? Madame agrees with me."

Max seemed distracted. He acknowledged her kiss, brushing her cheek, but kept talking to Fedor.

"At all events, with the international scene so uncertain, there won't be new trappings for a while. So cancel the order."

After Fedor had left the room Max said, "Don't forget, the Princess Matilde's friends may have their knives out."

"I'd match you against them any time."

"I'm afraid my 'sinister policeman' look, as you call it, would hardly subdue Plonplon or Matilde. But I promise not to let them eat you."

Max and Letty were both in excellent spirits a few hours later as they set out for the rue de Courcelles. As they traveled through the bright, gaslit Paris night, Letty, conscious again of the warmth and intimacy, surely a deepening love that she shared with Max, leaned closer and hugged him.

Letty expected liveried footmen, massive staircases, and all the formality of the Tuileries. Watching her face, Max was amused by her surprise when they were greeted in a dark foyer and had their wraps removed in a one-time powdering room.

Letty caught a glimpse of the heavily furnished rooms beyond. As in so many overfurnished houses, these salons bore witness to the princess's astonishing range of interests, from the Napoleonic wars to the Orient. The large rooms were cluttered, but Letty found them far more cozy than the polished and glittering elegance of the empress's suite in the Tuileries.

Eugenie's bedchamber and boudoir were pristine and perfect, but given her choice, Letty would much prefer to spend her time in Matilde's marvelous dining salon, to which they'd been ushered without the usual getting-acquainted period. A mass of greenery on this hot summer night, the room's Grecian pillars were half hidden by the climbing green vines, and slender young trees in ornamental tubs were set about the floor. A skylight over the trestle table reached a starry sky, whose luminescence was all but obscured by long tapers in the central chandelier.

A woman stood in the doorway of the dining salon, framed by the draped portieres—the green of which did nothing to enhance her muddy complexion—and surrounded by a chattering, excited coterie. Although it was clear that she must be the hostess, it nonetheless came as a shock to Letty when Max presented her with rigid formality to this ungainly, inappropriately dressed Matilde.

"Your Imperial Highness, may I have the pleasure of presenting Madame MacCroy? She wishes to thank you for your gracious invitation, and I would like to join in that expression."

"Handsomely said, Monsieur Max. Stiff but handsome. So. Are we to remain enemies, now that you will have sat at my table and partaken of my food? I assure you, it is not yet poisoned."

"I am enemy of no man who supports the dynasty, madame."

The Princess Matilde impressed Letty in a strange way. Perhaps it was her weight, or the way she moved, but there was something frighteningly solid about her—like a California oak, with spreading roots, even ugly. But an immovable presence nonetheless.

Her Highness changed the subject. "So this is the girl who captured you, Max. We had all thought you were quite unattainable." The princess extended her stubby, strong fingers to Letty, who made a graceful gesture of bringing them near her own forehead before releasing them.

"Your marriage came as a surprise to all of us. She is not quite *sauvage* though, as we might be led to expect of those who come from the desolate lands of the Middle West, I believe they call it."

Letty bristled but felt the pressure of Max's fingers on the nape of her neck. He said coldly, "I dare say the savagery of the Americans has as much basis in fact as the decadence of the French."

Princess Matilde motioned with her huge, Chinese ivory fan, attracting the attention of the gloomy-looking Plonplon, who came over and joined them.

"My dear brother, you are caught out in a lie. You told me distinctly that our Max had softened, but I find him just what he always was. And how fortunate! Life can become infernally dull when we lose all our enemies to death or other unpleasant fates."

Max bowed. "You see, madame? We can agree on one thing, at least."

Letty thought that if this went on it would end in pistols at twenty paces. She was overwhelmingly relieved when the princess turned to her, until she uttered her first words.

"You have led a strenuous and shocking life, I understand, Madame MacCroy."

"I b-beg pardon, ma'am?"

"Between all those cows and the red Indians, my dear," the princess said in a flat voice. "But come, all of you, or my chef will cut his wrists with rage, if the soup is warm and the fish is cold."

Letty would have preferred to enter the dining salon with Max but Princess Matilde ordered otherwise.

"Remember, my dear brother, she is to sit close on my left, just beyond the marquis." And to Letty she said, behind her fan but loud enough to be heard by others, "Alas, my dear madame, had you arrived only a year ago, how much an intelligent young woman like you would have had in common with my guests then! The incomparable Saint-Beuve, with his needling wit that he injected into every piece of writing, and those brilliant brothers, Edmond and Jules. The Goncourts, you know."

Who on earth?

"But death has scythed them down. First Saint-Beuve, and then that dear, clever Jules only last month. Never mind." She raised her voice. "Attention, all."

The murmur hushed as if a symphony conductor had signaled his orchestra.

"We have a charming little divertissement tonight. Something quite out of the usual way. But first, we dine."

The fact that the princess had taken such a pronounced interest in Letty might have been upsetting at another time, but with Eugenie's small mission to fulfill, Letty was glad Max had been placed at the other end of the table. Under the cover of chairs being eased to the table by lackeys, the rattle of silver and the tinkle of the crystal glasses, Letty attempted to engage the princess in conversation.

"I am told, Your Highness, that yours is the best table in Paris. I am persuaded your chef finds no rival at the Tuileries."

Over the head of the ancient marquis, who appeared to be hard of hearing, the princess agreed, as Letty had known she would.

"It is the Spaniard's fault. My poor cousin, the emperor, must endure agonies of the stomach. No imagination. No pleasant tastes and flavors. But what can one expect from that quarter? One of her ancestors was a Scot. My brother says that when he visited Spain he was forced to live on eternal pork and sherry. He knew the Spaniard when she was merely the Countess of Teba, before my besotted cousin set her over us all. One can but wonder at the blindness of men."

"How true, Your Highness." The creamy soup was ice cold, but no one seemed to notice. Perhaps it was supposed to be cold. Letty took a breath and plunged further, speaking audibly enough to be sure she was heard by several at the table. "Considering that she is Spanish, it is strange that Her Majesty has so little interest in war. One would think she might support the war talk against Prussia, but it has been quite the reverse. She is violently opposed."

"Indeed?" Clearly this was not news Matilde wanted to hear. "One would think she felt the danger to France. That is to say, if she regards it as her country, which I very much doubt. One wonders what *does* occupy her mind." Letty found the princess's laugh more cutting than her tongue. "And does she still have that prurient interest in magdalens?"

Letty was not sure how to answer. Did she mean prostitutes? Or was this some reference to characters in a book, or to the Gospels themselves? Her hesitation betrayed her ignorance. She gave Max a quick look and saw that his eyes had narrowed; this was no time to provoke him into fresh conflicts with the princess. Letty spoke quickly, smiling and much too cheerful.

"Had her Majesty ever spoken to me of magdalens, I should certainly have remembered. But perhaps you refer to the Church of the Madeleine. What a splendid edifice! I was so touched by all Her Majesty has done for the church and the poor."

"Priest-ridden," Plonplon said harshly. "Typical of all Spaniards."

The princess frowned at her brother, then said to Letty, "No, madame. I refer to the way she bored young Dumas, in our presence, by questioning him about the magdalens—prostitutes—from whom he obtained his information for *La Dame aux Camellias*. A disgusting curiosity on her part."

"Your Highness is quite correct, of course," Letty agreed and assumed a look of passionate devotion, a look she had cultivated for the role of Joan of Arc. "I was astonished that Her Majesty learns everything about the condition of these wretched women and very quietly gives them monetary aid or spiritual consolation. She has even persuaded medical men to help them."

"I did not know . . . that is to say . . ." and then Matilde was silent.

Letty took up the lance for her final thrust. She laughed as cattily as ever Princess Matilde could manage. "But you are right. Charity is such a bore. And spending one's time as the empress does in such causes—well, really, you and I are much too sensible, I am sure."

Letty's hand shook a little as she reached for one of the outside glasses from her place setting.

A few listeners chuckled, some exchanged looks and furtive smiles. The princess changed the subject to a discussion of Monsieur Gounod's *Faust* versus Herr Wagner's *Tannhäuser*. The debate became heated, but in this Letty was far out of her depth, never having heard either opera. So she concentrated on the endless wines which accompanied the many delicious courses of the meal.

She didn't see how any normal human being could possibly taste all of the fifteen or more courses, much less eat them, but the princess's friends not only ate everything in sight from caviar to soup, to fish, to beef, to vegetables and cheeses before the elaborate desserts, but they kept up their conversations and arguments at the same time.

When the meal was finished, the princess led the way to a salon with subdued gaslight and furnishings that looked rich but well used. Letty made her way through the knots of guests to reach Max and took his arm.

"Darling, you will never know how much I've wanted to be this close to you all evening."

He was in a better humor than he had been during her fencing with Matilde.

"You seemed to be doing very well. I was proud of you. What did you mean by all that talk of Eugenie's charities?"

"Isn't she involved in good works?"

"Very much so, but that business about the magdalens, harlots, streetwomen! It must have shaken Matilde. She is notorious for her own charities."

But Letty was not embarrassed; the woman shouldn't have taunted her. She and Max found hard, curved Empire chairs at one side of the long room but Matilde motioned them closer, gesturing to a loveseat just beyond her own crimson-cushioned chair with its regal back. Max hesitated, but Letty said, "We've annoyed her enough for one night."

When all the guests were seated—the specially favored grouped around her chair—the princess looked over to Plonplon, who was leaning negligently against the shining marble mantelpiece. He nodded back, and the princess waved the room to quiet.

"I promised you something not in the usual line of entertainment. No singers from the Opera, no elocutionists from the Comédie-Française. Our brilliant oddity comes from over the seas. A recitation of poetry written by an American, Mr. Edgar Poe."

The princess's heavy face broke into a smile as she pointed her fan at Letty. "A recital by one of your own countrymen, Madame MacCroy. . . . My dear friends, let me present for your entertainment that distinguished American performer, Monsieur Vincent Fairborne."

Letty sat paralyzed. Max turned sharply and she knew he was watching her. During the polite round of applause, punctuated by one or two muffled groans, she closed her eyes, muttering, "Oh, God, no!" Then she looked at Max.

He was expressionless. "Did you know about this?"

"Do you think I'm quite mad?"

When she saw that he had softened, she added, "Do you think he will betray me?"

Max shrugged, but he reached out and put his arm around her shoulder, crushing the silver-ribbed, white ruffle that outlined the low neck of her gown.

"A treat for your charming American wife," Princess Matilde said to him.

Max nudged Letty while he replied, "If the fellow is any good. Let us hope he doesn't put us all to sleep."

Vincent Fairborne entered the room and stood a minute between the two draped emerald portieres, as if in a picture frame. His tall, graceful figure was impressive and he had never looked more handsome.

Like all the women present, Letty was spellbound by the spare form in stark black and white, whose golden hair caught the lights like a halo. He looked as glorious as ever.

She twisted her hands nervously, praying under her breath, *Don't let him speak to me.* Betrayal would not only shame her but it could ruin Max and give the princess fresh ammunition against the emperor and empress.

Vincent bowed first to the Princess Matilde and then to Prince Plonplon, who turned away contemptuously and straddled his chair sideways. Several women sighed with rapture, never taking their eyes off the American Adonis.

A delicate-looking, long-haired gentleman got up from a chair at the side of the room and came forward, and Vincent announced in moderately correct French, "Her Imperial Highness has graciously designated one of your excellent poets, Monsieur Paul Ivry, to translate for me." He cleared his throat, opened a black leather book and began to read "The Raven."

It seemed an extraordinary choice, for it was somewhat monotonous when recited in Vincent's low, theatrical voice. The translation struck Letty as ludicrous, highly overdramatic, arousing an occasional titter among the less appreciative.

During the applause, desultory by the men but wildly enthusiastic by the ladies, Max leaned nearer to Letty. "So long as there are females, it appears he will succeed."

"He was always an excellent actor."

The princess opened her fan and said to Letty, in her clear, decisive voice, "One wonders that he can present such a gentlemanly appearance. He once produced a show with naked females, you know."

"Really?"

Vincent, about to start on his next reading, drank a small glass of white wine, set it back on the footman's tray and opened his black leather book.

"Fair Helen," he began and then looked up. He studied the painting over one of the long windows. "I dedicate this to one I once knew. A child of sorrow who blossomed like the fair Helen . . ."

Letty whispered to Max, "He loved Annabeth very much."

"Don't be coy," Max said. "I know the poem. It is you."

She hid her fingers in her skirt. They were shaking badly.

Vincent continued. "Your classic face, and naiad airs bring me home"—he raised his head, looked at Letty—"to the glory that was Greece, the grandeur that was Rome . . ."

Letty bit her lip to keep tears from falling. She almost lost control, but was brought to an angry sense of place by a low-spoken comment from Max.

"Pompous, isn't he?"

"He was taught to be that way. I mean—no such thing!" A woman nearby hissed her to silence; as if she had started this absurd business!

As the end of the reading approached, Vincent announced, "If Your Highness will forgive a personal note, I have recently been bereft of my dear wife. If I may, I will dedicate this farewell elegy to another lost love, 'Annabel Lee.'" The women throughout the room sniffled and grabbed for their handkerchiefs. The princess herself was seen to wipe the corners of her eyes with her forefinger as he came to the last "Annabel Lee."

As for Letty, she could see all too clearly the warm, lovely eyes of Annabeth Fairborne, and hear in the ever-repetitive line the tolling of bells for a lost friend.

Then came the congratulations and introductions, and surrounded as he was, Vincent Fairborne didn't notice Letty and Max, who remained on the outskirts of the crowd. But they had not counted on the persistence and determination of Princess Matilde.

"Come, Monsieur Fairborne. You must meet a compatriot of yours. A bride, in fact. The lucky man is our own man-about-prefectures, Monsieur Max MacCroy."

"Madame—MacCroy, you say? And Monsieur. A pleasure. I trust you were not entirely bored." Vincent smiled politely.

Since Letty was still speechless with nerves and the excitement of seeing him so unexpectedly, Max shook hands with him.

"We were anything but bored; isn't that true, my love?"

Letty looked into Vincent's eyes. The pain she saw in those gray depths made her guilty about every moment of passion she had enjoyed with Max.

"I will never—we will never forget such a splendid performance, Monsieur Fairborne."

Vincent reached for her hand and brought it up to his lips, still looking at her with that infinitely sad expression.

It was Max who rescued the awkward moment.

"Well, my love. Time to go home. Early to bed, you know, as your countryman so wisely observed." He tapped Letty's arm.

"What, Max?" Prince Plonplon asked with a jollity that did not suit his dour look. "Leaving already? And the evening just begun."

Max turned to Matilde. "If Your Highness permits."

The princess waved him away. "Certainly. How well I know such moments! My dear brother, do not detain them. You know how conscientious Max is when it comes to serving the empress—and his wife."

Everyone pretended not to understand this, and so far as Letty was concerned, the ghastly evening was over.

Letty was surprised at Max's excellent spirits on the way home, calling the evening "profitable in many ways."

"What on earth shall we do about him? Do you think he will try to see us?"

"I shouldn't be in the least surprised. But I trust you, my love. Just see to it that no one suspects you have known each other before. It should be simple enough. You are both actors, after all."

"You don't mind?"

"I think it is inevitable. You should make your meetings seem accidental, of course. And spontaneous. I don't think anything will come of it, if that is what you are concerned about."

CHAPTER *Nine*

*I*T SEEMED odd, considering Max's previous attitude, and certainly uncomplimentary, that he cared so little about the presence of Vincent Fairborne. She tried to speak to him about it.

"When the princess talked about the American entertainer I had no idea it was Vincent. When Calla wrote to me about Annabeth she warned me that Vincent might come to Europe."

"Warned you?"

"I mean, she—you know."

She wasn't sure she understood his smile, and they didn't discuss the matter again.

A day later Max arrived home unexpectedly early after an hour at the Paris prefecture.

"A special message for my wife. From an old admirer," he announced.

Her throat tightened. "Not Vincent. He knows he shouldn't. Not right now."

"Quite so. This message happens to be from another of your numerous admirers. This one may not be as young or as dashing as our noble Vincent, but he does wear a crown."

She groaned. "Oh, Max, must I see His Majesty alone?"

"Far from it. I have reason to believe one of the imperial lackeys may be in the pay of a fellow named Rochefort, who edits the radical republican sheet called the *Marseillaise.*"

"It sounds patriotic."

"Depends on the viewpoint. You are to play Eugenie for a brief moment. We are hoping Rochefort's spy or one of Plonplon's friends will print the rumor that Eugenie has spoken with a member of the Prussian embassy."

She began to see the reason for his intricate scheme. "Then you can show that Her Majesty was actually at St. Cloud all the time and that Plonplon and this Rochefort are liars. Nothing they say will be believed if we trap them several times. By the time they realize I was an impostor, it will no longer matter."

He pinched her chin and kissed her. "It will be too late. Their veracity will be in question. You see? You are becoming as crafty and devious as your husband."

"Insults . . . insults," she joked, loving their camaraderie, loving their moments together.

The prospect of masquerading as the empress again was exciting, and for a short time she forgot the problem of choosing between her idol, Vincent, and the husband to whom she found herself so ideally suited. She even swept aside the dreadful prospect of having the old Letty Fox revealed to the world.

"Someday," she said to Max, as they approached the Tuileries by the same indirect route they usually took, "I am going to walk proudly up through the main carriage entrance, as an imperial guest."

Max promised, "Certainly. As soon as we settle this crisis with Prussia over the Spanish succession."

"Will it be soon? I don't know why the Spanish can't settle their own affairs."

"Would it were so. His Majesty thinks it's just a matter of settling things with King William of Prussia. We've got to keep Chancellor Bismarck out of it. He'd like nothing better than to promote a war."

She saw that he was deeply concerned, but she didn't understand all the intrigue. "Why would Bismarck want war, for heaven's sake?"

"To unite all the little states of Germany under the Prussian flag. Louis Napoleon believes the rumor that Bismarck is supposed to be suffering from a nervous breakdown. I wish *I* thought so, but my agents believe he is waiting to pounce."

Letty wished he was a bit more optimistic. The possibility of war was frightening to her; remembering the Civil War in America, she knew life would never be the same again for either victors or vanquished.

Max left her in the capable hands of Doña Catalina and the young Spanish maid. The transformation into the Empress Eugenie was effected much more quickly this time. Letty was arrayed in a walking suit of spotless white linen with black lapels and a ruffled hem. She paraded up and down before the pier glass, enjoying once again her metamorphosis into the empress of the French.

A haughty lady-in-waiting came to escort her to an audience chamber where several men stood around, all of whom looked forbidding, even the emperor. Max lurked in the background.

One man, in the process of being dismissed by the emperor, made her uneasy. He struck her as pompous-looking with his overgrown side-whiskers, bushy eyebrows and pointed mustache. With great ceremony he bowed to her but said nothing, giving her a clue that he was not a close acquaintance of the empress.

As she had suspected, the man was from the Prussian embassy; this was the man she was supposed to be seen with at the window. She crossed the room, only half-hearing the emperor say, "Herr Baron von Eckhardt of the embassy. He was just leaving. He has made known to us His Majesty King William's views on the subject of the Spanish succession."

Letty knew this performance was critical. She moved across the threadbare carpet with Eugenie's celebrated glide until she was directly in the sunlight between the draped curtains. She offered the baron her hand, trying to give the gesture the elegant casualness Eugenie might have used, but very much aware that afterward it would be necessary for Baron von Eckhardt to realize no one had precisely introduced her as the empress. If he caught the French in a deliberate lie about her identity, there would be further hard feelings with Prussia.

Although Max seemed utterly at ease, Letty sensed the watchful attitude of the emperor and the curiosity of the baron's young blond aide. More than curiosity in the aide, she thought, knowing all the symptoms from her days in the theater. He was interested in the woman, not the empress.

She spoke in French with just a hint of a Spanish lisp, "We all know His Majesty is pleased to meet someone who brings conciliation and not talk of war."

"Quite true, Your Majesty. We in Berlin have invariably stood beside conciliation with honor. It is our inviolable rule."

The man was contemptuous, and Letty suspected his feeling was based on his suspicion that the imperial couple were cowards. She managed not to let her lip curl as she nodded to indicate that the interview was ended.

She turned to the emperor. "Let us trust, Your Majesty, that King William shares the baron's optimism."

Louis Napoleon said quietly, "Good day, Herr Baron. May we all trust in that optimism." His voice allowed of no question.

Another stiff bow, heels together, and the baron retired, moving in stately fashion past the lady-in-waiting, the blond aide and a footman at the door. The aide was the last to go. He looked back over his shoulder at Letty until someone, perhaps the baron in the corridor, tapped him on the shoulder. He smiled back at her, shrugged and followed his master.

Letty waited for her cue. The emperor made a small signal with his finger and everyone but Max left the room.

The emperor took both her hands and held them between his warm ones. "You were superb, madame. Max tells me our friend Rochefort has been seen in these halls today. I do not doubt that his ragged little propaganda sheet is already printing the story that my wife has influenced imperial policy with the Prussian embassy. It needs only that we contradict the story with the truth, that Her Majesty is at St. Cloud."

Max took her arm, making it impossible for the emperor to continue holding her hands, saying, "And also, my love, my agents discovered a few hours ago that the footman stationed at the antechamber door is in the pay of His Highness, Plon—I mean Prince Napoleon."

It seemed strange, all this intrigue, but Letty's chief concern was relief that her part had been a reasonable success.

Without warning, the emperor winced and doubled over. Both Letty and Max rushed to help him, but he straightened himself with an effort. His smile was steady, though Letty could see the perspiration on his forehead.

"Sir," Max began.

"No. You do see how important my health is at this juncture."

"Yes, monsieur. Even so, I wish you could have the operation. The sooner the better."

Letty cried out without thought, "We need you, sir. The country needs you. Please take care."

The emperor kissed the palm of her hand. "You have married a patriot, my dear fellow. We will not forget. Now, Max, you must reward this lovely patriot for her performance today."

"I intend to, Your Majesty. We are on our way to the Grand Hotel for luncheon. My wife has a passion to dine there."

Letty caught her breath. "Oh, I have! Ever since we passed it the day we arrived."

"I envy you. Well, go along, children, with my blessing."

At the door the emperor added a final word. "Max, submit the luncheon to your account. It will give me a vicarious pleasure in this happy occasion."

Within half an hour Letty was again dressed as Madame MacCroy, and they left the palace in the usual circuitous way. During the carriage ride to the huge hotel below the magnificent new avenue de l'Opera, Max pretended to be jealous of Letty's ravings about Louis Napoleon.

"My dear girl, he is a very human male. In fact, may I accentuate that? And you did him an enormous favor."

"Perhaps. All the same, he treats me like a lady. I wasn't always treated that way, if you'll remember."

"I hope you will admit that I have always treated you with respect." There was a cool edge to his lighthearted tone.

Letty apologized, assuring him that he was above the others.

Neither of them mentioned Vincent Fairborne, but he was very much in both their minds.

They rode around to the carriage entrance and Max escorted Letty in through the skylighted Winter Garden to a table in the center of the big room. Letty had been a guest at some splendid restaurants in the past, but as she was seated she became aware that she and Max were surrounded by extraordinary diners—the very correct waiters addressed them as "Your Grace," "Your Excellency," "General" and any number of "comtesses," and "ladyships."

"How lovely!" she cried.

"Adequate."

Now that they were here Max was behaving oddly; he seemed to be distracted and studied the various diners with narrowed eyes.

"You are not very well disguised, you know," Letty remarked.

"Disguised? Why should I be disguised?"

"Because you look exactly like a man about to arrest an assassin."

Belatedly, he grinned. "Well, there may be something in what you say. Paris seems to be a haven for all the disenchanted of the world. The Hungarians and Poles are hiding after their abortive revolutions. The Austrians and Russians. Some of these fellows may be heroes but many of them are nihilists, anarchists or unsuccessful assassins who failed to blow up the tsar, the emperor of Austria-Hungary, or the Turkish sultan. I'm not even counting all those Balkan terrorists."

She hadn't thought they would be surrounded by such an international assortment and began to look around, leaving the ordering to Max. A heavily bearded man with nervous black eyes attracted her interest. She leaned toward Max.

"There. Could he be an assassin?"

Max looked across to the far table. "Probably not. He is a Russian grand duke. Still, you never know." At that moment the grand duke saw him and inclined his head graciously. Max returned the greeting.

"Do you know everyone in Europe?"

"Not everyone, but I certainly know that fellow." His gaze had wandered toward the Winter Garden entrance, where a tall red-haired man had just entered alone. Max waggled his fingers, attracting the man's attention in a way very unlike Max's usual manner; it was almost effusive. Letty followed Max's waving fingers to the man in the doorway.

It was Vincent Fairborne.

It was an ecstatic moment of recognition for Letty. It brought her back to the days of her girlhood when she saw him like that, and he glanced her way. He looked romantically melancholy now, as he had at Princess Matilde's house, but his expression brightened as his gaze went from Max to Letty. He bowed to Max with rigid good manners.

Max signaled again. After a furtive look around at the chattering diners Vincent nodded with a faint smile and moved between the tables toward them. Max pulled out a chair before the waiters could do so. Everyone shook hands, and at Max's invitation Vincent joined them for lunch.

Letty hadn't said a word. When Max poured the sparkling white wine he had ordered, Letty reached for her glass with a nervous hand and tasted it. She managed at last to say, "We want to thank you for handling our relationship so well at Princess Matilde's house." She caught a message in Max's eyes and added quickly, "Mr. Fairborne."

"I would never betray you. Or MacCroy," he added as an afterthought. "That was understood."

"Of course," Max said. "How did you happen to be invited to entertain the friends of the princess? It seems something of a coincidence, to say the least."

"I told O'Halloran I wanted to get away during the summer. My dear wife died very recently."

"My condolences. She was a lovely person." Max's eyes traveled to Letty, and then he added, "I believe I may add my wife's condolences as well."

Letty nodded. She said finally, with difficulty, "Annabeth was very good to me. Even when you first—when I first came into the company, she accepted me. I cried when Calla wrote to me. Didn't I, Max?"

"I believe you did. Fairborne, you were saying it was O'Halloran who signed you for this affair. Was this your first European performance?"

A thread of a frown crossed Vincent's face.

"My first but, I assure you, far from my last. I already have offers from several of Her Highness's guests who heard me at her home. And next month I go to London." He added, with a proud glance at Letty, "I am to make what one might call a miniature tour of the provinces. I am particularly pleased because they have asked me to read Shakespeare."

She knew what that meant to him, and she really did want him to be happy again. "Oh, Vincent, how wonderful! You always dreamed of that."

"*We* always dreamed of it," he corrected her and then expanded on this after some slight motion on Max's part. "The entire Fairborne Company, I mean."

"Naturally," Max said.

Letty hurried to fill the breach. "It was a coincidence, as Max says. I mean, your being asked to perform at that particular house. You don't think they could suspect anything about us? About Letty Fox?"

"They've said nothing. Her Highness, while a bit brusque, is a very learned woman. She had been extraordinarily kind."

"Beware of Greeks bearing gifts," Max murmured.

"I beg pardon?" Vincent then turned to Letty to repeat, "So far as I know, it was purely coincidental that a man in the service of the princess's brother spoke to O'Halloran. He had seen me with the company in Chicago, so they say."

"Plonplon. I don't like that." Letty remained suspicious.

"Plonplon? I know of no Plonplon. Is it someone's name?"

"A nickname for the brother of Princess Matilde," Max explained and then, to their surprise, stood up as a man in a high-buttoned black surcoat came toward them. "This is an agent of mine. Forgive me . . . some business to settle. I'll be back before the cheese, I promise."

He bowed and went to join the stern-faced young man in the tight coat. As they left the room together, the interested gaze of several diners followed them.

Vincent too watched them leave before taking Letty's clenched fingers and pressing them. The warm light in his eyes was so familiar.

"How beautiful you look! I've never seen you so vibrant, so alive." He gave her a smile that was almost flirtatious, and he was not a flirtatious man. "Would it be too much for me to hope my presence in Paris gives you that glow?"

She was embarrassed by his false reading of her mood. The glow had been engendered by the praise of Max and the emperor over a job well done—by her pride of being something other than the naked Empress of Impressionists. Letty Fox had been forgotten until Vincent entered the room.

"We thought you read Poe splendidly. I was very proud of you."

"Were you, my darling girl?"

"I'm quite grown now."

He looked crestfallen. "Yes, you are, aren't you? I forget. For me you will always be that enchanting little creature I found in Virginia City. I'll never forget that night, the cold, crisp, clean air, the smoking lamplights. I confess I worried some about the money too, but I knew I had made the right choice."

"The right purchase?" she asked lightly. She didn't want to think about that night.

He was shocked. "Never. What a cad I'd be to remind you of that! Besides, your performances have paid the six hundred back handsomely." He hesitated, looked down at her hand where it rested on the table, and sighed, "And I truly did love Annabeth—"

"I know. Everyone loved her."

"But it is not the feeling I have for you, Letty. It never was." He looked into her eyes. "I know there must be what they call a decent interval, but can you give me some hope?"

She studied his features. This was the kind, gentle man who had rescued her from disgrace. She had owed so much to him.

"Vincent, I am Max's wife. We settled that in San Francisco."

"Yes, but surely it was only to help your career. We all thought that." His hand trailed away from hers and moved aimlessly across the table. She knew she had hurt him and couldn't bear that.

She said gently, "Vincent, I loved you when I married Max. He knew that. I used to pretend—never mind. But we can't just discard our lives today and return to the past. You said it wouldn't be fair to Annabeth. Now, I am bound in honor and affection to Max."

"I'm sure the man would understand. He knows why you married him. He can't be fool enough to imagine you love him."

She said nothing—any reply she made would be misunderstood.

He looked around helplessly, and returned to the central issue. "But we love each other. My God, Letty, it isn't fair! We had so many dreams, so many plans."

"We didn't want Annabeth dead, did we? And we don't want Max dead."

"No. But a divorce is possible. You weren't married in the Catholic Church, were you?"

She didn't know what to do or say. The turmoil had begun with Calla's letter. "Whatever we do, we must wait a year. By that time you may feel differently."

"A year to divorce him?"

"No. Out of respect to your wife."

He groaned. "I'm sorry. I forgot Annabeth for a minute. Of course. But you do love me?"

She touched his cheek gently. "I'll always love you, Vincent, in so many ways."

He settled back, relieved. "I can wait. My career is looking up, especially here in Europe. You'll be proud of me yet."

"I'm proud of you now." She spied Max returning to the table. Events had taken a turn that she found much too confusing.

Max greeted them in a most jovial way.

"Well, business is over. I spread the word, by the way, that we had met you first at Princess Matilde's house and were congratulating you at lunch." He looked from one to the other of them. "Have you finished reminiscing about the good old days?"

"All finished," Vincent agreed, "for now."

CHAPTER *Ten*

*A*N *AIDE* lit another of Louis Napoleon's endless chain of cigarettes while the emperor looked around the arm of his opera chair to speak with Max.

"Incredible how much the soprano puts me in mind of my Cousin Matilde."

Max wisely said nothing to that. He was courtier enough to know that one did not insult the sovereign's family, even to be agreeable to its detractors. Letty stifled a quick smile, following her husband's lead, but it was the first time since Princess Matilde's dinner party that she had felt like laughing spontaneously.

The two days since the luncheon at the Grand Hotel had been nerve-wracking. There was no logical excuse for Vincent to visit her, and she often thought Max was behaving in a very cat-and-mouse fashion, which didn't help.

The invitation to the opera had been the idea of Eugenie and Louis Napoleon as a reward to Madame MacCroy for her defense of Eugenie at Princess Matilde's house. The news of Letty's meeting with the Prussian baron had reached the empress at St. Cloud, and she had hurried back to Paris to say severely that the masquerade had gone far enough. But she had added to Max, "You must tell your charming wife how very much we appreciate her tussle with that woman Matilde."

Unfortunately, when the party had entered the imperial opera box, the first person Letty noticed was Vincent Fairborne sitting in the orchestra below. He stared up at the imperial box so long Letty saw the empress sign to one of her ladies and ask, "Who is that Adonis in the pit there? The one with golden hair."

Her lady had no idea, and it was she who turned to ask Max, "Have you any idea?"

Max's answer was brisk. "A gentleman of the American theater. Vincent Fairborne."

"Yes," Eugenie agreed after a careful survey of the American through

221

her opera glasses, "one would say he is of the theater. However, even at St. Cloud and Compiègne we have theatricals." Letty heard her light, chuckling laugh. "The gentleman might teach us his craft. Do you agree, Louis?"

The emperor, who had no part in her amateur theatricals, nodded, but his thoughts were elsewhere. He was obviously in pain, though making every effort to hide it. It would be calamitous if the citizens suspected the truth, with the threat of war so close.

Meanwhile, there was Vincent to worry about. Would he think she was greedy enough to love Max for his borrowed grandeur? He knew nothing about the reality of her life with Max in the house on the Left Bank—the laughter, the teasing, the passion they shared.

Am I too cowardly to tell Vincent the truth? She almost repeated her question to Max, but at times like this she felt a barrier between them in spite of Max's easy, confident attitude.

Letty and Max had taken their places at the back of the imperial box, since they were the only untitled pair attending on Louis Napoleon and Eugenie. This arrangement proved impractical when the emperor kept turning to exchange remarks with Max and distracting the other occupants of the box. Finally the empress frowned at her husband and whispered something.

Letty was amused by this wifely behavior and the wry look the emperor gave her. She took care not to acknowledge his attention by more than a tiny smile.

A short time afterward Max pointed out to her a group of figures in the box next to the imperial pair.

"Plonplon and the Princess Matilde."

She leaned far forward, over a row of ladies-in-waiting and a handsome Cent-Guard. She recognized Prince Napoleon's heavy, dark face, though it looked less gloomy tonight. Maybe he enjoyed opera. The heavyset princess wore a diamond tiara far more impressive than the empress's small, dainty tiara of diamonds and sapphires, but the result was not nearly so happy. Princess Matilde's dignity couldn't ever overcome her plain, almost dumpy look.

Matilde smiled as her brother whispered to her; she then looked over at the oblivious Eugenie and laughed openly. She nodded to Plonplon and settled back with satisfaction to chat while the ladies and gentlemen who surrounded her listened eagerly.

"Those two seem awfully satisfied with themselves," Letty whispered to Max.

Max raised his eyebrows. He too was concerned.

Gradually, Letty became engrossed in the story onstage, all about an old man who sold his soul to the devil in exchange for youth and then ruined a virgin, killed her brother and finally went to hell. Vincent had told her a story like that by a German author, but it had never stirred and thrilled her like this *Faust,* which Max said was the most popular opera in Paris. It had been performed over and over since its premiere ten years before, but Letty wasn't even surprised when some inspired young members of the audience cheered the final rousing trio.

Letty was enthralled. The virgin rose to heaven. Faust was dragged off to the fiery nether regions by an attractive Mephistopheles, and, as Letty said to Max, "It had a happy ending, after all."

Max seemed a little startled.

"I don't recall hearing that view of it before. There may be something in what you say. Though I am surprised that you of all people should condemn a man who led a woman into temptation."

For an instant she wondered if he was talking about himself. Then a more sinister meaning occurred to her. Was it possible he referred to Vincent? The idea deeply wounded her, that anyone could think the finest man in her life was guilty of ruining her. *Could it be true? Haven't I had the same thoughts lately?*

She was still scowling when the emperor and Eugenie stood up while the orchestra played what had become the imperial anthem, "Partant pour la Syrie," the tune written long ago by the emperor's mother, Queen Hortense. The pleasant tune always surprised Letty who had grown up with the idea that the passionate and rousing "Marseillaise" was the anthem of France.

It had been a shock when Max told her, "Singing the 'Marseillaise' is against the law. When you hear the 'Marseillaise,' my love, the game will be up. Either we are at war or in revolution. The song arouses far too much passion."

The emperor and empress passed Letty, moving out into the promenade, which was shrouded in old, worn velvet. They were immediately surrounded by fawning admirers. Letty thought it was rather like the Fairborne Players on opening night.

"Your gown is exquisite, Madame MacCroy," the empress said as Letty curtsied. "It suits you."

Letty watched Max's reaction. His bow was polite and he seemed pleased at Eugenie's attention to his wife. If there was anything between them they never displayed it publicly.

Letty's attention was caught by the curious behavior of a heavily jeweled group of opera-goers clustered around one of the long mirrors. They kept looking at the emperor and Eugenie, then back to something that covered the mirror. Their glances were sly and their laughter, behind cupped hands, sounded malicious. If ever she had seen a conspiratorial group, it was this one.

"Who on earth are they?" she asked Max.

"Bourbon or Orléanist royalists from the Faubourg St. Germain. They will do anything to bring down the government, even join the Marxists, I suspect."

Meanwhile, Louis Napoleon and Eugenie had moved quietly but desively out from the center of the throng surrounding them and started walking along the foyer, followed by the crowd. Letty had never seen so many reflected sparks given off by the dazzling array of jewels in the shuffling crowd.

Suddenly, the last of the smirking royalist group were gone and the long mirror that had engrossed them was free for all to see.

Here before the aristocrats of Paris, before the emperor and Eugenie, was one of Vincent Fairborne's advertising posters, like the one Max MacCroy had seen and despised the day Letty had met him in faraway San Francisco. Now Max's hand gripped her arm hard enough to make her wince.

"Some friendly soul has sent it to Paris," he said. "I have a notion the recipients were Matilde and Plonplon. As I told you, they bide their time. And this was their time."

Letty thought she was going to be sick, but Max's fingers, pressing hard, reminded her that she was not alone.

It gradually dawned on Letty that no one was paying any attention to her. They didn't associate this genteel, respectably dressed brunette with the auburn-haired creature on the poster, whose face was that of Eugenie de Montijo.

Eugenie's face had drained of color and her eyes were closed. Several ladies, including the Austrian ambassador's wife, the Princess Metternich, supported her while the emperor signaled Max, who had started forward, to stop. With remarkable calm, the emperor said to an elaborately liveried palace usher, "It seems to be an advertisement for an impressionist performer. Read the words there. The fine print."

"Majesty, the language is not French."

"Very true." Louis Napoleon stepped forward, ignoring the empress's stifled plea.

"No, no. It is something foul."

He peered at the legend on the poster, the words running down beside the naked half of the body. He read aloud in the calmest of voices, "Letty Fox, Empress of Impressionists . . . An impressionist," he explained in French, "is one who imitates, exaggerates and often ridicules the exalted. The advertisement begs us to watch this woman assume the personalities of the queen of England, the empress of Rome, the tsarina of Russia, and —" He paused. "The empress of the French."

Letty raised her head. He had omitted the name of Carlotta, empress of Mexico. It must still be too sensitive a subject, an affair in which his own conscience was not entirely clear. As Max had reminded her, this kindly monarch could be a devious man. But she was grateful that he hadn't looked in her direction.

A murmur ran through the crowd. Louis Napoleon added, washing his hands of the whole affair, "To enjoy this—er—lady's performance, one must journey to the city of San Francisco, in California of the United States." With a gesture to the usher he added, "I think we may safely burn this ordure in the stove. We leave the punishment of the perpetrators to the police."

The usher bowed again, and with his two white-gloved hands clawed the offensive paper advertisement from the mirror while the crowd's chatter echoed through the long foyer.

Letty, though badly shaken, was impressed by the empress's efforts to pretend this ghastly business had been merely a joke in bad taste. Her Majesty said little herself, but she nodded and laughed lightly at a remark by the Princess Metternich.

Out on the street in the foggy night, Max warned Letty, "I must return to the Tuileries when I've seen you safely home. Then we must discuss what is to be done about those who are back of this."

"I'll never forget Plonplon's smug expression tonight and all that whispering between him and his precious sister."

They settled back in the carriage seat. Fedor, seeing that serious matters were afoot, said nothing and took up the reins for a fast gallop across town and across the river.

Max shared her suspicions. "But who sent them the picture?" he said. "Probably Rissoli himself. And they waited for an opportune moment. It couldn't have been more public."

"Contessa Servandoni was in San Francisco. She and Rissoli are the only ones who knew about Letty Fox."

"Rissoli might have had an employer. At all events, it wasn't Pauline.

It would be the one way to destroy herself with the emperor." He was maddeningly determined to see the contessa in the best light possible.

"Is there any way you can punish the Bonaparte pair?"

"God knows, I wish there were."

She said after a heavy silence, "Could Vincent have given the princess and Plonplon that poster?"

To her astonishment he hesitated. "Vincent's not the type. He strikes me as an honest fool. He might blurt out something accidentally, but this is malevolent. Vicious. Someone in the pay of Plonplon or his followers."

"Thank you, darling." Another fear came to her then. "That wonderful honesty of Vincent's could spell disaster for you. They will know everything about me."

"That, I don't doubt. Poor devil—he has no idea what he let himself in for when he was hired by Matilde."

She returned to the subject later, at home.

"It's strange that you should pity him. You always despised Vincent."

"Ah, but now I have something he wants and I know how he feels."

Letty bristled. "If you are talking about me, I wish you would stop referring to me as if I were a piece of property."

He pinched her under the ribs. "Never underestimate yourself, my love. Incidentally, my agents from Berlin brought me news as we were leaving."

"I didn't see them."

He laughed. "They wouldn't be very good at their job if you had. We had two men in Berlin, one of them stationed in Bismarck's chancellery. They suspect changes were made in the message from King William. The missive was supposed to be a peacemaker."

"Well, then?"

"I'm very much afraid, my love, that what King William thinks and says may be very different from what his chancellor carries out in secret. The telegram the emperor is to receive tomorrow will be belligerent."

He kissed her goodnight and left for the Tuileries. Once he had gone, her private demons returned. Telegrams and international intrigue had little place in her life. How could she possibly be affected by events in a country like Germany, which she knew nothing about, except that the chancellor of Prussia was what Max called "belligerent"?

There were more important matters. Had Vincent given the poster to Plonplon? Perhaps in exchange for this new career of his in Europe?

Though she was inclined to share Max's belief that Vincent was incapable of such an act.

At the same time it was Vincent who had authorized the painting on that poster in the first place. If he truly loved her how could he have exposed her like that for money? She remembered Max's several hints to that effect and knew at last that he was right. Vincent had "hired" her, just as Max did, but used her far more vulgarly, never thinking of how it dragged her down into the mire. It seemed so clear now; why had she been so blind to this before?

Why did Vincent do it? For money. He wanted to sell tickets to the Fairborne Company's performances.

I owed him so much. But that has long since been paid back. The public display of my body every night cancelled that debt ten times over.

CHAPTER *Eleven*

*T*HE PROBABLE war with Prussia might be dreaded by the emperor and of great concern to Max, but the excitement it aroused in the public served to divert nearly all attention from the obscene poster. The poster merited no more than a couple of inches buried on the inside pages of a few of the little newspapers spawned by the new liberalism.

> A practical joke played upon Her Majesty . . . A garish nude painting seemingly attached to the empress's well-known features . . . Their Majesties treat the matter as a vicious and obscene bit of humor perpetrated by the extreme Left. However, Republican sympathizers in the Chamber of Deputies express shock and outrage and vigorously deny all knowledge of the original "humorist." Monsieur Thiers, long a critic of Her Majesty's well-documented pro-Vatican sympathies, promised the "artist" a sound thrashing, a reaction in which other anti-imperialists in the chamber join.

Genevieve Claudel had delivered two of the newssheets to Letty with breakfast, and lingered uncharacteristically in the doorway as Letty read. Letty threw the papers aside. She sat down at the table by the window to drink her chocolate and eat her croissant. Over the rim of her cup she asked, "You don't like me, do you?"

"No, madame."

The directness of that answer shook her. "Why? What have I done to you?"

Claudel shrugged. "We want the best for Monsieur Max. Your sort is unworthy. You do not love him. We saw at once."

I wonder. Or have I loved him since he excited me so much in San Francisco? Why else am I jealous of the empress to whom he is so devoted?

"And if I assure you I do love him?" Clearly, the woman didn't believe her. Letty added, "Why don't you hate the empress? Surely she doesn't love him—yet he adores her."

"If you mean to say, madame, that Monsieur has any physical interest in the empress, that is an insult to a great man. Monsieur would not dream of an affair with the empress, or with anyone else. Fedor and I have seen. He is fool enough to love the one woman. Yourself." She stalked back to her own sitting room.

It was with great wonder that Letty received this news. Max had shown her the delights of love, but even more important, he had helped restore her self-respect in regard to her body and her abilities as an actress. It was strange that she had never seen the difference between the debt she owed Vincent and all that she owed to Max. One man had saved her body but sold it, in a sense, to the audiences of the Fairborne Company. The other man, whatever his original purpose, had respected her personal dignity and made her his wife and social equal.

The Contessa Servandoni found Letty picking roses in the courtyard behind the contessa's apartment and brought her news that she couldn't quite believe.

"*Chèrie,* I do not know how you do it, I swear."

"Nor do I. What are you talking about?"

The contessa held her hands out daintily to the fountain and let the water splash over her fingers.

"You are a nobody. It is true, you need not deny it."

"I don't, except to remind you that I am now also Madame Mac-Croy."

"Understood. And as simple madame, you are invited where even myself, a countess, an intimate of King Victor Emmanuel of Italy and the emperor of France, is not truly welcome."

"And where would that be?"

The contessa shook her fingers: bright droplets of water flew through the sunlit air. "The Tuileries Ball, of course."

Letty caught her breath.

The contessa grumbled on. "Louis—I mean His Majesty—says my presence would upset his wife. As if I would upset anyone."

"You upset me," Letty confessed, "when you had hysterics over Max on Dupont Street."

The contessa giggled. "Of course. As Max assured me, I succeeded. But what an absurdity! As if I would fall madly in love with a poor man." She leaned toward Letty. "He *is* poor, you know. The emperor pays him a salary but no more. It is as the great Napoleon said—'One gives money to a policeman. One gives medals and honors to other men.' Perhaps Louis Napoleon shares his uncle's prejudices."

Be that as it may, it did not influence Letty, who had *not* married Max for his money. She was about to leave the garden but remembered the disgusting business of last night.

"Someone put up a poster of me at the opera last night. Did you find it in San Francisco and sell it to Plonplon?"

The contessa started. "But why to Prince Plonplon?"

"So he might use it to humiliate the empress."

"Our sainted Eugenie?" Then she burst into laughter. "Mother of God! They thought one of your portraits was Eugenie?" The contessa fell back against the wall. "Oh, it is delicious. What a pity I was not there! It serves me very proper for not enjoying opera."

"I do not advise you to claim sympathy with the culprit, contessa. What with my husband's opinion and mine, not to mention that of His Majesty, I am afraid there might be suspicion directed against anyone like yourself who shows animosity toward the empress."

"But I know nothing. I would never dream—no. It is not my method. I swear."

An hour later as she was going to lunch at Le Petit Prince next door, Letty found the sidewalk congested by groups, chiefly youths, shouting, giggling and screaming.

"Down with Prussia!"

"Vive la France!"

"On to Berlin. To Berlin."

Other expressions, some obscene, fueled the idiotic war fever. The Tricolor could be seen everywhere, and it took her a few minutes to make out Vincent Fairborne's tall figure as he walked along the quai. He saw her and had just waved when he was surrounded by a half dozen students from the Sorbonne.

Crossing the cobblestone street, Letty tried to make her way to him. She saw that the students were having their patriotic fun at his expense.

"Repeat," they demanded. "Say *'Vive la France.'* "

Vincent was looking cross but he shouted, *"Vive la France!"*

They parted into two lines and he made his way out from their midst with an unexpected *"Vive l'Empereur!"*

Several students laughed, and two or three repeated his shout. As Vincent joined Letty, someone began to sing, and the others soon joined in. "Don't you like it? It's the old hymn of what they call their grand Revolution."

"I know. The 'Marseillaise.' It's against the law to sing it."

"I don't see why. I must say, it is stirring."

She listened to the students; Max was right. The song did something, even to her.

"It heats up the blood," she said lamely, and laughed. "Doesn't it remind you of what happened ten years ago in our own country?"

"If you mean the War between the States, Letty, I don't find your comment amusing."

"Why should it be amusing? War is not a play on the stage of the Lyric Theater."

She turned and started toward Le Petit Prince with Vincent beside her, complaining of her remote air.

"Darling, I never taught you such frivolous views on serious matters."

"No, indeed. When I saw that poster at the opera last night, I realized exactly what you *did* teach me."

He made an impatient gesture. "That was disgusting. I heard about it. That poster was never meant to be seen in Europe."

"Then how did it get here?"

"Letty, for God's sake! You don't think I am responsible for bringing that poster to Paris? Why would I do such a thing?"

"Why would you do it in San Francisco, or Sacramento, or Gold Run, or any other place?"

"That was different. It was the only way we could attract business."

"With my body."

"Letty!"

Before he could open the door of the restaurant for her, she lowered the brass latch and walked in. She greeted her café friends, the waiter and the chef, absentmindedly, and Vincent was barely in time to pull out the bench of the communal table for her. He settled himself beside her. The refrain of the "Marseillaise" reached them from the street, reminding Letty of the disaster that might be brewing this morning in the Berlin chancellery and the Chamber of Deputies in Paris.

They were both startled. Pauline Servandoni stood expectantly at the end of the long table in an unspoken plea to join them. Vincent hesitated. Letty saw that he recognized her from San Francisco, but politeness won and he stood up, speaking in English.

"Please join us, countess."

She gave him a tight smile and seated herself on his other side. "Monsieur Fairborne, I cannot begin to express my admiration for your work in the theater. I was saying to the Princess Matilde only an hour since.

The dear creature was wretchedly concerned over the war talk. What nonsense! As though there were nothing better to speak of." Vincent looked puzzled by her interest in him.

"I wish to heaven there were," Letty said.

"The Princess Matilde has been very kind to me," Vincent said. "And speaking of kindness, an hour ago I received an invitation to a ball at the Tuileries, from an equerry in the service of Her Majesty the empress. She heard of my reading at Princess Matilde's house, and wants me to give her and her ladies the benefit of my theatrical experience when they perform their little plays at St. Cloud and Compiègne."

Letty recalled the empress's interest in Vincent at the opera house. It hadn't taken her long to make a move! Whatever Eugenie's much discussed celibacy, she certainly was flirtatious.

Vincent acted a bit smug as he asked Pauline, "Do you know the Princess Matilde well?"

"She is an intellect. I am not." The contessa's smile spread. "But what is infinitely more important, here am I, with no gentleman to escort me to the Tuileries Ball." The contessa's full lips formed a pout. "But you, monsieur, you are invited. Am I fortunate enough to find you without a lady on your arm?"

He was flattered but he glanced at Letty. The contessa cut in. "Oh, no, monsieur. Not Madame MacCroy. She arrives with her husband; isn't it so, madame?"

Letty nodded. She didn't know whether she was more amused or annoyed by the contessa's manipulative tactics.

Vincent offered the contessa his hand. "Tell me, countess, why does it mean so much to you, one more party at the old palace?"

"But why not?" The contessa pointed to the door. "If the war comes, it may be my last chance to dance at the Tuileries."

"Rubbish!" Letty said. "This is far from the last time. The Tuileries isn't going to vanish in a puff of smoke, you know."

The confusion of shouting and singing had now grown so loud it interfered with their conversation. When the waiter brought their dishes of Provençal onion soup he remarked, "I feel lucky today. I have ten livres wagered on war. The Tricolor will fly over the Berlin chancellery by September, mark me."

Letty bent over the soup plate, studying her spoon intently; she did not want to hear any more of this talk. With a jolt she realized that the most important factor in her fear of war was her fear for the life of the man she had married.

Don't let anything happen to Max, she prayed silently, and paid little attention during the meal to the arrangements made between Vincent and the contessa about the Tuileries Ball.

Letty was relieved when the luncheon was over and she could say good-bye to Vincent. "Until tonight," he added, in what for anyone else would have been a slightly coy manner.

That evening as Letty and Max were being driven to the ball, she recounted Vincent's fast conquest by the contessa.

That made him laugh. "You are very cruel to your ex-tutor, my love."

"It took me a long time to see that the Letty Fox he created was a vulgar display."

"I see." He said no more on the subject but she thought his dark features lightened. He stirred and sat up. "Here we are."

"This is worse than a first night in the theater."

"You'll do, my dear. Just remember the glorious staircase, and those shining Cent-Guards you admire so much."

An endless succession of lackeys, ushers and an occasional footman waited to pass them on through the halls, to remove Letty's ermine-trimmed white velvet capelet and Max's plain but correct evening greatcoat. Shaking badly by this time from nerves, Letty kept telling herself that this was only a performance and she merely one of the performers. Max was all business. Without turning his head he noted everything as they started up what had to be the longest staircase in the world.

She saw that his searching eyes missed nothing—every guest who swept grandly up the stairs, the Cent-Gards who lined both sides of the long flight, their cuirasses polished mirror-bright and the plumes of their helmets neatly laid back.

Though all the guests bowed and smiled at Max, Letty noted that their smiles seemed uneasy and the men, in particular, were anxious to move out of Max's range.

"They are all afraid of you," she whispered, not able to decide whether this made her uncomfortable or proud.

"It is very likely," he agreed.

The chandeliers hanging from the great, vaulted ceiling were a disappointment: gas lights had recently been added to parts of the palace and she thought that what had been gained in illumination did not compensate for the loss in beauty. They were not as pretty as Princess Matilde's crystal lusters. Still, the marble pillars and the highly decorated ceiling vault were reminiscent of the great cathedrals—only lighter. The ball gowns she saw were breathtaking.

Since Letty did not own a tiara, Claudel had unexpectedly arranged a wreath of baby roses from the courtyard. Letty was touched and thanked her profusely, though her gratitude seemed to have no effect on the Frenchwoman. But Letty was assured that she looked more charming than the stoutly corseted aristocrats festooned with diamonds.

When she and Max had passed beyond the draped portieres and were received into the reception line, Letty became aware that she was trembling again. She took a long, deep breath and raised her head proudly. There was nothing to fear. The emperor certainly liked her. When she curtsied before him he lowered his hand to her and raised her up, smiling. She thought he looked ill—his skin dark, almost yellow, his heavy eyelids swollen. But beneath those eyelids his eyes were alert, watchful, surveying her the way Max had surveyed the guests on the staircase.

"Good evening, Madame MacCroy." He added so low, even Max scarcely heard it, "Through the front door at last. A visit long overdue."

"Your Majesty is too gracious."

"For all your charm and beauty, madame, I suspect you are still concerned over the stupidity at the opera. You need not be. At my order Max long ago arranged that Letty Fox should die. We are in possession of her death certificate and the grave permit—so do not fret and redden those pretty eyes."

She was so startled she couldn't think of a word to say, not even thank you.

Letty's reception by the empress was more formal. Like her husband, Eugenie looked worried, but at least she was strong and healthy. Her Majesty was gracious and did not allude to the poster—maybe she still didn't know. Then, as Letty curtsied and again backed away, the empress said something totally unexpected.

"I believe you have a friend here, madame."

Letty looked around, puzzled. The empress added, "He may oblige us by giving my ladies and myself some advice on our amateur theatricals."

"Vincent Fairborne." She moistened her dry lips. "We met—"

"—Recently, at the Princess Matilde's dinner, I understand."

Letty stared into Eugenie's eyes, wondering if she had guessed the truth about her identity. She couldn't tell.

Max joined her a minute later, and whispered, "Bravo! You are doing splendidly." He raised his voice. "If it isn't our new friend Fairborne and his delightful lady, the contessa."

"Go along, you tiresome creature." Pauline Servandoni was sharp and antagonistic.

"She is only joking, sir," Vincent said. "How are you this evening, Madame MacCroy?"

"Very well, thank you. Are you to read 'Annabel Lee' for us tonight?" A second later she wished she hadn't said it. As it was, several guests standing close by had overheard her and began to urge him. "Do, monsieur. Give us 'Annabel Lee.' "

He smiled modestly but shook his head and walked over to the great doors of the ballroom with his companion on his arm. Someone standing next to Letty complained, "Such a bore, these palace parties."

"And they give their souls to be invited," Letty muttered to Max.

"True. But the flotsam rises to the top in bad times. Boiling usually skims it off."

Letty laughed. "You should have been a chef, darling—or should I say executioner?"

Although the buffets with their artful display of delicacies looked tempting, Letty heard a lighthearted burst of music from the ballroom and was far more interested in that. The orchestra began one of the Viennese waltzes of Johann Strauss.

"Shall we dance?" she whispered to Max.

He glanced around, his thoughts occupied with the problems of his profession.

"One dance?" she pleaded. She noticed that he exchanged nods with two men who stood in the receiving line, neither of whom looked much like a detective. One of them was fiftyish and wearing immaculate breeches and stockings. Correct in every way, he might have been an ambassador, except that his breast lacked decorations. Maybe the contessa was right, Letty decided. The Bonapartes employed policemen—they did not admire them.

The other, younger man, wore formal black trousers and seemed more obviously a member of the prefecture. He remained to the left and behind the empress—a warning presence, so to speak, much more so than the Cent-Gards, who were little more than window dressing.

Evidently Max was satisfied. "One dance," he said and swept her over through the great doors to the ballroom.

A pompous, stiff-backed usher tried to bar their way with a white baton as Max led her out onto the floor in the middle of the dance. Max raised a gloved hand and calmly pushed aside the baton. The usher stepped back, stammering, "My apologies, monsieur. I did not recognize you."

Max nodded, slipped an arm around Letty's waist and sailed her into the kaleidoscope of dancers. She loved dancing and in the old days some of her happiest moments had been waltzing with Vincent, who was a superb dancer.

As for Max, it was several minutes before she even noticed his dancing. Being held so close in his arms, pressed against his body, loving him, she forgot to ask herself whether he danced well.

He certainly did.

Max's control of his body was superb, and when they swung past Vincent and the contessa Letty could only marvel that she felt so little now about a man with whom she had been obsessed for nine years.

Max saw the look on her face and remarked. "Poor Annabeth. Her bereaved husband seems to have recovered rapidly."

She said nothing, more than a bit amused by his jealousy over nothing.

Vincent and the contessa waltzed by again. The men acknowledged one another with nods, but Letty and the contessa were all smiles—the contessa's triumphant, Letty's one of pure happiness.

To Letty's disappointment, Max didn't seem enraptured with the moment.

"A franc for your thoughts, darling."

He laughed shortly. "They aren't worth a sou. I'm just wondering how the Chamber of Deputies will react to the German telegram."

"Business again." She tried to act amused, but felt resigned. It would always be this way with Max. No matter. After almost twenty-four years alone she felt she had finally come home.

Letty looked around, wondering if anyone here could be as happy as she was. A bearded man with an elegantly dressed lady who looked English or American dipped and swung past them a bit laboriously. The gentleman nodded and smiled. She knew the face but couldn't place it.

"A new conquest?" Max teased.

"Who is he?"

"One of your countrymen. A dentist the emperor has taken a fancy to. You should remember—you met him."

"Good lord! Dr. Evans." She had completely forgotten the man who smuggled her out of the palace the day the emperor had his painful seizure.

"He is very democratic," she remarked.

"Who? Dr. Evans?"

"No. The emperor. Dr. Evans, a dentist, and Letty Fox, an impressionist, both dancing at the Tuileries."

The orchestra spun into a rousing finish.

Just as Letty and Max were leaving the floor, a stocky, heavily decorated man with a fierce mustache threaded his way between the dancers and headed for Max. Letty groaned—she knew the signs. Whatever had happened was sure to be shattering to everyone in this room.

"Max!" the uniformed man called. "Come quickly. You may be needed."

Following the marshal, Max and Letty passed Vincent and the contessa, who looked consumed by curiosity. Their Majesties had retired to an imperial study at the end of the gallery, and several other men joined Max as he strode through the great halls of the palace.

CHAPTER *Twelve*

*C*OMING THROUGH a doorway near the emperor's study was the well-stuffed figure of General Hugo Darlincourt. As the little group summoned by the emperor passed him, Letty saw that no one paid any attention to the man except Max. He gave the English general a long look, smiled unpleasantly and said, "You will not find Prince Napoleon here. That was your goal, wasn't it? He went abroad a day or two ago. Shall I send him your regards?"

"I don't understand, Max. His Highness scarcely knows me."

"But you do know some of his agents, don't you?"

The general's fat features crumpled. "No. I swear it, Max. On my honor."

"I advise you to be gone from the palace in five minutes."

The general nodded, spun on his heels and trotted down the gallery toward the grand staircase.

Letty wondered if there really was a connection between Plonplon and Hugo Darlincourt. After all, it had been the general who helped Max subdue the murderous Rissoli on shipboard. Was that just subterfuge? Had Darlincourt known Rissoli before? Did all the ties indeed lead back to Plonplon?

When the group of men poured into the study Letty followed Max; he made no effort to stop her. Letty was surprised to see Princess Matilde on one side of the emperor. The woman looked serious, but more angry than afraid. The empress sat in a stiff, straight-backed chair on the other side of the emperor.

Physically, the emperor looked very ill, but his manner was more controlled than Eugenie's, who despite her surface calm looked concerned about her husband. His sad, tired smile seemed to play down the danger, though his incessant reaching for cigarettes belied this.

In an unexpectedly harsh voice the emperor said, "Messieurs, as you have probably guessed, the Chamber of Deputies will call for war."

Each man seemed to catch his breath at the same time; only Max remained impassive. Letty realized that for Max this came as no surprise.

The marshal of France snapped, "Good. It is better not to wait. We have known it would come. These Prussians must be taught that they cannot rule the entire continent. We have permitted them to go too far as it is."

"That is all very well," Princess Matilde said. To Letty's surprise, the men listened respectfully. "Providing, of course, that we win."

For once, Letty agreed with Matilde, but Eugenie spoke for the others present. Generations of Spanish pride sharpened her reply.

"Of a certainty, we will win. Because to do otherwise is unthinkable."

The emperor stared at his shortening cigarette and took another puff.

Only one man, the notoriously pacifist premier, Olivier, argued against. "A mobilization perhaps, sire, but not war."

Eugenie cried, "It has gone too far! There is no turning back." The men around her nodded vigorously, but Max remained detached from this rhetoric. The empress continued, "The spirit of Austerlitz will lead us to Berlin. We must not be shamed before the world."

"But this is not the First Empire, Your Majesty," the premier said.

And someone added in a low voice, "Nor have we the first Napoleon to lead us."

The emperor puffed even harder on his cigarette. "We will call for a general mobilization." He looked around, sighed and shrugged. "My cabinet must vote with the chamber. I am a constitutional monarch, after all."

"Louis," his wife urged.

Other voices joined her in support of the emperor, who reiterated, "The chamber and cabinet will proclaim war, if it is to be war."

It ended as Letty feared it would. Letty had no doubt the cabinet tomorrow would also yield to the indignant demands for war. The French honor had to be upheld at all costs.

Two by two, they filed out soon after, vigorous in their support of Louis. Letty and Max left the Tuileries amid a confusion of running servants and men in uniform.

"Well, it's awfully exciting," Letty said. "I'll admit that."

"The emperor will probably appoint Plonplon as regent while he is at the front."

She didn't like the sound of that. "Isn't it better if the empress is appointed regent?"

He shook his head. "If Eugenie is appointed, it will be much more difficult to keep the people under some kind of control."

Letty knew what that meant, since Max's chief duty was to protect the empress. *But,* she thought, *if Max is needed in Paris he will not be sent to the front.*

Despite the late night, Max was up before dawn and off to the Paris prefecture to plan strategy for the declaration of war to come later that day.

The news itself, when it swept over Paris, was no surprise. Since dawn the streets and bridges had been filled with screaming, singing students, and among them many veterans of the Crimea.

Letty, walking through the streets that afternoon, was moved by the sight of aging veterans, some in blue uniforms, some in green, and many in baggy red trousers. Their age pronounced them members of that sacred fraternity, the men who had followed the Little Corporal sixty years before.

A tragedienne from the Comédie-Française had been lifted to one wall of the Pont Neuf. Her black hair streaming about her, the woman cried in a voice that would do justice to Medea, "Down with the Prussians! On to Berlin! Frenchmen, join me now. The emperor has made it legal to sing our beloved anthem. Join me now, for France. . . . *Allons, enfants de la patrie . . .*"

Letty, who did not know the words of the "Marseillaise," hurried on across to the Right Bank, just missing being hit by an omnibus that swarmed with soldiers and several of what looked like female furies right off the friezes of the Arc de Triomphe. Probably goodhearted harlots from the boulevards.

The optimism was contagious, but Letty, thinking of the Civil War, was well aware that no matter how many victories were won by the imperial eagles, the losses would be appalling.

I mustn't think this way. Max needs someone cheerful around him. It must be dreadful with the city in such confusion.

Along the rue de Rivoli arcades the atmosphere was equally charged. Voices were louder, the spending greater, the euphoria palpable.

Letty could see the Tuileries beyond the Louvre and wondered what Max was doing. The plaza around the Arc du Carrousel swarmed with soldiers in uniform and companies of cavalry, brightly colored and plumed, curiously reminiscent of the American cavalry she had seen in 1861. She hoped these men would have better luck.

When Letty returned to the house on the Left Bank she found the shouting and crying so loud, the hubbub infiltrated the ancient walls. But hearing a cry more immediate, Letty opened the door to find Genevieve Claudel weeping hysterically, a tray of broken dishes on the floor, and big Fedor trying to restrain her. He was handicapped by a faded chasseur's uniform, with a jacket far too tight for him and baggy blue breeches that somehow made him look bigger than ever.

Evidently Fedor, caught up by the patriotic fervor, was about to enlist, and Claudel objected. Letty's sympathies, for once, were with Claudel.

"Fedor, how can you do this? How unpatriotic!"

Claudel looked more hopeful, though it was clear she didn't understand Letty's argument.

"Yes. Not patriotic," Claudel said. "Listen to Madame."

Assailed on both sides, Fedor stumbled back against the mantel.

"I do not understand. I go for patriotic reasons. What else can I do?"

"You can stay in Paris and help Max. He is going to need you desperately."

He groaned and waved away her arguments.

"Too late, madame. I am enlisted. Signed. It is all finished. I did not think, madame."

"You did not think of me," Claudel wailed. "It is the old story. I am nothing."

Unfortunately, there was no way out of this impasse. An hour later Max stopped by briefly to have dinner with Letty before starting for the imperial residence at St. Cloud. After the meal he took Fedor aside.

"Fedor, do you want to be rescued from the army?"

"The shame would kill me more fast than a Prussian saber, monsieur. I know you will need me, as Madame says, but"—he straightened to his impressive height—"France needs me more. For me it is 'On to Berlin.' I owe it to the country that took me to its bosom when my own country would have taken me to the hangman."

"You see, Letty?" Max said. "You would not wish to deprive Fedor of a trip to Berlin, and paid for by the emperor himself."

The issue resolved with a good deal of celebrating on Fedor's part, during which Max opened a bottle of brandy vouched for by the Bonapartes. Afterward, in a quiet moment, he admitted to Letty, "Old Fedor will not end as one more casualty in some German field . . . or in a French field, if it comes to that. I'll see to it. He can be a patriot behind the lines. He did his part in the Crimea and at Magenta."

Letty was happy for Fedor and his lady, though Max warned her not to tell Claudel. As it was, Letty found her spontaneous defense of Claudel's position had made a fast friend of that lady. At least, the housekeeper now treated her a good deal as she treated Max, with respect and a neutral friendliness. A curious woman, Claudel was cold to all the world, including Fedor, whom she ordered about most of the time. But apparently she really loved the rugged, good-humored Fedor.

The departure of the emperor, who had ridden out to take command of the armies on their march to the Rhine, where they would stand between the German states and France, had placed the city in a state of emergency.

In spite of Prince Plonplon's fury and resentment the emperor, bearing in mind Plonplon's haphazard and confused conduct in the Crimean War, had decided to appoint Eugenie as regent of France. Plonplon's fury was boundless. Letty, like many, had been shocked by the news, but she was impressed by the way the empress took command.

Upon receiving reports of a minor skirmish on French soil near Saarbrucken, the empress began to organize hospital rooms in the Tuileries, and Letty felt that at last she might begin to earn her salary by helping in the wards. It was something Sylvie Benoit would have approved.

Claudel arrived shortly after, in rigid control of her emotions. "Fedor is to leave this afternoon. He would like it if you came to bid him good-bye."

"I? But you want to be alone."

Claudel shrugged. "So I reminded him. But he says he wishes to go as a hero, and it will look well if two women surround him."

Letty stifled a laugh. "He will be safe. I know he will."

"How do you know?"

"Never mind. I just know."

Claudel said nothing more about it, but she went out of her way after that to be polite, even friendly, in her dealings with Letty. She and Letty had been assigned to set up cots, and Claudel began to complain about the condition of the sheets and pillows. The latter were not only in short supply, many were filled with straw.

"These sheets are from ten years ago, the war in defense of Italy against Austria," she grumbled. "And in those days they were also torn and patched and stained, and we said, 'These are from the Crimean War.'"

"Holes at the end of the sheet," Letty said, sticking her finger through one. "I hate them. I used to find my feet going through the sheets just like this. No matter how many times I patched them."

Both women were silenced by the approach of the empress in a black bombazine dress and a pinafore. It was hard to see in her the hostess of the Tuileries Ball, the dazzling Spaniard in white tulle and diamonds.

As they began to curtsy, Eugenie said abruptly, "They are bad, are they not? We must obtain decent bed clothing. Perhaps from the palace itself, if these barbarians refuse to requisition it for us."

"The blankets are better, ma'am," Letty assured her.

But the empress looked at her vacantly, as if her thoughts were hundreds of miles away on the frontier, where her sick husband and her fourteen-year-old son were trying to find their way through a situation for which one was too old and sick, the other too young.

"Good," she said at last. "We will need them. I must see about the medical supplies—they are late. And the rolls of cotton and linen. They should arrive any minute." She started away, then hesitated, motioned Letty nearer. "Monsieur Max refuses to let me show myself in the streets. How else are the people to see that I have not run away? They need to see me. Tell him, please."

"Yes, ma'am."

"Why won't Max let her appear in the streets?" Letty said to Claudel after the empress left. "It *might* be good for morale."

Claudel leaned toward her over the bed they were making. "They dare not let her be seen. She would be attacked by the radicals and anarchists and those who want a republic."

"But why? What has she done?" It was bewildering to Letty, who judged everything by the one war she had lived through. No one had tried to assault Mrs. Lincoln—or Mrs. Davis, the wife of the Confederate president.

"Why do you think the empress hurried into Paris from St. Cloud at midnight last week? She had heard something."

"A defeat?"

"The Prussians, with the other German regiments, are in France now. They began to cross French fields two days ago, so it is said."

"But the victory," Letty said. "There was one. Everybody was celebrating." It had been a very small affair, and Max wasn't impressed, but Letty had felt better. Now it seemed that Max had been right. So much for optimism.

"That was a week ago. This recent affair was a major defeat. And on

French soil. The greengrocer has a son who was stationed at the front, near Metz. He was wounded and he says our men have no mounts, no horses to ride. The horses are on loan to the peasants to use for the crop harvests, the autumn work."

"Good God!"

"And the maps. No maps of France. Only maps of Prussia and the neighboring states, he says."

Letty burst into ironic laughter. "It is our Civil War all over again. Surely all wars must be run by the same madmen."

But it lent credence to Max's concern. He had grumbled to Letty, "The emperor refused to listen to my reports. Marshals and generals, he took their complacent word. Not the evidence of my agents. Now the poor devil is paying for it." Small wonder that Max had forbidden Eugenie to go about the city freely.

Letty and Claudel were dismissed from work barely in time to accompany Fedor to the East Station. Letty had hoped Max would be able to take time off to give the big bear one last embrace at the train station, but as she followed Claudel past the imperial guards stationed rigidly in the galleries, she discovered Max was busy elsewhere.

It had been a shock to see these palace guards in battle dress, and she saw Claudel hesitate in front of her just as a door opened. A slim, tough-looking Frenchman called in the guard. The door remained open a foot or so.

Claudel gasped; she looked into the narrow, crowded room and put a finger to her lips. Meanwhile, Letty realized where she had seen the tough-looking Frenchman before—he was one of Max's men, the one she had seen at the Tuileries Ball who exchanged signals with Max.

She moved to Claudel's side and looked into the room. A youth, his head bowed between his legs, cowered on a stool surrounded on three sides by men in plainclothes. The youth kept shaking his head and muttering. But the only person in the room of interest to Letty was Max, who stood with his back to the door.

In a voice whose casual quality chilled Letty, Max said, "You came with those who delivered cotton and unguents. Your pass was forged. Where did you get it?"

The youth raised his head, spat at one of the plainclothesmen, and another cuffed him across the head. Max pursued the questioning.

"Once more. You confess to this attempt? The pistol was purchased by you?"

"I do not confess it. I boast it. I am given Divine guidance. My hand would not have failed." His voice was shrill and horrifyingly confident.

"You confess you would have murdered Her Majesty. For France, you say?"

"Not murder. And not for France. For the world. All who wear crowns will die. It is God's will."

Nervously, Claudel picked at Letty's sleeve and whispered, "It is better not to see this."

They moved back into the gallery just as Max raised his tired voice. "It is enough for now. Jordan, let him sign. And for God's sake, get him out of here. There may be others. The entire palace must be scoured."

Letty followed Claudel down the grand staircase, which looked cold and forbidding, tomblike, by day. A half dozen soldiers requested to see their passes before they made it out to the street.

Claudel was frantic. "Fedor will be gone. Do hurry."

She obeyed Claudel absently. Letty's thoughts were still with the veiled brutality of the youth's questioning. The emperor and French law both forbade torture. But another facet of Max had been evident in those few seconds, and the sight was upsetting. She wished she hadn't seen him at his work.

Crossing over the footbridge, they then elbowed their way along the quais past the Place St. Michel, which they found overrun with yelling, screaming and sometimes sobbing students. Were these the same who had shouted and sung only a fortnight ago?

"When the first little thing goes wrong," Letty said, "everybody immediately blames the man they cheered yesterday."

"Not precisely little things, madame, if the rumors are true." She began to run.

They reached Max's lodgings just as Fedor was bidding farewell to the contessa Servandoni. This scene aroused Claudel's ire, but she was soothed by Fedor's delight at seeing her. The contessa turned at once to Letty.

"*Chérie,* your friend, the glorious Vincent, wishes to see you. He has received a most lucrative offer from Great Britain. He is to give his so-splendid recitations in certain aristocratic houses."

Rather than jealousy, Letty felt a surprising derision for Vincent. She had known since Vincent arrived in Paris that the debt between them was paid. But for him to depart now, at this precise time, suggested to her a form of caution that was almost cowardly. It wasn't fair of her to think this way, but the idea pricked painfully now; it hurt to despise someone she had once loved.

"My best wishes to Mr. Fairborne. And his companion. I take it that you are also thinking of a channel voyage. So wise of the two of you to make the trip, now that there is a hint of danger."

The contessa shrugged. "My dear madame, this is not my country, and I am told I speak English exquisitely."

"How true! I see no reason to meet with Vincent, but I am happy for him."

Letty was relieved when Fedor called, "Madame, will you come?"

On a note of finality, Letty, in a cool voice, wished the contessa well, "and, of course, Monsieur Fairborne. I trust you will find pleasure, happiness and, above all, safety across the channel. Ah, Claudel . . . Fedor, shall we be on our way?"

A profound sadness over the breaking of her last ties with Vincent suddenly engulfed her. He was the man who had been tutor, father and lover to her and he now meant nothing. She would never have believed it possible.

Fedor was anxious that Letty see what Max had sent him. Letty was touched by Max's gesture—that he took the time out from his nerve-wracking responsibilities to remember his old friend. Fedor opened a flat, leather purse and extracted a piece of paper, which he read aloud.

> Should things go ill, use these. The gold is a talisman anywhere. The names are those of citizens who will help you both in the Western German states and in France, though it is unlikely that you will find yourself in the front lines. You and I have shared danger too long for *le bon Dieu* to separate us now. *Bonne chance,* old friend.

"Good old Monsieur Max." Fedor sniffed mightily. He then slipped the worn leather purse inside the breast of his jacket, shouldered his military pack, which was rolled into a heavy cylinder, and took the arms of his two ladies.

The approach to the Gare de l'Est became more and more difficult. The square in front of the station swarmed with recruits, relatives, military bands and brightly dressed females hoping to make an honest franc from the departing soldiers.

Fedor was late, and the two women rushed him through the massive echoing station and past the *fourgons,* the baggage cars now loaded with troops.

Letty said, "You two go on. I'll go out to one of those cafés across the square and drink to Fedor and the others. Look for me there, Claudel."

"Yes, madame."

Letty kissed Fedor's rough cheek, received a rib-crushing hug in return and went out, making her way among the endless files of uniformed men. Their high spirits were touching; were they the only people left in Paris who felt that there was hope ahead?

There was some singing and more than a little drunkenness, but she laughed with them, wished them well and let two of them grab her, swing her around and kiss her. Around her the usual incantations to victory rang out: "On to Berlin!" "Long live France," and "Long live the emperor!" But there were no cries of "Long live the empress!"

She suspected that the chauvinistic Parisians hadn't changed greatly since the terrorist days of '93. If one spark set the furies off, they would shout "Down with the Spaniard!" and worse. Her crime? She was not French.

It seemed that everyone confused Eugenie with Marie Antoinette in this crucial moment.

Letty hurried out of the deafening station.

Across the street there were two sidewalk cafés separated by a wood partition on which the chef had glued the day's menu, scrawled with a spattering pen. A soldier and his girl got up from their table; the girl lovingly hung his pack on his back and made the sign of the cross on his forehead. They started over to the station holding each other tightly. The girl was crying.

What would it be like if she had to come here with Max and watch him ride away in a crowded baggage van, or even a coach, to heaven knew what fate? Thank God Max was still safe in Paris!

The train must be ready to pull out. Everyone had deserted her side of the café and probably the other side as well. She ordered a demitasse of espresso and a slice of lemon tart sprinkled with sugar. If the war came closer such luxuries as sugar would be in short supply.

Nibbling at the pastry, Letty considered the passing of Vincent Fairborne from her life. In retrospect it seemed that she and Vincent had severed their ties that night at the Italian restaurant on San Francisco's Ocean Beach. If their relationship was "eternal," the great, all-consuming love she had thought it to be, Vincent would never have permitted her to go off with Max.

Although sometimes sickened by Max's dreadful profession, Letty was certain of her love for him and equally convinced of his love for her.

The sound of voices filtered through the wooden barrier; there *were* people in the adjoining café. She began to discern the topic of the conversation and realized the group thought they were entirely alone in the café. One voice was suddenly raised.

"But it is absurd, this talk of removal—by knife, gun, poison or otherwise. The Parisian mob is a far more likely weapon."

Some responded unintelligibly. Again the louder voice: "On the contrary. Control is more simple. The hopeful republicans will do our job. They are already gathering their followers for an onslaught, an outpouring of good citizens to mingle with the Paris mob. Every village, every hamlet in the France is being combed. I have seem them at work."

"Shouting for a republic." Another voice, laughing, female. "But the Spaniard is still in the way. A foreigner ruling France! And a woman, at that."

"True. She will fight. She is acting dictator at this minute—the ultimate danger. Everyone knows that Spain is in league with Prussia."

"If the Prussians—let us include the other German states—are on French soil, the empire is dead. When the Spaniard is removed, we step in."

Several voices began to wrangle over whether the invasion of France would help their cause or not. Letty looked around anxiously; it was vital that Max should know about the conspirators.

The argument across the partition continued. The woman urged, "Above all, the Spaniard must be eliminated."

Across the street Claudel came down the steps. Holding her trailing skirts, she raised her other hand, about to signal to Letty, who shook her head and pointed to the street beyond the cafés. Claudel understood at once, and after a single glance at the group beyond the partition swept across the street, skirting a horse that drew a closed carriage away from the station.

Letty met her on the corner behind a kiosk. "It is vital. You must bring Max and some of his men. These fools are planning treason in broad daylight."

"Half of Paris is plotting treason, madame," Claudel said in disgust.

"They are discussing the best way of eliminating the empress. Tell him so. In the Café de la Gare."

"Very well. I will go. I will say it is life or death."

"Hail a *fiacre*. Pay anything, but hurry. And tell him to take care when he comes. They may be dangerous, even here."

She nodded. "I will say it is not your imagination, madame. Leave it to me."

Claudel, who rarely hurried, rushed over to the opposite corner and hailed a big, lumbering wagon.

Meanwhile, there was nothing to do but wait. If Claudel brought help, someone must remain here to point out the direction the conspirators took. Letty thought of returning to the café, but was afraid Max might walk up to her there and thus alert the conspirators. Letty looked around. Two young women turned the corner and stood there beside her, gossiping about the purchases they had made at the splendid Galeries Lafayette. This might be the safest place to wait. A crowd would eventually gather to wait for the next omnibus.

Letty began to grow restless, but continued to watch the café. Suddenly one of the men got up, stretched, and looked around. He glanced her way, but she was a half block from him and it was unlikely he associated her with any danger. A short man, he was well dressed, not at all what she imagined a traitor to look like. A woman arose, smoothed the man's collar and made a fuss over the back of his neck. She looked young enough to be a student; probably was. Her hair was close-cropped, mannish, but her manner was flirtatious.

A big man came next, and Letty ducked behind the kiosk. She could not mistake General Hugo Darlincourt.

CHAPTER *Thirteen*

*D*ARLINCOURT STRETCHED out his arms above his head, said something to the young woman, and another man, nondescript, waved a hand. Everyone began to argue once more. Letty watched them from behind the poster-covered kiosk.

Another omnibus approached, drawn by horses that were as fractious as the people pushing their way into the vehicle. Letty tried to remain undercover, but it was inevitable that General Darlincourt should look over toward the busy kiosk.

The conspirators embraced each other and began to stroll east, away from the station. Letty surmised they would separate soon, and there was a distinct possibility of their vanishing in the warren of little medieval streets beyond.

Letty plunged across the street between an omnibus and a tumbrel of vegetables, and as cautiously as possible moved toward the two cafés, which were beginning to fill up. She sauntered along, grateful for the dark homespun gown and jacket she had worn to the Tuileries that morning. Her bonnet shielded her face as she mingled with the hurrying crowds around her.

Ahead of her the conspirators dissolved into the crowd. Passing the second café, Letty was trying to pick up the group again when a hand grasped her arm at the elbow and yanked her around. She half expected to see Max, but the well-dressed, sloe-eyed young man was quite definitely not her husband.

She swallowed hard and tried to assume a look of hauteur, but he ordered, in thickly accented French, "You will walk with me, signora. Do not turn the head."

"How dare you!" she cried in English. "Are you a thief? Do you want my purse?"

He stopped, bringing her to an abrupt halt as well.

"You were following me," he said. "I saw you a few minutes ago. Now you are still here."

"Who is following whom? I am an American tourist. I have a perfect right to walk over and see the St. Martin Canal if I wish." Several passersby heard her shrill protests and grinned, but made no effort to interfere. Very much like citizens the world over, she thought in angry desperation.

The man hustled her along, evidently unsure of what to do next, but determined not to let her go. As he half-dragged her, she spied General Darlincourt and another man going into an upholsterer's shop across the street and a block away. Where was the woman?

A well-dressed gentleman of fifty or so came toward them, strolling along, looking into the shops. It was not until he was almost in front of them that Letty recognized him as one of Max's agents.

Ogling a pretty Parisienne, the man stumbled over a broken cobblestone in front of Letty's captor, bringing them to an abrupt halt.

"Je m'excuse, monsieur," he apologized in the face of her captor's cursing.

The agent had barely risen from the sidewalk when two arms circled the conspirator's throat and shoulders from behind. The agent made a grab for the conspirator's pistol, which clattered to the street.

Letty was elbowed out of the way in the ensuing scuffle, and Max, who had the fellow in a stranglehold, ordered his agent, "See if there are others."

"There are," Letty said breathlessly. "In that three-story house with the mansard roof. The upholsterer's shop."

Several interested bystanders had gathered around them, but by this time the conspirator stopped struggling and Max turned him over to the agent. With her back to the crowd Letty pointed out the house in the next block and then, to her astonishment, was shoved roughly against an equally surprised plasterer whose powdery white hands caught and held her.

Letty's heart stopped as she caught sight of the long-bladed dagger Max was twisting from the grasp of a young woman. The dark, goodlooking woman of the conspiratorial band. Max was using only one hand.

"She got him. Look. The blood."

It was true. A wet stain was already seeping through Max's coat sleeve, close to the shoulder. He didn't seem aware of it. "Is this one of them?" he asked.

She nodded. "Oh, Max, are you—?" She broke off, noting that people were listening, and tried to compose herself. "Monsieur, she is the one. I saw her with the other four. I heard what she said. She left with the others, and when I passed the café a minute later it was empty."

Max was all business. Not unexpectedly, he looked a trifle pale, and she knew he must be in pain. She was frantic to know how seriously he had been hurt by that dagger meant for her.

"Very good, madame. You will accompany us, if you please."

An police officer in uniform thrust his way through the crowd and collared the female. He followed Max's agent and the foreign prisoner up the street and around the corner. Another agent remained, at Max's order. Letty lowered her voice and said, "We should have a doctor. It might be serious."

Max ignored her. He motioned the other agent to him. "Clear the street. Get rid of this crowd." He turned at last to Letty. "The upholsterer's house?"

Until he had all the conspirators there was no use in asking him to be sensible. The bystanders scattered, with several looking back over their shoulders, perennially curious. The agent returned while Letty was pointing out the house in the next block.

"One of them was your friend, General Darlincourt."

Max raised his eyebrows but said nothing. Surely, Letty thought, he must be remembering the murderer Rissoli and how Rissoli died the instant he was in the general's hands. Perhaps the general hadn't wanted anyone to hear Rissoli's confession.

"Daubigny's reinforcements should be here any minute," Max said. "Meanwhile, I am confident my wife will do us a patriotic service. I'd like her to wait up there at the corner and tell my men where we have gone. And that is *all* you do, young lady."

This heroism was maddening to Letty, who at this point cared a great deal more about Max's injury than about hunting down the conspirators.

"I'll do it gladly. But Max, at least let someone else capture the general and the others, whoever they are. You need someone to attend that wound."

"You realize, Max, there are probably more in the house than the two that madame saw," the agent said.

Max shrugged his left shoulder, frowned, and said to Letty, "Soon. Don't worry. But we can't let them get away when they are so near. There is something pernicious spreading through the city, and these bastards are at the bottom of it. The people want someone to blame for our lack of preparedness at the front, and unfortunately they have chosen the empress as their scapegoat."

Having heard the conspirators today, Letty felt Max was right in his analysis of the situation. She could only pray that he knew his limitations.

The agent vouched for the baker in the shop on the corner, and Letty was strategically posted to wait for Max's men. While Letty and the agent watched the street, the baker's wife made a pad out of clean cloth used to lift the big trays out of the ovens. She bound this around Max's upper arm at the shoulder. The cloth immediately began to stain, a sight that the men assured Letty was a good sign.

"Best thing in the world for a wound," the baker said. "Drains all the poison out."

Letty found this hard to believe but she simply followed everyone's advice and relaxed. When Max and the agent left, she stood in the doorway, wondering if the minutes had ever passed so slowly.

Less than ten minutes later the gentlemanly agent, Daubigny, came around the corner, having removed his frock coat to reveal an old, faded blue smock like that of a hundred other men in the district. It looked as though it had been dipped in a flour sack. Daubigny saw her in the doorway at once.

"Are you alone?" she asked him anxiously. "They may need more men."

"Across the street, madame. The fellow with the straw broom and the drunken old vagabond. Our Monsieur Max, has he attacked the house?"

"The upholsterer's. Max went around to the back. The policeman entered the front of the shop."

Daubigny was gone at once.

Letty and the baker and his wife, plus an elderly male customer all watched the street. A boy rushed by some minutes later and shouted, "I heard 'em shoot. They're shooting each other."

Letty had heard nothing from this distance and could only pray that Max was not in the line of fire. Her relief was enormous when she saw him and several uniformed policemen come around from the rear of the upholsterer's shop with two men in their custody. A couple of plainclothes agents walked out the front door with another prisoner; one of the agents was limping. Two closed carriages approached and the manacled prisoners were loaded in.

After a seeming eternity Max returned to her, looking very much his tough, lean self. The capture had done wonders for his health. He put his good arm around her, winced when she hugged him with thoughtless affection, and kissed her lightly to stop her endless questions.

"All right. I agree. Someone signal a *fiacre* or a horse and buggy. Anything."

In the *fiacre* he was more serious. "Hugo Darlincourt wasn't there."

"But I know I saw him. I couldn't be mistaken about that mountain of flesh."

"I don't doubt it. No. He must have gone through the house and right out the back of the cellar. The men are looking for him now. It's clear that Rissoli was his man, and when Rissoli was in danger of talking, Hugo strangled him right in front of us. Rissoli had told Hugo of your resemblance. We've always suspected Rissoli informed someone."

"I thought all along it was the contessa."

"It didn't really matter. Your job was to confuse Plonplon and his friends about the presence of Eugenie. You succeeded to some extent, even if Plonplon was aware of your resemblance. You made a fool out of the radical editor, Rochefort, with the scene between you and the Prussian emissary. They didn't dare plant evidence of treason against Eugenie when there was a possibility you would be their victim. It could too easily be exposed for what it was. Yes, my darling, our scheme was a success."

She felt a certain pride in her part, even if it had been somewhat abortive. Maybe there would be moments in the future when she could truly help Max.

He laughed as he thought about Darlincourt. "Those who want to bring down the empire certainly did not need a second Eugenie. My mistake was in thinking Hugo, and especially Rissoli, might simply be tools of Plonplon. But our Prince Napoleon would never try to bring down the empire itself—he would be reduced to nothing without his cousin on the throne. These fellows and their charming female accomplice are interested in different stakes, some sort of Red dictatorship. An anarchist commune, perhaps."

"But I can still be of help. I feel as if I know His Majesty now. And the empress. And I do want to show you how useful I can be."

He took her hand in the fingers of his right hand. "But we won't have any more of that. Not after today. You are going to be under guard at all times."

It was frustrating to hear him talk of her safety when he did so little about his own. She tried to call his attention to the badly soaked pad at his shoulder but this only increased his impatience.

"Never mind it. It has stopped bleeding. I'll have the wound treated when we reach the Tuileries, but first I make my report to Her Majesty."

She sighed and gave up.

Several aristocratic ladies were on duty in the hospital ward, and they all fluttered around Max. He ignored them as he had ignored Letty's helpful arm. He stalked past the ward, looking for the empress, after ordering a jolly, red-cheeked man to keep an eye on Letty.

The conversation among the conspirators was transcribed by a young man who took down scrupulously every word Letty could recall. She felt rather proud of herself until she realized that her contribution was small and merely fitted into the general pattern of usefulness.

Once she reached home she had to find the agent a place to sleep. Claudel, who approved of the presence of this innocent-looking guard, suggested the flat just below the MacCroy apartments.

"Old Madame la Marquise will not return while the war goes on. She visits her daughter and her daughters husband in Brussels."

During the following days Letty learned that stab wounds were considered no more than minor inconveniences to Max and his men. Max went about with his left arm in a sling for several days, looking rather dashing.

"Suppose the dagger had been poisoned," she suggested once, but he just laughed and said, "Only half of me would have gone. I am right-handed." He refused to discuss it further.

Letty's guard informed her that the captured conspirators had confirmed, more or less, everything she had overheard. How and by what means they confessed, she did not ask. They all agreed that their ringleader was General Hugo Darlincourt, whose escape they resented. "Typical English trick," they had agreed, and evidently Max had used that sentiment as a wedge to get their confessions. The knowledge that the fat general was somewhere undercover, perhaps waiting for the opportunity to strike again with a more successful tool than Rissoli, was unsettling.

The worst news from the front—and Letty heard very little good news—seemed less nerve-wracking than the uncertainty in Paris. Rumors were everywhere.... The Spaniard had sold out the army.... She wanted the Prussians to win because her grandmother was a Scot. The Scots were British, and everyone knew the British sympathized with the

Prussians. After all, Queen Victoria's daughter was the crown princess of Prussia.

Another rumor had it that Eugenie was so violently religious she wanted to bring the pope to Paris. Every move she made originated with His Holiness. (This rumor proved more salable to the public.)

The wounded began to arrive from battle, details of which were unknown to most citizens. The first casualties—the "heroes," over whom a fuss was made—were brought in by train. Later, in steady streams, came the tumbrils, wagons and carriages—and the bodies.

It was during one of these exhausting, discouraging days that Vincent paid his final call on Letty. He had followed her to Max's house and caught her on the stairs after an argument with her red-cheeked guardian.

Vincent looked astonishingly like the man who had rescued the young Letty in Virginia City ten years ago. So handsome, so noble, a shining knight. No blood, no dirt, no cow dung or filth on this courtier. He was vastly different from the men she had been attending in the makeshift hospital ward at the Tuileries.

"You look just like a hero in a novel," she said, too tired to wipe the sweat off her face.

He was pleased but he brushed this aside to comment on her own looks, which obviously shocked him.

He took her by the shoulders, pulling her resistant body to his. "My poor child, what has he done to you? You look so thin, so ill."

"I've never felt stronger. And my husband is not responsible for my looks, Vincent. Maybe the king of Prussia. Or the emperor of France." She pushed against his chest and freed herself. "Or you. When you traded me for a job in Chicago."

"Letty!"

That had hit home. Letty had so many more immediate worries that she no longer cared how he felt, but he did deserve an honest explanation.

"We aren't the people we were when we left San Francisco. You are a stranger here, a successful and admired actor. England is going to love you." He started to speak but she put her hand over his mouth.

"No, Vincent. I am different. As long as Max remains, these are my people. As they were my mother's people. And my father, whoever he may have been, gave his life to the Bonaparte cause. You might say it's in my blood."

He made a cutting motion. "Eugenie is through. This playactor who calls himself an emperor—they say his armies are surrounded. He may surrender any day. Then what becomes of you? I can't leave you here alone."

"Alone?"

"Vulnerable to attack by invasion armies or these crazy Frenchmen."

She started up the stairs, but her conscience troubled her and she turned back, holding out her hand.

"Dear Vincent, we had some wonderful years together. I owed you and Annabeth so much."

"My dearest." He took a step, gently framed her head between his hands and pressed his lips on hers, holding her there. Letty recalled the countless times she had prayed he would hold her like this, in gentle command, confessing his love for her. She tried to respond, willed her body to respond, but she felt only a terrible sadness for what was gone. Her youth. Her idolatry. She found herself ready to cry and knew he would misunderstand, thinking she still loved him.

"No. It's over. You do see that, don't you, my dear?"

He stood there without words, staring up at her. Then he blinked, turned away, walked down the stairs and out of her life.

Letty climbed the last flight of stairs and went into Max's apartment. Five minutes later she was sound asleep in a chair.

Later in the day a boy arrived with an urgent message from the Sisters of Charity.

"They need you, madame. New wounded expected by nightfall. Monsieur Max, he's sent an *agent de police* to walk back with us."

She returned with him, aware, however, that today she had said goodbye to a large part of her girlhood—the naive, dreaming child.

Working in the wards beside the empress every day, and occasionally witness to her autocratic handling of various advisers, cabinet members and the Chamber of Deputies, Letty knew that the rumors about Eugenie were lies. Her Majesty's real fault, and a disastrous one, was her manner toward the men who surrounded her. They were not used to taking their orders from a female, and a foreigner at that. But Eugenie made no allowances for wounded self-esteem or ancient prejudice.

"My husband has just sent General Trochu to assist me. Very well, messieurs. This does not mean that he should be placed in command of Paris. I am still the regent of France. General Trochu is a loyal soldier and will take his orders from me."

Letty and a dozen others overheard this discussion in the halls of the makeshift hospital, the only place where Eugenie could be caught briefly during her swift-moving supervision of the wounded.

Letty knew nothing about French generals. But she was a bit shaken by the fact that Max and the empress had an argument shortly afterward on the subject of Eugenie's safety. Max insisted, "It is all arranged. You have only to give the word. A carriage and horses will take you to Bordeaux. Set up the government in the west where you can trust their loyalty. I have taken the preliminary steps. Your government will go on, but from a safe distance away from Paris. Trochu will take care of Paris. You cannot depend on the Parisians. They are too volatile, too easily aroused to extremes."

When she refused, he added, "Then go to the north, closer to the channel and safety, if it is needed. Once you leave Paris and head for the coast you will be safe."

"You are offensive, Max. You imply that my own people, these citizens of Paris, are my enemies. They show me every respect. They salute, they bow every time I pass a window. I am still their empress."

"They bowed to Marie Antoinette only hours before the National Guard went over to the mob. You cannot count on the National Guard either. They have short enlistments and they are not soldiers trained in the field. They haven't seen combat. They will either turn traitor or run."

"I cannot reorganize the National Guard at this date."

"You must recall army troops for the protection of the palace, the government. And yourself."

"I am ashamed of you, Max. Recall men who are fighting for France, in order to protect one woman?"

"To protect the empress of the French."

She waved him aside. To Letty she had never looked more like the imperious Spaniard so much disliked by the common people of Paris.

"That is the most contemptible reason of all. In any case, they will not hurt me. I represent the empire, and France."

"Another queen thought that, madame."

Letty saw Eugenie shiver and remembered that time weeks ago when Eugenie spoke of her haunting fear that she would walk the same path as Marie Antoinette. But the reminder only made her more angry.

"My husband left me in command as trustee of the empire. I will not fail him. Make what preparations you like, Max, but not for me."

Their argument ended with a sharp wave of dismissal.

Max said nothing of his plans to Letty, but a few days later she came upon him in the courtyard below the gallery that connected the Louvre and the Tuileries. He had just given orders to an old man who was hauling away furniture that had been badly damaged by a long-ago fire in that wing. It must have been in storage for years; it looked worthless.

The trashman kept scratching first his tobacco-stained beard, then his baggy breeches. When he saw Letty he saluted her in a flip way, adjusting his stiff-billed red cap, and took up the reins.

Letty watched the wagon rumble away and was surprised when Max said, "Look! Across the Seine. Toward the Palais-Bourbon." He swung her around.

She looked, startled by his tone.

"I don't see anything."

They must have stood there a full minute before Max relaxed and Letty demanded to know what he meant by his behavior.

"Because, my love, I didn't want you calling attention to the old man and his tumbrel."

"Of burned-up furniture?"

He said nothing. She looked around and then behind her at the great gray walls of the Louvre. The truth struck her with the force of a fist in the stomach. That old wooden tumbrel had carried more than furniture. Priceless Louvre treasures. They began to walk along the quai.

"Are things that bad?" she asked.

"Eugenie has ordered the crown jewels placed in safety. More Louvre treasures will follow. She gave her personal jewelry to the Austrian ambassador's wife, Princess Metternich, today, wrapped in yesterday's edition of the *Moniteur*."

Not wanting to ask the obvious, "Have we lost the war? Are we about to be invaded?" she said instead, "Should we all learn German?"

He gave a short, angry laugh. "It's not the Prussians we have to fear."

When they returned to the Tuileries they found the empress moving through the hospital wards in her graceful, disciplined way. She wore a nun's habit and its severity emphasized her drawn, almost haggard look.

"Strange, madame," a bearded man murmured in English to Letty as he passed her in the ward, "These days you look more like Her Majesty than she does."

Letty was puzzled and then recognized the strong American accent. Dr. Evans, the dentist friend of the emperor. She admired his loyalty—it was in short supply these days. And he was right about Eugenie, who seemed never to sleep.

The fortification of Paris began under the empress's order. To Letty and the rest of Paris it was a frightening sign that invasion and siege were expected. Letty saw the rebuilding of walls and the reinforcing of the great Paris barriers by which sellers of produce and taxable goods came and went, along with millions of tourists in good times. All this activity pointed to a fear that the enemy might soon be within range to pound Paris with the huge and terrifying Krupp gun that Chancellor Bismarck had been so proud to exhibit at the Paris Exposition of 1867.

Letty had gone home to wash and change, one September day, after twelve hours at the charity hospital, when she heard a sound like the rumble of distant thunder. She looked out over the quai. The autumn air was humid and gray but there seemed to be no storm in sight. Still, the thunderous roar grew louder.

Then she saw the crowd pouring onto the quai. Parisians of every class and race headed along the quai toward the Palais-Bourbon, the meeting place of the Chamber of Deputies.

Letty remembered that the conspirators at the café had spoken of mobs "persuading" the deputies. Of what? The fall of the empire, obviously. And the conspirators could manipulate this mob. Passion had less to do with their noisy shouts and gunshots than simple politics: they were being used, and from their numbers, it might be too late to stop them.

By the time Letty reached the Tuileries that evening the crowds around the Palais-Bourbon were chanting in an obvious effort to intimidate the deputies, "Down with the empire!" "Down with the empress!" and more and more frequently, "Death to the Spaniard!"

Letty reached the Louvre where she was relieved to find that the guards had prevented any gatherings. Letty had no idea what most of these people stood for. Her prejudices came from books, mostly fiction, and her ignorance made her emotions much simpler.

As she entered one of the great galleries of the Tuileries, she met Claudel, who pushed her into a niche behind one of the marble pillars.

"Madame, he is safe."

It was the only good news Letty had heard all day.

"Fedor? Thank God! How do you know?"

"We invented a code. One of Monsieur Max's agents got it through. Fedor was one of the men chosen to smuggle the little prince imperial through the German lines into Belgium. Fedor is in Belgium now."

Then it must be nearly over. The suffering and the useless slaughter. The pointless, silly war.

"Have we surrendered?"

"Hush." Claudel looked around nervously. "The way to Paris is open to the enemy."

Letty closed her eyes. The worst days were still ahead.

CHAPTER *Fourteen*

*L*ETTY HURRIED along the corridor, looking into each room. She found both Max and the empress in the theater/hospital.

"You cannot count on the Chamber of Deputies, Your Majesty," Max was saying. "May I remind you, they voted down every effort at preparing the army and then cried for war? If they defend Your Majesty's position now they will have become heroic overnight. It is not in their nature."

The empress waved her hand. "We do not desert, Monsieur Max. It is absurd, you waste words. Can you imagine a Bonaparte riding out of Paris in a *fiacre,* like that coward, King Louis Philippe? If I ask sanctuary of the deputies, even they cannot refuse me. Meanwhile, General Trochu can meet with these so-called communes in the Hotel de Ville. They have no consensus among them, after all. I am the only legitimate ruler until the emperor's return."

Max looked at one of his agents, who shrugged. Max said quietly, "That coded telegram gives Your Majesty the answer. You must believe it. His Majesty is a prisoner in the hands of the Prussians."

"Don't. It can't be true. He is not capable of surrendering. He is the nephew of Napoleon." She began to walk up and down between the cots of the wounded. She caught her black skirt on one of the cots and stopped, smiling at the young male patient who watched her with adoring eyes, while Letty untangled her skirt. Eugenie then turned to Max and became once more the proud empress, fighting every inch of the way to regain the post to which life, ambition and perhaps her God, had brought her.

"Max, Louis Napoleon would never surrender, no matter what the provocation. He would die first. This is a forgery. My husband is no coward."

"He is not well, madame. He has been in agony. Then there was an ill-equipped army, thanks to the Chamber of Deputies and His Majesty's own deafness . . . He would not listen to our reports."

She raised her hands, palms toward him. "Not now. It is too late. Are you sure my son is safe?"

"Reasonably sure. They were to cross the border yesterday, madame. It is you who are in danger. We know from the confessions of the group my wife overheard that they want your death. We have to plan for all contingencies."

The empress brushed past him. "Have the National Guard put in readiness in case of attacks on the Palais-Bourbon. The Chamber of Deputies is in as much danger as I am. Order the National Guard around the Hotel de Ville and the prefecture of police as well."

"And the Tuileries, madame?"

She nodded. "General Trochu is still in control of the city. He won't let the Guard go over to the mob."

Max looked doubtful. Later, walking along the corridor with him, Letty asked, "Is she really in such danger?"

He was grim. "I warned Louis Napoleon many times, as I've warned Eugenie. They are like a home guard, these National Guardists. They are not an army—they are totally inexperienced. Many of their friends are among the rebels. In my opinion, the first time the Tuileries is threatened, they will go over to the rebels. And there are too few of those pretty Cent-Gards. The trouble is, Eugenie insisted on sending every able-bodied soldier to the front." He breathed deeply, then smiled at her expression. "Don't worry. We've survived these revolutions before. They come. They go."

"But my father was killed in one of them."

He said nothing. But Letty felt that he had been humoring her, the way Vincent might have done.

An hour later Max, a chamberlain and two trusted secretaries of the imperial service gathered in one of the emperor's studies to analyze private papers before burning them. Letty assumed the official papers would come later.

Desperate to get away from bad omens and misfortunes, if only for a few minutes, she left the palace and passed through the barrier between the public and imperial sections of the Tuileries Gardens. The humidity had lifted and the early September evening was mellow and glorious. She walked among the strollers, astounded that no one spoke of the war. Perhaps they were, like Letty, seeking escape.

Walking out to the rue de Rivoli, she remembered the first day Max drove her along that street, the first time she looked up at the imperial insignia on the gates, the first time she saw the emperor's flag snapping in the hazy sky over the Tuileries. This evening, placards were set up beside the stacks of briskly moving newspapers.

EMPEROR PRISONER!

A mob was pouring down the rue Royale from St. Honoré, at least half of which sang revolutionary songs and waved weapons in the air. Backing away, she returned to the grounds of the Tuileries.

When the mob reached the rue de Rivoli she saw that most of them carried straw brooms and axe handles. Very few guns or even swords. This observation didn't afford her much relief, however.

Shouts of "The old fox is captive," "The empire is dead," "Long live the Republic," and "The emperor is a prisoner" shattered the air. Then came the terrifying power of the "Marseillaise," and Letty fled into the palace.

More wounded were unloaded late in the evening when the streets had thinned out, so Letty remained at the Tuileries all night. She knew very little about the care of sick people, even after weeks of working in the Tuileries ward and the charity hospitals of the city, but she was proud of her usefulness when it came to cleaning up and doing what some called in her presence the menial tasks. Some of the wounded even looked at her as if she were that Florence Nightingale who had been so beloved during the Crimean War. One young soldier said, "I'd rather be washed and my sheets changed by you, madame, than get all the doctoring in the world."

She treasured that.

When she was dismissed that Saturday night, she curled up on the very settee she had once shared with Louis Napoleon. Max looked in on her several times, and at one point they talked about the episode of the emperor's romantic hands.

"It seems such a long time ago," she said. "Now with the poor man a prisoner, I almost wish I had let him—"

"What!"

"Never mind. Do you think the empire will fall?"

He busied himself locating a decanter of brandy stored behind the bookcase to the left of the big wall-map display. He poured the dark, smooth liquor into small glasses, and she studied the brandy.

"I remember this. Max, I like that poor man. He was my first friend in Paris."

"Oddly enough, mine, too." He clicked her glass with his. "Long live France!"

"Long live the emperor." She added thoughtfully, "And the empress. I think Mother would have said so. She had a deep feeling about legitimacy. In government, and otherwise."

Sipping the brandy and sharing the settee, they looked around, busy with their own thoughts. Outside the windows the world waited in the darkness, very still, pregnant with a terrible fate that was waiting, Letty thought. Waiting for the dawn. She shook off forebodings and yawned.

"Think of it," she said. "Letty Fox of Virginia City, Nevada, slept in the Palace of the Tuileries. No one will ever believe it."

Max stared into his glass. "I wonder if anyone else will ever sleep in it."

"You are afraid for the empress, aren't you?"

"I am afraid for you as well. And for many things." He swallowed the last of the brandy and set his glass back. His smile was a bit twisted. "No. I wanted you from the first. But I was just wondering whether you and I ever guessed how happy we would be. We have been happy, haven't we?"

"Yes . . . yes, we have." She said it passionately, surprised that he did not know. Something in his voice, that pinprick of doubt, touched her deeply. She added, "No matter what happened, or will happen, these last two months have been the happiest in my whole life. Because of you."

They were silent. Then he said suddenly, as if imbued with new vigor, "Well, it was a good run while it lasted."

"What? Our marriage?"

"Good God, no! I expect that to last considerably longer. I was talking about the Second Empire. Somehow I never quite thought it would last. He did it very well. He kept most of his promises, and even to the end I believe the French people loved him. It was Paris that he couldn't conquer."

"What will replace the empire?"

"God knows. I only hope it isn't one of the Red communes they are preaching about on the streets tonight. A respectable republic, probably. In time." He laughed. "You know, it's rather funny. They're all comparing him to the first Napoleon. But the First Empire only lasted ten years or so. This one doubled that." He sighed and got up. "However, I don't suppose that will count in the long run. Drama is everything in this game, and unfortunately for Louis Napoleon, the end of his reign is sad and pitiful, not grand and tragic. Eugenie would have made a better figure of tragedy. She has the talent for it."

She did not ask what would become of the empress. The problem was too close at hand, the possibilities too horrifying.

Max left to find the empress for the burning of the official papers. Letty curled up on the settee in the emperor's study, trying in vain to ignore the many incursions by officers, foreign dignitaries, and the Cent-Gards who repeatedly woke her up to demand her identification papers. Somehow the Cent-Gards looked far less romantic than they used to.

Just before sunrise she awoke from a doze, blinking in the light from the gallery as a tall, blond gentleman opened the door.

"Madame," he said, "I cannot reach Her Majesty at the moment. She is deeply involved. Will you please tell her that her escape is vital to the life of the empire."

Letty sat up, trying to straighten her cap.

"I beg your pardon?" Belatedly she recognized the Austrian ambassador, Prince Metternich, whose wife was one of the empress's close friends.

"If we can assist in any way," he began again. "Ah! Monsieur Max's wife."

Letty unwound her feet from her skirts, got up and curtsied to the prince. It was an effort. Her knees felt stiff after much standing and the discomfort of the settee. Prince Metternich bowed and left her.

She walked slowly to the windows and drew back the portieres. Only the usual vigorous morning walkers were out in the still shadowed square between the Louvre and the Tuileries.

What could she do to help the woman she had seen working so hard in the hospital and at the council tables?

During the frantic activity in the palace that morning she tried to reach the empress with Prince Metternich's message, but Eugenie was always tense and hurrying, constantly listening to reports and dismissing those who asked her to leave the palace.

In the afternoon of that crisp, splendid autumn Sunday, Letty watched Eugenie give orders at last to her frightened and confused followers.

"Monsieur Max tells me the rebels have occupied the municipal offices of the Hotel de Ville and the red flags have gone up. I am sending General Trochu to meet with them. We will hear their grievances and redress them. If they refuse our offer, then will be the time to debate our next move. As a last resort, General Trochu and his men will escort me to the Palais-Bourbon, under the protection of the Chamber of Deputies."

"May I remind Your Majesty," one of her cabinet said, "that this is precisely how King Louis the Sixteenth and Marie Antoinette were put into the hands of the mob."

Someone else objected. "The Chamber of Deputies is hardly the equivalent of the Revolutionary Assembly."

Letty had very little idea of what they were talking about. She relied on Max's reactions. The situation was regarded as serious, though the shouting, singing mobs throughout the city were no nearer than the Place de la Concorde, where they presumably intended to camp while they prematurely celebrated the Red Revolution. The area around the Tuileries and the Louvre remained free of disturbances, and surprisingly enough, well-dressed strollers still promenaded around the square.

"Most of them are tourists," Max said in answer to someone's remark. He then took Letty aside.

"I am giving orders to Daubigny to take you away from here. There is a lodging house off the Place St. Michel. Wear your hair as unlike the empress's as possible. And keep your face covered. You have a deep bonnet with you?"

"Yes. But where will you be?"

She knew the answer, but he said, "As soon as we have gotten Eugenie out of the city I will join you."

"Couldn't I go with you and the empress?"

"No, my love. Definitely not."

"You think she may be attacked? Outside Paris?"

"Not beyond the barriers. The problem is getting her out of sight of the Tuileries."

She wanted to cry, "Don't tell me these things. Give us all some hope," but said instead, "All right. I suppose there is a lot of danger to you, isn't there?"

He pulled her to him, raised her chin. "Just kiss me, sweetheart, and leave my job to me. What do you think they pay me for?"

Letty wanted to impress upon her memory his touch, his warm, vital mouth, his hard body against hers, but the moment was shattered by the sound of broken glass; a heavy china épergne seemed to explode on the sideboard. Max set Letty firmly in the far end of the room by the corridor doors. Following the wall he edged his way around to the windows. His laugh relieved her.

"Some fool of a rebel is running away. Dropped his rifle. One of the

Cent-Gards picked it up and he's after the fellow now. Well, there is bound to be more of that. Maybe Eugenie will listen to me at last."

She wanted to see the activity but he kept her out of sight of the window. "Now, Letty, I am going to send you off with Daubigny and I want you to stay until I come for you. If anything happens and I don't reach you—no, don't interrupt me—go with Daubigny. He knows where my accounts are in London. Not large, but they will keep you."

"But what about you?"

"I've no time now, sweetheart. I'm about to practice some magic, transform myself into an aged cabby and, I hope, get the empress out of here as my widowed fare. But I can't do anything until I know you are safe and out of this labyrinth."

Her pleas were to no avail. She finally said, "Never mind me. Promise me you won't do anything stupid."

"Of course."

Everyone in the palace seemed to descend on Max. He turned her over to the agent, Daubigny, who was in a room with anxious, babbling cabinet ministers, foreign ministers and a scattered few of the glamorous Cent-Gards. Letty saw no signs of soldiers or National Guardsmen.

The rats had left the sinking ship.

Daubigny was nervous and somber as he took her arm. As they reached a wide staircase she looked back and saw two men talking to Max with great animation. When he saw her turn and stare at him he raised his fingers to his lips in a small, intimate gesture. She understood and went on.

Before she could descend the stairs she saw Prince Metternich hurrying up past her. Ignoring Daubigny's bow he addressed Letty.

"I am here to help Her Majesty. Where is she?"

"In the Council Chamber," Daubigny replied. "To your right."

The prince went on.

The shouts of the crowd somewhere in the sunset outside took on the menace of many roaring beasts.

Suddenly the uproar sounded much closer, beyond the doors at the foot of the stairs. Daubigny was looking out the window onto the street and the muddy green River Seine.

"Messengers from the Hotel de Ville have arrived. That is where the insurrection has its headquarters."

Then, with a frantic signal he sent her back into the gallery. "We can't leave by these stairs. We are too late. Crowds are gathering below and they might mistake you for the empress."

Not knowing what to do, she backed off, turned and started along the way they had come. Daubigny took her arm, pulled her back. "Hush! The empress."

Eugenie de Montijo did not see them. She came rapidly through the gallery and past them, her black skirts swinging around her as she entered the big audience chamber beyond. More than a score of people followed her, so closely that two of her ladies-in-waiting were crowded out to the doorways of the chamber. Among those herded into the back of the gallery were Letty and Daubigny.

The empress looked shaken and pale, but she retained her characteristic straight carriage and proud Spanish demeanor. Eugenie lowered her hands to the desk in front of her, her fingertips pressing hard on the leather desktop.

"I am gold General Trochu has brought a message back from the Reds who have seized the Hotel de Ville."

A small, thin man in uniform stroked his white mustache nervously. "To be precise, Your Majesty . . ."

"Yes, yes. *Madre de Dios!* Where is General Trochu?"

"Your Majesty," the old officer began again, trembling. "General Trochu is not here."

"Is he dead? Have they assassinated him?"

"What we are trying to tell Your Imperial Majesty is that General Trochu now calls himself the president of the provisional government of national defense. He has, in fact, betrayed you. And France."

The empress swayed but steadied herself on the desk. No one touched her. "General Trochu has gone over to the mob? Very well. What else is proposed by anyone here?"

One of the men on the outskirts of the crowded chamber called out, "Your Majesty will be safe in our midst. The Chamber of Deputies will swear to your protection."

"Honor demands no less," another voice added. "If Your Majesty will make ready to remove herself to the Palais-Bourbon immediately, we will pledge her safety."

"Not so," called a voice from the doorway.

Letty turned with everyone else to stare at the Cent-Guard who had hurried in from the gallery, clutching his sword in its scabbard at his side and breathing hard.

The empress asked in a voice hoarse and deep enough to be that of a male, "Why, may I ask?"

"Your Majesty, the mobs have surrounded the Palais-Bourbon. The deputies are their prisoners. The mobs demand that they proclaim a republic. They are crying, "Death to the empress!"

CHAPTER *Fifteen*

*G*HASTLY SILENCE. Then the furor broke out: every man present had something to say to Her Majesty.

Daubigny whispered to Letty, "It is too late. We must leave with the others. Perhaps it will be safer."

Meanwhile Prince Metternich joined the chorus urging Eugenie to leave before the palace was surrounded on all sides. One of her ladies set down a small, elaborate black valise with the imperial crest in which, she explained breathlessly, "Your Majesty will find everything for her overnight needs."

An old, limping man pushed his way through the crowd amid the mumbled protests. It took a moment for Letty to realize that it was Max, a totally unfamiliar Max in a coachman's caped greatcoat that reduced his height and made him appear a trifle hunchbacked. He wore a gray mustache like an old veteran of the Napoleonic Wars, and wisps of gray hair stuck out from under his top hat. He hadn't seen Letty and Daubigny, and made his way to the empress.

"Max, what is your advice? Do I travel as your postillion?" she asked.

Ignoring the empress, Prince Metternich and the Italian ambassador, Nigra besieged Max.

"Monsieur," the prince said, "Signore Nigra and I believe that we might leave in separate carriages, diverting the attention, with Her Majesty in my carriage "

"No carriage with armorial bearings—anything of that nature will be suspected at once. I have a horse and cab waiting for Her Majesty near the bridge. As you see, I am the cabby. She should leave in a plain cloak and deep bonnet by the east portico. The activity is all in the west and along the river."

"What of the palace hospital?" Ambassador Nigra asked, just as the afternoon sun dropped suddenly behind the trees of the Champs-Élysées and plunged the room into evening.

From the rue de Rivoli came distant shouts, and one of Max's men stationed at the windows called, "They are breaking down the fence into the imperial section of the gardens. Monsieur Max, they have the hospital. They won't harm the sisters, but Her Majesty can't get through them now."

Max reached for the empress's arm and drew her toward the door; she was too surprised to protest. Letty suspected no one in her life had ever treated Eugenie so roughly. Max nodded to Prince Metternich.

"Escort Her Majesty. Someone give her a bonnet and veil."

Prince Metternich offered Eugenie his arm. "Exactly my thought. Did you hear, Majesty? They are inside the grounds."

Eugenie hesitated. Ambassador Nigra offered an arm on her other side.

"Your Majesty, permit me."

She crossed herself. A slow smile lighted her face, relieving it of that pinched, starved look everyone had become used to in the last month.

"With pleasure, messieurs."

The empress moved out into the long gallery between her two escorts, but looked back to say to Max and the others, "I yield to force. Mind that." She nodded to a chamberlain who announced formally that the imperial audience had ended.

Eugenie signaled to Max. "No massacre, Monsieur Max. No defense to the death. Tell the guards."

Max bowed and spoke to the nearest Cent-Guard. "Order the duty guards to ground arms."

They were deafened by a metallic crash from outside; the imperial insignia had been ripped off the great metal gates and the crowds were pouring into the grounds toward the tightly bolted formal entrance of the Tuileries.

Max spoke rapidly to the prince. "Not the great staircase. Take the gallery into the Louvre."

"I don't understand."

"Through the museum galleries to the portico. Here is a set of keys." He handed them to the empress. "I will be waiting with the carriage. We must know the carriage is safe and waiting for you. Descend to the street facing the Church of St. Germain l'Auxerrois. Wait for my signal from the carriage box." He raised his head, looked around at the rest of the courtiers.

"Separate into small groups on leaving. If I am taken before you arrive and you don't get my signal, leave by the cellars and use these passports." He gave them to Prince Metternich. "They are English. Take the route through Passy."

Daubigny was looking frantic. He whispered to Letty, "What shall be done about you, madame?"

"Don't let him see us. We can't delay him."

The agent nodded. He and Letty crowded into an alcove beside the great doors of the audience chamber.

They heard the empress say calmly, "I know Passy. His Majesty's dentist lives in that direction."

Max didn't give Metternich a chance to speak. "Afterward, Her Majesty will leave Paris by the Porte Maillot. One of the inspectors there is an agent of mine." He left them abruptly, pushing his way through the nervous, frantic group. A moment later the cabby was gone.

The empress said, with a wry expression, "Our escape from the palace then depends on our facing the Church of St. Germain. I do not like that omen." But she went with her escorts. The rich and impressive valise remained behind on the floor, forgotten in the scuffle of departure. Her Majesty had nothing but the clothes she wore.

As they followed, Letty whispered, "What did she mean by 'omen'?"

"Across the street is the church whose tocsin signaled the St. Bartholomew's Day Massacre against Protestants."

"Oh, no." They began to run after the others.

In spite of her cloak, bonnet and heavy cashmere skirts, Letty felt icy cold, but as they crossed the gallery from the Tuileries to the Louvre she found some of her courage returning. She glanced at the few pictures remaining on the denuded walls as they passed and wondered suddenly why some very uninteresting landscapes and even worse portraits were hung in the Louvre.

A bestial roar came rolling up from the Arc du Carrousel and the square beneath the windows. Daubigny hurried her on through the long vista of museum galleries. At the far end of the next gallery they saw a desperate knot of people gathered before two closed doors.

The Italian ambassador said, "Some fool must have locked the doors."

One of the men looked out the window and began to sob, a low, strangled sound that irritated everyone and made them all more nervous. Only Eugenie seemed calm.

Eugenie glanced out the nearest window and saw her personal flag lowered. She said, half to herself, "If they did not want me as empress, they might at least have kept me on as a nurse." She smiled. "I was a very good nurse."

One of the ladies-in-waiting became hysterical. While the men pounded on the doors, shouting, the empress raised the ring of keys Max had put into her hand.

The empress tried two keys. Neither worked.

Everyone's eyes were on Eugenie's hand as she stuck a third key, an odd, wiry-looking key, into the keyhole.

"It's in. Now, someone push."

Several men heaved, and one of the doors creaked open. Hysterical laughter spread through the group as they filed through, and the roar of the mob seemed to fade. The empress's party was now within the thickest, most ancient walls of the Louvre, built to withstand the ferocity of medieval warfare.

Before entering the Gallery of Antiquities, Metternich gave the order for the groups to separate. He motioned all the attendants, officers and ladies-in-waiting to scatter. "Use all service exits, crawl if you have to. Only one lady attend Her Majesty. We don't want to call attention to a larger group."

Letty called out, in a faraway voice she barely recognized, "I'll go with Her Majesty."

Metternich made no objection to this or to the inclusion of the Italian ambassador in the imperial party. They had played the amusing gallants at court and would serve to strengthen Eugenie by their presence, at least until she and Letty were safe in Max's horsecab.

Letty realized that the ambassadors were perhaps the only pair in the small group who were not in personal danger during this last and most dangerous part of the flight from the palace. It was unlikely that the mob would risk adding the menace of the Austro-Hungarian empire and the kingdom of Italy to the approaching Prussian armies.

Eugenie went along the line, embracing each of her ladies, then giving her hand to each man. Last, she gave Letty a flickering smile.

"So there *is* some loyalty in the world." Then she turned away from the others and did not look back.

Daubigny and the two ambassadors escorted the two women through the Egyptian gallery. Letty could not help thinking how these ancient artifacts and mummified remains represented the fall of empires long ago.

Prince Metternich went to the long windows overlooking the ill-famed church across the street. "I see the horse and cab. And the signal! Monsieur Max gives the signal!"

Letty gave silent thanks that Max had not been seen or recognized.

With the most perilous moment of their escape at hand, Letty found surprising resources within herself. Walking erect and proudly, she followed Eugenie down the stairs.

Daubigny opened one of the street doors. Beyond the east portico and a browned patch of lawn the street was deep in shadows. The gas lamps had not yet been turned on, and the empress and Letty, surrounded by Daubigny and the two ambassadors, made their way out between the noble pillars of the portico, confident, at least, that their pale faces were not visible.

Letty looked across the street at Max, who had stepped down from the box. He started toward the empress and her companion, his hands in his great patch pockets. No doubt he carried pistols.

Seeing how a newsboy on the corner stared at the empress, Letty turned away, making an obvious gesture of concealment to attract the boy's attention. Daubigny, realizing what she had done, seized Letty's arm and separated her from the empress and the two ambassadors. They started toward the street through the patch of grass. Letty could see the usual strollers a block away, acting as if the carnage around the Tuileries didn't exist. She was astonished that parts of Paris seemed to be conducting business very much as usual.

The rest of the imperial party was swallowed by shadows under the portico. Letty suddenly remembered how she had passed this way and at this hour on her first night in Paris. How different it had been on that exciting night when she first met the emperor!

They reached the street. Sounds of rioting in the Concorde area and along the rue de Rivoli were clearly audible. The newsboy shuffled toward Letty and Daubigny, holding up folded newspapers known to be either radical or republican. The boy assailed them.

"Emperor captive! Emperor surrenders! Empire falling . . . Read about it, m'sieu?"

Daubigny pulled away impatiently as the boy persisted, but Letty turned her head just as the gas lamps flared on, illuminating her face for an instant. The boy gasped, then shrieked, "Sneakin' out. Trying to hide your face! I saw you. You must be . . . It's the empress . . . Help! She's escaping . . . The emp—"

The two ambassadors had suddenly materialized. Nigra clapped a hand over the boy's mouth.

Across the street and just beyond the church a stroller stopped, looked their way, then hurried on, trying to avoid involvement.

At that moment Max, having helped the empress into the cab, materialized. His eyes widened as he recognized Letty, but he remembered his role. His warning to the boy was rasped out.

"Why did you cry 'Long live Prussia!'?"

Ambassador Nigra removed his hand. The boy swallowed nervously.

"N—no, m'sieu. Not me."

"You, my lad. I heard you."

Daubigny recovered his wits. "We all heard you. Including my American wife."

Taking the hint, Letty said in her broadest Western drawl, "We sure did, kid. You guys think you can betray a nice country like France to the Prussians?"

The boy was livid with terror now. He wiped his runny nose on his sleeve. "I d-didn't! I swear it . . ."

Ambassador Nigra played the genial, benevolent foreigner. He said to Daubigny and Max, "I think we may forget what the boy said, for the time being. These French have their problems tonight. Let us not add to them."

Everyone acted agreeable. Nigra bowed to the group and said clearly in accented French, "Pleased to give the personal regards of Italy to your American compatriots."

The two ambassadors strolled away, their pace becoming more rapid as they turned a corner.

"What now, monsieur?" Daubigny asked, breathing deeply.

As they returned to the horse and cab, Max said, "I assumed you couldn't get out in time." With his arm around her, Letty felt secure for the first time since the flight began. "Never mind. It's a damned great relief to know where you are at this minute. Darling, are you all right?"

"Of course. . . . Somebody had to go with her. There was no one else."

His hand squeezed her waist. "That's my girl. We'll see this thing through, with any luck at all." Over his shoulder he said to Daubigny, "Remove that fancy frock coat—you are going to be my postillion."

"Me, monsieur?"

"With a pistol at the ready."

"Very well, monsieur."

"As for you, sweetheart—"

Max opened the cab door and half-lifted, half-dropped Letty in a bundle beside the empress, who stretched out her arms to help her.

Seconds later the carriage started forward with a lurch. The empress startled Letty with a sudden outburst of hysterial laughter.

"And I used to despise King Louis Philippe because he left Paris like a coward, in a common *fiacre*. Yet, here I am, sneaking out in exactly the same way." She added, looking out the window, "I wonder if we shall make it."

"Max will get us out, Your Majesty."

CHAPTER *Sixteen*

*T*HE HORSE-DRAWN carriage made its way through silent streets whose gas lamps flickered in the September breeze, lending eerie shapes to buildings and trees. The strollers and tourists had vanished by nightfall. Few people were out in an area that had seen wild activity an hour ago. It seemed evident that the respectable, nonviolent majority of Parisians were wisely hiding behind their shutters.

Occasionally, at a prominent cross street, running youths raced in the direction of the Tuileries, shouting and laughing.

Eugenie stared at them through the lowered window, remarking, "Nothing political about them. Undoubtedly hoping to get rich by looting the palace. I wish I might have taken some of my son's things, his cradle, the—well, no matter." Remembering that she might be a target, the empress drew back from the window and sat there with an expression so carefully cultivated by years of experience that it might almost have been called boredom.

"Monsieur Max will see us through. You must have faith in your husband."

"Yes, madame."

It was easier to have faith when they reached the silent residential districts of Paris, which had darkened with the onset of night. The road was lined by delightful garden-mansions, and there were no signs of revolutionary activity.

But as if to give the lie to Eugenie's confidence and Letty's renewed hope, they both heard the sudden pounding of hoofbeats behind the carriage, a deafening echo in the night. Several resounding bursts that could have been rifle shots were followed by pistol shots from either Daubigny or Max. Perhaps both.

The horse and carriage raced on. Letty and the empress exchanged a quick glance then looked away, ashamed of what they saw mirrored in each other's eyes.

Scarcely two minutes later the hoofbeats were following again. Unable to remain passive, Letty looked out and saw the great moon face of General Hugo on horseback, trying to manage both his reins and the heavy pistol in his right hand. If Letty uttered a sound she did not hear it.

The general screamed, "Halt! Prisoners of the Commune. I demand —" He raised his pistol and fired toward the carriage box, the bullet speeding past Letty's face; she heard the answering shot from the box. She drew back in a hurry. A second or two later the fat general's body lurched against the carriage door and crashed to the road, landing between the carriage wheels. The cab bumped to a halt, throwing Letty and the empress against each other.

The door was wrenched open. Max reached in and pulled out Letty, then the disheveled empress.

"Daubigny is dead. Those were the first shots you heard. Hugo and two cutthroats seem to have been the only ones to guess you would leave by the east portico. One is down. The other will be along, I expect."

"Why?" the empress asked wearily. "What can I do to them?"

"Those who blame you for the war, madame. Some would like to see you tried as a war criminal. Hugo's men probably intend to use you to bargain for a high place in the new government. Quickly, now."

He thrust them both toward a hedged garden beside the road. "Madame, do you know the mansion of an American dentist named Evans?"

"Yes. On my boulevard—the boulevard de l'Imperatrice. Are we near?"

"It is behind you. Go to the next street. Turn right for a short distance and then right again on the boulevard."

"I know the house."

"I'll meet you both there."

He looked at Letty. "Sweetheart, take care of her." Then he knelt beneath the coach wheels and dragged out the limp mountain of flesh that was the general.

"Is he dead?" Letty whispered.

"Unconscious. Her Majesty will be safer if he is dead."

To the horror of the women, he pulled a pistol out of the leather pocket beside the carriage box. He had cocked it and lowered the barrel to Hugo's temple, clearly intending to give General Darlincourt the coup de grâce.

The empress put out a shaking hand. Her voice was hoarse, almost unrecognizable.

"I forbid it! Don't add his blood to the other crimes they charge me with. Leave him and let us be gone."

He shrugged, but pushed the bloated body under a privet hedge with the toe of his boot and returned to the carriage box. The women watched him lift the body of the agent Daubigny and lay him gently beside a rose arbor. He spoke some quiet words over the body of his friend and then swung up onto the box again with his greatcoat flying. He looked back at the two women.

"Remember. Keep in the shadows. Don't venture into the road. The Evans house."

Letty nodded. He waved the whip at her and then signaled the mare to move on. The sturdy creature answered with a fair gallop.

The empress, badly shaken, managed to say, "Come, madame. We must rely on our wits now."

They stumbled away, keeping always in the deep shadow of hedges and trees.

Letty was still shocked that the general, of all men, should have guessed the empress would be taken out of the palace by the east portico, and that he had come so close to capturing her. There was probably an informer in the empress's suite.

She took Eugenie's arm as they made their way through nettles, weeds and a thorny hedge that caught and held their skirts.

The sound of another horseman on the road stopped the two women. They knelt behind a staked line of rose bushes and watched breathlessly as a single man rode after the horse and cab.

"Max has only one to contend with now, thank God!"

"Unless General Darlincourt's other man has notified the barriers," Eugenie grumbled. "Radical or Republican, they are all enemies."

Eugenie looked around in confusion. "We are on the wrong side of the road. At the avenue we turn to the right."

They hurried across the road. They had just begun to stagger along the road again, dragging the weight of their heavy skirts and tired bodies, when the silence was again broken by hoofbeats, this time a small contingent of mounted men. Only two were in uniform, one a National Guard, the other a chasseur.

Letty pulled the empress into the darkness of a sweet-scented garden. Eugenie whispered, "The gazebo. To your left."

But the tiny white pavilion was the first place they would look for the women. It seemed to glow in the starlight.

"No," Letty said. "Retrace our steps. They may have seen us cross. They will expect us to try and go on."

On a sudden impulse she ripped off one glove and threw it to the side of the road beyond the gazebo. Then she seized Eugenie's hand and dragged the startled empress back in the direction they had come.

As she feared, the troop must have caught a glimpse of the women, perhaps in silhouette as they crossed the road. The leading horsemen pounded past the women and drew up at the gazebo. One of them shouted, "The Spanish bitch is hiding here. I saw them both."

He did not dismount. His bay mare made its way to the garden, its hooves hunting for a safe path up the two steps of the gazebo.

The four remaining men trampled down all the flowers and grass in the garden. They circled, arguing among themselves, each move bringing them closer to the two women, who hid in the shadow cast by a chestnut tree and a dozen clay pots of drooping red amaranth.

One of the National Guardsmen backed his mount into a clay pot and the noise of breakage brought questions from the leader circling the gazebo.

"What are you about, you fool? We need you here. I'd swear I saw them pass this end of the garden."

"I thought I made out something moving near my boot."

Letty held her breath. A faint movement on Eugenie's part told her the empress had crossed herself.

Someone bellowed, "Can't wait to cut off the Spaniard's head, eh, Jacques?"

"My father voted for the death of Antoinette. I'll do better than that. It's the Spaniard who sent my boy off to war to be cut down by the Prussians. Give me an axe. I'll finish the old harridan soon as I lay a hand on her."

Letty barely stifled a gasp at the pointless hatred in that vow. Out of the corner of her eye she saw Eugenie's face, frozen.

The man who boasted of axe-wielding had led his mount so close Letty could have reached out and touched its mottled gray flanks.

"There it is again," the horseman claimed. "Made my horse shy away." Another clay pot fell over as the horse sidestepped.

Letty prayed in silent panic.

The answer came more quickly than her waning faith would have expected. The bloodthirsty horseman kicked his heels into the flanks of the horse and shouted, "Body of Christ! They've got rats like wolves in this place. Steady, Khalil. Steady, lad. It's only a rat or two."

He led the horse out into the road just as a new horseman came galloping along to join them.

"It's the general. He's up and conscious and riding like the furies."

There was no mistaking the huge man riding the stallion and carrying his arm in a sling. General Darlincourt drew rein just beyond the gazebo and said, "What in hell are you doing here? That devil has only one man after him, a mere recruit. Follow him, I say. He is sure to meet the women again."

"But my general, Santerre thought he saw the Spaniard bitch and her maid along here."

Letty saw Darlincourt's face as he moved along the road in the starlight—a pallid, pudding face, but the little black eyes glittered unpleasantly.

"We must move," Letty whispered. "We are too close to the road." She took Eugenie's hand.

The empress made no reply but obediently let herself be led past the broken clay pots until she and Letty were standing in the spot where the horsemen had been prowling around minutes before.

Darlincourt barked, "Well then, finish your search and be done. We've no time to lose."

The empress jumped as a small, furry creature scampered across her instep, but she said nothing. Her fingers clung painfully to the heel of Letty's hand.

The men peered into the space around the chestnut tree where the women had stood only minutes before. Then the guardsman called out, "I've covered the area. It's full of rats. Come away."

General Darlincourt had moved on. He now leaned down, groaning at the effort, and pointed to something in the road.

"There. What did I tell you, imbeciles? A glove. Her precious Majesty's glove. She could be gone from the district after all this time. Get moving, at the gallop."

The two women dragged themselves through the grass, past the gazebo and on along the road, careful to remain as much in shadow as possible. Once in a while the lights from a large country mansion gleamed through half-closed portieres of unshuttered windows and Letty caught glimpses of Eugenie's face.

She looked gaunt and ill. The bones of her celebrated face seemed barely covered with flesh. She started onward, stumbled, and caught her skirts on thorns of a rose bush, crying, "*Sangre de Cristo!* Is there no end of this?"

Letty jerked the empress's skirts free and they made their way onward, across dark gardens haunted by weird, botanical shapes, until they reached a cross street.

"Ah! To the right. We shall be there in no time. Dr. Evans will help us. He is American like you, madame. And we shall meet Monsieur Max again, if God is just."

Letty took the empress's arm again but her thoughts were wrapped around Max. Where was he now? Dead in the road somewhere this side of the Paris barriers? Had the pursuing horseman shot him?

After the last few months, she could not imagine life without him.

The rising moon silhouetted the stately houses with their mansard roofs and English gardens. Now and then individual gas lights illuminated carriage paths or porte cocheres opening into the gardens beyond.

The empress stared both ways along the wide and beautiful thoroughfare. She remarked, "I wonder how soon they will be changing the name of this street. To the rue de Madame Thiers, perhaps. Or Madame Gambetta. Solid Republican names, all."

The names meant nothing to Letty. What did matter was that they must be close to Dr. Evans's mansion by this time. What would be waiting for them there? Had the revolutionists guessed their destination, just as General Hugo had discovered the method of their escape from the Louvre?

The empress guessed what she was thinking. "You must not be concerned, madame. Only you and I and Monsieur Max know we are going to Dr. Evans."

It was reassuring.

The empress clutched her wrist suddenly. "There! Before us."

Letty saw the carriage entrance of a large, impressive house almost overshadowed by its surroundings of noisily splashing fountains, a greenhouse and a forest of perennials that perfumed the night.

The two women ran toward the heavy door. Further along the avenue, toward the Arc de Triomphe and the heart of Paris, they heard a roaring noise that seemed to be drawing nearer.

"The mob," Eugenie muttered. "The mob of my nightmares." She raised her hand to ring, saw that her fingers were shaking, and laughed harshly.

The women waited, looking anxiously over their shoulders at the approaching sounds. No one responded to the empress's ring, so she reached for the knocker.

Letty stepped back, saw that though the portieres were nearly closed over several upstairs windows, light glowed in those rooms. Someone was at home. Suppose the American thought the rescue of an ex-empress might cause international complications for his country. The empress whispered, *"Por Dios!* It cannot be."

At last, the door opened, gingerly. The man who stared at them showed every sign of being about to slam the door in their faces. A servant of some kind.

"We must see Dr. Evans," Letty said. "It is urgent."

"Dr. Evans does not see patients at night, especially tonight. He entertains the members of the Hospital Ambulatory Committee to dinner. You understand? No other guests."

The empress swept forward with something like her old grace. Her light, flirtatious manner astonished Letty.

"We are old friends of Madame Evans and the good Thomas. It was the emperor himself who introduced us. May we wait, if you will be so kind?"

She succeeded where Letty had failed. The man may or may not have recognized her but he certainly was not immune to her charm. He stepped aside, waved the women in.

"Mesdames. I am the personal valet to Dr. Evans. If you will please step inside and wait for the doctor. As I have said, he entertains tonight. But before the guests arrive I hope he will be informed of your presence."

The empress moved slowly over the rich carpeting, her torn and dusty skirts swaying rhythmically. She was followed at a short distance by Letty, who kept looking behind her. Every slight sound made her hope against hope that Max would come striding in.

Eugenie held up remarkably well until she and Letty were alone in the upstairs library with a place of macaroons, a pot of tea and glasses of madeira. The empress drank the tea, but Letty needed the madeira. The room was pleasantly disordered, full of books, comfortable, all the furnishings obviously well used. There were several paintings and a complex tapestry that Eugenie admired.

"It must be very expensive," Letty said. "I can think of no other reason why a rich man would have it."

Eugenie smiled. Letty was glad something could amuse the empress, even if it was Letty's ignorance about art.

When the door opened Letty's heart leaped, but the man who entered was not Max. Dr. Thomas Evans was dressed for the formal dinner at which he was about to preside, but he remained very much the good-hearted, sensible man Letty had twice encountered in the Tuileries. He smiled at Letty as he crossed the room and bowed to the empress, bringing her fingers to his lips.

Letty thought the empress looked exhausted and ten years older than she had early in the day, but Eugenie managed a radiant smile.

"Ah, monsieur, you see before you a poor fugitive, begging your hospitality."

"And your rescue, madame. Have no fear. It will be contrived. That mob will not think of this house yet, I trust. You hear them? At this moment they are tearing apart the mansion of the Baronne Darville. They know we are Americans, however. Our flag will be honored by revolutionaries."

He explained that it had been too late to cancel the dinner party. "Besides, they will be watching all the exit barriers of the city tonight."

Each ring of the front bell by the arriving guests raised Letty's hopes that Max had arrived. Feeling numb, she finally resigned herself to the fact he was not coming.

Eugenie's assurances were useless. Some food and drink had done wonders for her optimism.

"You will see, my dear. Monsieur Max will not fail us. I only wish I had sent him to the front with the emperor. There would have been no capture. No disgrace. My poor Louis."

"Will they . . . hurt His Majesty?" Letty asked, realizing that the empress had not one but three lives to worry about, those of her sick husband and her fourteen-year-old son, as well as her own.

Eugenie looked grim, but she sipped her tea and added, "Kings do not kill kings. He is safer in the hands of the Prussian king than in the bloody hands of these revolutionaries."

A click sounded somewhere. Eugenie was looking over Letty's shoulder toward the door and suddenly her face lighted. She set her cup down so quickly it fell to the thick carpet.

"You see, madame? I was right to believe in him."

Letty swung around and saw two men in the doorway. Dr. Evans pushed the other man inside, closed the door and crossed the room to join the empress. The dentist and Eugenie were both smiling as Letty stared at the other man, a wretched, elderly cab driver whose wig was askew, mustache lopsided, greatcoat stained with something that might be blood. But the eyes belonged to Max, and the mouth and the grin. He held her so tightly as they kissed that she thought her ribs might be broken, but a dozen broken ribs would be worth this moment.

Over her head he greeted the empress, who had gotten to her feet to welcome him. He kept an arm around Letty while he kissed Eugenie's hand.

"The fellow who followed me is dead. It took a bit of doing. He was a troublesome flea. And he was the one who murdered Daubigny."

"He deserved to die," the empress said flatly.

Dr. Evans nodded, but said, "Our task is to get Her Majesty to the coast and then to England. I have it on some authority that Her Majesty will be accepted there until this war with Prussia is over. But there is one problem—Her Majesty will need a passport from Queen Victoria's government."

"I have it," Eugenie put in, waving the passport papers Max had given her before the departure from the Tuileries.

"Excuse me, sir," Max said, "but we are faced with a more immediate matter. The enemies tonight and at the barriers of Paris are not Prussians but Frenchmen."

"Unhappily, yes."

The dentist rustled about pouring liqueurs and offering them to his guests. Max took his, said brusquely, "Their Imperial Majesties!" and drank his down. The dentist said, "Amen!" and drank, but Letty couldn't swallow hers. She was too excited over Max's return, anxious over the new dangers ahead.

"What were your own plans, sir?" Max asked.

"This all happened so quickly. But I have a friend here tonight, a Dr. Crane, whom we can trust. He is seeing to my guests' departure now. He suggests we make it a masquerade. Crane as Her Majesty's physician, Her Majesty the patient, myself as her husband—"

"Her brother?" suggested Eugenie.

Everyone agreed hastily.

Max asked, "And my wife?"

The doctor had not thought of that. "Ah, Madame MacCroy . . ."

"Why not my nurse?" Eugenie suggested once more. "Incidentally, what is my illness?"

"Hysteria," Dr. Evans said.

Eugenie thought this over. "Well chosen, all considered."

The men were so busy planning that Letty suspected they had forgotten about the condition of the imperial "patient." But presently the dentist arranged for Eugenie and Letty to rest in Mrs. Evans's bedchamber.

"My wife will be flattered," he assured the empress. "I asked her to remain at Deauville while Paris is in this turmoil. She has many acquaintances. Wives of yacht owners along the Norman Coast. One of them will take Her Majesty and her attendants."

Max said, "That should answer."

Sleep was impossible. The events of the past few hours crowded in on Letty and the events of the next few hours did not bear thinking of. She suspected Eugenie didn't sleep either, but the empress closed her eyes and remained quiet until shortly before dawn, when the men came to prepare them for the journey.

Dr. Crane, a serious, businesslike gentleman, seemed dedicated to their rescue. Max trusted him.

Dr. Evans asked the empress is she had slept. Eugenie shrugged and smiled, but added, "I am ready, messieurs."

She needed no actor's props to look the part of an hysterical and half-insane patient. The past sleepless nights had given her eyes a peculiar glitter, as if it were an effort to see things clearly. Her plain black gown had not been changed during the last forty-eight hours, and even its neat white collar accentuated her pallor.

Her role was explained to her while she attempted to eat the breakfast Dr. Evans's cook had prepared for the group. As a stimulant for the ordeal ahead she drank black coffee, which she had not done in weeks. When the moment of departure arrived, the household staff lined up before her, and she bestowed on each a word of thanks, particularly to the stout cook and the butler.

They were all silent, hardly breathing. She turned, beckoned to the pale, rigid Letty.

"Come, Madame. We shall take a short carriage ride." She flashed a smile that would have done credit to a Tuileries reception. "I have a longing to enjoy the sea air."

Two carriages with teams waited in the courtyard, the horses fretting. The doctors helped the empress into the Evans landau, making sure she was seated on the side opposite the one the border officials would probably approach. Max and Letty stood for a minute or two beside the carriage.

Max looked into her face, cupping it between his hands. "I wish you were a thousand miles from here." He added with a sudden, unexpected grin, "But I'm glad you aren't." He kissed her, and she clung to him, thinking how her future would be if something happened to him, if he was recognized as the head of the imperial prefecture.

Dr. Crane tapped Max's shoulder. "Time to go, Monsieur MacCroy. Trust us. We will see that no harm comes to Her Majesty. Or your wife."

Dr. Evans slapped him on the back. "As for you, up on the box there, my friend. We will win through yet."

Letty climbed into the carriage, followed by Dr. Evans, who said, as he took his seat, "The good God bless us all."

Letty looked out the window, saw Max on his high perch shake the reins.

The carriage lurched backward, then forward, and then moved off.

The city was barely awake as the horses trotted through empty streets. The violence of the mobs had not reached this far and Letty suspected that most of these early risers were not even aware of the imperial overthrow. Now and then they were passed by a tumbrel loaded with produce for the city. And the four in the landau could not help but remember the other tumbrels that had carried the condemned to the guillotine not so long ago.

Letty watched Dr. Crane lean forward. He motioned them all to silence.

"Porte Maillot, ladies. The barrier."

The dentist looked out. "They would appear to have doubled inspection." The tension was palpable. "Are you ready, ladies?"

CHAPTER *Seventeen*

MAX DREW up the team and climbed laboriously down from the coach box, like an old man. With back bent he shuffled to the door.

"Dr. Evans, there is a newspaper on the floor. Hold it up as though you were reading it. It will conceal the—the lady's face."

Dr. Evans obeyed.

"I've heard from another traveler that there seems to be a troop of horsemen about two kilometers down the road. They may be Hugo's men. They have probably visited the railroad stations and the other barriers." He reached in and touched Letty's hand, then shuffled back to his coach box. Ahead, the long line of carriages and wagons moved forward.

Before Letty had time to think, the carriage had stopped again, and an unknown face loomed at the window, young, nervous, and scowling. One of the renegade National Guards.

"Out. You." He gestured at the dentist with his bayonet, but the hard eyes stared at Letty.

Letty pulled herself together and burst into a Western drawl.

"We are Americans, mister. Yankees. I'm Nurse Fox. We're taking this poor widow lady home to bury her husband. This is our patient's doctor here. And Mr. Evans, her brother. Dr. Crane, you tell this good-looking fellow what ails her."

"Hysteria. Her husband's death has badly shaken the poor woman."

Letty saw that Max came up beside the guardsman. His hands were once again jammed in the pockets of his greatcoat.

The guardsman peered in at the two women.

"Set down the paper."

Dr. Evans did so, slowly.

"Wouldn't catch me so close to that female," Max mumbled.

The guardsman kept staring at Eugenie's drawn, haggard face. Without moving his head, he asked Max,

"Why not? What's wrong with her?"

Max's rasping voice sunk to a loud whisper. "I heard the husband died of the cholera. Ain't supposed to be known."

"Nonsense!" Dr. Crane snapped.

Letty heard a gasp from the empress but luckily her pallor, her staring eyes, and her nervous state suggested that she might be suffering from any disease. The guardsman thrust all the passport papers into Dr. Evans's palm, and shouted at Max, "Go! Get on!" He slammed the door shut.

Max climbed back onto the box, gave the signal, and the coach moved on.

No one in the coach breathed for a moment.

At the moat bridge beyond the ancient stone barrier, a second inspector marched out in an officious way to stop them but caught a signal from the guardsman and waved them on.

The coach rumbled through the bright autumn woods of the countryside. Gradually, it seemed to Letty that they were traveling at an excessive speed. She glanced at her companions and saw they shared her concern. The men kept looking out the window, and then quickly down, avoiding the women. The empress looked straight ahead at nothing, but her gloved fingers were tightly laced together.

It was near midday when Max pulled up the tired horses at a country inn and relay station. While the hostler saw to the team, Max came back to the coach. His false mustache was gone by now, but mustache or not, he looked like a god to Letty. At Dr. Crane's anxious question, he promised, "The hostler and the innkeeper are loyal. That isn't our problem. We were being pursued until we reached the Malmaison road. A troop of horsemen. One of my agents was there in a guardsman's uniform. He demanded that his farm lads inspect the troop. He accused them of running to rescue the Spaniard. But he can't hold them long. We've no time."

"I understand," Dr. Evans said. "Give us five minutes. For the ladies."

"Five."

The two doctors helped Eugenie out of the coach and took her inside the inn, deserted at this hour.

Max lifted Letty down and held her against him, then sent her after the empress with the promise, "I'll get some food."

"I couldn't eat if I wanted to," she called as she hurried away.

Led by Eugenie, the group was back in the landau a few short minutes later. Max was checking the new team, a pair of stout-hearted farm nags, and receiving last-minute instructions from the innkeeper as to their care.

As the landau started off again on its race to the coast, Dr. Crane raised his head and forced a smile.

"My imagination, I'm afraid. I thought I heard horsemen behind us. I beg your pardon, ladies."

The empress said, "Please don't spare us, doctor. I hear them as well."

Max was urging the team along at a breakneck pace. Shortly afterward, the coach and team swung off the Imperial Highway and proceeded along a heavily rutted dirt road through the sunlit woods.

The pace slackened, and they began to breathe again, to look at each other and, on the empress's part, to make jokes. She found it amusing that their carriage was emblazoned with the *E* for Evans.

"Appropriate, don't you agree, messieurs? It is what I have been used to. Of course," she added with a mock elegance, "mine was surmounted by a crown in those days. At present, I think I prefer the good doctor's."

Everyone laughed, and Dr. Crane produced a bottle of wine that had been provided with the scarcely touched basket of food from the inn. He offered a half-filled glass to the empress. Just as he was pouring for Letty, the carriage bumped over a tree limb in the road and the empress spilled a few drops on her lap. She tried to make light of it, but said, "I hope that is not an omen of spilled blood."

As they plunged on into the damp, salty air of the channel ports, the sunny weather of the Norman landscape began to change to rain. No one complained; it meant they were approaching their destination.

They made a longer than usual stop near dawn at a posting house to give the tense and pallid empress an hour's rest. About to leave, the party was just coming down the creaking stairs from the small private parlor when a half-dozen men in the uniform of a local army regiment poured into the taproom demanding cognac and Calvados. Two of the riders began to sing a local tune, while another bellowed out the "Marseillaise."

Hearing the anthem she dreaded, Eugenie stopped just behind Max as they passed the open doorway of the taproom. For a terror-filled minute no one could move. The men in the taproom stared at the black-clad woman whose eyes were wide and blazing with defiance.

Then Max nudged Eugenie into the dark passage. To her astonishment he pulled her hat off. Letty thought she understood and untied the strings of her own bonnet. The women traded hats as they moved along the passage.

Suddenly, one of the soldiers, waving a small, heavy glass, shouted a command from the taproom doorway.

"Halt, in the name of the republic! You, the female in the hat." The doctors immediately hurried Eugenie to the coachyard door. With Max's hand under her elbow, Letty walked up to the soldier, now joined by two of his companions. She thrust out her chin and hid her trembling fingers in her mantle, while she stared at the soldier. His face looked hard and weathered, but he reeked of Calvados and had the truculent attitude of a hardworking fellow interrupted in his relaxation.

"You called the lady, monsieur?" Max said.

"Come here. Into the lamplight. Raise your head."

Letty did so, trying to look surprised. She took her cue from Max, who explained to the soldier, "Madame is Nurse Fox. She is escorting the family of a cholera victim back to the United States."

The soldier flinched, exchanging looks with his comrades, who began edging away. One of them mumbled, "She's not the Spaniard. It's the drink working, Pierre."

"Spaniard? Indeed not," Letty rattled off in English with a nervous laugh. "Can't you tell an American when you see one? My passport—oh dear, where did I . . . ?"

The soldiers retreated, except their leader, who insisted, "Somebody hold up the lamp. Let me see her face."

Max's body was close to hers. He removed his fingers from her elbow and she felt his hand slip into the pocket of his big coat.

The light blinded her for a few seconds. With her chin out and her mouth a tempting, sensuous pout, she tried to look as unlike Eugenie as possible.

"The Spaniard never looked kissable to me," one of them jeered.

The rest of the men murmured agreement.

"We're wasting time," someone else said. "It's back on duty in two hours. You there, Anatole. My glass is empty."

Pierre shrugged and let Letty go with the warning, "We take our orders from the communards, not the republic. So be on your way. We want none of your foreign aristos around here. We're cleaning up the nation."

Letty couldn't forget that final warning.

"He mentioned the commune. They are sure to help General Darlincourt if he gets this far."

"Then we'll hope Hugo doesn't get this far," Max said lightly.

But they both knew that he was unlikely to stop before he found Eugenie.

CHAPTER *Eighteen*

"**T**HERE IT is, the way to freedom." Dr. Evans made a sweeping geture toward the vessels at anchor along the quai de la Marine. "I'll go back to the hotel and tell the empress. Poor woman—she must be frantic with worry. We were lucky not to have met anyone while I was getting her to my wife's rooms."

Beyond the busy harbor of Deauville-Trouville the channel waters looked choppy, gray and rather sinister in the night fog. But Letty silently echoed the American dentist's optimism.

Things had looked bad for a few minutes when they approached the owner of the most suitable and seaworthy yacht, a forty-ton cutter. The owner, an English man named Sir John Burgoyne, refused to take on the empress as a passenger, claiming he did "not want to become involved in French politics."

Luckily, his wife was either more charitable or more curious and managed to change his mind. She insisted that they set out immediately to obtain supplies more suitable to an empress. Barring some unforeseen calamity, they would all be safe on British soil by this time tomorrow evening.

"I had better see to the trustworthiness of the crew," Max said to Letty. Dr. Evans and Dr. Crane had hailed a horse and buggy and gone back to the fashionable resort of Hotel du Casino where Mrs. Evans and the empress were resting.

In the guest cabin, Max began to tease Letty. "When we arrive in England, your duties with the empress are over. Will you divorce me then?"

"Good heavens! Why?"

"Your friend Vincent the noble-hearted is there reciting Shakespeare, isn't he?"

She hadn't once thought of Vincent since the day before yesterday—or was it a hundred years ago—when they had made their escape from the Tuileries with Eugenie.

She gripped his sleeve and shook his arm. "How can you be so nasty? You know I would die if anything happened to separate us. What would I do with that—that actor?"

"I leave that for you to figure out. Meanwhile, sweetheart, don't go on deck—one of those boisterous fellows in the cafés on the quai might mistake you for you-know-who."

"Would the people themselves attack the empress?"

He shrugged. "Probably not. But it's a gamble whether they would defend Eugenie or the soldiers, and I don't want to take the risk."

Alone and uneasy, she looked around at the little guest cabin of the *Gazelle*. Furnished in the elaborate, fashionable British style made popular by the late German consort of Queen Victoria, the cabin was cluttered with walnut furniture and antimacassars, little spool stands and a large, flower-painted chamberpot. It was nonetheless a true haven after the vicissitudes of their flight.

During her imperial reign, Eugenie in a private capacity had often visited England and particularly Scotland. According to Max, she had traveled alone except for a few ladies-in-waiting and a couple of agents, so it would not be an unknown country she entered tomorrow night.

Letty heard Max in the passage outside talking to one of the six crewmen of the *Gazelle* and opened her cabin door a few inches. A sturdy windburned sailor tipped back his cap and scratched his tousled head.

"Ye don't say now, sir. O'Reilly here. And me born not a hop-skip below County Sligo. I'll be that pleased to make your acquaintance. Seeing as I'm Sir John's mate, and sometimes messboy, I might be of service."

They shook hands and Max said, "Precisely. Here are the precautions."

Still talking in low voices, the two Irishmen moved down the passage toward the companionway.

Letty waited anxiously for the next half hour, looking out the porthole every few minutes. The sight of a dozen raucous, singing and shouting soldiers in a tavern across the quai was not reassuring. And Letty was further distracted when she overheard a discussion between several men in blue, probably port officials, and one of the *Gazelle*'s mates on watch at the top of the gangplank.

"Inspection," she heard repeated several times in French.

Presently, the mate motioned to someone on the deck above Letty. A minute later Max, wearing borrowed trousers and a respectable frock coat over a white shirt and waistcoat, crossed the gangplank to lead the group aboard. One of the French officials addressed him as "Sir John," and thus Letty resolved to be Lady Burgoyne.

Looking into the shaving mirror on the chest of drawers near the bunk, she pinned up her hair in a severe bun and mentally rehearsed the accent she had used in her Queen Victoria sketch.

Someone rapped on the cabin door.

"My dear, it's I," Max called to her, sounding very British. "May these gentlemen view the cabin?"

She was all weary patience and politeness, quintessentially British. "Of course, dear. Do come."

He jiggled and shook the door, then entered with two young blue-uniformed harbor officials behind him.

"Pardon, Lady Burgoyne," the Frenchman murmured, bowing with great respect. "A mere formality."

The men made a pretense of looking around, then ducked out, bowing again. Max remained long enough to grin at her before closing the door.

She leaned against the bulkhead, wondering if they had really escaped danger.

There was a bumping noise against the ship's hull and someone called out in French, "Boarding party!" Presumably, the French intended to search the vessel from two quarters.

She dusted herself off and once again became Lady Burgoyne, keeping in mind that she had to be imperious but not imperial. She was only a baronet's wife, not the Queen of England.

She heard the door of the owner's cabin open and close gently. Seconds later there was an officious knock on the door of her cabin.

"Who is it?"

"Port inspection, madame."

"You've already been here once. Very well." She breathed deeply. "Enter."

The passage lamp was out, leaving the passage dark. The man who squeezed in was General Hugo Darlincourt, closing the door behind him with his shoulder. Though one arm was in a sling under his cape, the other carried a pistol that he aimed steadily at Letty's head. The sight of his long-barreled, heavy pistol cut short the cry that rose in her throat.

"Good evening, general." Her lips were dry; she moistened them and tried to smile—a feeble response to the general's big friendly grin. "You are marvelous, sir. Do you have nine lives?"

His fleshy red lips spread in self-deprecation. His body, shrouded in a heavy black cloak, looked like that of a lumbering bear. He was fully as dangerous.

"Letty Fox, Nude Empress of Impressionists. Charming, charming. I knew you would mean trouble for me. From my first correspondence with poor Rissoli, of unhappy memory. I recognized that two Eugenies were at least one too many."

"How you hate her!"

"Not at all. But I had to bring down the Bonapartes if my own party was to succeed to power. And how better than to divorce that poor ignorant Plonplon from the imperial family."

He was close enough that she saw the sweat on his upper lip. Either he was not as confident as he looked, or his exertions had cost him a great deal. Her terror thawed ever so little; if she could keep him occupied, appeal to his vanity, she might gain time.

"How clever of you, general, to help the Prince Napoleon humiliate the empress. How easy to cause suspicion between the emperor and his cousin!"

"It brought them both down in the eyes of the French people."

"Are you actually going to proclaim yourself emperor?"

He pressed the icy steel of the pistol against her temple. She shivered. His grin faded.

"Dear little Nude Empress, you are my most persuasive weapon against Max. And I would not be the first general to crown himself. Now, you must be patient and wait for Max. He will rescue you, then obligingly make a trade. The Nude Empress for the Spaniard."

The brave Darlincourt was getting nervous. She winced as the mouth of the pistol pressed harder against the bone of her temple.

Letty heard the timber creak as the vessel rolled at anchor, and above this sound a man's heavy stride in the passage sounded almost deliberately accentuated.

The knock on the door was followed by a well-loved voice. "Letice, it's Max." The door opened and Max stepped into the cabin. He never called her Letice; it had to be a signal that he knew of Darlincourt's presence.

Max stopped with the door ajar behind him. "You! How did you get here?" He appeared tense and nervous but did not overplay his surprise.

"A dory, my boy. And a fool of a sailor who paid tribute to my—shall we say, my Oxonian accent. It is hard to refuse a general. Even at sea."

"My wife is not your target, Hugo. Let her go and we'll talk."

Max started deliberately across the cabin but stopped as Darlincourt cocked the pistol.

Letty swallowed hard. A thousand ideas crossed her mind and were banished; she could pull away, or drop, or faint, or turn to plead hysterically, yet in that second the pistol could be discharged.

Max looked pale, unlike himself, but his voice remained conversational, under control.

"Is this a cat-and-mouse affair, Hugo, or do you want to get to business? How do I get my wife back?"

"An exchange, Max. Your Nude Empress for the Spaniard."

"Then we will have a long wait. Her Majesty won't be here until just before dawn. We sail at seven."

Hugo took the pistol from her head and waved it. "Don't waste time in lies. I know she arrives within the hour." He brought it back against Letty's head again with some care.

"You didn't use your men to capture Her Majesty because you want the sole honor. It will make you a hero," Max taunted.

"It will make me master of my party," Hugo corrected him. "And eventually, the master of France."

"My wife has nothing to do with this. I'll oblige you."

Hugo grinned. "You are quite capable of rousing those volatile fishermen and those good citizens wandering around the quai. They might even defend the Spaniard. But not if the little actress is in my hands. When the coach comes with your Yankee friends and their prize we are going to walk off the gangplank down to the carriage. When the Yankees have gotten out I will get in. I will give orders to start. Without having seen the prisoner my men will provide my escort back to Paris. You, my dear Max, and your little strumpet here may go to the devil."

Letty did not believe for a moment he would let them or the doctors go free. His men would probably shoot them.

But the general was no gambler. He and his men might capture Eugenie and her party only to have the empress rescued by the French people themselves. As the general admitted, no one knew how the public would react on the quai if they were harangued by Max into defending

Eugenie. It would hardly enhance Hugo's figure as the savior of France.

"It seems I have no choice," Max said. "But I promise you, I'll have the empress free before the week is out."

"A gallant boast. You say what is expected of you. Come along. You first, Max. I will be close beside the actress. Very close."

Letty felt her knees buckle and she gritted her teeth desperately. If she fell now the pistol would discharge by the general's reflex action.

Max opened the door into the passage. It was still dark. He stepped out, followed by Letty, held near the general's great body by the steely chill of the pistol. But the general had forgotten one thing—his size.

He squeezed through the doorway, found the sling of his injured arm in the way and turned sideways to accommodate it. For an instant Letty was free of the hard, metallic pressure against her temple. Everything seemed to happen at once. Someone behind her in the dark clouted her across the shoulder, pushing her hard to the deck.

She crouched there expecting to hear a pistol shot reverberate through the tight space. Three men scuffled above her, breathing hard, one of them cursing in what sounded like Gaelic.

When the pistol shot finally came, it was curiously muffled. A huge weight crumpled to the deck across her legs and she pulled her feet up with an effort. Pushing the cabin door open so that lamplight slanted across the passage, Letty saw a monstrous heap shrouded in black, the fingers of one bloody hand pressed to what remained of a face.

She shuddered and looked away, retching. Seconds later Max stepped over the body and knelt beside her, drawing her close. She thought nothing had ever felt so loving and so safe as this moment.

"Sweetheart, I should have realized the fat slug wouldn't walk up the gangplank like any other human being."

O'Reilly, the Irish mate, protested, "Who'd be thinkin' anything that big could board a vessel out of a dory? Damned if I don't admire the bastard . . . Sir, he can't stay here when the great lady comes . . . Do we weight him, shroud him and toss him overboard?"

Max did not seem to hear him. He kept murmuring words that warmed Letty's chilled and shaking body.

"My sweet. My poor darling. Those were the worst minutes of my life . . . When the idiot crewman told me he'd admitted that animal and I realized he might have you—"

"Sir," O'Reilly persisted, "we've a bit of a problem here and little time to dispose of it, as ye might say."

Letty sighed and stirred in his arms, facing reality. "The doctors must be leaving the hotel with the empress about now. And the Burgoynes will return with the supplies."

Max looked behind him at the motionless heap and slowly let Letty go.

"I'm afraid you're right. It's back to work. I don't suppose Eugenie would want to see this bloated carcass." He helped Letty to her feet. "All right, sweetheart? Any bones broken?"

"No, no. Please get rid of—that."

She stumbled back into the cabin and closed the door. Even with the door between them she could hear the whishing sound as they wrapped and then dragged the huge body to the companionway.

Scarcely fifteen minutes later Letty heard the wheels of a *fiacre* rattle along the quai. She rushed to the porthole in time to see the empress's party descending from the carriage. The two doctors were followed by Lady Burgoyne, and last came an unobtrusive woman in black, her face concealed by Letty's bonnet: the ex-empress of the French.

The empress and her guardians crossed the gangplank, followed almost immediately by Sir John and Lady Burgoyne.

The women were escorting Eugenie down to her cabin when they met Letty in the passage. Eugenie was too tired to do more than reach out as Letty curtsied. Letty arose and the empress took her hands, pressed them between her own chilled fingers, and said, "You are as gallant as your husband, Madame Max. You will find him on deck. I am sure he is waiting for you."

Letty went up on deck, her face slapped by the late night air off the channel that promised freedom and safety. The empress's words of thanks, brief as they were, had been like the Legion of Honor. Max was with O'Reilly, who had just given orders to cast off.

"Done, sweetheart. He goes over the side when we get out into the channel. We don't want him bobbing up in Deauville like a beached whale."

One by one, the vessel's ropes—its ties to France—were loosened, and at last the sails filled and they slipped away from the mooring. *And likewise,* Letty thought, *are my ties to France dissolved.*

Max hugged her but his eyes were on the harbor lights receding in the distance.

"Will I ever see those shores again, I wonder?"

"Of course you will. They'll find they can't get on without you."

He laughed, but she could see in his eyes that a part of his life had been left in France and would always be there.

It was her task to replace that life with a future equally important to him. His embrace tightened around her, and Madame Max responded lovingly.